PRAISE FOR RITA CIRESI AND
BLUE ITALIAN

"HONEST, EARTHY, WARM, AND FUNNY—AS WELL AS
HEARTBREAKING. HIGHLY RECOMMENDED."
—*Library Journal*

"Ciresi keeps the humor flowing while never shying away from
the painful emotions, the fear and the regret, that intimacy
brings."—*Booklist*

"Who is Rita Ciresi? And how has she kept me up half the night
devouring this book? It is not enough to say this novel is real or
captures the Italian-American experience or the spirit of a
generation, all of which it does. THIS IS A WELL-CRAFTED,
EVOCATIVE TALE THAT ENVELOPS THE READER,
TAKING US TO ANOTHER WORLD, WHERE WE
BEFRIEND GARY AND ROSA, WHERE WE LAUGH AND
CRY. AND EVEN AFTER WE CLOSE THE BOOK, WE
DON'T FORGET THEM."—Ken Auletta,
author of *The Highwaymen*

"ENTERTAINING READING . . . There is real substance in
this tragicomic story of two people with smart mouths and
starved hearts."—*Publishers Weekly*

"Ciresi captures through the dialogue the hidden agendas and
cross-purposes beneath the most mundane conversations."
—*The Columbus Dispatch*

"SURPRISINGLY FUNNY, POWERFULLY SAD, AND
SCRUPULOUSLY HONEST."—Frederick Busch, author of
Harry and Catherine

"Ms. Ciresi . . . gives us parental lunches and trousseau shopping
. . . that make us laugh, cringe, and identify all at once."
—Elinor Lipman, *The New York Times Book Review*

Also by Rita Ciresi

Mother Rocket

blue italian

Rita Ciresi

Delta
Trade Paperbacks

for Jeff

acknowledgments

I am grateful to the Ragdale Foundation and the Virginia Center for the Creative Arts for providing the solitude and support to finish this project. Appreciation is due to Hollins College for granting me funds to attend these colonies.

I thank Carol Bonomo Albright, Jeff Lipkes, Geri Thoma, Jeanne Wilmot Carter, and Daniel Halpern of The Ecco Press, and Kathleen Jayes for their editorial advice and encouragement.

For love is strong as death; jealousy is cruel as the grave.

—Song of Solomon, 8:6

blue

italian

prologue

Gary Alan Fisher had cancer. He was thirty-one years old and he was going to die.

It felt like an earthquake when the doctor told him. Not that Gary had much experience with cataclysmic events. But once, when he was eleven, his parents took him on a trip out west. While visiting cousins in L.A., the Fishers went walking on the cliffs above Santa Monica Beach. Gary remembered some intense discussion between the East-Coast and West-Coast relatives about which afforded the more spectacular view—the palisades that towered above the calm Hudson River or those that overlooked the huge, green Pacific Ocean.

Then, all of a sudden, Gary felt his feet start to vibrate. The lampposts and park benches quivered and the asphalt path shifted slightly to the right. Gary looked up at his parents. Their mouths were moving, but he couldn't hear what they said because their voices were overwhelmed by a low and deep rumbling that seemed to come from the center of the earth. The ground was a wave of soil, and for a moment, the cliffs seemed ready to slide into the ocean.

The earthquake was the scariest thing that had ever happened to the Fishers. But it also was oddly comforting. After the ground ceased to shake, Artie grabbed Mimi's hand, and Mimi grabbed Gary's hand, and they stood there, in the middle of the path, surprised the sun was still shining and they were all still alive.

The California cousins were amused. They called out numbers— 3.5, maybe 4.0 (anything more and glass would have shattered in the condominiums across the street)—as if the earthquake (*tremor,* really) were a short quiz show, staged by God, to test how accurately they could recognize the different gradations on the Richter scale.

Clearly it was not the thing to be alarmed. So Gary claimed the earthquake was cool. God, it was the coolest!

Mimi's face went pale. She pinched her son on the back of his neck. In her book, there was nothing cool about dying, nothing cool about being on the verge of disappearing right off the face of the earth. Gary could have been killed—he could have been crushed to bits, like ice in a Waring blender.

The West-Coast cousins indulged in mellow laughter.

The week after they returned home to Long Island, the Fishers gave a dinner party. Drinks and unsalted cashews were served on the patio. When asked how he had enjoyed the trip, Artie immediately launched into the story of the earthquake. He pulled out a small, vibrating pillow that Mimi had given him for his birthday to help soothe his bad back and pressed the pillow against each guest's cheek. The pillow let out a low tremolo of pulsation, making the jowls of each person shiver and shake. "Now that's an earthquake," Artie said. "That's what it feels like."

"We felt like ice," Mimi kept repeating, "being crushed to bits in a Waring blender!"

"And how about you?" the guests asked Gary, as they chewed on cashews and rattled their mixed drinks. "Did you like it?"

Gary watched Artie press the vibrating pillow against the heavy cheek of Itzie Katz, Gary's dentist and just about the biggest dog-breathed moron ever placed on the planet. Gary was appalled. Now he never would be able to whack off with that pillow again! His father was a fool. These dinner parties, which his mother forced him to attend, were absurd. The guests were cretins and the conversation was inane.

Gary curled his lip and answered, "Yeah, the earthquake was cool. It felt like the earth let rip a big, killer fart."

The silence was so sustained that Gary could hear the ice cubes melting in the mixed drinks. Mimi gave Gary a murderous glare that promised some form of dire punishment and a long lecture on the inappropriateness of discussing abdominal disorders—i.e., *farts*—while having drinks out on the patio, or, for that matter, at any other point of a dinner party. Artie looked puzzled, then laughed. His son was such a joker, a real wisenheimer! He should be a stand-up comic. He should write for Hollywood pictures. Then he could live in L.A. and be a kid for the rest of his life. Because, bar none, Artie had never seen so many adults acting like four-year-olds as he had in California.

"You should have seen Meem's cousins," Artie told his guests. "The ground was shaking like crazy and they just stood there and laughed like hyenas, as if the whole world were a Technicolor movie, and everything would come out all right in the end."

For some odd reason, Gary remembered the earthquake, and that conversation out on the patio, when the doctor told him he had cancer. *As if the whole world were a Technicolor movie . . .* he kept hearing his father say.

Gary sat in a straight-back chair opposite a light box that displayed the results of his ultrasound. Each of the five black-and-white images showed a different angle of his prostate gland. An ominous shadow, its position slightly shifted in each picture, darkened every screen.

The doctor was Indian. Dr. Harish Mehta. In a high, singsong voice, he described Gary's tumor as if he shared it. *What we have here is. . . . We seem to be looking at. . . . We face surgery. . . .* Dr. Mehta's voice became higher and thinner as he continued to speak, until the sound disappeared, reminding Gary of the dog whistles he used to see advertised on the Bazooka chewing gum comics: *A pitch so high it is indecipherable to the human ear!*

Gary no longer heard the doctor. He felt himself freeze, then hum, as if he had covered a comb with wax paper and was playing it like a harmonica, until his lips and face and then his whole body started to vibrate. Yet this sensation did not seem to originate within himself. It came from some outside, unknown force. It was the world itself. It was the voice of the universe, playing Gary like a ventriloquist played a dummy.

Gary felt the vibration inside him for several seconds. Then it disappeared as fast as it came, and Dr. Mehta was asking him if he understood, and Gary had to say, "I was listening. Swear to God. But I didn't hear you. God, could you start all over again?"

So Dr. Mehta took his finger and pointed at the first ultrasound. And Gary, whose photographic memory had gotten him through Simon Wiesenthal Academy, Columbia, and the majority of Yale Law with straight A's, was so dazed he had to ask Dr. Mehta for a piece of paper and a pencil. He sat there in his chair, staring at the first ultrasound image as if it were a world map or a periodic table of the elements, and he took notes on his own illness. He even raised his hand when he had a question. "How do you spell that?" he asked when Dr. Mehta said *prednisone.* "How long is the surgery? How many stitches?" He scribbled with his pencil and then looked at the sheet of paper. He did not ask the real question nagging inside of him (*Christ, why did I get this?*) but only "Is it going to work?"

Dr. Mehta pulled out all his stock doctorly phrases. *We have excellent chances of recovery. But no guarantees. First, surgery. And then we must have faith.*

Dr. Mehta's calm, lilting tones soothed Gary. If Gary closed his eyes, he almost could imagine himself conversing with a Brahman on a hillside. Gary liked this doctor. He wanted to like him. Yes, he fervently did, because he had read somewhere, long ago, that having a good relationship with your physician was an essential ingredient for recovery from cancer or any other grave illness. He wasn't sure where the article had appeared—in some magazine he had perused while waiting to have his eyes examined—*Psychology Today* or *American Health?* Or had it been in some unlikely source, such as the *Times* magazine or *Smithsonian?*

Ah, he was sick, he was sick! His memory already was starting to fail him.

Gary shook Dr. Mehta's hand and went out into the waiting room while the receptionist, who avoided looking him in the eye, got on the phone and made an appointment with an anesthesiologist and then an oncologist. Gary sat on a wooden chair and stared down at the oak-laminated coffee table. He was seriously ill. He had cancer. And yet *Reader's Digest* still continued to unfold the drama of real life, *Time* and *Newsweek* had competing stories on the fall of Communism, and *People* showed Princess Di modestly peeking out from beneath her blond bangs as the headlines once again shrieked that her marriage was finally over.

The entire waiting room, from the glossy magazines to the fake ferns, was an insult to Gary's sorrow. And yet it was now his place. It would be his place to sit on kelly-green plastic chairs and mauve and grey sofas, waiting for his name to be called. He would spend hours lying on gurneys, pushed in and out of surgical suites and recovery rooms, propped against X-ray plates and slid through scanners. He would be injected with saline and dye, zapped with radiation, forced to take pills that would make his hair fall out and hollow out his stomach faster than a case of food poisoning. The hospital would become his home. It already *was* home. He felt like he was surfacing out of a womb as he walked down the wide halls, got on the elevator, dropped to the lobby, and went out onto the street to the parking garage.

He was so dazed he did not even remember he could have stopped right there in the hospital to see his wife. Rosa's office was on the first floor of Yale New Haven Hospital, just off the hall from the main lobby. All morning and afternoon, patients streamed in and out of the social work office—the soft, sad old women from the Dominican Republic, the crack-house mothers from Dixwell Avenue, and the paroled men who hung out on lower Chapel Street in front of the Horowitz Fabric Store, begging the women who went in to buy Butterick patterns to spare them some change, please.

Rosa did not need another sick person in her life, Gary thought. She already had her hands full of seriously ill people. But not his kind. They were the miserable ones, the ones who did not fight back. Rosa complained about that sometimes, the way her clients seemed to dumbly accept their medical condition as if it were another bill presented to them which they couldn't pay. "Of course," she always added, "who's to say what's going on inside them? Who's to say how anybody is supposed to act when they're told they have a brain tumor or AIDS? You have to handle it some way. I mean, much as you might want to, you just can't go berserk. You can't start screaming and yelling like a wild animal put in a cage." Then she paused and said, "I would go bonkers, of course."

Doctors supposedly liked passive patients—dumb and docile, the kind who didn't dare ask questions or expect miracles, the kind who knew how to make nice with death. But Gary already knew he was going to be a pain-in-the-ass patient, the kind doctors and nurses complained about in the privacy of the lounge or cafeteria. He was going to talk a lot. He was going to fight. He was going to be the kind who lived like the rest of his life was a ball of yarn spiraling down a flight of stairs. He would run—frantically, uselessly—to catch it, crashing down upon himself at the bottom.

Of course, no one had said it was terminal. Dr. Mehta only had said it was rare in men of his age. Yet Gary had been trained to hear violins when the words *rare disease* were spoken. Rare meant freak. It meant fatal. It meant all your relatives, after they found out, would talk about you for weeks.

Gary was so preoccupied, so stunned by the knowledge of his illness, that he walked right past the hall to Rosa's office and went out onto the street. He walked past the mailbox, the newspaper stands, and the hot-dog stand with the pigeon-pooped umbrella, where he and Rosa once bought two franks with sauerkraut. The little old Italian man who took their money merely pointed to the yellow squirt container when Rosa asked for mustard.

Cigarette butts, gum wrappers, crushed Coke cans, and rain-drenched copies of the *New Haven Advocate* lay in the gutters in front of the parking garage. Gary forgot which level he was on, 2A or 2B. When he finally found the Subaru, he put his head down, briefly, on the steering wheel, then backed out without even looking behind him. He gave the parking attendant a dollar bill instead of a five. The man kept his hand out and Gary stared at it until the man said, "Three-fifty, buddy, three-fifty!"

He remembered nothing from the ride home, except that on Whalley Avenue there were a couple of red lights, and the Subaru stalled out by a kosher deli.

Gary went home to wait for Rosa. The three flights of stairs that led to the apartment seemed extraordinarily steep and dark. Did he imagine it, or was he puffing for breath? Was that a pain in his upper leg? And what about that throbbing in his groin? Maybe he just had to piss. All that water from the ultrasound . . .

He dribbled a little, on his underwear, before he made it to the bathroom. Ah, God, the indignity was starting already.

He went into the living room. It was a mess. Rosa had been nagging him for weeks to clean up his papers and books, and look, they were all still there. He sat down on the horsehair sofa. Then he tried one of the chairs. But it didn't feel right. So he did what sick people were supposed to do. He went into the bedroom and lay down on the bed. He stared at the ceiling. The bare facts of his life seemed to hover oppressively above him. Born in Flushing, New York. Thirty-one years old. Married three years. No children.

He thought, *I have just written my own obituary.* Then, amazingly—perhaps to protect himself from going completely crazy—he fell asleep.

When he woke up, the apartment was soaked in the grey light of a January dusk, and the afternoon seemed like a bad dream. If only it had been a dream. . . . But he patted his shirt pocket and heard the paper that detailed his illness crinkle beneath his fingers. Yes, it was true. It had all happened, all of it. Gary Fisher was a lawyer. The paper, the ache of his bladder, the wild beating of his own heart, provided sufficient proof. Hard evidence.

chapter one

Rosa Salvatore knew that even after her husband was dead—after they had topped him with a yarmulke, wrapped him in a prayer shawl, and sunk him into the ground in a Long Island cemetery—she never would admit to anyone how the cancer had fooled her. Was it love—or just plain paranoia—that had crazed Rosa into mistaking a massive tumor for another woman?

The error was easy enough to make (she told herself). After all, illness and boredom manifest themselves in exactly the same way: with fatigue.

Gary obviously was tired. He was studying for the bar. He was helping some hotshot at Yale write a bunch of legal briefs. And he was teaching a classroom full of overanxious, underachieving little shits and schnorrers (his words) at the University of Bridgeport. *Eth-ics and Eth-nics,* Gary had dubbed the course. "Most of it has to do with quotas," he told his parents over the phone. "You know, caps on immigration, Berkeley putting limits on Asians—What? I talk about Jews, Mom. *Mom.* Mom, I talk about Jews, don't worry!"

It was the dead of winter. Grime tinged the cuffs and hem of Rosa's camel-colored coat, but she didn't take the coat to the dry cleaner. Why bother? The bare limbs of the trees stood out against the heavy grey sky, the snowbanks on the side of the roads were filthy, and the slush of the season seemed as if it would stick around forever. Rosa felt fat and sluggish. She went to bed early and let herself hit the snooze button three times before she dragged herself into the bathroom in the morning. Gary also seemed to be lagging. He came home and sank down on the couch as if he had no intention of ever getting up again. "I'm tired," he said, when Rosa asked him what was the matter.

"Maybe you're getting sick," Rosa said.

"More like I'm getting old."

Rosa went into the kitchen. She had a whopper case of PMS, and the last thing she wanted to hear about was another one of Gary's weekly midlife crises. While she tossed a salad, Gary lay on the couch, enumerating the possible causes for his malaise. It had to be stress. Or it could just be the gloomy weather. No, it definitely came from squinting at the fine print of the legal briefs and gazing at all those bored faces in the classroom. Or maybe it arose from guilt, from simply driving by after taking a hurried glimpse at all the shivering, homeless people on the benches of the New Haven Green. *Exercise,* that was it. He needed to walk more, take more Vitamin C, eat more complex carbohydrates, drink less coffee.

Rosa took her sweet time making the salad. The longer Gary talked, the more goodies she slipped into her mouth on the sly. She polished off the Kalamari olives, then took a fork and went after her mother's marinated peppers. She dipped into the canned artichokes and scooped out half a jar of pickled eggplant. By the time Gary was done, Rosa had ingested at least 400 or 500 calories and God knew how many grams of fat. She wiped the olive oil off her lips and went into the living room. "Maybe you should see a doctor," she said as she set the salad on the table.

Maybe he should stop worrying, stop kvetching, stop dwelling on it. He continued to do all three, until one night his throat started to hurt and his spirits picked up. "Don't kiss me," he said as he came in the front door. "I'm definitely coming down with something." He smiled as he unpacked the contents of a white drugstore bag onto the kitchen counter: cherry-flavored Sucrets, Listerine, Chlor-Trimetron, Tylenol. Rosa bit her lip, irritated that he had not bought generic. She winced as he glugged and gargled in the bathroom, breathed his hot cherry breath in her face, and left glasses half-full of water around the apartment, wherever he had found it convenient to pop another pill.

A week later, he was back to square one. The cold or flu kept on coming but never got there. He grew irritable and always had a pinched face, like the people on TV commercials who needed relief from constipation. He shrugged Rosa away. "I don't know. I'm just not interested. In much of anything. Lately."

He started coming home late. He flopped on the couch and sometimes fell asleep, until Rosa got so angry she went into the kitchen and emptied the dishwasher, deliberately letting the spoons and forks clatter as she dropped them into the silverware drawer, waking Gary up. Then he got off the couch and sat at his desk, surrounding himself with a circle of papers, a wide, white moat that Rosa could not cross. Rosa went to bed by herself. She put on the stinky pink flannel pajamas she had worn for four nights running and pulled the covers over her head to block out the light that shone beneath the bedroom door. She wept soft wintery tears, the kind she would color dark olive if asked by a psychiatrist to translate her emotions into art. Meanwhile, Gary stayed up late in the living room and kept the brightest lamp going.

Then he started getting up every night. She heard the creak of the bed as he sat up, the groan of the floorboards, the click of the bathroom door, the long silence before his urine hit the bowl. Sometimes it sounded like nothing more than a short dribble; other times it was a long and steady stream. One night she counted; he got up four times.

In Rosa's book, that meant one thing: VD.

Rosa felt blood pulse from her temples down to her pinky toes. She felt her inner organs—was it the stomach, the liver, or the spleen?— fill up with some dark green, blood-tinged bile that was a combination of anger, envy, and shame. Getting a cold? Ha! More like he was getting it on, with some cheap little commuter student from Meriden or Windsor Locks, a size-two bitch with a pert butt that fit perfectly into the palms of his hands, and soft, sweet breasts that didn't smother the man lucky enough to nuzzle them. He was hitting on students, like some lech professor in chinos and tweeds who was bored with his thin but wrinkled faculty wife (the kind with frosted hair who made a career out of passing the peanuts at cocktail parties).

What did Gary say to this girl—this woman—the Other Woman? Did he complain about what a nag Rosa was, about how she had a little cellulite pouched on her thighs? Did he tell her, *My marriage is as moldy as a piece of week-old provolone left out on the counter*? Did he act wise and mature, explaining the Cuban missile crisis to this hot little babe, who surely had been born post-1970? Yes, this wide-eyed weasel twisted her lithe body into positions that defied gravity as Gary recalled great historical moments, such as Neil Armstrong bobbing up and down as he took his first steps on the moon. She sighed deeply as Gary explained the Summer of Love. And didn't it just tickle her little twat when Gary admitted he was standing in front of the unicorn tapestries at the Cloisters when John F. Kennedy was shot? What an orgasm, to sleep with someone who actually remembered Vietnam (albeit only through the body counts on the nightly news), who could define the My Lai Massacre and give a geographical accounting of the Ho Chi Minh Trail. Wasn't Gary so mature? So authoritative? So much like her—*dad*? Weren't she and Gary just the perfect combination—better than beer and pizza, chips and salsa, yin and yang?

This girl—Rosa refused to think of her as a woman—grew up in a ranch house. In high school she dated boys named Kenny and Randy who liked her because she was cute, optimistic, and only smart enough to be elected senior class secretary. She went to Boston College or Providence and then came home to work in her dad's real estate agency, where she filed and answered the phone and studied for the night classes she took at University of Bridgeport. She wore size-A pantyhose in every brand from L'eggs to Hanes. She got her shiny hair cut every four weeks and wore pale peach nail polish, perfume, mascara—all the things that Gary claimed to hate. She worked out at the gym every night in pink-tipped Reeboks and coordinated leotards and tights, and even after an hour's worth of step aerobics, the cologne she dotted between her breasts failed to go sour from sweat. She was Irish. Her name was Heather or Jennifer. She was everything Rosa wanted, but failed, to be.

Rosa suffered under the weight of who she was and where she came from. She had grown up on the shore, in a neighborhood known as Pizza Beach, where two- and three-family houses were jammed on narrow lots, and in the tiny backyards, clotheslines on squeaky pulleys crisscrossed every garden. Rosa's father Aldo was a plumber. Her mother, Antoinette, dressed every morning in a white sleeveless blouse, doubleknit grey slacks, and a gingham cobbler's smock spotted with tomato sauce—clothes that she called *practical* and that Rosa, behind her back, called *hideous*. Antoinette and Rosa used different words for just about everything, and it was not just a question of Antoinette resorting to Italian and Rosa insisting on English. Antoinette called eating pasta four times a week *thrifty*. Rosa called it *cheap*. Antoinette called marrying a neighborhood boy *sensible*. Rosa called it *instant death*.

On Pizza Beach, Rosa had been surrounded by relatives who had the grimmest possible view of what it meant to be a human being. Italians were supposed to be happy-go-lucky, but Rosa's family always seemed braced for famine and disaster. If Rosa or one of her cousins happened to complain about something, a voice always rang out: "Eeh! Just be glad you're alive!" or "Thank God for good health, who can ask for more?" As if life were nothing more than breathing—parcelling out the hours according to the song Rosa's uncle, Zio Louie, used to sing. At parties Louie would tilt back a quart of dandelion wine, honk his red nose, then squeeze his accordion and recklessly sing:

> *Oh lucky, lucky, lucky me!*
> *I'm a lucky sonofagun!*
> *I work eight hours*
> *I sleep eight hours*
> *I have eight hours of fun.*

That song seemed to represent everything that Rosa found wrong with her family. The men worked like mules, then came home and snored like pigs. Fun was a game of bocce on Sunday afternoon, the faded balls clacking hollowly against one another in the driveway. Fun was a few turns at *briscola* and *scopera* while smoking Dutch Master cigars. It was getting a run in pinochle, a strike in *pochero*. Fun for the women was winning the twenty-three-pound turkey at the Thanksgiving Bingo. It was sitting around the table eating too many prune cookies and then complaining about men and indigestion.

By marrying Gary, Rosa had escaped the awful fate of becoming a woman who leaned out of a second-floor window, her heavy upper arms jiggling as she hung out on the clothesline the white flags of laundry, like so many signs of surrender. And so she was all the more determined to nip this affair—beat out the Other Woman—and hang onto Gary. For Gary wasn't just her husband. He was a whole way of life.

But trying to nail him was difficult. Rosa inspected his underwear before she threw it into the washer; she personally delivered his coats and shirts to the dry cleaner, scouring the pockets before she handed the clothes over the counter. Nothing. She thought she might find a telephone number, a love letter, hotel matches, maybe some lipstick on a white collar. What other evidence could there be?

Rosa was on shaky ground. She had no direct experience with extramarital affairs. Her parents hadn't gone in for that stuff; her brothers were too boring to even dream of such things. No one she worked with seemed to have time for any of it. The only way Rosa knew of such illicit romances was through reading the advice columns in the newspaper.

Ann Landers became Rosa's god. Every night Rosa picked up the *New Haven Register* and turned straight to Ann to see what sage words she had to offer on the subject. Ann shot straight from the hip: *Tell that man to shape up or ship out. Wake up and smell the coffee, honey.* One of her standard lines became a refrain in Rosa's head: *Are you better off with him or without him?*

With him or without him? Rosa could not decide. She knew, for certain, that her marriage with Gary had lost its pizzazz, like a shriveled helium balloon forgotten in the corner of the living room three days after a birthday party. Gary and Rosa never went out to lunch anymore. His occasional phone calls at the office—once the high point of her afternoon—had become mere annoyances. At night she found herself moping around the apartment until he got back; then once he was there, she wished she were alone again. Some nights, just before she got home, she was seized with the desire to turn the steering wheel and drive in the other direction. But where would she go? What would she do? There was only so much shopping one woman could accomplish before she fell into the deep, dark hole of debt. And it was not safe to walk downtown alone, even to the library or to a movie theater.

Maybe he wasn't having an affair, Rosa reasoned. Maybe he just felt the same way she did, tired and a little confused by the utter boredom of his life. Maybe he came home late because he wanted to sit by himself in the library or the cafeteria for a while, be on his own, not have anyone bother him. Rosa herself often went downtown on her lunch hour to one of the Greek diners, where she sat in a back booth, brooding over bitter coffee and a sticky-sweet baklava. At times like this, she actually felt happy—no one knew who she was, where she was, or what she was thinking. She had no responsibilities.

Maybe Gary wanted a few moments of that sort of heady freedom, too. Yet it did not seem likely. He was an extrovert, even a party-hardy. He loved being in the limelight and in control. It was inconceivable to think of him sitting morosely in one of those boothes with the ripped vinyl seats and quarter-a-song jukeboxes, nursing his problems. He liked to talk about things, get them off his chest. If he had a problem, he would take it to a psychiatrist.

A psychiatrist. Now that was an idea. At work, Rosa had access to the hospital files. One touch of the computer and she could trace any appointment Gary had made with any doctor at Yale New Haven Hospital.

When she got back from her lunch hour one afternoon, Rosa shut her office door. She punched in Gary's name. Three Gary Fishers were on file. She selected Gary Alan. The first page of the file came up, displaying Gary's birthdate and their home phone number and address. Rosa was listed as the emergency contact.

Rosa pressed the return to display the next window. The file reported two visits—both within the last week—to a urologist.

Rosa sat there staring at the physician's name—Dr. Harish Mehta—and her heart dropped to the bottom of her stomach. Although she did not have access to the diagnosis and treatment files, she found this sufficient evidence of Gary's philandering. He had gone to a doctor. He was being treated for VD. Now Rosa, too, probably had some sexually transmitted disease. He had given it to her. Then he would leave her for the girl who had passed along the clap, and she'd be stuck high and dry with herpes or genital warts, without the prospect of ever getting another man again.

Are you better off with him or without him?

Rosa cleared the screen and typed in her own name, just as she had done hundreds of times before. There it was: Salvatore, Rosa— her own chart, the ultrasounds, the visits to gynecology and obstetrics, the admission to emergency, ending with the D&C. On her own computer, Rosa was just a number, another woman who once had been pregnant and then lost her baby.

Rosa cleared the screen again and left her desk. She went down the hall and sat on a toilet in the ladies' room for ten minutes. She watched different sets of feet—Hush Puppies, Red Cross pumps, tennis shoes, work boots—walk in and out of the adjacent stalls. She listened to the pull and pucker of the toilet paper and the bellow of the hand dryers. Then she got up and spent three or four minutes in front of the sink, mindlessly running warm water over her chapped hands. When she glanced at herself in the mirror, she panicked. Her skin was dull as recycled paper. Her mouth looked uncertain of its proper position on her face, and her eyes seemed scared of her own reflection.

Rosa was thoroughly, totally undesirable.

So maybe Gary *was* having an affair and *was* only a half-time husband—it wasn't like there were any full-time replacements waiting in the wings. Rosa clenched her fists, then stretched her fingers out into crooked claws. She decided she had to keep him, if only out of pride, if only to torture him for the rest of his life for this cruel betrayal!

Rosa marched back to her desk and pulled out the Yellow Pages. She called a beauty salon on Chapel Street and made an appointment with a stylist. "It's an emergency," she stupidly said. She worked the rest of the afternoon in a daze. Then she pleaded illness and left work an hour early so she could get to Scissor Wizards and scour the women's magazines for information on how to save her marriage.

Rosa sat in a sleek chrome chair and flipped through the magazines, sneezing every once in a while from the smell of the perfume strips. In each and every article that she read, happy couples testified that communication was the key to a long and healthy union. "Once a week, we hire a babysitter and go out to dinner together," Susie Smith, of Tulsa, Oklahoma, reported in *Redbook*. "Without the hectic noise of all the kids, we can catch up on news, chat about future plans, and rediscover why we fell in love with one another. We almost always end the evening in bed!"

McCall's carried this testimony from Jerry Polansky, a forty-six-year-old auto mechanic from Bergenfeld, New Jersey: "Years ago, my wife Angie and I made a vow never to go to sleep mad at one another. We sit down at the kitchen table and talk it out until we reach some kind of compromise. Angie makes hot chocolate and we laugh at how silly we've been. Then we go to bed."

Cosmo-girl Janet Keilman, an executive for a nightly news program in Manhattan, offered these bits of wisdom: "With a day that begins at 5:00 A.M. and often ends just after 11:00 in the evening, I come home *exhausted*. My husband Larry, an executive in a Silicon Valley computer firm, and I have a bicoastal marriage. Still, we make it a point to chat on the phone *every* night (the phone bills are *horrendous*, but *worth* it!) and once a week we join each other *somewhere* in the United States (and sometimes out of it, too!). We talk for *hours*. Needless to say, our conversations *always* end in bed."

Rosa despaired. These articles made marriage sound like machinery: the way to keep the system smoothly running was to talk and screw, talk and screw, and talk and screw some more. Rosa detested the psychologists who offered their wisdom on the topic and the average Joes and Janets who gave their personal testimony from all points of the United States. No one ever admitted that it might be hopeless; that it wasn't worth the energy; that perhaps the best solution would be separate vacations and a firm vow never to take your spouse home to visit your family on holidays. Nobody ever got to the heart of the problem, at least in Gary and Rosa's relationship. And that was simply the word *Oh.*

The *Ohs* were indicative of everything that was wrong with their marriage. I had a miscarriage, Rosa said, and Gary said, *Oh.* You know, Gary said, you should turn off your headlights before you turn off the engine, otherwise you're gonna kill the battery. *Oh.* You know, I don't like it when you talk to me when I'm brushing my teeth. *Oh.* I have a headache. *Oh.* I have diarrhea again. *Oh.* My sinuses are killing me. *Oh.* I have a real dislike of you, *oh,* when you talk too loud or when you act so stubborn, so *cafone,* so much like your father, *oh,* yeah? And you act like your *mother.*

Rosa looked and felt exactly like her mother when she sat down in the beauty salon chair and the hairdresser—Mr. Charles, he called himself—asked her what she had in mind. Rosa had in mind another life for herself, another body, another chance at Gary, maybe, or maybe just another face, one that did not have tight, pinched lips and dark, dissatisfied eyes, that did not have the beginnings of a double chin or goofy, crooked eyebrows that came from not heeding her mother's advice to tweeze only on the bottom. Yes, Rosa looked like her mother—discontent with the whole world.

In the mirror, over her shoulder, Mr. Charles waited with one hand on his hip and a pink plastic comb poised in the air.

"I just need something—" Rosa began.

And luckily, Mr. Charles, who had heard it all before, nodded, and finished her sentence for her. *"New,"* he said. "I know. You need something fresh, something original, not so dull. You want—*striking.*" He began to pull the comb through Rosa's hair. "The body is fab," he said. "The texture is great. Italian?"

Rosa nodded.

"Italians have the *best* hair," Mr. Charles said, glancing down at Rosa's Pappagallos. "And great shoes, too. And the jewelry. I'm going to blunt it up a bit in the back, give you a little bang in the front to take the attention off the jaw—"

"My husband likes my hair long," Rosa ventured.

"Men," Mr. Charles said. "What do they know? Over to the sink."

Rosa liked Mr. Charles. He took charge. He shampooed and clipped and trimmed and tickled Rosa when he shaved the back of her neck. "Sideburns be gone," he said as he brought his scissors to the side of Rosa's face. He clicked his tongue. "Sallow skin. You need some blush. You have a hair growing in your ear. I can't stand it, I'm going to clip it. *Out of here.*"

Rosa watched her black curls falling, in tufts, onto the purple smock Mr. Charles had tied around her neck. Her face looked chubby, white, and extraordinarily pale in the bright lights of the salon. Mr. Charles pulled down two strands on either side of Rosa's face and measured them against one another. "Assymetrical," he said. "Assymetrical is what you need. For too long you've been trying to find a balance. Don't tell me. You're a Libra."

Rosa nodded.

"Moi aussi," Mr. Charles said. "Omar says we're on the verge today. 'The scales will tip to one side,' he said, 'and you will find yourself on the cusp of a new beginning.' So maybe I'll win the lottery. Or who knows, maybe I'll just finally clean the mold out of my fridge!"

Mr. Charles switched on the blow dryer and blasted the purple smock with hot air. Rosa's hair clippings flew to the floor. Then he turned the dryer on Rosa and sang "Some Enchanted Evening" while he styled her hair. "Okay, here's a trivia question for you!" he shouted at the other stylists. "Everybody listening? Who played the Frenchman in the original cast of *South Pacific*?"

Mr. Charles stumped everyone in the salon. "Rossano Brazzi!" he brayed, then switched off the blow dryer. He blew a kiss at Rosa in the mirror. *"Perfecta, cara mia.* Good enough to eat."

Mr. Charles had tamed Rosa's curly hair into a sleek little bob with feathered bangs and a flip at the bottom. Rosa liked it. She was so grateful to Mr. Charles that she handed him a ten-dollar bill with her Visa. Then she let him talk her into buying shampoo, mousse, gel, and conditioner.

"Tell all your friends Mr. Charles has changed your life," he said and slipped the money into the breast pocket of his silk shirt. "And remember—free bang trims."

Rosa clutched the white paper bag full of hair-care products and went out to her car. The night was cold, and beneath the streetlights she could see small drops of condensation beginning to form into raindrops or wet snow.

Rosa drove home in the dark, blasting "Bolero" on the cassette deck. She felt like a new person, pounds lighter, freer, more independent, and in control. She was ready to take on Gary. She was going to pounce on him the minute he opened the door and confront him. He would go down on his knees and beg for mercy. Then he and Rosa would sob in each others' arms and renounce the folly of their ways. They would fuck each other senseless, then raid the refrigerator and eat pimento olives and baloney sandwiches, then fuck some more and fall into a deep sleep that would result in a bright and beautiful new tomorrow. Gary would court Rosa and kiss her and hug her lots, the way he never did anymore, and Rosa would cook him lasagne and baked ziti and double fudge brownies and call him at work and do heavy breathing, and they would go to the movies and buy the gallon container of hot buttered popcorn and afterwards they would paw each other with their greasy hands as they danced around the apartment to Billie Holiday singing "A Fine Romance."

Rosa drew close to home. They lived on the top floor of a three-family house on Emerson Street, just off of Edgewood Park. The neighborhood around Edgewood—and the park itself—had changed dramatically since Rosa was a kid. The grand old houses set back from the street on steep hills now were split into three- and four- and five-family apartments that housed students from Yale and Southern Connecticut, retirees who lived on Social Security, and blacks who were trying to move up in the world but could not afford any better. The park was full of youth groups by day and drug dealers by night.

By six o'clock in the evening, there was hardly a parking space to be found on the wide streets. Rosa had a tiny blue Honda Civic but a mortal fear of parallel parking. She went around the block two or three times before she found enough curb space to pull in headfirst.

"Where do you park your car?" Gary once asked her after they came back from a restaurant.

"The next street over," Rosa said. "Just to get a little exercise."

"You don't get *exercise* in this neighborhood," Gary said. "You get *jumped*. So listen to me and don't do it."

Whenever they went somewhere together, Gary always drove. Rosa was ashamed to tell him that she had not parallel parked in close to fifteen years, the first and last time being when Mr. Arcadi, her high school driving teacher, had taught her to turn the wheel Right-Straight-Left while chanting, "Right for Russell, Straight for Stover, Left for Licorice," as she bucked and bonked the driver education car into one tight parking space after another on the outskirts of the New Haven Green.

Thinking about the long, red, and chewy whips of Russell Stover Licorice made Rosa ravenous. She got out of the car, clutched her purse against her chest like a baby that needed protection from the wind, and hurried down the dark street toward home. She climbed the steep set of stairs that led to the front door and fumbled for a minute as she dug her keys out of the tangle of junk in her purse. She had to lean against the heavy wooden front door of the house to let herself in.

The dim hallway was lit only by a bare forty-watt bulb. Rosa unlocked the metal mailbox. Half of the mail toppled onto the floor. Among the clothing catalogs, bills, solicitations from charities, and white envelopes from credit card companies, Rosa found a yellow slip that indicated a package, in her name, had been left with Mrs. Luigi Sansone on the second floor.

Rosa trudged up the steps. Mrs. Luigi Sansone was a widow who unfortunately attended the same church as Rosa's mother. Not knowing her real first name, Rosa simply called her Mrs. S. to her face. Behind her back, she and Gary called her La Luigi. "Code Red," Gary whispered, whenever he and Rosa went by La Luigi's door. "Lower your voice. Do not display any marital discord. La Luigi knows—and tells—all!"

Rosa's mother, it was true, seemed privileged with information about Rosa's marriage that could only have come from La Luigi's cracked pink lips. "Don't you make your tomato sauce on Saturday?" Antoinette asked Rosa, in an accusing tone which betrayed that she already knew the answer. "You let your husband take his shirts to the dry cleaner? You don't iron them?"

Rosa knocked on La Luigi's door. The door immediately opened, as if La Luigi had been standing right on the other side, waiting.

La Luigi did not waste any time getting to her point. "You got your hair cut," she said. "What for?"

"I needed something—new," Rosa said.

"He's not gonna like it. He likes long hair."

"I don't care what he likes," Rosa said.

"So what'd you cut it for?" La Luigi shook her finger at Rosa. "Men always like it long. You see. You call me in fifteen minutes, after he takes a look at it."

"He's not home yet."

"He's home."

"The lights are off," Rosa insisted.

"I heard the bed creak a few minutes ago," La Luigi said.

Rosa flinched. La Luigi was listening to their bed. And what the hell was Gary doing in that bed? Was he by himself? What had La Luigi heard? Nosy bitch!

"I got a package for you," La Luigi said. She bent over and reached behind the door.

Rosa looked at La Luigi's large rear end, which Gary confidentially referred to as *whole Boston butt*. Did Rosa, too, look like that from behind? The front was bad enough. Rosa thought she had breasts heavy as meatballs and thighs wide as tires. When she looked into the mirror she saw one of those Playtex models from the 1960s, the *full-figure girl* in desperate need of *extra support.* It had been fine—it had been fun—to be a bit plump when she was pregnant. But she had lost the baby and never lost the weight. Rosa had stopped eating breakfast, stopped eating potato chips, stopped eating desserts. She went vegetarian for two weeks. She bought a calculator and tried, futilely, to figure out the percentage of calories that came from saturated fat. Occasionally, in her more desperate moments, she closed her office door during the lunch hour, picked up the phone, and ordered, in hush tones, some overpriced, overplastic, fat-busting gadget she had seen advertised on TV.

It was one of these packages—postmarked from Muscatine, Iowa—that La Luigi handed her. The long thin box announced in bright green letters: ROSA SALVATORE, YOUR GUT BUSTER IS HERE!

Rosa blushed as she accepted the gut buster from Mrs. Luigi. "This is for Gary."

Mrs. Luigi crooked a finger at Rosa. "I was gonna say. You trying to lose weight. No good when you're trying to get another baby. You wanna come in? I just made cannoli."

Rosa leaned her head forward and smelled the fried oil, the rich ricotta, and the sweet powdered sugar. Her stomach yearned. But she shook her head and hurried upstairs. The moment she entered the dark apartment she tossed the gut buster to the bottom of the hall closet and yanked a coat off the hanger, dropping it to the floor to cover the box. Later, when Gary wasn't around, she would tear the box into shreds and bury the torn wafers of cardboard at the bottom of the kitchen wastebasket, underneath the coffee grounds, eggshell shards, and old newspapers.

The apartment was completely dark. Rosa's confidence, which had started to waver in the car, now was completely extinguished. She switched on the hall light and walked to the door of the bedroom. Gary was nothing more than a dark outline in bed.

"Ro?" he said. His voice sounded scratchy. "I gotta tell you."

She nodded. A lump formed in her throat. She was all prepared. She was already a jilted woman.

"I have cancer," Gary said.

Rosa leaned against the doorway and stared at his dark figure. Then she slumped down on the bedroom chair, her coat on, her purse still in her hand.

"Oh," she said.

And he said, "Jesus, what'd you do to your hair?"

chapter two

The other woman. The cancer. Either one meant life without Gary, and Rosa had a hard time imagining it. Yet not so long ago she had been completely on her own, convinced she would never find anyone to share her life. When Rosa's mother—shaking a dull silver garlic press big enough to crush a bull—used to ask, "Who's gonna marry you? What kind of man would put up with your nonsense?" Rosa had been hard pressed to answer her.

What kind of men did Rosa meet while working, for years, as a social worker for the city of New Haven? Alcoholics. Crack addicts. Black sanitation workers who had lost their jobs when the white mayor was ushered in, and white sanitation workers who got the boot when the black mayor was elected. For months at a time no man approached her except for the sorry guys who hung around the New Haven Green, who wanted a dollar—*just a dollar, baby, gimme a dollar*—to get a little something in their stomachs.

When she landed a much better position in the counseling division of Yale New Haven Hospital, Rosa was elated. This was a clean job. A nice job. She had an office with a tolerable-smelling carpet, a computer, and a phone with ten buttons for predialed numbers. Her colleagues washed their hands and didn't smoke. The cafeteria was subsidized. She was convinced she would meet dateable men— doctors and researchers and administrators and even lawyers who were involved in some of the bill disputes. But she sat in that office for over a year before she met Gary.

It was a sunny September afternoon. At two minutes before five, Rosa was hunched in front of her computer, backing up her files, when the phone in the outer office started to ring. Rosa's secretary ignored it. Rosa sighed. Donna Computo was just so *tricky* to work with. Donna took a couple of hours—and a couple of sweet rolls and coffees—to grow into a rational person every morning. Civility peaked just before lunchtime. Then, as the sugar and caffeine wore down, Donna once again became a sullen creature. Her tote bag was packed at 4:30 and her desk locked by 4:45. Donna always devoted the last fifteen minutes of the work day to redoing her face. She wore gobs of black mascara, dark brown blush, and deep and dramatic lipstick which she obviously thought made her look sultry— and which made Terry, one of the other social workers, tell her, "You look like a *slut,* girl."

"Phone, Donna," Rosa felt obliged to call out. "Get the *phone."*

Donna slowly adjusted her silver belt two inches to one side. With great deliberation, she smoothed down her denim mini skirt. Then, not minding what she looked like from the rear, she reached far over her desk and snatched up the receiver to comply with hospital rules: secretaries must answer all phones before the fifth ring.

Donna switched the phone onto the speaker mode and put down the receiver. Rosa could hear the caller's voice echo hollowly on the other end of the line—loud, fast, and New Yorkish.

"I'd like to talk with one of your social workers—"

Donna was feeling cocky because the boss already had gone home. "What for?" she asked.

"Whattayamean, what for?" the caller asked.

"I mean, in regards to what?" Donna said.

"What's with this 'what for' and 'in regards to' stuff?" the caller asked. "What if I had a problem I wanted to keep confidential?"

"You definitely got a problem," Donna said. "But you aren't doing a good job of keeping it under wraps."

"Look, I'm calling from Legal Counsel, you know, the office on Congress Avenue? I'm supposed to help one of your clients, a guy with a kidney?"

"All our clients got kidneys," Donna said. "How do you think they use the john?"

"A kidney *problem* this guy has. And he can't pay his bills. Look, is somebody named Rosa Salvatore there?"

"Salvator-ay," Donna said. "You pronounce the last e." Donna leaned her thick body into Rosa's doorway, and made a crazy sign next to her head to indicate her opinion of the caller. "*Whom* should I say is calling?" she asked.

As the man on the other end of the line gave his name, which Rosa didn't catch, Donna switched the phone off the speaker mode. She asked Rosa, "You wanna talk to this dickhead now, or should I tell him to call back in the morning?"

"I'll take it now," Rosa said. She closed down her computer and picked up her phone. "This is Rosa Salvatore."

"Rosa? Hey, I really like your secretary."

"She seemed to really like you, too," Rosa said. "What can I do for you?"

"My name is Gary Fisher. I'm calling from Legal Counsel, you know, the office on Congress Avenue?" He seemed to have this speech memorized. "I'm supposed to help one of your clients, a guy with a kidney? And don't tell me all your clients got kidneys."

Rosa waved good-bye to Donna. "I have two clients with kidney problems," Rosa said.

"This guy's from Haiti."

"Oh, Ivory White."

There was silence on the other end. "Isn't that name redundant?" Gary finally asked.

Rosa didn't quite know how to answer. So she kept silent, and to fill up the gap, Gary said, "Hey, don't get me wrong, it's an okay name, I guess, if you're an albino—"

Rosa clucked her tongue. "This conversation is getting less than professional," she said.

More silence. Then Gary Fisher said, "So keep on talking."

Rosa gave Gary a bare outline of Ivory's story. Ivory was HIV-positive and had only one kidney. Sometimes he did not have the ninety-five-cent bus fare to come in and get his dialysis. There was a problem with his naturalization papers and the state was withholding some funding. Someone would have to process the right forms and maneuver some kind of legal fol-de-rol before Ivory could get his treatment covered. In short, a case for Legal Counsel and Rosa to work on together.

"You'll have to come in and pick up a photocopy of Ivory's file," Rosa said. "I'll leave it with my secretary."

"Oh, don't do that," Gary said. "I have a feeling I didn't make a very good impression on your secretary."

"You didn't."

"Let me get on your calendar. I might make a better impression on you."

Silence. How long had it been since anyone she was really interested in had said anything even remotely flirtatious to Rosa? Eight months? No. God. Nine, *nine*.

Rosa wrapped the phone cord around her hand. "What'd you say your name was again?"

"Gary Fisher. I'm calling from Legal Counsel—"

"Jesus! I know that! Tell me something else."

"I'm a volunteer here. I just started law school."

"University of New Haven?"

"No. Yale."

"Oh," Rosa said. "So that explains your behavior."

More silence on the other end of the line. Then a little snort, a few vague references to town-and-gown tensions in New Haven, and Gary Fisher was off the phone and on Rosa's calendar for 4:30 the next day.

Rosa went home and tried to forget about him. But she was bored, and her Le Menu Lite dinner—honey-mustard-glazed chicken nuggets with waxed green beans, mashed potatoes, and a dubious speck of brown that was supposed to taste like fudge—was hardly satisfying. There was no harm in dreaming a little, was there?

Rosa turned on the radio, lay on the couch, and daydreamed to *Fantasy on a Theme of Thomas Tallis*—WYBC presenting an hour of uninterrupted classical music, for your listening pleasure.

The next morning when she got out of the shower, Rosa put on a black-and-white herringbone dress. The princess seams seemed to puff out along her belly and pull against her breasts. She took that dress off and then put on another. And another. God! She was acting like a character in a woman's magazine cartoon. *How can my closet be so packed,* the woman in the bra and panties would despair, *and yet I still have nothing to wear?* Rosa took off yet another dress and stuck out her tongue at herself in the mirror. It wasn't the clothes that were all wrong. It was the body. And the face. Too late to change that. Work began in twenty-five minutes.

Rosa put on her navy linen suit, which she fortunately had sent to the dry cleaner the week before, and her cream silk T-shirt with the jewel neck. Gold button earrings? Too predictable. Pearls? No, God—totally *librarian.* But wait. Wouldn't everyone at work notice she was dressed to the nines? Wouldn't she get all sorts of comments? "Expecting royalty?" Donna would say. "Up for a promotion?" Terry would offer. "Big meeting today with the Veep?" Alejandro would ask. And their boss, Tony Callone, better known (behind his back) as the Baloney, would say, "Make sure you don't spill your coffee this morning," with enough bite in his voice to indicate he was still pissed that Rosa had turned him down, over a year ago, when he asked her out on a date. Perhaps Rosa had refused a little too quickly, without making the proper excuse that she did not like to get involved with her co-workers. But the truth was, the Baloney was looking to get married, and being Mrs. Tony Callone of Fair Haven, Connecticut, was not one of Rosa's highest priorities in life.

Rosa looked at the clock, grabbed the phone, punched in the office number, and started to strip. On the fifth ring, Donna picked it up and mechanically mumbled, "Social work office, how can I help you?"

"I'm having a closet crisis," Rosa said.

"Hold on for the Gay Hotline—"

"No, Donna, it's me, Rosa. I'm gonna be late."

"Again?" Donna asked.

"Am I on the speaker?"

"No. Regular phone."

"Cover for me," Rosa said. "Tell the Baloney my car wouldn't start—"

"You used that excuse last time—"

"You got something better?" Rosa asked.

"How about: Rosa's got another run in her pantyhose because she refuses to buy the size that fits?"

Rosa clicked her tongue. She rued ever telling Donna that secret. She asked Donna, "How about my telling the Baloney you take a coffee break that starts at four o'clock every afternoon and doesn't end until five?"

"I work!" Donna said. "I got that phone yesterday at 4:58."

"And you were rude to the guy."

"He was an asshole—" Donna stopped, then hissed, "Baloney alert!" Loudly, she added, "Okay, Rosa, so good luck at the garage where you're gonna get your car fixed and we'll see you around nine-thirty, okay?"

Rosa hung up the phone and carefully returned her linen suit to the hanger, covering it with the dry cleaner's plastic bag. She wrinkled the silk T-shirt as she struggled to get it over her head. This was ridiculous. She was late for work and jeopardizing her job all because she wanted to dress just right for this appointment. All because of this Gary Fisher! All because of a penis! All right. All right. This was the last straw. This was it. This was the final time Rosa would ever compromise herself for a man. "I dress to please myself," she muttered. Aware of how foolish it was, how this potential relationship was based upon the thin threads of imagination and fancy, she still said aloud, "Love me or leave me!"

Rosa ended up wearing what she felt most comfortable in: fat clothes. PMS clothes. Clothes that didn't make her feel any more bloated than she already was: an oversized royal blue turtleneck sweater, black stirrup pants, and Van Eli flats. She fastened on gold hoop earrings that she had gotten at the going-out-of-business sale at Michael's Jewelers and put on her favorite shade of peach lipstick slicked over with a big blob of Vaseline. She blew herself a kiss in the mirror; then, noticing her crooked eyebrows, she stuck out her tongue at herself again. God, she could sweat and toil for years and still never transform herself into a knock-out—so why bother?

Rosa drove the long route into work. On Whalley Avenue, she was about to sail through a yellow light when a red Subaru rounded the corner off a side street and cut her off. Rosa slammed on the brakes, leaned on the horn, and gave the driver the finger. He looked in the rearview mirror and gave her the same sign language before he cruised down the street. "Stupid sonofabitch!" Rosa said. At the hospital garage, she charged her Honda up the ramps, parking on the deserted top level. Then she ran down the dark, dirty stairwell before a man could jump out of the shadows, pull a gun on her, and rape her. Someday she would move out of New Haven. But until then, better safe than sorry.

When Rosa got into the office, she made a big deal out of how filthy the Whalley Avenue bus had been. How crowded! She had just about gotten a seat. "And it's going to cost 200 dollars to fix the brakes," she told Donna loudly.

From inside the Baloney's office came a sarcastic voice. "I thought it was the muffler."

"Oh, that too," Rosa quickly said.

The Baloney leaned back in his office chair and glared at her.

"If you need anything done late in the afternoon, Anthony," Rosa said, "I'll be working late tonight."

His look seemed to say that yes, Rosa *would* be working late and if she didn't watch it, she may not be working there at *all* much longer.

To show her sympathy, Donna tapped her orange fingernails on her computer monitor as Rosa walked by. Rosa blew her a kiss when she got into her office. Then she gave Alejandro a dirty look when he came by and said, "*Guapa* earrings. But *chica,* your shoes just don't match your pants."

Rosa sighed and switched on her computer. When the first screen came up, an icon of a phone and a little ringing sound greeted her. The Microsoft Mail message was from the social worker next door, Terry. It said: *If it's hump day, then why can't I get laid?*

Rosa shrugged. It seemed to her that every Wednesday she or Terry asked one form or another of this question. A preoccupation with sex—or the lack of it—formed one of the few bonds between Rosa and her co-workers. No one in the office was married, and no one had an ongoing relationship except for Alejandro, who had just acquired a steady boyfriend. Rosa had met the boyfriend one Saturday in the cosmetics department of Macy's, where he and Alejandro were trying on aftershaves. The man, whose name was Dirk, wore a blue suede belt that Rosa could have died for. Apparently she hadn't done a very good job of keeping her lust under cover, because on Monday morning Alejandro tut-tutted at her. "Why did you keep staring at Dirk's pelvis?" he asked. He didn't seem to believe Rosa when she told him that Dirk's belt would have perfectly matched her pastel blue lambswool dress. Yet he must have gone back and reported this information to Dirk, because the next morning Rosa found the belt neatly cinched around her computer.

Rosa clicked on her Microsoft Mail icon and sent Terry a message: *Why are all the good men gay?*

Why is the grass always greener? Terry answered.

Rosa's mail icon rang again. This time the message was from Donna, who claimed insider knowledge of the Baloney's motives and actions because, after all, she was related to him—being a very close fourth cousin.

Don't worry, he won't fire you, the message said. *He likes looking at your tits. Ever since he was small he's had a boob thing.*

Rosa furiously stabbed at her keyboard and deleted the message. Then she tore off the top sheet on her calendar. Another day, another sixty-eight cents to Tony Callone's two-bit prick of a dollar.

Rosa filled out paperwork until ten. Then clients came in every half hour until four, with an hour in between for lunch. Most of Rosa's clients were either blacks who had grown up in the New Haven area or recent immigrants from Haiti, Puerto Rico, Cuba, and the Dominican Republic. They could not pay their bills. It was Rosa's job to help them process the necessary papers. The clients always hesitated before they came into Rosa's office, and the half-hour sessions always consisted of lots of head-nodding, blank faces, and Rosa repeating in her textbook Spanish, *"Mi entiende, mi entiende?"* The men did not look her in the eye. The women smiled weakly. That afternoon, at the conclusion of a session, one overweight woman pressed her hand on Rosa's and said, "*Usted es* too skinny." That made Rosa's day.

After her last client, Rosa went to the bathroom to powder her nose and clear her bladder. Then she played "Wheel of Fortune" on her computer—blacking out the screen when the shadow of the Baloney passed by her office window—until four-thirty. It was four-thirty-five. Four-forty. Gary Fisher was late. Rosa found herself angry, as if she had been stood up on a date. She was dying to get up; she was dying to take another piss, but she didn't dare leave her desk. The Baloney would be watching her every move, making sure she was chained to her computer until 6:00 P.M. If she did get up, Gary Fisher surely would arrive. Then Donna surely would call out to Terry, "You seen Rosa?" And Terry surely would holler back, "She's in the can. That girl's got a bladder the size of a peanut."

Rosa's intercom buzzed. "Somebody here to see you," Donna announced.

"Send him in."

"It's the guy who called yesterday at five o'clock—"

"Send him *in*," Rosa said.

Gary Fisher knocked on Rosa's door and then opened it before she could even call out for him to enter. This annoyed Rosa. She stared brazenly at him. He was better-looking than she thought he might be—about five eleven, with jet black hair and a full beard. He wore jeans and a denim shirt and over it, a brown tweed coat in the rough, nubby fabric that reminded Rosa of her father's winter hats. Rosa stood up and held out her hand. He looked vaguely familiar, but she couldn't quite place him.

"Sorry I'm late," he said. "The garage was full and I had to park on the street." He looked out the window. "They wouldn't strip a Subaru, would they?"

When he mentioned his car, Rosa recognized him. Stupid sonofabitch! She pointed to a chair and Gary Fisher sat down.

"So," he said. He gestured outside. "Nice neighborhood you got here."

"About as nice as the one Legal Counsel is in," Rosa said.

"Yeah. Whew! I feel like I oughta be carrying around a shotgun when I walk back there."

"You're probably one of the few who doesn't."

"You're probably right."

They looked at one another for a few moments. Then Rosa asked, "If you're in your first year of law school, why are you volunteering?"

"I'm smart. I'll pass. All right, so I'm not modest. I'm just not going to go crazy studying."

Rosa shrugged. She appreciated honesty. At least he didn't give her some pukey philanthropic line about the need to *give back to the community*. And at least he didn't start throwing around a bunch of legal terms about which she was clueless. What the hell was an *assize* anyway? And why did the word for wrongful action—*tort*—sound like a pastry?

"So you just got here?" she asked. "How do you like New Haven?"

"Great pizza," he said, leaning back in his chair, "but the rest of it I just don't get."

"What's to get?" Rosa asked.

"Oh, I don't know. Little things, like why does your secretary have purple lips?"

"It's Revlon," Rosa said. "I think the shade is called Violet Passion."

Gary Fisher shifted uncomfortably in his seat. "And what's your shade called?"

Rosa hesitated. "Mango Bango."

Gary laughed. "Well. Miss Mango. Miss Bango. Shit. Oh man. You got the file on this Ivory Black guy?"

"Ivory *White*," Rosa said.

Gary knocked his head with the palm of his hand.

God, what a jerk! Rosa thought. *I wonder what he looks like in his underwear.*

While Rosa took her sweet time looking for the file, he said, "You know, you look awfully familiar to me."

"Is that right?" Rosa said.

"I'm not trying to hand you a line or anything," he said. "But I know I've seen you somewhere before." He held up his hand. "No, no—don't tell me—I've got a wonderful memory, I pride myself on it, it's photographic."

"Then you ought to be able to place me," Rosa said and looked him straight in the face.

"Do you buy vitamins at that health food store on the corner of—?" Rosa shook her head.

"Are you taking a class at Yale? Do you study on the third floor of Sterling?"

"No. No."

Gary sat back and looked at Rosa. "Was that you in the Stop & Shop the other day, feeling up the bread?"

Rosa curled her lip. "I don't feel up bread."

"Well, somebody did, because when I got home my loaf of Italian was crushed to bits." Gary looked frustrated. "Give me a hint."

"It's got something to do with a car," Rosa said slowly.

Gary snapped his fingers. "Oh, I got it, you were behind me the other day at the DMV—how'd you like that woman behind the counter with the dragon breath?"

Rosa shook her head again. Then she smirked when she saw the little light bulb—forty watts and pretty damn dull—go on over his head.

"Hey, you gave me the finger this morning," he said.

"No, *you* gave it to *me*," Rosa said. "And I had the right of way."

"The light was turning, you should have stopped—"

"You should have waited," Rosa said.

"What for—kingdom come before I made a right turn on red? Where'd you learn how to drive, Kansas?"

"Where'd you get your license?" Rosa asked. "Sears Roebuck?"

"No, I just told you, at the DMV on State Street—"

Rosa paused and glared at him. In the distance she heard the ringing of Microsoft Mail messages, and she suspected Donna of alerting Alejandro and Terry that a *cafone* with a New York accent was in Rosa's office, giving her all kinds of grief. Rosa held out Ivory White's file to Gary Fisher, which he accepted with a sheepish smile.

"I'm sorry I gave you the old finger," he said. "I mean—whoa— oh my God—" the contents of the file went scattering to the floor "—you know, flipped you the bird—Jesus, what am I saying? How about helping me pick this shit up off the floor?"

Rosa mechanically obeyed. Her head knocked against his as she bent over to retrieve the contents.

When he left—fifteen minutes later—Donna was still hanging around at her desk.

"Quitting time," Rosa reminded her.

Donna watched Gary Fisher's butt as he walked down the hall. "That guy wants to dick you," she said to Rosa.

"Cut it out," Rosa said.

They watched as Gary stopped in the middle of the hall, then turned around and started to come back.

Rosa blushed. "He forgot the folder."

Donna smiled. "Dick you *bad,*" she said.

When Rosa left work at six, she practically collided her Honda into the Baloney's Dodge, which was pulling off the fourth level onto the ramp. She waved and smiled weakly at Tony, purposely pumping her brakes as if to test them as he followed her, a little too closely, down to the exit. What a beautiful fall night it was! And such excellent timing. Macy's was having its semi-annual lingerie sale, and after much deliberation, Rosa spent sixty-eight dollars on two pale pink silk push-up bras and a week's worth of matching bikinis.

chapter three

"You like Progressive?" Gary
Fisher asked when he called her at the office at exactly 9:01 the next
morning.

"Progressive what?" Rosa asked.

"Progressive *Pizza*."

Rosa tried not to sound dubious. "That's a Yalie hangout," she
said.

"So next time you can show me some local place," Gary said. "An
authentic hole in the wall."

Rosa thought about the pizza parlor down the street from her
parents' house, Il Giardino, where the owners played tapes of Ca-
ruso in the kitchen and hollered at each customer who came in the
front door, "*Che sa dici, goomba?* You want the usual?" Photos of
the Colosseum—the bright blue sky of Rome faded to vanilla—
graced the walls, and a cluster of wax grapes grew dusty by the man-
ual cash register. Rosa was sure that Gary Fisher, even though he
had grown up in New York, would not be able to handle it.

Progressive Pizza turned out to be what Rosa's family called a
"beards-and-glasses" joint. The waiters and waitresses all had close-
cropped hair and high cheekbones, a strong sign that they had just
graduated from Yale Repertory or Paier School of Art and now were
forced to tote around pizza and beer while waiting for their lucky
break. The women customers wore batik shirts and pendant neck-
laces. The men were tweedy in the extreme. Everyone in the restaurant—from the hostess who said, "Non-smoking, I hope?" to the
five-earringed bus boy—gave off overly educated vibes, like their

idea of a good time was drinking Foster's Lager and listening to loon calls on the stereo.

Definitely not Rosa's kind of place.

The hostess led them to a dark booth in the back. The plastic covering on the bench made a melancholy fart sound when Rosa sat down. Considering this was their first date, Rosa thought it prudent to ignore it. She moved the yellow candle closer to the middle of the table and squinted at the menu that the hostess placed in front of her. All her suspicions were immediately confirmed. Progressive offered pizza with pineapple, broccoli, and avocado on top, and calzone stuffed with peaches and mangoes. Rosa shook her head with sorrow. Anything beyond mushrooms, peppers, black olives, and sausage seemed complete sacrilege.

"What do you like?" Gary asked.

"What do you like?" Rosa countered.

"I asked first."

"Guess," Rosa said.

As if he were a fortune-teller, Gary leaned over the table and gazed deep into Rosa's eyes. Then he glanced down at the menu and looked intently at Rosa again. Rosa had to suppress the urge to stick out her tongue at him and waggle it.

"You're sporting a very dark aura around your head," Gary said. "This indicates you're revolted by the very idea of baked beans and sauerkraut on your pizza."

"So far you're on target," Rosa said.

"You cringe at the thought of a jicama—and/or any other root vegetable—defiling your tomato sauce—"

Rosa nodded, grateful he had defined *jicama*.

"—and you crave an old-fashioned pizza—dependable and trustworthy as a Republican cloth coat—with plenty of mozzarella—"

"*Mootz*-a-relle," Rosa corrected him. "Pronounce it right."

"—with lotsa onions. Unless you got an ulcer. Got an ulcer?"

Rosa had a spastic colon, but she was damned if she was going to admit it. She shook her head.

Gary smiled at Rosa. Rosa smiled at Gary. Gary flipped through the menu. Rosa also flipped through hers. She was reminded of the song she used to sing at Girl Scout camp:

The other day
I met a bear
Out in the woods
Away out there!

In the song, the bear looked at the hiker and the hiker looked at the bear, and then the bear smiled at the hiker and the hiker smiled at the bear. Each verse of the song related another version of this Monkey See, Monkey Do game, until in the final verse the bear decided to go off somewhere and steal a picnic basket or—if the Girl Scout leader was out of earshot—take a shit in the woods. And that was her and Gary, out on their awkward first date.

Rosa looked around the restaurant at all the other couples, who seemed to be conversing so smoothly and naturally. She was relieved when the waitress came over and Gary put in their order, although she got flustered when he asked her if she wanted a pitcher. For a moment the only thing she could think of was baseball. Then she nodded vigorously, although she seldom drank beer, and said, "Love it," when Gary asked if she liked Black and Tan—even though she hadn't the vaguest idea of what it was and thought it sounded like some nightmare bowel movement.

Rosa was glad she was locked inside her own body and could not see herself from the outside. She knew she would disapprove. She would cringe! All the other women in the restaurant seemed to be arching their eyebrows at the men, deliciously licking their teeth as they delivered cutting, seductive little barbs that made the men reply, "Touché." And what was Rosa doing? She was dreaming about running into the bathroom to loosen her too-tight belt. She was holding her stomach to keep it from making funny noises. She was hoping Gary would not get close enough to her tonight to see the one age spot on her face, and she was trying oh-so-desperately not to stutter when she spoke to him. But it was impossible. Rosa belonged to the Porky Pig School of Love. Put her next to a man—an attractive, eligible man—and she immediately started to st-u-t-t-t-er.

Rosa regretted that the waitress had taken away the menu, because her hands had nothing to fiddle with and she actually had to look at Gary.

Gary stared at Rosa. Rosa stared at Gary. Gary leaned back. Rosa leaned back. Each of them smiled. Then, mysteriously, each of them sneezed. They had to use paper napkins to blow their noses. Rosa, who usually carried the contents of half a pharmacy in her handbag, had forgotten to pack Kleenex.

"Do you have allergies?" Gary eagerly asked.

Rosa shook her head.

"Oh. Well. Do you like your job?"

Had he also prepared questions in advance? Rosa wondered. She half nodded, half shook her head. "I'd like to think I'm helping people," she said. "But deep down I know I'm just a paper pusher."

"Ivory White said you were helpful. And nice."

"You talked to him?"

"Yeah. He calls you Lady."

"He always calls me that," Rosa said. "Even to my face. It's kind of touching. Like I'm a lady-in-waiting or something."

"I had a dog named Lady once," Gary said. "A beagle. But she crapped all over the carpet and my mother had her put to sleep." Gary looked at Rosa. "Did I say something wrong?"

"No. Go on."

"That's all there is to the story. Except that my mother told me the dog had run away, and I've had a grudge against her ever since."

"Oh, I know all about grudges," Rosa assured him.

"Don't you get along with your parents?"

Rosa shook her head.

"What's the matter with them?" Gary asked. "Are they vicious? Neurotic? Moronic? Or just totally dysfunctional?"

"What if I said all of the above?" Rosa said.

"I'd say you got yourself a major problem."

Rosa shrugged. "What about your parents?"

"They're very much—*alive*," Gary said. "In fact, I don't think they'll ever die. They wouldn't give each other the satisfaction."

"Don't they get along?" Rosa asked.

Gary shrugged. "They have a big house. They tolerate each other."

"Do you have brothers and sisters?" Rosa asked.

"No," Gary said. "I'm an only child. And yes, I *am* a spoiled brat."

"I didn't say that," Rosa said.

"But you were thinking it."

"You're a mind reader?" Rosa asked.

"No, I'm a sleeve reader." He leaned across the table, stretched out one finger, and gently placed it on Rosa's upper arm. "You wear your heart right there."

Rosa felt her face grow hotter than a metal lawn chair left out in the afternoon sun. She looked down and noticed a long groove on the wooden table that absolutely was begging to be traced, slowly and carefully, with her fingernail. Before she got to the end of the groove, the waitress came with the beer.

Black and tan turned out to be a smooth, creamy mix of stout and champagne. Rosa liked it on the first sip and liked it even better two glasses later. It helped her forget about looking and acting like a dope. She actually loosened up and told Gary stories about her wayward cousin Connie and tales about the Baloney and the other characters at the office. She laughed and laughed and she even snorted once—kind of loud, just like a hog—and she didn't even care. The pizza had a thick sauce with a strong taste of basil, and a firm and substantial crust with air bubbles that crackled when Rosa crunched down on them. Hey, this was pizza. Why bother to be polite? Rosa let the black olives fall on her lap and got a green pepper stuck in between her front teeth, which Gary gallantly fetched out with his fingernail.

"More beer?" Gary asked.

Rosa shook her head. "Go ahead if you want to."

"I'm the designated driver."

Rosa pointed to his plate. "Don't you eat your crusts?" she asked.

"Yeah, all at once," Gary said. "At the end. Like a pile of bones or something. Don't ask me why." He broke one of the crusts in half and munched on it. Rosa picked at a black olive on the one last remaining piece of pizza, then harvested a mushroom before she realized how gauche this was.

"Eat this piece," she said to Gary.

"I can't. You do it."

"No way."

"We'll bring it home," Gary said.

"Okay," Rosa said. It seemed like a good solution, until she started to think about what was being implied. Whose apartment was home? And what would transpire there? Rosa felt herself starting to worry, until she suddenly recalled a record album that belonged to her mother. The cover showed blond-out-of-a-bottle Doris Day flinging out her hands in coy acceptance of whatever would come her way. Rosa felt inclined to agree with Doris—*Che sera, sera.* Whatever will be, will be.

Gary stopped eating halfway through his crusts. "I ate too much," he said.

"I have something for heartburn," Rosa said. She fumbled in her purse and pulled out a roll of Tums.

"You like *Tums*?" he asked. He held up one hand to decline, and with the other he pulled out of his pants pocket a roll of his own. "Mylanta is definitely better."

"You get calcium from Tums," Rosa said.

"What are you worried about calcium for? You just ate a ton of cheese. Here, try these."

Rosa took one of the tablets that Gary offered. The powder that dissolved in her mouth tasted artificially minty.

"All right, a half hour from now I'm gonna check in with you and see if you're a convert," Gary said. He put the roll back into his pocket. "Can you wrap that piece?" he asked the waitress, who looked down at them condescendingly as she whipped a strip of aluminum foil out of her apron pocket and plunked it down on the table with the check. Gary pushed the foil toward Rosa and snatched the check before she could grab it, "Cut it out," he said. "I'm taking you out."

"You don't have to," Rosa said.

"Whatta you mean? Of course I gotta take you out."

"Why? Because you're a guy?"

"Well, why not? Because you're a feminist?" He pulled out his MasterCard and then he looked up. "*Are* you a feminist?"

"I don't know," Rosa said. "I go to church. I mean, from time to time." She paused. Was that or was that not what they called a *non sequitur*? Did he notice? Did it matter? Rosa smiled. She was drunk. She was having fun. She was a hit. She felt so mellow she forgot to use the Ladies Room before they left. When they got back in Gary's Subaru and he suggested that they drive somewhere quiet to walk off some of the pizza, Rosa considered running back into the restaurant and using the toilet. But she was too embarrassed. She was a big girl. She could hold it in. It was important to have some dignity, a little sophistication, an air of style and grace.

Gary's car had a stick shift and he drove New-York style. Each sudden shift was a jolt to Rosa's bladder. She tried to distract herself by watching the red taillights of the other cars. The traffic signals and street lamps seemed to glow hopeful colors—green, yellow, bright white.

It was 8:15, a cool September night, when Gary pulled up on Prospect Street in front of the Divinity School, which he claimed was the only safe place in all of New Haven to take a walk after dark. When she got out of the car, Rosa stepped into a huge pile of leaves. She kicked her foot upwards, and leaves scattered in the air. But then she slipped and Gary held out his hand to steady her. It seemed natural to hang on to his hand afterwards and even to squeeze it when he put pressure on her palm. His fingers, wrapped around hers, felt big and comforting.

"I like fall," Rosa said.

"Me too," Gary said. "The air smells like new shoes. It makes you feel like a different person."

They walked up the stone steps and passed through the wide

white gates. Rosa felt compelled to whisper, as if she had just entered a church. "I've never been back here," she said. "We used to drive past the gates when I was a kid, on our way to visit cousins, and I always was intrigued with the name. Divinity School. Like Divinity Fudge, whatever that is."

"You never had it?"

"I don't like sweets that much," Rosa lied.

"Oh yeah?" Gary asked. "God, every single girl I've ever known has had an absolutely neurotic relationship with chocolate."

"I guess I have a weird thing for doughnuts," Rosa said.

They continued walking along the poorly lit path. "My Aunt Sylvia used to bring back fudge every year from the Catskills," Gary said. "It came in a white box with gold letters on it, and it said *Divinity Fudge—Everybody's Idea of Heaven!*"

"Was it?"

"What?"

"Your idea of heaven?"

"Jews don't believe in regular heaven," Gary said.

"What do they believe in, then?" Rosa asked.

"That you live on in other people's memories."

"So what happens if everybody gets Alzheimer's?" Rosa asked.

"I guess you're kaput. Forever."

Rosa listened to their footsteps on the brick path. Then Gary's hand was on her forearm, stopping her. Rosa closed her eyes and tried not to cringe, knowing it would be a godawfully clumsy kiss. And it was—slightly off-target, hesitant, complete with nose-bumping and dual uncertainty about when it should stop.

When it finally, mercifully, was over, Gary hesitated. Then he asked, "Can't we do better than that?"

They tried again. This time the embrace was firmer and the kiss had more conviction. Rosa was sorry when it stopped, especially since the minute it did, she remembered she needed to pee. Desperately. Lights were glowing in one of the buildings on the hill. She pointed up the hill and they continued. The path was dark and scattered with leaves that crunched beneath their feet.

As they climbed the hill, Rosa thought about the whole idea of Divinity School, where, she assumed, Protestants trained to become priests—uh, that was, *ministers*. Other religions made Rosa feel uneasy and uncertain. In the comparative religion course she took at Southern Connecticut State College, Rosa had learned all about indigenous peoples who worshiped goats and cows and goddesses with eighteen arms and two heads. But she only had a vague idea of what Protestants worshiped and why there were so many different sects. She hadn't the foggiest idea what the difference was between a Methodist and an Episcopalian. She didn't know what Baptists and Fundamentalists believed in, besides TV. And who *were* those boys in white shirts and black pants who periodically drove their bicycles up and down the streets of Pizza Beach, knocking on every door to spread the word of God, only to have the doors slammed in their faces?

"Are your parents really religious?" Gary asked.

"Oh, men aren't really Catholic," Rosa said. "Italian men, that is. Only women go to church."

"And your mother goes to church every Sunday, right?"

"No, she goes every day," Rosa said. "Once my father got really mad at her and told her she should throw all her clothes in a sack and go live in one of the back pews, like a bag lady." She paused. "What about your parents?"

Gary reached up and pulled a leaf off a tree. He twirled the stem between his fingers. "My father owns stock in Red Lobster. And my mother, she *hates* Jews. Real Jews, you know, the religious kind."

This was a subject that obviously was very dear to Gary's heart, because he continued to talk about it until they reached the buildings at the top of the hill. Gary said his parents didn't believe. In anything. They said the very idea of God was ludicrous, and the people who bought into it were clutching at straws. "Do you think God really cares about the blister on your ankle?" his mother used to ask him when he was small. And his father, who suffered from a sore tush for the great majority of Gary's childhood and adolescence, used to say, "Why place faith in a God that permits hemorrhoids?" for which Gary always found himself substituting the word *holocaust,* an event that seemed to have totally passed by his parents—or been sliced out of their cultural unconscious—because they never talked about it. Whenever Gary referred to it, his mother told him it was extremely tiresome to dig up the past, as if having a memory meant you didn't have sophistication.

Once, after his own mother died, Artie took Gary to temple. Gary was fascinated by the whole thing. But he didn't get the Hebrew, and at one point in the service he leaned over and pulled on Artie's sleeve, eager to find out what was meant by the words they kept repeating: *Baruch ata Adonai.* "Dad," he whispered. "What's Adonai?"

"You mean, *who* is Adonai?" Artie whispered. He waved Gary away with his hand. "I can't tell you right now."

"But who is it? Who is it, Dad?" Gary kept on whispering, and Artie leaned over and said, "Hold your horses, you gotta wait."

Outside, Artie told Gary that Adonai was God.

"So why didn't you just say so?" Gary asked.

"Because they use that word to signify God. Because it's wrong to say his name."

Gary puzzled over that one. "You say God all the time at home. You even say goddammit—"

"Enough," Artie said. "I don't say it in temple."

"But why is it okay to say it at home but not in temple?"

Artie shrugged. "That's the rules."

"But Dad," Gary said. "Dad, it doesn't make any sense, Dad."

"So maybe you think a god nailed on a cross makes sense?" Artie asked. And he never took Gary to temple again.

"Now I'm messed up," Gary told Rosa. "I don't know what I believe in. I mean, if my parents wanted me *not* to believe in God, they should have raised me religious. Then I would have rebelled against it. But now I feel deprived. I want to *be* something. Deep down I know I'm *something.* But I had to go to college. I had to read Freud and Camus. I had to learn about that stupid *uebermensch.* But none of that stuff really touched me. I can't help it. I'm a sap. I like Batman and Robin and the Old Testament God. When they sing 'Anatevka' in *Fiddler on the Roof,* I feel like crying. But then the next minute I go completely irreverent again—I'm driving down the expressway and I see a Hasidic Jew driving a Coupe de Ville and I crack up laughing, I can't help it, I'm a complete nonbeliever, and I think what kind of sense of humor does God have anyway? It must be pretty sick to let all this stuff go on, like planes falling out of the sky and earthquakes and floods and Hitler."

Rosa kept silent. She believed in God. *Somebody* had to have made the world—and who else could have thought up all the goofy stuff in nature, like hummingbirds and Venus fly traps, penises and zebras? Who else could have performed miracles like having a son's voice duplicate the tone and timbre of his father's?

"When I was a kid," she said, "I wanted to die for five minutes, go to heaven to see God, and then come back again."

"I wanted a yarmulke," Gary said. "A lot of kids in our neighborhood used to wear them on Saturdays. They used to cruise around on their banana bikes with these little skullcaps on their heads and they looked so happy! Like they knew exactly who they were and felt at home in the world. My mother called them peasants. She never wanted me to play with Conservative kids. But I had to have friends." Gary's voice took on a pleading tone, as if Rosa somehow could change the past by sympathizing with him. "In the fourth grade," he said, "I knew this kid—he had a horrible name, Peter Wiener, pardon me, but those are the facts, ma'am—and he came over to my house and we messed around for a while and then he stayed for dinner. My mother's a really good cook. She made beef stroganoff and Peter, he was kind of a pig, he ate three plates of it. Then he went back home and told his mother what we had for dinner and Mrs. Wiener called my mother up and my mother had to hold the phone away from her ear because Mrs. Wiener was shrieking so hard, cussing my mother out for keeping an unclean kitchen and mixing beef and milk and feeding it to her son. My mother held out the phone toward me, looking all smug and know-it-all, and she hissed at me, 'This is the voice of the God you want me to believe in. Listen to it. Listen to it. Do you like what you hear?'"

"Jesus," Rosa said.

"I found out later Mrs. Wiener made Peter go in the bathroom and stick his finger down his throat." Gary shuddered. "He ate three plates, three *plates* of it. Man, can you imagine?"

Rosa was totally grossed out. But in spite of herself, she laughed, and the laughter made her bladder ache even more.

"I gotta go," Rosa said.

"Home?"

Rosa shook her head. "To the bathroom."

"Didn't the Mylanta work?"

"Pee," Rosa said. "I just have to pee."

"All right. Just asking. Sit down. I'll go see if one of those buildings is open." Rosa watched him hurrying across the courtyard in the moonlight. It seemed as if she had known him forever as she watched him run up the steps, try the doors, then run down the steps and up the stairs of the next building, pulling at the doors, to no avail.

Rosa ended up peeing behind a bush. Although she had gotten as far as Advanced Botany in college, she still could not correctly peg the plant that hid her from Gary. Was it a rhododendron or a mountain laurel? And what was she doing—how had she gotten there—squatting behind this magnificent woody ornamental, which fortunately had a lot of leaves, praying to the God whose sacred seminary she was defiling that no security guard would be making his rounds right as she dropped her pants?

Some craziness had taken over Rosa. Was it the beer? Or did it come from the air, which smelled heavy and fertile and delicious, or the clouds, which muddied the sky and hid the stars and then let loose a few big drops of rain that splattered on the brick walks? The wind shifted and the rain became a steady, cold shower that made them laugh and run back down to Prospect Street. Rosa's hair was limp and her shirt was plastered against her chest by the time they got back to the car.

In the front seat, Gary said, "Come home with me, and I'll fight you for that extra slice of pizza."

Rosa bit her lip. Things were progressing at a fairly rapid clip. But *things* were bound to happen sooner or later. Why not sooner? Why not? She was wet, and the splatter of rain on the roof of the car was romantic, and she liked Gary, she truly liked him. She already knew it. The sonofabitch. She loved him! She was crazy for him! Why else—before he came over to pick her up—had she spent a good ten minutes trying to shove that slippery five-year-old diaphragm up into her? Why else had she smiled at herself in the bathroom mirror when she finally got it into place? What the hell. She was lonely. She was *lonely.* She was tired of having weird dreams in which she was a huge deep green Pontiac Le Mans, and an immensely attractive man leaned over her with a hose, filling her tank with unleaded. And she was sick of eating powdered crullers in bed on Sunday morning and then taking the sheets to the laundromat where she read, word for word, the fairy-tale fortunate marriage announcements in the *New York Times,* then watched her dingy underwear tumble in the dryer.

Gary started the car. Letting the engine idle for a minute, he pulled out his shirt tail and wiped the rain off his glasses. "You can put on some music if you want," he said.

Rosa leaned down and picked up the grey cassette case on the floor of the car. The selection on one side of the case was mixed: Handel, Benny Goodman, the Barry Sisters, Heifetz. The rest of the case was filled with rock: The Band, Jefferson Airplane, Madonna, the Doors. Did he really like this shit, Rosa thought, or did he just listen to it when he felt horny, the way she herself did, tapping her fingers on the steering wheel as she went flying over the Ferry Street Bridge on the way to visit her parents?

"You said you liked classical," she told him.

"Yeah, I've got *Carmina Burana* in my record collection," Gary said, "but that doesn't mean I want to listen to it."

Rosa picked up a tape. "You like the Doors?"

He put the car in gear. "Yeah, it's good fucking music."

Rosa held the cassette in her hand, wondering whether Gary was using *fucking* in its adjective or verb form. And what would happen if she put the tape in, and Jim Morrison hollered out, *Come on, come on, come on, come on, now TOUCH me, baby!* For in truth—it must be admitted—Rosa was afraid.

Rosa hesitated.

"You like it?" he asked.

"What, fucking?" Rosa asked and dropped the tape. It fell to the car floor.

"No. The Doors." He looked quickly over his shoulder before he pulled out onto Prospect Street.

"I guess," Rosa said, bumping her head on the dashboard as she retrieved the tape.

He laughed at her. "The other is a given."

Perhaps the Black and Tan still had its hold on Rosa. Or maybe she felt feisty from all those onions. In any case, it felt like someone else, someone more bold and daring—and certainly more reckless—who said to Gary, "Depends on who it's with."

She sneaked a look at him. He kept his eyes on the road, but he was smiling. "What about with me?"

"What about it?" Rosa asked.

"Give me a half hour and I'll leave you begging for more."

"Oh yeah?" Rosa said. "You wait until I get done with you. You're gonna be outta commission."

"What are you going to do, wear me down?"

"To a pulp," Rosa said. She smiled. It had been a long time since she had used the language of Pizza Beach—the idle threats issued over the chainlink fence of the school yard, the filth whispered in the Saint Boniface bathroom in between Latin and catechism. Coarse sounds pleased Rosa—the smack and slap of the blackboard erasers against the brick wall, the hollow bounce of the four-square ball, sneakers pounding the pavement, the scuttle of the Progresso pureed tomato can on the blacktop as she came racing out of her hiding place, kicked the can, and hollered *Ollie ollie all home free!* Most of all, she loved the kidlike mix of Italian and English, coarse and bitter as coffee grinds, which once had been her everyday language and which she had grown to scorn, but now knew she sorely missed.

Rosa liked talking dirty. After all, that was the real her—the girl who grew up saying things like *Don't like it, don't look at it! Cram it! Eat it!* and *Up yours!,* the girl whose throat burned deliciously from a Marlboro sneaked behind the ashcans of her father's garage, the girl who carelessly called other girls sluts and cunts before they could call her the same, and whose tongue vibrated with the sin of it the first time she was alone with a boy and said, "Well, if you're gonna dick me, come on, get on with it." Yes, this was the real Rosa, the girl who had grown into the woman who dreamed about fantastic, five-minute quickies as she stared at the blank computer screen, and who once was so taken by a doctor's sinewy forearm at a meeting that she had to stop herself from leaning over, touching his wrist, and whispering, "Fuck me. Hard."

The *fuck me* was understandable—a basic human desire—but where had the *hard* come from? From the real Rosa—the one who craved something deep below the humdrum of the everyday world, who wanted it to make her ache so badly that tears came to her eyes and the muscles in her calves burned and vibrated.

Rosa felt born to be some brazen slut—two legs in the back of a Chevy Impala. Instead, she went to college. There, she did not meet a single boy that she liked. She may have dreamed about armies of men as she sat in front of her computer, but in real life, she had only been with three men—or two and a half, since one was a badly bungled blow job. ("I told you not to nip 'em in the nuts," her cousin Connie reminded her afterwards. "The slightest hint of teeth and they never call you back.")

The first time Rosa did it—the momentous stripping of her virginity—consisted of some minor wrestling in a dorm room, where Rosa availed herself of the Catholic girl's form of birth control— three Hail Marys and two crossed fingers—while next door Van Morrison sang "Tupelo Honey" on WAVZ. The boy was from Moosup, Connecticut. Rosa hated his guts immediately afterwards.

The second man was the blow job. Enough said. The third was a highly unsatisfying affair that dragged on for seven months until Rosa finally had the courage to tell the man—who worked undercover for the New Haven police—that he was a bore and she really preferred men who showered on a regular basis. After it was all over, Rosa missed the marijuana he had stolen from the precinct, which they always smoked together. She felt incredibly lonely, and for months afterwards, she still dreamed about making love to him, his loaded gun resting beneath the bed.

Ah. What a pathetic sexual history.

Rosa jabbed the Doors tape into the cassette deck, leaned back, and watched the wipers swish back and forth across the windshield. The song was "Riders on the Storm." Appropriate. Gary pulled out into the left lane on Whalley Avenue and whizzed through a yellow light. Rosa relished the rain, the music, and the sleepy-beery feeling that enveloped her.

Gary also lived off Whalley, on Emerson. A stone staircase with a black enamel railing led up the steep hill to the three-story house. The front hallway was dark and cluttered with umbrellas and boots that probably belonged to the first-floor tenants. Gary put his arm around Rosa and escorted her and the extra piece of pizza up the bare wooden steps. Their footsteps echoed hollowly in the stairwell.

Gary had the third floor to himself. Like Rosa, he also had two deadbolts on his apartment door—a gold key for the top lock and a silver for the bottom. Rosa went into the apartment first and waited for Gary to turn on the light. But he closed the door behind him and the only illumination in the room came through a curtainless window, from a floodlight attached to a house across the way. Rosa heard the rustle of the aluminum foil as he put down the pizza. She tried to make out the outlines of the furniture, but after a moment the only outline she was aware of was the dark shape of Gary, which felt very pleasing as he backed her up against the wall, his hands on her hips, and kissed her surprisingly gently on the lips. Rosa slipped her hands beneath his jacket, settling one hand on his butt and the other just above his belt loop, on the small of his back. He leaned in further and Rosa tilted her hips so she could feel him better. Yup, it was all there—stiff and substantial—the very thing Rosa had been longing for. She felt satisfied. Anticipation always made her so much happier than action. She could have stayed pressed against the wall forever, just imagining how blissful she could be.

Gary rubbed his face against hers, and the prickle of his beard felt like rough wool on her skin. For a moment Rosa thought he was going to tell her that he loved her. But he whispered, "Are you—uh—*protected*?"

If it hadn't been such a practical and responsible question, Rosa might have slapped his face.

"Mmm-hmm," she whispered. Then it was her turn. "Got any deadly diseases?"

"I'm clean. *Et tu*?"

Rosa nodded.

Gary took her down the hall. The bedroom was completely dark. Rosa tripped on something that felt like a shoe and banged her knee on the edge of the bed. Some of her hair got caught underneath Gary's elbow and she tried not to grimace from the pain as they French-kissed. Finally. Ah. Here came the good stuff. The removal of clothes—above the waist—was slow and exciting and Rosa relished every hook and button. Below the waist, things become awkward and ridiculous, complicated by zippers and belts and shoes and socks—what were you supposed to do with socks, yank them off the man and throw them aside like dirty laundry? or let him take them off himself? or keep them on? and was there nothing more foolish than the thought of somebody's bare behind moving up and down on top of you, two dark, stockinged feet positioned at the end?

Oh, shut up, Rosa told herself. Shut up and enjoy yourself. Get naked! Make noises. *Ooh. Aah. Ya.* Shit, she sounded like a German tourist at the top of the Statue of Liberty.

Neither one of them spoke, but had they verbalized their thoughts it might have gone like this:

Watch your knees.
The hook's in front.
Hurry up.

What's your rush?
I'm supposed to like this? Mmm, tongue. I like this.
Relax, baby.
I hate the bottom.
Quit the wrestling. I'm getting on top.

But none of it got said. There was a lot of concentrated breathing, calculated kissing, and then Gary became all hands and mouth, and Rosa became all breasts and belly and hips and thighs, which stretched and grew tense until her feet, which barely could turn out during the bastardized fifth grade production of *The Nutcracker,* stiffened with more pointe than a prima ballerina with the Bolshoi Ballet. She was sopping wet. Gary penetrated her and Rosa ground herself down on him until she felt she would scream, the way she used to holler when she and Connie drove through the West Haven tunnel, the wind whipping through their hair and the radio blasting as all the lights in the world seemed to go out.

It was over in six minutes. Six minutes. Rosa knew. Perhaps because neither one of them wanted to assume the dominant position, actual intercourse took place kneeling on the bed, which afforded Rosa an excellent view of Gary's digital clock. There was oral stimulation and approximately a baker's dozen and a half of overly dramatic thrusts. All parties involved orgasmed, although not simultaneously, a magical feat which Rosa had never experienced and did not quite trust was possible, although she had read about it in novels and sex manuals and seen it on the movie screen, to her envy and disbelief.

Gary pulled Rosa down next to him and covered them both with the blankets. Rosa lay with her head on his chest and her thigh flung over his. Rain spattered the window, but beyond that, the world seemed so quiet that Rosa almost could have believed that she and Gary were the only two people on the planet.

"Well," Gary finally said. "I wouldn't give that one a standing O." He laughed. "Still. It was good. It felt good."

"Yeah," Rosa said. "It felt nice."

He smoothed his hand through her hair. "Don't go anywhere," he said. "I make good pancakes."

"But you probably have lousy shampoo," Rosa said. "Men always do."

"And I fall right asleep," Gary said lazily.

"And snore?"

"Like a pig, baby."

"And what do you dream of?" Rosa asked.

"You, of course. You."

Within a minute his breathing was steady and measured, and Rosa, although she still was in his arms, suddenly felt grossly alone. She extracted herself from his embrace and turned over. She tossed. She turned. She could not get to sleep. Finally, she groped her way in the dark toward the bathroom, where she turned on the light and continued down the hall to the living room. Where was it? Where was that frigging last piece of pizza? Rosa felt along the table until she heard the crinkle of aluminum foil. Then she peeled the foil back, and standing naked in Gary Fisher's living room, she devoured the slice in seven big bites, dabbing with her index finger to catch the little bits of sausage and mushrooms that had fallen on her naked breasts and that might leave a telltale sign on the carpet. How in the world would she explain the missing piece of pizza to Gary in the morning? Could she tell him she had a long history of post-coitum pigout? Could she tell him, *I once scarfed down half a bag of circus peanuts after screwing a member of the New Haven Police Department*? No! No! Some secrets were sacred! She groped through the dark and found her way back into bed, settling down in the sheets. Maybe Gary would just forget about the pizza. Maybe she would dream up a great, amusing excuse for her greed. For Rosa suddenly felt sleepy. But as she sunk her head into the feather pillow, she smelled the fresh scent of detergent. She held the sheets up to her nose. Same thing. Before he picked her up that evening, he must have changed the sheets. Just for her.

Cocky sonofabitch, she thought.

Sometimes Rosa dreamed in Italian. As she slipped into that odd, amorphous world between waking and sleeping, she had a soft, blurry vision of Gary tucking clean sheets under a mattress. And then, suddenly, Rosa was checking into a hotel, some rundown *albergo* in Rome, and the concierge, who was missing two front teeth, sarcastically asked the dream Rosa, *E certo? Vorrebe un letto matrimoniale?*

Ripeta. Repeat. Are you sure you want a double bed?

chapter four

Gary had a waffle iron he had bought for three bucks in the Jewish thrift shop on Whalley. The next morning—after Rosa had risen and pissed and surreptitiously brushed her teeth—he made her waffles and pancakes. They ate them silently. Then, standing at the sink, they let the dishes clatter against the drain, licked the maple syrup off each others' lips, and went back to bed to mess around some more. Mmmm. Aaaaah. So nice it ached. But all good things must end. Rosa took a long shower and put on her clothes from the night before, which made her feel grungy. She longed for clean underwear. And Gary *did* have bad shampoo. Men always did. And no hair dryer or mousse. Rosa felt lost without them.

"Hey, did you chow down that last piece of pizza?" Gary called out from the living room as Rosa tried to do something—anything—with her wet curls.

Rosa pretended not to hear him.

Around noon, Gary and Rosa went walking in Edgewood Park. They entered from the main parking lot by the ice-skating pavilion and walked along the banks of the creek, throwing in sticks and stones to hear the water splash. Then they crossed over the arched bridge that spanned the creek. The hollow sound of Rosa's pumps on the wooden slats reminded her of the fairy tale where the goats went trip-tripping over the bridge—Father Goat, Mother Goat, Baby Goat.

Ah, they walked! They talked! For hours, they explored the utter misery of their childhoods and adolescences, their foul relationships with their parents. Rosa began her life story by telling about the time her mother left her screaming in the crib, terrified and thoroughly convinced that Foghorn Leghorn was living in the bedroom mirror and was going to peck her to bits. She ended by telling Gary that she was worth nothing—absolutely nothing—in her parents' eyes because she was single and had no kids.

Gary said if he had to write the story of his life—his autobiography, his coming-of-age, his own personal *bildungsroman*—he would have to start at the most embarrassing part. He had been born in Flushing. "Sounds like I came out of a toilet bowl or something," he told Rosa. But although the name of his *città natale* was foolish, Gary still viewed his years in Flushing as a kind of paradise. Even though the folks who lived in the row houses were ugly and coarse, even though the delicatessens still had cracker baskets and pickle barrels and the drugstores sold too much castor oil and vinegar douches, there was a real sense of community.

Of course, Gary's mother didn't want to have much to do with the neighbors. She looked down on the other women, who wore gingham aprons and fuzzy slippers as they swept the front porches every morning. She thought their husbands—all small businessmen—were just that: petty. And she was not fond of the neighborhood kids, who ran in packs up and down the narrow sidewalks and alleys. Yet it pleased her to see that her son was extremely popular. Gary always was elected pitcher or quarterback or head cowboy when it came time for play. Once he was even chosen to be both Lewis and Clark when the kids played explorers, and he got to kiss Pocahontas—Judy Leitner, a pretty little thing with flaxen curls who looked nothing at all like the dark and fearless Indian squaw of Gary's imagination—twice. Whew! Life was good.

Not having any brothers or sisters, Gary's best friend and sibling equivalent was his cousin Benny, who lived four blocks over. Benny's father, Uncle Len, had a car dealership in Whitestone. Sometimes on Saturdays Gary and Benny would go to the showroom and horse around in the cars. Don't ask Gary why—he didn't quite understand himself why two Jewish kids would be so obsessed with acting like Italians when this was all pre-*Godfather*—but Gary and Benny used to climb in the silver Oldsmobile 88s and pretend they were a couple of mobsters.

Benny was the driver; Gary was the Don. Their names were Chooch and Looch and they *tawked like dey had mah-buls in der moufs.* By day, Chooch and Looch imported olive oil and balsamic vinegar into the harbors. By night they became cold-blooded killers, feared by all the Flushing *paesani* and respected by the rival families of the mob. Each night they popped off a couple of traitors to the family, roughed up a few insubordinates, and then swung the Oldsmobile 88 into a Bayside steak house, where they chowed bloody prime ribs, baked potatoes smothered in butter and sour cream, whole loaves of garlic bread, and a jug of dark Chianti. The restaurant was dim and red and empty and the waitress's name was Maria. After dinner Chooch and Looch took her in the back room and took turns sucking her big boobs on the black leather couch, her weak cries of *No, no, no!* quickly turning into a breathless string of *Yes, yes, yes.*

"You stupid kids!" Uncle Len used to holler. "Keep your fingerprints off my dashboards!"

Flushing was a boy's world. If they didn't go visit Uncle Len, they'd drop in on Gary's father Artie at his shop. Artie sold eyeglasses. Gary and Benny sat on the revolving stools and twirled around and around, then tried on all the spectacles, from the heavy tortoise-shell frames to the pink spangled jobs with the rhinestones on the ends. They giggled and laughed and did imitations of Groucho Marx, to Artie's amusement and the disgust of Naomi, the bookkeeper/receptionist who had thick black eyebrows that looked like they were going to coil up off her face like a couple of hissing snakes. Artie never yelled at them. He never said a word about fingerprints, even though Gary and Benny left smudges all over the mirrors and counters.

"Your father really loves you," Benny once told Gary.

And Gary, embarrassed, replied in his best Looch voice. "Whattaya tawking about?" because he was afraid if his dad loved him too much, then he would turn out to be—like, *homo* or something. The possibility was all too real with a father who was such a softie.

Artie had a tendency to get worked up over things. Once when he was cutting open a lemon to put in some cocktails, his bottom lip started to quiver, and when the four-year-old Gary asked him why, Artie said he was remembering the first time his mother brought home a lemon from the street market, and they all held a slice up to their lips to savor the new taste. "America," his mother said, screwing up her face from the sourness of it. "It's really something." Another time, tears came to Artie's eyes when he showed Gary a prayer shawl that his father—Gary's grandfather—had brought over from Poland. "See, look," Artie said, holding out the fringes. "Wax from the candles. He used to light them every Friday night. We used to make bets on which one would burn the longest. Those days are gone now."

Yes, Artie was a real soft touch. And Gary's mother?

For as long as Gary could remember, his mother Mimi had been addicted to snooker. Artie claimed Mimi first got hooked on the game during their honeymoon. Artie and Mimi went on a cruise to the Bahamas and Artie got seasick the very first night. Mimi was forced to go down to the buffet table alone. There she met a couple from New York who befriended her. The man was a snooker champion. "She spent the rest of the cruise banging balls in the game room," Artie said, "while I was sweating and burping on the upper deck."

Sometimes Gary tried to picture the guy who taught Mimi snooker and he imagined exactly the kind of guy his mother professed to despise: a sleazer from Queens, a sharpie from Brooklyn, with thick, built-up shoulders and a little mustache that quivered as he tried to sell you a flat of maple syrup or a crateful of pantyhose for half price. The Snooker Man had a shiny belt buckle and a toothy smile. Clean cuffs and bad intentions. A tolerant wife, who played canasta while her husband leaned over Mimi in the pool room, showing her how to guide the cue between her fingers and make a sharp, clean break.

"I don't know what happened," Artie sometimes said. "The minute I married her, I could hardly keep her out of the pool halls."

"Well," Mimi said and laughed—she had that brittle, false little laugh that for years had grated on Gary's nerves—"I got addicted, Artie. I was hopelessly addicted."

She was embarrassed by the whole thing, but also proud, as if she knew that her lust for snooker was the one thing that made her human.

When Gary went off to elementary school, Artie bought Mimi a snooker table. They had to move the dining room table into the front parlor to make room for it. Gary remembered relatives being a little taken aback by the arrangements. "I don't know, Artie," Uncle Len said. "It doesn't seem natural. It doesn't seem Jewish." But Artie shrugged and said, "You know women. Eccentric." Implying that if it wasn't snooker, Mimi would have found something else, maybe something even worse to get obsessed with: alcohol, housecleaning, overeating, nagging, a religious conversion. Best to live with a known vice.

Mimi had to have something to do with her life, besides rearranging the furniture every season. She was good at snooker and she won the trophies to prove it. Snooker was all hers. "She never once offered to teach me how to play," Gary told Rosa. "The thing I remember her saying to me most when I was growing up was, 'Stand back, Gary, you're in my way.' God, other kids would come home and find their mothers making cookies and brownies. I'd get a glimpse of my mother's rear end as she leaned over the table, squinting and calculating her next move. 'Don't break my concentration,' she'd warn me. And then came a loud crack. She'd stand up, her eyes still on the ball as it disappeared into the pocket. 'Well, hello, dear,' she'd say. 'How was your day?' And as the ball fell with a thud, she'd smile and start her interrogation. She had a lot of questions, and I had to report in, truthfully, or risk having my snack—two graham crackers stuck together with olive and pimento cream cheese—taken away.

"She wanted to know what I got on the last math test," Gary said.

"Was I—or was I *not*—the last child to be standing at the spelling bee? With whom had I played during recess, and what did his father do for a living? Were they Conservative or Reform? Who was the girl who said hello to me when she dropped me off at school that morning? She was very pretty. I didn't think so? Maybe I wasn't telling the truth. Maybe I was embarrassed? No? Well, maybe I was too young for that sort of thing. What was the going fad now? Was it still dinosaurs (goodness, those teeth on Tyrannosaurus Rex) or was it baseball (those tiresome, tobacco-chewing Mets) or had I progressed onto bigger and better things, like Kasey Kasem and the top forty?

"She was always so scornful of everything I was interested in," Gary continued. "She called everything a fad. *Gary's latest,* she said, whenever she wanted to describe to someone *what I was up to these days.* She got impatient when she had to drive me somewhere for practice or take me to the hardware store for more Super Glue. She got mad at me when I said only wimps used seat belts.

" 'Buckle up,' she said. 'If I have to stop short, I don't want to see you go flying through that front windshield like a rocket.'

" 'Sounds like fun,' I said and she shrieked, 'God, I am sick of men and Apollo Seven!' "

That was fine by Gary. Because he was sure he and Artie were just as sick of Mimi as she was of them. Didn't Artie and Gary have a rip-roaring good time whenever Mimi wasn't around? "She always complicated things. I'll never forget the time she got sick and had to go to the hospital. When I asked her what was the matter, she got all flustered and said it was something that only happened to women. So I dropped the subject right there—I mean, I was mortified to ask anything else. The maid—all right, so my parents have a maid, I didn't hire her!—watched me all week after school and Dad took me out to eat every night. I sort of had the feeling he liked having my mother gone, too. When we got home from the deli or the Chinese place, he played 78s on his wind-up Victrola, the kind of records my mother hated. There was one that simulated a radio broadcast. 'And now, from atop of the Loews State Theatre in New York City—the

B. Manischewitz Company, world's largest matzoh bakers, proudly presents your American Jewish Hour—Yiddish melodies in swing!' The drummer hit the down beat and the trumpets started to blare and my father snapped his fingers and be-bopped around the living room, munching on some of the Cracker Jacks he had bought me. In the meantime, I was playing with a blackboard and chalk on the floor, something I never dared to do with Mom around because she hated the sound of the chalk on the board and she said I got the carpet all dusty.

"Dad was totally into his records. He listened to Richard Tucker and Moishe Oysher and the Barry Sisters while I screwed around with the Cracker Jack prize and whined until he gave me a big bowl of chocolate ice cream to shut me up. It was ten o'clock before I got into my pajamas and I never had to brush my teeth before I went to bed.

"On Saturday—just to keep me amused—he took me to Playland in Rye. I acted horrible, a grade-A brat. I remember throwing some fit about some cotton candy and refusing to get off the kiddy train because I wanted to ride again. He had to put his hands underneath my armpits and drag me off. 'All right, that's it, we're going home,' he said, and on the drive back he kept on squinting like the sun was in his eyes, but it was cloudy and I knew I had given him a headache. That night I heard him tell my mother on the phone, 'Meem, I don't know how you do it,' and because he didn't have the phone all the way up to his ear, I heard my mother say back, 'Now you see. You see how he really is, what I have to deal with, every day.' And I realized then, right at that moment, that I would never have any brothers or sisters. That was fine by me. I didn't feel like sharing my toys. After my father hung up the phone, I decided I would be even more obnoxious for a while—throw a few fits, narrate whole baseball games to my mother, bug my father about getting a horse—just to make sure they didn't change their minds about having more kids.

"When Mom came home from the hospital, Dad walked her in the front door. 'Here's your mother,' he said, 'all rested up,' and she winced when I kissed her. Then she looked around and complained about how messy the house was—had I been playing with the black-board on the carpet, after she had told me a million times not to? And where were the pillows that belonged on the couch, she had told me a million times not to jump off the stairs onto those pillows and now look, now look! 'Artie,' she said, 'you let him run wild, he's completely out of control, you probably fed him nothing but sugar the whole time I was gone, and I told you, lots of grains and milk, and every other day or so, give him some fish for brain food,' and then she turned on me and said, 'What are staring at?'

" 'You look different, Mom,' I said and my father stood behind her, making motions at me to just leave the room, while she shrieked at me—yes, she shrieked, like an animal—to just get away, get out of her way, the sight of me made her sick!

"That was her first face lift," Gary said.

Rosa clucked her tongue sympathetically. "Your mother sounds horrible," she said.

Gary snorted. Horrible? She was harmful. Mimi Fisher was ra-dioactive waste. You had to arm yourself with gloves and goggles before you handled her. You could try and bury her, but she would continue to burn in the bowels of the earth. When Gary was grow-ing up, he always felt like there should have been showers in the halls of their house—you know, like the kind they have in the chem-istry labs, in case you spill some deadly chemical on yourself? He just never knew what kind of mood Mimi was going to be in or when she was going to turn on him and explode, with all the violence of one of those cartoon characters who swallows a firecracker.

What was Mimi Fisher's problem? Gary was no psychologist, but the other day when he was in Sears Roebuck—buying underwear, he was quick to assure Rosa—he noticed a sign over by the lady's lingerie department claiming that eighty-nine percent of American women were wearing the wrong bra size. Perhaps Mimi was in this large majority, which contributed to the tension she seemed to radi-ate. Or maybe she just felt trapped. The Fishers were not a good match. Artie was short and Mimi was tall and thin and liked to wear high heels. So far as Gary could tell—and he wasn't privy to much information—his parents had been introduced at some party. Artie was ten years older than Mimi. His business was starting to take off. And Mimi wanted to get out of Brooklyn, where she had been born and raised. "She could have been just another Flatbush fishwife," Gary said. "Instead, she married my dad. She learned how to use birth control. And now they're sitting together on Long Island, just a little confused—if they ever stop to think about it—about how they ever got there."

Rosa and Gary walked off of the asphalt onto the dirt path that led to the duck pond.

"You told me last night your parents weren't religious," Rosa said.

"They aren't," Gary said.

"But then you said your father showed you the prayer shawl. You told me you went to a private school for Jewish kids."

"I did."

"You said you went to kibbutz," Rosa continued.

"I was seventeen years old."

"What's that got to do with it?"

"Seventeen," he said. "Long Island girls." He drew a light bulb above Rosa's head. "I wanted to get laid."

"Well?" Rosa asked. "Did you?"

Gary got a dreamy look on his face. "Her name was Rachel Pinsk. She was from Camden, New Jersey. She gave me the best blow job of my entire life."

"You told me I did that this morning," Rosa reminded him.

"Oh," Gary said. "Well. I stand corrected."

For five weekends in a row they went walking in Edgewood Park, and Rosa put off introducing Gary to her parents. She didn't mind telling story after story about Pizza Beach—about how she and her cousin Connie, both the youngest in their families, both the only daughters, and both obviously accidents—used to filch their fathers' cigars and swipe money from their dads' cash bags to attend the Saturday matinees, where they would swoon over the muscled, oiled men who played the swarthy Jews and the Roman slaves in

Barabbas, Ben-Hur, Exodus, and *The Ten Commandments.* Yet she objected to actually showing Gary where she came from, for fear he would go flying in the opposite direction.

Rosa was forced to bring Gary home much sooner than she ever would have wanted. Once a month Rosa forced herself to drive back across the Q Bridge to her parents' house and eat Sunday dinner, which was served at noon. Rosa showed up around eleven to chop the tomatoes and peel and slice the cucumbers. Her mother seemed angry about something. Whenever Rosa tried to start a conversation, Antoinette answered only in monosyllables.

When the pasta turned soft, but not limp, Antoinette opened the china cabinet and fetched a white porcelain bell, painted with violets, off the second shelf. She opened the back door and shook the bell furiously in the direction of the garage where Rosa's father Aldo was working. "Chowtime!" she hollered. Rosa cringed. The only thing that saved her from rebuking her mother was the fact that the neighbors shouted even worse things out their doors. Down the street, Mrs. Piscitelli used to chase her son around the backyard with a metal spatula, yelling, "I'm gonna whack your can!" Across the way, Mr. Guidici—short, dark, and stocky as a fire plug—sprayed his teenage daughters with abuse, calling them *putane* and hot pants.

When Aldo came in from the garage, what little conversation there was between Rosa and her mother ceased. He answered Rosa's hello with merely a grunt. A grim wrinkle appeared between Antoinette's eyes, and the meal, as usual, was eaten in silence. When they were halfway through the ravioli, Antoinette finally said, "Zio Dino said he saw you the other night. In Athenos Pizza. With a man with a beard."

Rosa kept quiet.

"Zio Dino, he came to visit yesterday," Antoinette said. "And he goes to me, 'Rosa finally got herself a fellow?' " Antoinette held her fork sideways and split a piece of ravioli savagely in half. "What was I supposed to say to that?"

"What did you say?" Rosa asked.

"I had to act like I knew," Antoinette said. "Like I knew all about this man with the beard." She grabbed the parmigiano cheese and shook it angrily over her pasta. "You could bring him home to meet your parents," she said. "Unless you're ashamed of us. You ashamed of us?"

"I'm not ashamed of anybody," Rosa said. "And why doesn't Zio Dino mind his own business?"

"He's your family," Antoinette said. "You're his business."

Rosa stopped eating. "I haven't brought him home because we haven't been seeing each other that long."

"How long?" Antoinette asked.

"I'm not keeping track," Rosa lied.

"Did you hear that, Aldo?" Antoinette said loudly. "She's not keeping track."

Aldo took the loaf of Italian bread that sat in the center of the table, ripped off a large hunk, and used it to mop up the sauce in his bowl.

"What does he do?" Antoinette asked.

"He's in law school." Rosa peeled forth the facts slowly, aware that each bit of information was a strike against Gary. "At Yale. He's from New York."

"*Come si chiama?*"

Rosa bit her lip. "Gary. Gary Fisher."

Then there was silence, broken only by the sound of the forks squeaking against the bowls of ravioli. "That's a Jewish name," Antoinette finally said.

"No shit!" Rosa answered.

Aldo shook his fork at Rosa. "Watch your mouth!"

Antoinette shook her head. "*Managgia.* What next?" She kept quiet for a moment, as if trying to decide what to do. "Next Sunday," she finally said, as if challenging Rosa to a rumble. "Here."

"What time?" Rosa said.

"Same as always."

"What are you going to cook?"

"What does he eat?" Antoinette asked.

"Food," Rosa said.

"He like Italian?" Antoinette asked.

"Obviously," Aldo said, only half stifling a burp.

"Where'd you meet him?" Antoinette asked.

"At work," Rosa said, reluctantly.

More silence. Then Antoinette made tssking noises with her tongue. "At work. She meets him at work. Did you hear that, Aldo? I told her, when she took that job, I said, you better watch out, at Yale Hospital they do abortions!"

"Oh, Mother. For Christ's sake, what do abortions have to do with it?"

Rosa got up from the table. She picked up her plate and dumped the rest of her ravioli in the wastebasket, where it fell to the bottom with a thud. The tomato sauce splashed back and spattered Rosa's new pointelle-lace sweater, which she had bought at Macy's—and not on sale—just the week before. Rosa couldn't wait to go home— her own home—and wash the stain out.

She dreaded telling Gary about the invitation to dinner. "Hot *dog!*" Gary said, when Rosa told him. He was thrilled. For weeks he had been hounding Rosa to meet her family. He went through Rosa's photo albums and was touched—no, honest to God, really touched—by the pictures of Rosa and her cousin Connie walking solemnly down the aisle in their white bouffant dresses to make their First Holy Communion, and by the photographs of Rosa standing in front of her father's plumbing truck in her Easter outfit, complete with white wicker purse and bubble hat. "Your father's pretty good-looking," Gary said, and Rosa squinted at the pictures, trying to see the man that Gary saw. "But your aunts look like the ladies on the pizza boxes—you know, La Donna and Mama Celeste."

Rosa did not want Gary to meet Antoinette, because all the magazine articles she had ever read on mother-daughter relationships said that young women inevitably turned into their mothers. What if Gary had read the same articles? He would see the hard knot of tension, dark and ugly as a mole, that formed at the back of Antoinette's neck as she bent over the kitchen sink and scrubbed the zucchini with a vegetable brush. He would see her ankles, swollen from water retention, and the rings that circled her throat like a choker, which came from not moisturizing the skin on her neck. Antoinette's harsh voice and bossy commands ("Go on, siddown! Help yourself! Eat!") would grate on Gary. The minute Antoinette rang that cheap porcelain dinner bell out the back window to announce dinner time, Gary would realize that this hideous spectre of a woman—a battle-ax right off of prime-time TV—would haunt him for the rest of his days, and he would turn tail and run. Just run. Rosa would never see him again.

"I can't wait to go to your house," Gary said. "What do you think I should wear? What's on the menu? Think your father will talk to me? Think your mother will slap me on the back of my head and say, 'Shut up and eat'?"

"Maybe she'll just say 'shut up and shut up'," Rosa said, and turned a deaf ear on Gary. Why did he have to talk so much? God, she had never met any man who jawed so much in her entire life.

This became all too evident on the Sunday they went to Aldo and Antoinette's for dinner. Gary insisted on driving, although he had never taken the Q bridge before and was not aware of its many sharp curves and little room for maneuvering. As he accelerated onto the ramp, Rosa closed her eyes to block out the sight of the traffic and the view far below of the grey and pink oil tanks that lined the shore. Rosa wished she could block out the smell of the harbor. The brackish odor of low tide seeped in through the closed windows of the car and made Rosa's nostrils quiver.

"Relax," Gary said. "It's just your parents."

Rosa leaned back in the car seat. God. This was a nightmare. On top of mega-menstrual cramps (which she already had medicated with too much Motrin), she was developing a throbbing headache, an aching bladder, a sore throat, and the initial abdominal rumblings that always signaled the prelude to a spastic colon attack. Rosa clutched the car-door handle. They would just have to turn back. They could not go to her parents' house. They would have to go to the emergency room, where Gary would hover over Rosa for hours in the lobby until the nurses finally called Rosa's name. Then Rosa would be ushered into an examination room, stripped of her clothing, and forced to don a scratchy gown that reminded her of the paper tablecloths her mother used to put on the park tables during Fourth of July picnics. Another hour would pass until a doctor finally came in and asked her what was the matter, and Rosa would clutch her stomach and whisper, "I was born."

"Other symptoms?" the doctor would ask.

"I have Italian parents," Rosa would say.

Rosa would be released on the spot.

Rosa opened her eyes and found Gary tailing a Pontiac with five inches to spare.

"Not so fast!" she said.

"Relax," Gary said. "I know how to drive, I'm from New York."

"You'd better behave," Rosa warned him. (See. Listen. Already. Her mother.)

"Don't worry," Gary said. "I know how to make normal conversation, even if I never do it with you."

"So now it's my fault you're a *chiacchierone*?" Rosa asked.

"What's a *chiacchierone*?" Gary asked.

"A diarrhea mouth," Rosa said.

"Oh," Gary said. "I knew I didn't like the sound of it."

Rosa sighed and stared out the window. Occasionally she said, "Turn right" or "Left at the light" as Gary, not daunted in the least by the implication that he had a tendency to chatter, launched into another one of his stories. Gary thought he was the Aesop of Long Island. Trouble was, his stories had no morals. Even more trouble was, his stories had no point. He remembered all these weird scenes from his childhood and he could describe them to Rosa for hours. These stories always were character-driven and usually began like this: "There was this kid in third grade named Mark Rabinowitz. . . . " "The summer between sixth and seventh grade, there was this girl named Esther Lieber. . . . " Rabinowitz was purported to have done it with a dog, a German Shepherd named Queenie. Esther Lieber was purported to have done it with Mark Rabinowitz, but her armpits were so utterly *pee-yew!* that nobody else wanted to take a turn.

As they drove to Rosa's parents' house, Gary launched into a long one about a rabbi at a summer day camp designed to introduce secular Jewish boys to the least superstitious forms of their heritage. The rabbi wore a dashiki and love beads and made the campers sing international songs like *Zum Gollie, Gollie, Hava Nagila, Alouette,* and *Up, Up With People!* to the accompaniment of a bongo drum. By the time they approached the East Haven town line, Rosa had an ache sharper than a cleaver slicing through her head and Gary was crooning *Kumbaya.*

Rosa started a new verse. "Someone loves the sound of his own voice—"

"Kumbaya!"

"Someone's not watching where he's driving—" Rosa began to sing, then gasped. Gary was staring out the window at the houses; the Subaru swerved on the street and a rusty station wagon missed them by about half an inch. The driver leaned on his horn and Gary flipped him the finger.

"Whoa," Gary said. "Someone's praying now, Kumbaya."

Rosa sighed. "Turn down this street, keep on going until I tell you to park. Keep on going, would you please look where you're going!"

Parallel parking was not Gary's forte. The Subaru stalled out twice as he tried to jam it back against the curb. Gary laughed. "God, did I ever tell you about this kid in driver education class—"

Rosa glared at him. "Shut up," she said.

Gary looked hurt. "And all this time, I thought you loved me for my mouth."

"Guess again."

Gary turned off the ignition. "Then you must love me for my big, fat, throbbing—"

"Ha!" Rosa laughed, perhaps a bit too scornfully for Gary's comfort. "Who said I loved you?"

"Who said you didn't?" Gary asked. He got out of the car and slammed the door.

Rosa supposed this was a declaration of sorts, a new twist to the—uh, *situation*. Rosa did not use the word *relationship*. She also had read in countless women's magazines that men were turned off by this word and any other combination of vowels and consonants that implied they would have to give up all the manly pleasures in life—belching, farting, and yelling, "Oh my God, fourth and goal on the one!" as their team struggled its way into the Super Bowl playoffs.

Gary seemed embarrassed when Rosa got out of the car. He was looking down at the street as if he had never seen asphalt before, and he was rubbing his toe against it to test its resiliency. Rosa just stood on the curb. Goddammit. Let him make the first move. Make him say something. For once, Gary seemed a little tongue-tied. Then—perhaps on the principal that actions spoke louder than words—he came over to the curb and gave her a long, delicate kiss.

"Mmm, good one," he said. "Tastes like marinated mushrooms or something."

Rosa pushed him. "Get outta here."

Rosa had made Gary park his Subaru far down the street from her parents' house. In this neighborhood, *ci compra Americano.* They bought Detroit. Gary's was the only foreign car among the fender-dented Fords and Chevrolets lining the curbs.

Gary worked on Congress Avenue and had been in and out of the back entrance of the hospital several times, with plenty of chances to observe the bad straits of the surrounding neighborhoods. Still, Rosa doubted he had ever been in a neighborhood such as Pizza Beach, where tomato plants drooped on hand-cut stakes, chipped statues of the madonna (lit by eerie green or yellow spotlights at night) defended the front yards, and charms against the *mal'occhio* hung on the front doors. Here and there you could still find the rotten lumber from the now-defunct outhouses, or coils of rusty wire from the old chicken and goat pens. The air smelled of cattails and salt from the marshes a quarter of a mile down the road. The foundations of the houses rattled and the contents of the china cabinets—the dishes, teapots, and porcelain statues of the bride and groom plucked off wedding cakes—vibrated whenever commuter planes buzzed into Tweed–New Haven Airport.

Here the peeling paint and scanty, weedy front yards could not be blamed on discrimination or lack of equal opportunity. The poverty in Rosa's old neighborhood came not from unemployment but from working too hard at jobs that paid too little and that were too mindless to even talk about at the end of the long day. The privation came from saving every spare penny that did not go towards Catholic School tuition for elaborate wedding receptions with open bars and five-piece dance bands, and for silk-lined lead coffins that served as the centerpiece at lavish ten-limousine funerals. On the shore, the want and need for something better made itself manifest not in loud car radios and open drug-dealing on the street, but in occasional alcoholic binges and the ever-present blue glow of the living-room TVs.

Yet the people in Rosa's old neighborhood who were conscious of their slender means were not ashamed of them. They wore their poverty like a badge of honor. They were the little guys, the ones who made the country go, and they proudly announced their bad straits through the worn-out dishrags hanging on the clotheslines, the buckled blacktop driveways, and the shattered stones of the sidewalk, which little girls used as hopscotch tokens and which little boys delighted in crushing and grinding beneath their feet. One of Rosa's father's favorite sayings, besides *Nothing beats a really good tomato,* was *Hey, everybody take care of their own backyard.* This meant the sidewalks went to pot until the city officials came out in their shiny white cars and forced the owners to fix them.

Walking down the street, Rosa saw the neighborhood through Gary's eyes, then saw it again through her own. Each readjustment of her vision made the picture seem worse. Her heart pounded as they passed by the houses she knew so well, and she sunk her nails into her palms as they walked toward her parents' house, past her father's green Chevrolet sedan out on the street, and in the driveway, his big square truck emblazoned in red with *PLUMB EASY, Aldo Salvatore, sole proprietor.* Heaps of plumbing supplies sat to the side, waiting to be loaded onto the truck. In the middle of the faucets, joints, and pipes sat a pristine white toilet bowl that made Rosa despair. It seemed like a symbol, an advance announcement of everything that was ridiculous about her family.

Gary was polite. He looked at the toilet bowl and then looked away.

From the driveway, Rosa could see Antoinette standing behind the lace curtain in the kitchen window, sizing up Gary—his corduroys, Rockports, work shirt, and beard. It made Rosa furious. "My father's probably in the garage," she told Gary. Sure enough, Aldo was sitting at a worktable he had improvised out of a sheet of plywood and two wine barrels. On the wall above him hung a faded felt Yankees pennant. And next to that—a small detail that Rosa had forgotten about—hung a black-and-white portrait of Benito Mussolini which had been on display in her father's garage for as long as Rosa could remember. The photo had belonged to Rosa's grandfather, who stoked coal for the railroad when he first came over, and who liked the notion that Mussolini, unlike Conrail, had the ability to make the trains run on time. After her grandfather died, Rosa had suggested that her father take down the picture. Aldo merely grunted, as he did whenever anyone mentioned making any kind of change, and Antoinette said, "You never know, we might be related."

Gary's eyes lingered for a moment on the portrait. "Whoa," he said, beneath his breath, and Rosa felt herself turning hot and red. But there was no time to deal with Il Duce, because Rosa's father had looked up when they came in the garage. Aldo did not get up from his stool.

"I got dirty hands," he said when Rosa introduced Gary. He took a rag and made a big deal out of wiping the grease off his fingers. After he shook Gary's hand, he tossed Gary the rag and motioned toward a wooden chair.

Gary sat down and asked him what he was doing. Aldo showed him how he was fitting the pieces of the faucet together and replacing the worn threads. He ignored Rosa. Since there was nowhere to sit, Rosa just stood there, and within the space of a minute, she had become the outsider. It was just the two men talking at the worktable, with Rosa hanging off to the side, wanting to take a pick and chisel to the fat lip and watchful eye of Mussolini and listening to the clatter coming from the kitchen. Antoinette was scraping the pots and crashing the lids around on the pans, angry because Rosa hadn't introduced Gary to her first.

When all three of them finally went into the house, Antoinette welcomed Gary by clutching both his hands and holding them so tight she seemed to paralyze the rest of his body. Then she ushered him into the dining room and held out a chair for him. The table was set with a white Venetian lace cloth, Antoinette's light pink hexagon-shaped wedding plates, some crystal glasses Rosa had never even seen before, and the heavy Towle silverware that usually sat wrapped in burgundy velvet in the wooden box on the buffet. Antoinette held up her finger and went back into the kitchen. Over the sound of the faucet running, Rosa heard her father say in Italian, "What are we expecting, royalty?"

"Wash your hands," Antoinette hissed back in Italian.

"I'm washing 'em!" he said in English.

Rosa's face turned as pink as the china. She gave Gary a pleading look. Gary sat back in his chair and folded his hands over his stomach, the very picture of some fat burgermeister in an illustrated fairytale book. Aldo came in and sat at the head of the table. Antoinette pushed Rosa into a chair and then rushed back and forth from the kitchen, so fast and so often her apron came undone in the back. She announced each dish as she set it on the table. "Fennel slices. Cucumbers and tomatoes with basil and oregano. Here you got your stuffed artichokes. Your mushrooms in oil. Your meatballs. Your sausage and peppers." After she lowered the last heavy dish to the table, she took off her oven mitts and wiped the sweat off her forehead with the back of her hand. "Baked ziti," she announced. *"Mangiamo."*

"Where's the bread?" Aldo said.

Antoinette looked flustered. She rushed into the kitchen and came back wielding a fat crusty loaf, which she set down directly on the tablecloth. Antoinette took a plate and heaped a little bit of everything onto it. Then, to Rosa's dismay, she plopped the plate down in front of Aldo instead of Gary. She served Gary next, then left Rosa to fend for herself.

Aldo took the loaf of bread and ripped off the end, passing it to Rosa. Rosa looked at her mother. With her right hand, she tried to make a discreet sawing motion. Antoinette looked confused.

"Knife," Rosa started to silently mouth at her. But then, fearing her mother would answer, *What's the matter, too good to use your hands?* Rosa defied etiquette. Crumbs scattered over the table as she ripped off a hunk of the bread. Gary smiled at her as she passed him the loaf. He took a large piece. He had to put his piece on the table-cloth because Antoinette had loaded up his plate.

Everyone began to eat. After a couple of vain attempts to start a conversation about the weather, Rosa gave up and decided to concentrate on the meal. Aldo chewed as loud as a cow. Out of nervousness, Antoinette started to hiccup. She held her clenched fist to her chest and repeated *"Scusi! Scusate!"* Gary was the only one who seemed relaxed. He sat back in his chair and ate in peace.

After her hiccups had subsided, Antoinette told Gary, "I got a cousin in New York."

"Who?" asked Aldo.

"My Aunt Theresa's oldest. His real name's Cesarino. They call him Johnny for short."

"He the bum that owns the bar?" Aldo asked.

"Hey, nobody owns a bar in my family," Antoinette said. "Johnny, he's got a good job, working for a liquor importer. Of course, he plays the dogs every now and then." She turned to Gary. "They say New York is a big city."

"My parents live on Long Island," Gary said.

Antoinette looked confused. "You said he was from New York," she told Rosa.

"He is from New York," Rosa said.

"He just said Long Island," Antoinette said.

"New York *State*," Aldo said, impatiently. "Where'd you go to school?"

"Same school as you!" Antoinette replied. She shook her finger at Rosa. "When people say New York, they should mean New York. The real thing. The city." She pointed her fork at Gary. "I don't get it. Where you from? Tell me where you're from."

"I grew up in Flushing," Gary said.

"Like flushing the john?" Antoinette asked.

"Yeah," Gary said. "Mmm, these meatballs are good."

"Have some more, have some more."

"And then my parents moved to Manhassat—" Gary added.

"That's a funny name, too," Antoinette said.

"Let him talk," Aldo said.

"He is talking," Antoinette said. "*Ascolti.* Listen to him. You got brothers and sisters?"

Gary shook his head. And Antoinette shook hers. "That must of been hard," she said. "You had to do all the chores!"

Yeah, real hard, Rosa felt like saying. With a maid and all. But Gary nodded and kept on eating and Rosa let it go.

"Rosa's got two brothers," Antoinette said. "Frankie and Junior. And then she got her cousin Connie, she lived in back of us, they grew up like sisters. She tell you about Connie?" Antoinette clucked her tongue. "Divorced. Two kids. But now she's getting back on her feet again. She's assistant manager of a store—do you believe it?— where everything costs a dollar."

"Ninety-nine cents," Aldo corrected her.

"Ninety-nine, a dollar, what's the difference?" Antoinette said.

"It's the extra penny," Aldo said. "People think they're getting a bargain."

"People don't know how to add up ninety-nine cents in their head," Gary said. "There's been all sorts of market research—"

"You ever been in one of those stores?" Antoinette asked. "I never been. Pina—that's Rosa's *zia*—Rosa's aunt—she said she'd take me. But it's all the way out toward Branford. I don't know, I said. Lemme think about it. What am I gonna buy there? I thought.

I got everything I need. I got everything I needed when I got married."

"And you never threw any of it out," Rosa commented.

Antoinette glared at Rosa. "She doesn't like my cutting board," she said to Gary. "So it has a few cracks. I can live with it. They say we're a disposable culture. I read about it in the *Register*—you read the article in the *Register* about the guys—scientists, they call themselves, garbologists, who go digging through people's trash? They want to see what people throw out. *Madonna mia,* how'd you like to have that job?"

"That's not a real job," Aldo said. "That's some crackpot stuff they do, with money from the government." He pointed his knife at Gary. "What line a work your father in?"

"He sells eyeglasses," Gary said.

"He got his own shop?" Aldo asked.

He's got thirty, Rosa felt like saying. But she sat there and waited to see how Gary would answer the question. He did it with a noncommittal, "Mm-hmm. Yes."

"It's hard to stay in business," Aldo said. "There's no room for the little guy. The little guy is getting crushed. People are going bankrupt right and left. All this Walmart and K-Mart stuff. The chains are running everybody out of business—"

"Gary's father owns a franchise," Rosa said.

Aldo grunted. "Smart guy," he said. "Knows which end is up."

"Forgot the water!" Antoinette hopped up from the table and came back with a pitcher of ice water. The ice cubes rattled and hissed as she slopped water into the glasses. She dabbed at the wet tablecloth with a corner of her apron and sat down again.

"So you're gonna be a lawyer, huh?" she asked Gary.

"That's right."

Antoinette narrowed her eyes with displeasure. "People gonna go to you when they want a divorce?"

"There are all kinds of lawyers," Gary said. And for Antoinette's benefit, he went through the categories alphabetically—accident and health insurance, aviation, bankruptcy and debtor-creditor relations, civil rights, corporate, criminal, divorce, environmental, general litigation, immigration, labor, malpractice, patent, real estate, taxation, wills and probate. Little did he realize, Rosa thought, that all the categories were the same to her parents, who considered divorce and taxation on a par with bomb threats and shopping-mall mass murders, and who believed anyone who even stepped within a court room was guilty of the great crime of *rocking the boat.* They should be thrown in jail just for being troublemakers.

When Gary was done with his little speech, Antoinette looked dubious. "*Managgia,* they got their nose in everything these days, these lawyers," she said. "What kind are you?"

"I'm still a student," Gary said.

Antoinette shook her head. "You go to Yale," she said. "That's a bad neighborhood."

Before Antoinette could launch into a story about the numerous relatives who had been mugged on Chapel Street, Rosa said to Gary, "Tell her what kind of law you want to practice."

"Immigration," Gary said. "Immigration law."

Aldo grunted. "These days, you get off the boat and you got all kinds of rights."

Rosa sighed.

"We came here," Aldo said, "with nothing. And we took it on the ear. What rights did we have? Nowadays, there's all sorts of groups, all hollering about how they want this, that, and the other. They want their rights? Go ahead. Give them their rights. They got the right to go back where they came from!"

"Maybe some of them didn't want to come here in the first place," Gary said.

"Don't kid yourself," Aldo said. "Everybody wants to be American."

"Yeah," Gary said, "even some Americans still want to be American."

"What do you mean by that?" Aldo asked.

"Well—uh—sir, do people always treat you like an American?" Gary asked.

"I pay my taxes, same as everybody else," Aldo said.

"He's not American," Antoinette said. "He's *Italiano*. He belongs to the IA Club on Fox Avenue. By the way, you got the bill, your dues are due, don't forget to pay them—"

"Okay, so you belong to the IA Club," Gary said to Aldo. "You live in New Haven, there's a huge Italian-American population, you're surrounded by tons of people who are just like you—"

Antoinette held up her hand. "We got nothing to do with the Mafia."

"Ma! Cut it out!" Rosa said. "He didn't say that."

"What do I care what he says? I care what he's thinking."

Gary ignored them. He leaned across the table at Aldo. "Say you moved to, uh, I don't know, some other place in the United States, Tennessee or South Dakota—"

"What for?" Antoinette asked.

"Just pretend," Gary said. "I mean, people might treat you like a foreigner."

"They say Columbus was here first," Antoinette said. "And they also say first come, first served—and if you don't like it, tough tomatoes."

Gary paused. He looked like he was trying to find an intelligent response to that comment. Finally he said, "You know, that's why I want to go into law. Say somebody treated you unfairly, because they didn't like the color of your skin or hair, or they treated you differently because you were a woman—"

"Hey, there's a difference between men and women!" Antoinette said.

Gary put down his fork and smiled. "I know that," he said.

Silence fell over the table. Rosa blushed. Aldo took his fork and chopped a meatball in half; little specks of tomato sauce splattered onto the tablecloth. Antoinette looked over at the table at Rosa and glared at her, as if Rosa had the nerve to go out with a man who was fully cognizant of the difference between the sexes and who probably acted upon this difference, with her daughter, no less. Then Antoinette looked back at Gary. He just sat there, looking a little bit obtuse about the whole thing, and Rosa felt like leaning across the table and telling him that the ultimate taboo at her parents' dinner table was not politics or religion—after all, it was a free country, and everybody had a right to their own fool opinion about God or government—but one thing, dammit, that you did not talk about, did not acknowledge, was sex.

Surprisingly, it was Aldo who smoothed things over. "Aah, these days, you don't like the way somebody looks at you, you go to court."

"You're gonna do good business," Antoinette said to Gary. "I can tell. You got a big mouth. You're gonna be a good lawyer." She looked approvingly at his plate, which was almost empty. "You like Italian food?" she asked.

"If I'd known you were such a good cook," Gary said, "I would have asked Rosa to take me here a month ago."

"There," Antoinette said to Rosa triumphantly. "You see? He wanted to come." She turned to Gary. "You want *più*? You'll have more? He wants more, Aldo."

"So give him some, and stop *chiacchieroning* about it," Aldo said.

So, within the space of those two or three minutes, Rosa could see that her parents accepted Gary, not because they could tell that Rosa loved him, but because they suspected she had kissed him, maybe even let him cop a few feels above the waist—through the clothes, of course—before he dropped her off at her apartment. They could not know—and perhaps did not have the capacity to imagine—that just a few hours ago, Rosa had woken up in Gary's bed, completely naked, her breasts bruised from Gary's mouth and her crotch raw from the night before. If only they suspected! Antoinette would look sorrowful and tell Rosa that she would pray for her. Then she would get into the habit of calling Rosa's apartment early on weekend mornings to see if Rosa were there or not, and maybe she would even show up at Gary's door, unannounced, wielding a large jug of cranberry juice which she would offer her daughter as a cure for those inevitable urinary tract infections. Aldo, on the other hand, might grunt. He might fantasize about putting

Rosa in a cage, where all loose women rightly belonged. He might fantasize about sinking Gary's Rockports into a tub of cement and throwing Gary off the Q Bridge into the dark depths of high tide in the New Haven Harbor. Rosa didn't know what he would do if he found out about their relationship. But one thing was for certain, he would take down the picture of Mussolini now. Rosa was sure of it.

Just then the phone rang. "Let it go," Aldo growled when Antoinette pushed back her chair. "We're eating dinner."

"Who's still eating?" Antoinette called out from the kitchen. "Just him." Gary looked up from his plate guiltily, then shrugged and began to reattack the ziti. "Besides somebody might of died, how do you know?"

"So let 'em be dead on the answering machine," Aldo said.

Sick and tired of answering the phone at all hours of the day and night, Antoinette and Aldo had finally "joined the space age," as Antoinette called it, and purchased an answering machine for the plumbing business. It took them hours to figure out how to hook it up, and they never did determine how to silence the outgoing message or adjust the volume of the speaker. So the hollow echo, beep, and hum of the outgoing and incoming messages created more noise and trouble than a persistently ringing phone that needed to be picked up.

In the kitchen, Antoinette got to the phone before the machine caught it. "Hello," she hollered into the receiver. Then she moved the phone over so she could get a good look into the dining room. "No. No. No," she said. "Yes. No. No, he's still eating."

Gary looked up, observed once again that he was the only person still stuffing his face, shrugged again, and went back to his dinner.

Antoinette continued to say yes or no. Then she knocked her hand against her head, quickly pointed at Gary, and lip-synched to Rosa, "Does he *capisce* Italian?"

Rosa refused to answer.

"Pssst," Antoinette said, her hand over the receiver. This time she gestured with her head towards Gary. *"Parla italiano?"* she hissed.

"Guess!" Rosa said through clenched teeth.

Antoinette dissolved into a flood of Italian. Gary started to look nervous. "My Aunt Pina doesn't speak English very well," Rosa said.

"What are you talking about?" Aldo said. "She speaks it as good as I do."

"Tell Ma to get off the phone," Rosa said.

"I already told her," Aldo said. "Since when does she listen to me? She got a real *testa di cavolo,* that one there, head hard as bricks."

"These cucumbers are really good," Gary said, as Antoinette detailed, in rapid-fire Italian, Gary's height, probable weight, hair color, eye color, beard color, skin color, father's profession, and estimated value of that business. Antoinette didn't know—she wasn't sure what these eyeglass stores were worth—but one thing was for sure, Gary was going to Yale, and that meant somebody in his family had the bucks, and plenty of them.

Rosa was mortified. "Get off the phone, Mother," she said.

Antoinette nodded and waved at Rosa. "I gotta go," she said in English. "I don't wanna be rude to our guest."

When Antoinette came back into the dining room, all smiles for Gary, Rosa could have easily stretched out her two hands and strangled her.

"Aunt Pina wanted to know what I made for dinner," Antoinette said. "I told her we had a visitor."

"You forgot to tell her Gary's the only child," Rosa said.

"Oh, *madonna mia,* I completely forgot. I'll call her back later." Antoinette sat down and nodded approvingly at Gary. "Look at him, look at him go. It's like watching one of your brothers eat."

Gary's fork stopped in midair.

"Let him eat," Aldo said. Then, without any explanation, he got up from the table and went through the kitchen out the back door.

When Gary looked questioningly at Rosa, Antoinette told him, "You gotta excuse my husband, he's got the gas. You better stop eating now too, before you get it. Save room for dessert." She took the fork out of Gary's hand and pulled his plate away. "I got zeppole, you like the zeppole? I got a dozen, you gotta have at least two."

"What the hell is zeppole?" Gary whispered while Antoinette was in the kitchen.

"A pastry that looks like a tit," Rosa whispered.

"Do I have to eat two if I don't want two?"

"I don't know," Rosa said. "Do what you want. What do I care?"

"I don't want to offend anybody," Gary said.

"Who's to offend?" Rosa whispered. The phone began to ring again.

"I'm gonna get it!" Antoinette called out.

"Let it go!" Aldo hollered from the back porch.

Rosa felt her eyes fill with tears. "I told you my family was crazy," she whispered to Gary. "My mother's a moron, my aunts are busy-bodies, my father's bombing the big one out on the back porch, and you really think somebody's got the right to criticize if you don't want to eat a couple of pastries that look like boobs?"

"I just want to do the right thing," Gary said. "You know, when in Rome—"

"Then eat them and shut up," Rosa hissed.

"Sir! Yes, sir!" Gary said and gave Rosa a mock salute, as the answering machine picked up the call. There was a long, breathy silence, and then Aldo's voice came through in halting rhythm, "This here is—uh—Plumb Easy—expert plumbing and repair—at your service—Monday through Friday—and emergencies only on weekends. Leave your name—and number—and what's your problem—and I'll call you back—yeah, I'll call you back. Here comes da beep."

The beep screeched and there was enough heavy breathing to qualify for an obscene phone call. Then Rosa's Zia Fifi said, "Am I talking to the machine? I'm talking to the machine. Are you there? Antoinette, you there?"

"I'm here, I'm here!" Antoinette said. "I hear you."

"Mother, she can't hear you," Rosa said, "unless you pick up the phone!"

"How'm I gonna pick up the phone? The machine already did it for me!"

"Lift the receiver," Rosa said.

Zia Fifi was under the impression that she had to talk much louder to a machine than to a human being. "Antoinette," she bellowed. "I just talked to Pina. I'm gonna do my tomatoes this afternoon, I gotta have another colander and Pina says she can't spare her *collino* for a few hours, I know you got more than one and you don't mind if I come over and borrow it—"

Rosa put her head down on the table and cradled it with her hands.

For symmetry's sake, Gary ate two zeppole, and Zia Fifi, when she came over to gawk at him, took a napkin and wiped the powdered sugar from his beard. "You got some ziti in there, too," she said, dunking the napkin into Gary's water glass and scrubbing the pasta out.

"Get your hands off of him," Aldo said. "You don't even know him."

"What, you want your daughter to do this?" Zia Fifi asked. "You don't mind, do you?" she asked Gary. "A handsome guy like you, walking around with your dinner all over your face?"

"I really appreciate your concern," Gary said. And to Antoinette he said, "It was a great dinner."

"You come back next Sunday," Antoinette said.

"Sure," Gary said, before Rosa could stomp on his foot underneath the table.

"You bring him," Antoinette said to Rosa. "I'll get the zeppole again, special for him. You like lasagne, I'll make lasagne."

Rosa frowned. And then she grew resentful of all this deference given to Gary, all this kowtowing and cleaning his beard. Why didn't they just get some oil and wash his feet? All because he was a man. A man. And a man was meant to be waited upon. His wish was their command. It was sickening.

Rosa went into the kitchen and started to wash the dishes. Discovering that Gary liked classical music, Antoinette got out her Liberace albums, and Rosa scrubbed the ancient aluminum pots to the bombast of the *Warsaw Concerto*. Aldo sulked in his La-Z-Boy lounger because he was missing the Yankees game. Zia Fifi, no longer making any pretense about the nature of her visit, plopped her fat behind on the faded chintz couch and complained about her varicose veins. "You got the veins, too?" she asked when Gary expressed his sympathy. "So young. But young people nowadays are getting everything, tonsillitis, this AIDS thing—"

"Nobody we know has that," Antoinette said.

"—and cancer even. It's horrible. But it's God's will. We never know, do we, when God is gonna call our number?"

"Yeah, it's kind of like the lottery," Gary said.

"Or Bingo," Antoinette said. "You like Bingo? What do you mean, you sang the song but never played?"

Liberace gave way to Sinatra, and Sinatra melted into Tony Bennett, who, in Rosa's opinion, had left his heart so many times in San Francisco, it would be a mercy if he just flung himself off the Golden Gate Bridge. Rosa kept on waiting for her mother to come in and help with the dishes. But everyone ignored Rosa. She got all the way down to the silverware before Zia Fifi came into the kitchen and nodded at her. Rosa looked her up and down, from her calico housedress to the fleshy support hose that always sagged around her ankles, and remembered all the injustices she had suffered in her childhood at the hands of Zia Fifi's spoiled-rotten sons—the way they used to gang up on her during Kick-the-Can and make her be the Monkey in the Middle—and Rosa realized, for the first time in her life, just how much she despised Zia Fifi, absolutely loathed her.

"Nice of you to come over," Rosa said, tossing a knife onto the pile of silverware stacked up on the drainboard.

"Anytime," Zia Fifi said, heading for the back door.

"Where are you going?" Rosa asked. "You forgot your *collino.*"

"So I did!" Zia Fifi went over to the cabinet—Rosa's aunts all knew each other's kitchens as well as they did their own—and pulled out a dented colander, the very one that Rosa's mother once had thrown at Rosa's head, missing her by half an inch.

"*Adio,* everybody!" she hollered before she slammed the back door.

Rosa steamed and fumed, like a sauna gone haywire. Then she

shuddered, feeling something wet on her underwear. Jesus! Everything that could possibly go wrong was messing up today. Rosa wore Super Plus—paying the same rip-off amount as Regular, when there were ten less in the box—and still those stupid tampons always leaked. It was the ultimate end to the afternoon. Rosa grabbed her purse and walked through the living room.

"Where you going?" Antoinette asked.

"To the bathroom," Rosa said as Tony swelled out the final bars of *San Francisco.* The tiny little bathroom was decorated with pink and black square tiles and cramped by a huge free-standing bathtub that looked like it dated back to King Henry the Eighth. Rosa's father was a plumber, but do you think anything in that bathroom ever looked good or worked right? The toilet was gurgling from the last flush and the faucet on the tiny sink plopped a drop of water onto the rusty silver drain about every other second. It was the only bathroom in the entire house, situated right off the living room, so everybody could keep *au courant* about everyone else's business. Through the door, Rosa heard Aldo ask Gary, "Enough of that music. Who you for in the series?"

Rosa listened for a moment to Gary and Aldo talking baseball. Rosa had always assumed that Gary, like herself, knew jacksquat and cared even less about the goings-on of the American League. Now Gary was out there talking about earned-run averages and RBIs. Was he putting Aldo on? Or did Gary read the sports page, maybe even look at baseball on TV when Rosa wasn't around? Ugh, Rosa thought. He watches *baseball.* What would happen later in the fall—if Gary and Rosa were still going out together then? Would Rosa, now old hat to Gary, have to compete with the Knicks and the Jets? Would Rosa have to sit through four quarters of football at the Yale Bowl, shivering underneath a buffalo-plaid stadium blanket, watching a bunch of Ivy League weenies running up and down the field trying to act like they were first-round recruits of Miami and Notre Dame? In any case, if she went to the Bowl with Gary, she would not be able to run down to the fifty-yard line, as she used to do with Connie, and holler, "EX-LAX! EX-LAX! GO HARVARD GO!"

Rosa surfaced out of the bathroom, all fake smiles, to find Aldo and Gary in a heated argument over the salaries of professional baseball players.

"Bunch a bums," Aldo was saying. "Three million for tossing a ball around all day—"

"If someone gave it to you, would you turn it down?" Gary asked.

Rosa positioned herself in front of the Zenith console TV, which dated back to her grade-school years, and adjusted the aluminum foil on the rabbit ears that sat on top. "I think it's time to go," she announced.

"What's the rush?" Antoinette said.

"We're going," Rosa firmly said.

Antoinette pushed her hand against a cushion, gave a great heave-ho, and catapulted herself off the couch. "Bring back some ziti," she said. "I made too much."

"Time to go," Rosa repeated as Aldo and Gary kept on swapping their heated opinions.

"Just a second, just a second," Gary said. "I gotta finish this argument."

Rosa followed her mother into the kitchen. Antoinette ripped off a large sheet of aluminum foil, spooned a generous helping of the ziti onto it, wrapped the foil, and creased it on the end. "Here," she said, holding out the package to Rosa and cocking her head toward the living room. "For him."

"For him?" Rosa asked. "What about for me?"

"You know how to cook. He's a bachelor."

Oh. The bachelor. The all-wise and all-wonderful and (most important) all-*eligible* bachelor, who had to be lured into the family circle using those all-important feminine arts: lasagne, stuffed shells, *braciole,* eggplant parmesan, roasted peppers, manicotti, and fifteen thousand zeppole. "He can eat a TV dinner," Rosa said.

Antoinette looked alarmed. She held onto the aluminum foil packet and called out into the living room, "*State zitti* out there. I got a present in here, for the big-mouth lawyer."

Rosa grabbed the packet and felt the macaroni squishing beneath her hands.

On the drive back, Gary said, "Wow. That was some ziti. And your mother's got a great *tzatchke* collection. My favorite is that planter of Mary and baby Jesus with that sick-looking spider plant growing out of the top of Mary's head. And the ashtray with the picture of the Pope at the bottom. Set that Holy Father on fire! Speaking of which, your mother definitely has the hots for me, but I don't think your father likes me very much. He really seemed put out that I'm for the Mets instead of the Yankees. I mean, let's get real, the seats are so much more comfortable in Shea Stadium."

Rosa stared sullenly out the window all the way across the Q Bridge and blinked back bitter tears at the hideous sight of the rusty New Haven Coliseum. She swallowed back lumps of dissatisfaction all the way down Whalley Avenue, and after Gary suggested a walk in Edgewood Park to temper some of the evil effects of too much ziti and zeppole, she finally dissolved into great heaving sobs as they circled the algae-ridden duck pond.

"Oh my God," Gary asked. "What are you getting all hormonal about?"

"My family is ridiculous," Rosa said, fumbling in her purse for a Kleenex.

Gary shrugged. "They were okay. A weenie bit on the Fellini side, but basically well-intentioned."

But Gary could not know, Rosa said. Words could not describe the hardships and horrors of her childhood. Rosa took the Kleenex and made a loud honking noise with her nose that sounded suspiciously similar to the angry sounds coming from the orange-billed geese that pecked for food on the other side of the pond. She blew and blew into the tissue, and instead of snot, nothing but self-pity came squirting out.

Rosa had grown up wearing hideous homemade clothes that her mother had sewn from piece fabrics that cost twenty-five cents a yard. She was forced to eat escarole and beans every Friday night or go hungry. She wasn't allowed to shave her legs until she was sixteen, and when she finally, on her fifteenth birthday, stole her father's razor and mowed it all down, she had cuts all over her calves and thighs for weeks. Her parents had warped her, the world was confusing, and the God Rosa was supposed to believe in was not on her side. Rosa wanted ready-made clothes from the Edward Malley department store downtown. She wanted a hug more often than the every five years she got one, namely, on her First Holy Communion and Confirmation and high school graduation. But what did she get? Her mother gave her a groddy old SOS pad and a can of Bon Ami to scrub the ancient clawfoot tub in that shitty little bathroom off of the living room. Her father practically gave her brain damage from all his whacks and slaps. Rosa's childhood was hell. She had to snap beans until her wrists ached. She got called a *stupida* even though she brought home straight A's. Her mother told her not to read so much, she'd have to get glasses and you knew how much those cost. Rosa was oppressed, depressed, repressed. And here, here, on this very spot—right in this very park—a man had exposed himself to Rosa, frightening her half to death!

Rosa told this story Gary-style, in great detail, describing the costumes and the scenery, all in an effort to recreate the wrenching emotions she had experienced on that cold winter day when she had wandered away from the ice-skating pavilion on a Girl Scout field trip. Rosa recalled how her ankles wobbled and the soles of her feet tingled after she shed her freshly polished figure skates, put on her flat boots, and walked out of the pavilion down to the arched bridge. She remembered how the thin white layer on top of the creek shifted and cracked as the cold, clean-looking water burbled over the rocks and filled the pockets of the ice. Then she remembered the man, who stepped out of the trees as quietly and dramatically as the Savior first stepped forth onto the stage during a Passion Play. The man wore a red-and-black buffalo-plaid jacket and a bright red hat pulled low over his ears.

Rosa felt her feet go numb as he lifted the jacket and slipped down the zipper of his trousers. What he showed her seemed as pale and prehistoric and dirty and dumb as the withered, dusty old rhinoceros fenced in at the Bronx Zoo. The rhinoceros had blinked its tiny grey eyes and stomped its hooves as it lowered and picked up its ugly head. Rosa had simply stood there in the zoo, licking an orange Creamsicle, staring at the rhinoceros. So, too, she stared at the man's fleshy appendage, until he found it prudent to put it away and quietly slip back onto the hiking trail. He left Rosa standing behind on the arch of the bridge, her nose running from the cold and her heart beating faster, suffused with the vague and confusing feeling that all the troubles in her life—and all the excitement and heartbreak and pleasure—now would date from that moment.

When Rosa was done relating this significant memory and had dissolved into another fit of tears, Gary was quiet for a moment. Then he said, "It was just a prick."

Rosa could have slapped him. Instead, she stomped her right foot, and the heel of her shoe came down square on the ground, squashing a pile of duck shit. Gary did not understand! He was completely obtuse, a dinosaur, an emotional moron!

"All right, all right," Gary said. So he was a man. He wasn't ashamed of it! Rosa was the one who was ashamed, who suffered from a complete lack of self-esteem, who needed to chill out about her bad childhood, or at the very least, stop being so goddamn melodramatic about it.

Rosa continued to cry. Gary made ineffectual clucking sounds to try to soothe her. "Hey, you want to see quality fruitcake, you can come to my house," he finally said. "Come on. Shut up. I love you, all right? Stop crying. I'll take you to New York."

Rosa took out an old Kleenex and wiped a gob of snot off her upper lip. "When?"

"Next weekend."

"You told my mother we'd go to her house," Rosa said.

"So call her tonight and tell her you're coming to mine."

"She'll call all my aunts," Rosa said. "They'll think it's getting serious."

"Well? Isn't it?"

Rosa's last view, before she closed her eyes and pressed her salty mouth against Gary's, was of the deep blue sky and the slick green pond. The honking of the geese and ducks echoed in her ears, like a far-off warning, the last sound you might hear at the beach, a life-guard's whistle or the urgent calling of a mother, before you dove into too-deep water.

Too late. Rosa went under. She was a goner.

osa should have known something was fishy about the trip to his parents' house when Gary casually told her, "Bring your bathing suit."

"Are we going to the beach?" she asked.

"No. My parents have a pool."

Rosa's idea of a pool—dating back to the hot summers of her childhood—came from visiting neighborhood kids lucky enough to have those four-foot-high, dented metal structures in their backyards. The pools were painted bright blue, with warped wooden decks perched precariously against one side. Half-deflated tubes and rafts, littered with the wet bodies of wasps and flies, floated in the too-cold water. The filters gurgled sluggishly and the chlorine burned the swimmer's eyes and nose. Yet any child lucky enough to have a pool was instantly popular when the temperature surged above seventy degrees. Rosa and her cousin Connie had cultivated many a friendship based upon pool ownership.

Now, on hot summer days, Rosa and Connie sometimes paid five bucks to camp out on Lighthouse Beach, where an excess of seaweed and jellyfish often prevented them from going in the water. Rosa owned one black tank bathing suit, which unfortunately had lost much of its elastic snap in the back, so that Connie always whispered, "Butt alert! Cheeks on view!" whenever Rosa stood up from her towel.

This was the bathing suit that Rosa was forced to toss into her bag as she packed to visit Gary's parents for the first time. Rosa sighed. It was too late to go shopping. They were leaving for Long Island in half an hour and spending the entire weekend there.

Rosa thought a weekend visit was a bit much. "You don't understand," Gary finally had told her. "I can't visit my parents for just one day. I gotta stay overnight, eat a huge dinner, do the whole shebang, otherwise I get a big doo-rah from my mother and my father about how I never visit them."

Rosa was running late that morning. Clothes were strewn all over the place and Rosa was only half-dressed when Gary got to her apartment.

"Bad hair day?" Gary inquired.

Rosa glared at him. "I haven't even done my hair yet."

"When do you plan to be ready? Next August?"

"Shut up," Rosa said. "Go get a book out of your car and study."

"Worried I'm gonna bomb out of law school?"

"If you keep on watching basketball."

"I just happened to have the TV on the other day when you called—"

"You should have muted it."

"What for?"

"What was the final score?" Rosa asked.

"112–106, the Knicks."

"You see," Rosa said. "When I called, it was still the first quarter."

"So I study and watch at the same time," Gary said. "God, it's the Knicks! Besides, I don't like it when you're not around. It's too quiet. The TV keeps me company."

Rosa and Gary were getting used to one another. It seemed natural to Rosa to take her time putting on her makeup and doing her hair while Gary sat in the armchair in her living room studying. Each time she sneaked a look at him, she was flooded with fond feelings. He looked so sexy in jeans. He had the greatest butt, and a warm smile. He liked to laugh. He was smart, funny, kind, considerate, a good storyteller—my God, how lucky could she get?

Rosa smiled when Gary glanced up from his book.

"What are you staring at me for?" he asked. "I got a snot in my nose or something?"

Rosa turned away. He really was a pain in the ass.

Just before they left, Rosa took her bag into the bathroom, opened the cabinet below the sink, and went into a closed box in the back where she had hidden all of her stomach medicines the minute she had started to go out with Gary. Rosa slipped Pepto Bismol, Maalox, and Extra Strength Gas-X into her bag. Anticipating trouble, she took a big swig of Immodium, swished her toothbrush around in her mouth once for good luck, and announced she was ready to go.

"You look like you're ready to throw up," Gary said. "Come on, relax. My parents'll love you, if only because you're living, breathing proof that their son is not a faggot."

Gary's parents set themselves up as liberals. But the one thing they couldn't handle, Gary said, was that their nephew Benny was homosexual—and that their son might someday turn out that way, too. Artie and Mimi worried because Gary had spent so much time with Benny when he was growing up. "It doesn't matter that I hardly ever see Benny anymore," Gary told Rosa once they got onto the highway. "It doesn't matter that we don't have a damn thing in common. It doesn't matter that—well, you know, I like girls! My mother and father still think Benny's some kind of evil influence. The last time the whole family got together—at my cousin Eileen's wedding—my parents sat on both sides of me at the reception, and Benny had to sit across the table in between my Aunt Sylvia and my Uncle Len. It was like the grown-ups were determined to keep us apart. What were they afraid of—that we might ask each other to dance? Benny looked bored and miserable and I looked bored and miserable and we both drank too much, and halfway through the dinner, when people started getting up and making toasts to the bride and groom, I looked over at him and thought, *God, Chooch, you could be dead in a few years. For all I know, you're dying of AIDS right now.* And I don't know—must've been the wine—but I got all teary-eyed just thinking about it."

Rosa nodded, only half listening. She began holding her stomach halfway down 95 and bit her lip all the way down the Cross Island Parkway. Gary blasted the Doors and accelerated another five miles per hour every time Jim Morrison asked, "Don't you love her madly?" As they pulled into Manhassat, he flipped off the tape deck and hummed to himself. He liked to sing show tunes. This one was "Summertime."

Rosa silently tried to reconstruct the lyrics. *"The daddy was rich, right? and the mama? Good-looking?"* She gazed out the windows at the neatly manicured gardens and unnaturally green grass—courtesy of Chemlawn—and the large houses set back from the quiet, wide streets. "This is a beautiful neighborhood," she commented.

"Mmm-hmm."

"Who lives there, movie stars?"

"No. Just plain and humble folk." He laughed and turned the steering wheel. The Subaru sputtered up a long, curved driveway. "Like me."

Gary stopped the car in front of the house and turned off the ignition. Rosa tried to keep her jaw from falling open. She had expected something nice, something modern, something along the lines of some TV sitcom house—maybe a split-level or a ranch, with a smooth driveway and attractive landscaping.

This house, however, was beyond expectation. It was a two-story Mediterannean—white adobe with big, grated windows, a curved tower, and a red-tiled roof. Cacti and jade plants grew in the neat stone garden on either side of the front steps. The massive wooden front door looked like something people got tortured on during the Inquisition.

Rosa turned to Gary, who was smiling like a kid showing off a new toy. "Welcome home," he said.

"You sonofabitch," she said. "Why didn't you tell me?"

They got out of the car. Rosa looked down and was dismayed by the sight of her wrinkled blouse and chinos, and the scuffed heels of her pleated leather flats. It really was too late to go shopping! The front door opened and Gary's mother came down the short stairway. She was a thin, willowy woman who would have been Rosa's height had she not been wearing gold criss-crossed sandals with two-inch heels. Mimi wore a white gauze blouse and patterned palazzo pants that floated like silk. Her hand, when she held it out to Rosa, was perfectly manicured, with pink blush nails.

"You must be Rosa," she said. "I'm thrilled to meet you, dear."

"This is my mother," Gary said. "Mimi Fisher."

Rosa bit back the urge to reply, "Oh, I thought she was the maid." She smiled and shook Mimi's hand. Mimi released it very quickly. She put her hand on Gary's arm and gave him a half-hug and kiss. "You should have called. I thought you were in an accident."

"Don't start, Mom."

Before they could get any further, Gary's father came out of the house. Rosa could tell he had a good ten years on Mimi. He wore pastel-green slacks and white shoes, and his hunched shoulders seemed too small for his white shirt. Overall, he barely reached Rosa's shoulder.

Rosa was afraid she would say something totally moronic to him like, *God, you're a midget!* Or *You're not supposed to wear white shoes after Labor Day.* But instead, she smiled, and Artie smiled back, revealing some charmingly crooked teeth. He shook Rosa's hand vigorously. Rosa liked him right away. He reminded her of her Great-Uncle Eddie, a short little *scooch* who used to greet the childish Rosa by patting her full petticoats and pinching her cheeks.

As if he were consciously trying to imitate Great-Zio Eddie, Artie took Rosa's face in his hands and looked sorrowfully into her eyes. "No glasses?" he asked. "Not even contacts?"

"Dad," Gary said.

"He always goes out with girls with perfect vision," Artie told Mimi.

"Artie, really," Mimi said. "Step aside. Get the suitcases, Gary." Mimi took Rosa's arm. "Come inside, dear. I'll get you something cool to drink."

Gary was instructed to leave the bags in the *foyer,* a black-and-white tiled entrance area which seemed larger than Rosa's entire apartment. Or maybe it was the mirrors that made the hallway look huge, and made Rosa feel as though she had fallen into the jaws of a mighty whale as she stepped into the two-story-high living room, which was flooded with sun from the skylight and trimmed with a wooden bannister that wrapped around the upper balcony. The fur-

niture was sleek and modern and low to the ground, the most striking piece being a sectional sofa made of creamy vanilla leather.
There was a de Kooning-like picture hung on top of the fireplace—
not a print, but a canvas encrusted with blobs and swirls of actual
paint—and what looked suspiciously like real Picasso drawings
hung above each built-in bookcase. Rosa tried not to look at anything too hard. She turned back to look for Gary and met only
Mimi's quizzical face.

"Yo," Gary said. "My mother asked if you wanted ice in your lem-
onade."

"Yes, that would be—" Rosa couldn't find the right word. Excellent? Lovely? "Fine," she blurted out.

Mimi glided off, her palazzo pants skimming the top of her thin
ankles.

"You look good, Gary," Artie said.

"Thanks, Dad. So do you."

"Go on. You know I'm an ugly duck. How about it, Rose?"

"Rosa," Gary corrected him.

"You're a pretty girl," Artie said to Rosa, and Rosa blushed.
"She's pretty, Gary."

"Yeah, well, she's not up for grabs, Dad."

"Aah," Artie said, "I wouldn't even try to compete with you.
What do you say, Rosa? He's a hard one to beat."

Rosa must have looked stupefied, because Gary pinched her.
"Earth to Rosa," he said. "Here's where you're supposed to tell my
dad, 'Your son is perfect, what can I say?' "

Rosa remained silent.

Mimi came back in with two tall frosted glasses clinking with ice
and topped with lemon wedges. "For you," she said as she handed
one to Rosa, "and you, *you,* we're so happy to see *you,*" she said and
pecked Gary on the cheek. "We never see him anymore," she said to
Rosa. "I told Artie just the other day, I said, 'Artie, we have lost him
to New Haven.' "

"I'm two hours away, Mom."

"And we're thrilled to meet you, Rosa," Mimi repeated. "Now

let's all sit down. Unless you're tired of sitting, in which case we'll give you a little tour of the house."

"Oh, let's have the grand tour," Gary said. "And get it over with."

"All right," Mimi said. "Let's. We'll start in the dining room."

Mimi strolled up and down the halls like a museum docent, pointing to key *objets d'art* and lecturing about certain antiques or treasures brought back from abroad. She had the right costume for the role, and even the right jewelry, Rosa thought—real ding-dong stuff that looked like something dug up at an archeology site. Her necklace was made of alternating bone- and mud-colored beads inscribed with some sort of hieroglyphics. Miniature brass fish dangled from her ears. Around her wrist hung a string of tarnished gold coins in a currency that had been rendered useless centuries ago.

The downstairs consisted of the living room area, an excessively formal dining room that glittered with glass and chrome and was full of hard edges, a galley kitchen with an eat-in sunroom, a hallway leading to what Mimi called "the maid's quarters," and an oddball area she referred to as the "recreation room," which was dominated by a sea-green pool table. "This is my vice," Mimi said, stroking the felt top.

"I already told Rosa you play snooker," Gary said.

"And don't get in her way when she's playing!" Artie called out from the living room.

"She's been state champion twice," Gary said. "She wins hideous trophies."

"Which I have the good taste not to display," Mimi said.

"Come on, Mom. Show Rosa how mean and fast you can break."

"I will not," Mimi said.

"She'd love to see you in action," Gary said.

"Well, she'll have plenty of chances later. You are staying until Monday, aren't you?"

"Sunday night, Mom. I told you on the phone."

"I must have heard you incorrectly," Mimi said. "Get the suitcases and I'll show Rosa upstairs."

The staircase was made of bare, shiny blond wood and was carpeted with an Oriental runner tacked down with brass rods. The walls were hung with wooden spears, shields painted with bold brush strokes, batiks with colors so vibrant the wax still seemed hot, and flat grass baskets. A row of hollow-eyed, open-mouthed masks stared at Rosa as she went by, and she was tempted to stick out her tongue at them.

Upstairs were three bedrooms. Artie and Mimi's was understated but elegant, with a white carpet and a white satin bedspread. Mirrors lined two walls of this room. Rosa tried hard to ignore this. There was a much smaller bedroom, which apparently had been Gary's room when he was young, but which no longer bore any traces of his childhood except for the tiny twin bed. Then there was the guest room, which rivaled the master suite with its blatant emphasis on simplicity. The room was dominated by a queen-size bed. There were matching nightstands and brass reading lamps, a sitting area with a white loveseat and a coffee table stacked with magazines, and a cherry writing desk. Six mirrored panels along the back wall seemed to hide a long walk-in closet.

"Well," Mimi said, "suppose I leave you two here to get settled?"

"That's fine," Gary said.

"Do you need anything?"

"I don't know," Gary said. "Did you put toilet paper in the bathroom?"

"No," Mimi said pointedly. "Pilar did."

Gary flopped a magazine onto the coffee table, took the glasses from Rosa, and put the lemonades down on top of the most recent issue of *The New Yorker.*

Mimi pointed to the drawers of the cherry writing table. "Coasters," she said. Then she issued an invitation for them to meet her and Artie out on the patio for drinks and hors d'oeuvres in five minutes. "Five minutes," she told Gary and shut the door.

Rosa looked at Gary after Mimi had left. "We're both sleeping in here?" she whispered.

"Unless you want me to sack out in the bathtub."

"They don't care?"

Gary shrugged. "They voted for McGovern. They give money to Planned Parenthood and Save the Whales."

"What's that got to do with it?"

"I mean, hey, they're like—modern. Hip. They know I do it."

"Just because they know doesn't mean they have to approve of it," Rosa said.

"Sweetie, my parents aren't your parents. They *want* me to be happy. I've slept in here with all of my—"

Rosa glared at him. Then she silently put her bag on the bed, trying to figure out just how many girlfriends had been in this room with Gary before.

"Three," he said after a moment.

"Three what?" she asked.

He laughed. "You want to know their names? I already told you about one."

"The skinny redhead who couldn't eat MSG or she got migraines?"

"Yeah, her."

Rosa wished she had a voodoo doll so she could stick a needle in its head and give that skinny bitch a killer headache right that very minute.

"I don't want to hear about the other ones," she said.

"Good," Gary said. "Because I don't want to bore you. Or me." He reached over and slapped Rosa on the butt.

"Cut it out." Rosa yanked open the zipper of her bag and pulled out a pile of clothes, giving Gary just enough time to cop a good long look at the Pepto Bismol and Maalox and Extra Strength Gas-X.

She thought for a moment that he would look discreetly away. But he simply asked, "Oh, ho ho, what have we here?" and leaned over further to inspect the goods more carefully, even picking up the Gas-X to read the label, as if to challenge its claim to dispel pain, pressure, and bloating.

"This is one serious supply of rear fuel injection," he said.

"I have a spastic colon," Rosa defended herself.

"Okay," he said and shrugged. "Since it's true confession time."

He heaved his gym bag onto the bed and unzipped the top. Inside, hidden underneath his chinos and plaid shirt, was a goodly cache of antihistamines, decongestants, breathalators, and other forms of relief for the suffering schnozz.

"I've got sinus problems," he said. "My mother's perfume aggravates it."

"Are you a hypochondriac?" Rosa asked.

"Are you?"

Rosa didn't answer.

"You should buy generic," she finally said.

"It doesn't work as well," Gary said. He lowered his voice and gave Rosa an uncanny imitation of his own father. "You get what you pay for."

Rosa walked over to the window. She moved the lace curtain aside and gazed down at the pool, the tiled deck, the beach cabana, the meticulously landscaped garden. "You should have told me about all this," she said.

"Sorry, babe. I didn't want you to love me for my money."

He laughed, a little. Maybe he was kidding around. But Rosa heard uncertainty in the laugh, and maybe even an element of mistrust. Well—and why not? He was the only child. He would inherit his father's business (obviously worth a small fortune), this very house, and whatever else was involved in it all. Rosa was not sure, but she suspected there was something even bigger beyond this, in the way of things her relatives never could even dream to dabble in—stocks and bonds, securities, trust funds, real estate. It would all be his.

And what was Rosa's? An almost paid-for Honda Civic, and 4,500 dollars in savings after working full-time for five years (2,000 of which Rosa had earmarked for a facelift). Rosa could quite easily be seduced. She could easily forget about New Haven, the sooty brown buildings and the mud-flecked city buses, the homeless people camped on the Green, the rocky sand at Lighthouse Beach, the Catholic churches on every corner. She could easily forget about Sunday dinners with her parents, the endless obligations to attend the funerals and baby showers and weddings of every fourth and fifth cousin, and all the shit she had to put up with working at the hospital. She could kiss that goodbye forever, without a shred of regret.

Gary opened one of the nightstand drawers and put some of his clothes inside. "Do you like this house?" he asked.

"No," Rosa said. "It's too cold. And calculated. And there are too many mirrors."

Gary laughed. "She's sunk a fortune in plastic surgery," he said. "I guess she wants some return on her investment."

"What's with all that ugly stuff hanging out in the hall?" Rosa asked.

"Concrete evidence of their travels," Gary said.

"It's like living in the Peabody Museum of Natural History."

"Yeah, every time I come home, I feel like I'm entering some sort of tribal culture that I don't truly understand. I just go along with the rituals."

Gary went into the bathroom and arranged all of his sinus medicines on top of the toilet tank. When he came out, he put his arms around her from behind and pressed up against her, kissing her neck. The kiss seemed too insistent and utterly humorless. As he broke away from her, Rosa thought that some odd psychology— some weird vibes—were clearly at work in the Fisher household. And as if to confirm it, when Rosa looked down at the yard through the lace panels, she caught a glimpse of Mimi, standing by the pool with a tray of drinks and food in her hand. She was looking straight up at the window, right at Rosa.

Ah, what a game it all seemed to be in this house. Rosa was determined to play it as well as all the rest. She raised her hand and waved at Mimi, who could have pretended not to see. But the wave must have caught Mimi off guard. She nodded at Rosa, a little grimly, and Rosa turned away from the window, feeling as if she had just won her first battle.

Downstairs, by the pool, Rosa sat in the chair directly opposite

Mimi. Bad choice. The reflection of the sun on the cool, blue water made her blink and squint, until Artie, reminding her of the damage done to the cornea by the sun's rays, forced her to stand up so he could reposition her chair.

"You need sunglasses," he said.

"I forgot them at home," Rosa said.

Everyone else had some kind of protection. Gary's glasses were tinted a very light brown. Artie had photo-grey lenses that turned so dark Rosa could not see his eyes. Mimi, who had worn tortoiseshell glasses when she met them at the door, now had on rose-tinted glasses with pearl-white frames that looked flattering against her tanned skin and frosted blond hair.

"You need to shield yourself from the UV rays," Artie said.

"Let's not talk shop, Artie," Mimi said.

Artie held up an imaginary key and locked his lips. "I've got to listen to my best customer," he whispered to Rosa.

"Mom's the Imelda Marcos of eyeglasses," Gary told Rosa.

"Oh, stop it," Mimi said. "I am not Imelda."

"Come on, Mom. You change your glasses the way some women change earrings."

In spite of having a hundred different ways of looking at the world, Mimi did not seem to enjoy the view. She pressed her thin lips tightly together as if she had just tasted a spoonful of vinegar. "We each have our own little peccadillos, dear, most of which are not polite to point out," she said. She leaned forward, and Rosa noticed how graceful her movements were, as if she had taken years of posture lessons and ballet. "Have some of these canapés, Rosa, before these men do them in."

Rosa reluctantly leaned over and selected an hors d'oeuvre that looked like a cheese puff. She was afraid she would spill something on her clothes and was all too aware that she had neither worn the right outfit nor had she brought the proper wardrobe for tomorrow. What had Gary been thinking of when he told her to just throw some jeans and a T-shirt into a suitcase? My God, *he* might—and did—look great in such an outfit, sitting by the pool, totally comfortable in this familiar environment, but Rosa felt like a slob, some kid from the Fresh Air Fund brought in to get a taste of the more genteel life. Rosa was not exactly shining in this conversation. Better clothes might have made her feel more confident that she could hold her own.

Mimi poured champagne, and to Rosa's surprise, she proposed a toast to her after passing around the drinks. "To Rosa," she said. "We have you to thank for this visit."

Gary grinned and raised his glass high to Rosa. Artie raised his glass even higher, and then Gary one-upped him again, until Artie said, "Aah, you win, I'm too short."

Rosa took a long sip, which made her nose tingle.

"We can't tell you how much we appreciate seeing Gary again," Mimi said, as if Rosa had been keeping him in a cage.

"I'm two hours away," Gary said again.

"He hardly ever calls anymore," Mimi said. "Artie wants to call him every night—"

"Come on, Meem. You're the one with the hand on the receiver."

"—and I say, no, no, leave him alone, do you want him to flunk out of law school? Let him study. We had no idea—that this—"

"What's *this*, Mom?" Gary asked.

"Well, dear, when you called—we were surprised, that's all." She turned to Rosa. "That Gary was—seeing someone from New Haven. In New Haven. This is news to us, we said."

"Good news," Artie added and winked at Rosa. Rosa smiled back.

"And someone so established," Mimi said. "And committed."

For a moment Rosa heard *committed* in the mental institution sense. Then she realized Mimi was referring to her work, the nature of which Gary must have painted a slightly different shade than the reality.

"You're on the right side," Artie said. "We need to help each other. We owe it to each other."

Rosa, whose cynicism about social work was about as thick as one of her college textbooks, merely nodded. What in the world had

Gary told them about her job? Rosa heartily wished she knew, especially since the next moment Mimi said, "Tell us about your work,
dear. We admire what you do so much. It's so courageous."

Gary raised his eyebrows at Rosa and squirmed a little in his chair.

"Your parents must be proud of you," Artie said.

"Sure, Rosa," Gary said, taking another sip of his drink. "Tell us
how proud your parents are."

For a moment Rosa had a picture of Antoinette on the phone,
talking with one of her out-of-state cousins. "Yes, Rosa is still down
on Dixwell Avenue, trying to save a few hopeless *melanzane,*" Antoinette said. "No, she doesn't have a boyfriend yet."

Rosa glared at Gary. He looked penitent. He put down his glass,
then leaned over and squeezed her hand. The attention made Rosa
feel uncomfortable, and she was glad when Gary took his hand
away.

"I push papers," Rosa said.

"Come on." Gary nudged her.

"Well, that's what it feels like," Rosa said.

"Give yourself credit. You do more than that."

"There's certainly a lot that needs to be done in New Haven,"
Mimi said and held out the plate of hors d'oeuvres toward Rosa.

"Do you go there often?" Rosa asked, selecting another cheese
puff.

"All of once," Gary said.

"There's not much to go back for," Mimi said.

"How about to see me?" Gary asked.

"It's a pleasure anytime," Mimi said. "But not in those surround-
ings."

"The town's a dump!" Artie said, and Rosa, in spite of herself,
laughed.

"Glad you were so impressed," Gary said.

"To think that we were so happy when you got into Yale," said
Mimi.

"Yeah, there were just so many drawbacks to Harvard," Gary
said. "Starting with the fact that they didn't accept me."

"Don't downgrade yourself," Mimi said. She turned to Rosa. "He's always so critical of himself. Yale is better for law. I read it in the *Wilson Quarterly.*"

"The Republicans go to Yale," said Artie. "FDR, JFK—they all went to Harvard."

"Sorry to disappoint you, Dad."

"Who's disappointed?" Artie asked. "If you hadn't gone to Yale, you wouldn't have met Rosa."

"Come on, Dad," Gary said. "You're making her blush."

"She's got a nice smile. I want to see it. Here it comes, just look at it. Look at it."

"It breaks my heart," Gary said.

"Oh, honestly," said Mimi. "Rosa, just *ignore* them."

"Mimi's been trying to do that all her life," Artie said.

"With limited success," said Mimi.

Gary reached over and patted her hand. "You love us, Mom."

Mimi looked point-blank at him. "I don't know what I'd do without you." She turned to Rosa. "So tell us about your family, dear. Your father's a contractor, Gary told us."

"Not really," said Rosa. "He owns his own plumbing business."

"It's called Plumb Easy," Gary said.

Rosa gave Gary a dirty look. Artie chuckled and whacked his hands down on the table. "That's good," he said. "I like that."

"Well," Mimi said. "It's very hard to find a good plumber these days. Almost as hard as finding a good housekeeper."

"What's the matter, Mom, Pilar threatening to quit again?" Gary asked.

"She's making the usual noises," Mimi said.

"She'll never leave us," Artie said. "We'd go to pot without her."

"I'm sure your father is very successful at what he does," Mimi told Rosa. "You know, Artie started out on a small scale, too."

"I went door to door during the Depression," Artie said. "I carried a black suitcase full of eyeglasses, like the Fuller Brush Man."

"And now look at him," Mimi rushed in. "Head of his very own successful chain."

Artie leaned back in his chair. "You're looking at the American dream," he said.

Gary put his hand over his heart, as if to pledge allegiance, and Artie shook a finger at Rosa, as if she were the one being the smart-ass. "Don't laugh," he said. "Hard work pays off. That's the one thing I've never been able to drill into Gary."

"Dad, you drilled me so hard I'm like a piece of Swiss cheese."

"What are you talking about?" Mimi said. "He was far too liberal with you, much too lenient. He never hit you."

"He did," Gary said and looked down at his champagne. "Once."

"I don't recall that."

"You weren't involved, Mom."

Whatever lay behind this obviously was a sore point both for Gary and Artie, because they avoided each other's gazes. Artie said, "These days, of course, education is the ticket. Look at you." He pointed at Rosa. "Your parents didn't go to college."

"Don't pry, Artie."

"Who's prying? You asked on the phone and Gary told us." Artie turned back to Rosa. "And look at Gary. His father peddled eye-glasses, his grandfather pushed furs around the garment district. And now, he and his cousins, they've all got their degrees, they're all gonna be doctors and lawyers—"

"Don't forget Benny," Gary said.

"Oh, Benny," Mimi said. "You know what they say about Benny."

"No, Mom. What do they say?"

Mimi looked pointedly at Rosa. "He's a musician," she said half under her breath.

Gary took his finger and pulled down a corner of his right eye. "E-*nough* said."

"Well, what do you want me to call him?" Mimi asked.

"Try *queer.*"

Mimi clucked her tongue. "Why do you act like this?" she asked.

"Vulgar. And illiberal. Unliberal, whatever the word is. The complete opposite of everything we brought you up to be—"

"Because that's what he calls himself," Gary said. "Benny stood up at his brother's bar mitzvah—"

"It wasn't his bar mitzvah," Mimi said. "It was Simon's birthday party."

"All right already," Gary said. "He stood up at his brother's birthday party and announced it to everybody. He said, 'Ma, Dad. Ma. I'm queer.' My Aunt Sylvia started to cry. My Uncle Len spit chopped liver halfway across the room. When he finally found his voice, he said, 'So you want a medal?' "

"Gary has always been a great storyteller," Mimi said. Her eyes were focused on Rosa, but the comment seemed directed more at Gary, a warning which of course he did not heed.

Gary laughed. "Uncle Len was so flipped out by the whole thing that he went out and bought one of those chairs—you know those chairs?—the kind that invert you so more blood goes to your head? We'd go over to their house and Uncle Len would be hanging upside down like a bat. Meanwhile Aunt Sylvia would be lying on the couch, narrating her migraine headache like it was the light show at the Hayden Planetarium. 'Oh, it's the green,' she'd moan. 'Oh my God, it's the blue. I can't stand it, here comes the red!' "

"Stop," Mimi said. "You're making that up. Fabricating. It's true that Sylvia cried. After Benny told her."

"Who could blame her?" Artie said. "Any mother would cry."

"Would you?" Gary asked. "Would you cry, Mom?"

"I don't know what you mean," Mimi said.

"What if I stood up, right now, and told you I was gay?"

"I don't believe that's your problem," Mimi said.

"Damn right," Artie said.

"Although you may have others that I'm unaware of," Mimi added.

"Answer, Mom," Gary said. "Come on, answer. What would you do?"

"Well," Mimi gave a false little laugh, "for starters, I might point to Rosa as evidence to the contrary."

Rosa shifted in her chair.

"Say she wasn't sitting here. Say it was just you and me."

"Well," Mimi said. "I would be—disappointed. But I would—*we* would—still love you and support you."

"I'd crack your head open," Artie said. "I want grandchildren."

Rosa suddenly got interested in the bubbles rising in her champagne glass. Gary reached over for the bottle and slopped some more champagne into her glass, then refilled his own. "Cin-cin, Dad. At least you're honest."

"You know we would still love you and support you," Mimi repeated. "You know I've never interfered with your life. We've never interfered."

Gary laughed. "And I'm a Vienna choir boy," he said. "Did you know I was a Vienna choir boy?" he asked Rosa.

"Parents are supposed to interfere," Artie said. "If you don't, you're not doing the job right."

"You cried when I went off to Columbia," Gary said to Mimi. "You held my arm so tight it ached for days. You made weird monkey noises. You said, 'You can be whatever you want to be as long as you don't become a rabbi or—or—or—a ballet dancer—' "

"Even I remember that," Artie said.

"God, she did it right in the hallway of the dorm! I was the only Jewish kid on the whole floor, it took me the entire freshman year to live it down, you better believe it."

"How could you be the only Jewish kid on the floor?" Artie said. "At Columbia?"

"I told you, he should have gone to Princeton," Mimi said. "It would have been safer, and more prodigious."

"How many times do I have to listen to this, Meem?" Artie asked.

"You still fight about it?" Gary asked his parents. He nudged Rosa. "They still fight about it, four years and eighty fucking thousand dollars later—"

"Don't remind me," Artie said.

"And no vulgarities," Mimi added. "This is not a French film. And we don't need to reveal all of the family secrets at once."

"That's right," Artie said. "They come out by themselves fast enough."

"And what doesn't come to the surface, your son will be sure to blab away," Mimi said.

"What's to blab?" Artie asked. "The next time Rosa comes, we'll give a party. She'll meet the whole family face-to-face."

"Come on, Dad. I like her. I don't want her to run in the other direction."

"It's true." Artie nodded. "Lennie can come on a little bit strong."

"Lennie!" Gary said. "How about Aunt Sylvia? She jumps on me—and—and *licks* me—slobbers all over me—like a dog—every time she sees me. It's major assault and battery. She has this thing for men, for manhandling men." He turned to Rosa. "Benny had something wrong with his windpipe when he was growing up—"

"That's too bad," Rosa said sympathetically.

"And she used to chew his food in her mouth to make it soft before she fed it to him. She used to spit on his shoes and polish 'em with wax paper, remember, before he went on stage for his recitals? He used to play the violin. Now he plays crumhorn—it's this weird instrument that sounds like a fart—"

"How many times do I have to tell you—" Mimi began.

"—in a Renaissance band," Gary continued.

Artie shook his head. "They sent him to Cornell. Now he wears pink tights."

"But not to fear," Gary said. "All the good stuff gets covered by the codpiece."

"You will change the subject, thank you very much," Mimi said. "Goodness. What sort of impression have we given Rosa?"

Everyone turned and looked at Rosa. There was a long silence.

"Psst, you missed your cue again," Gary whispered as Pilar stepped out on the porch and announced dinner.

Rosa, who hardly had been able to wedge a word into the conversation, had ended up swilling far too much champagne. She had to steady herself on Gary when she got up from her chair, and Artie and Gary made jokes about her falling into the pool and having to be fished out, and then Gary sang a new version of the old camp song, *There were two jolly Fisher men!* and Mimi kept on saying, *Honestly, Rosa, just ignore them,* and then Artie and Gary came up behind Mimi and shouted, *Fisher, Fisher, men, men, men!* and she turned on them with a mean, icy look that instantly convinced Rosa that she really had been the 1968 New York State snooker champion.

During dinner, it became apparent that all this back and forth, this bickering and challenging of one another, was the usual Fisher family shtick. Artie praised and joked along with his son when he wasn't scooching Rosa; Gary goofed it up with Artie and twisted whatever Artie and Mimi said into a challenge of their rights as parents; and Mimi weaved herself in and out of their jokes, cutting off the conversation when it displeased her. Crackling beneath the surface was a strange sexual tension that Rosa had never seen at work in any other family, and which she did not understand, although she was sure that Freud could have done a heavy number on it. So this was what Gary had meant when she asked him if his parents loved him, and he said, *So bad it strangles. And they don't want anyone else to break in.*

It was, ultimately, too tight of a game for Rosa. Still unsure of the rules, she ate her dinner in silence in the cold, high-ceilinged dining room, and every time she looked up she saw Mimi's face, tight and stiff as a Punch and Judy puppet, directly opposite her, and then, in the mirror behind Mimi, Rosa saw her own face, and then another reflection, from the opposite mirror, of Mimi's face yet again. It was like being in the mirror room of the Seaside Heights funhouse, only no one's reflection was distorted. It was simply multiplied. They all were who they were, over and over and over again, and everyone could see one another too many times and too clearly, and nobody was laughing.

They all had too much to eat and drink, and after dinner they sat out on the tiled patio, sipping decaf and watching the fireflies dot the dark lawn with brilliant yellow specks of light. Reclining on a chaise longue, Rosa could see several silver stars and a round speck that Mimi said was Venus, hanging just above the dark outline of the trees. The water filter on the pool hummed and gurgled, the leaves rustled in the wind, and from inside the kitchen there came the comforting and comfortable sounds of somebody else cleaning up. Artie sighed contentedly, smiled at Gary and winked at Rosa. Rosa also sighed when Gary refilled her cup of decaf and leaned over, rubbing the back of her neck with his hand. Mimi leaned back and crossed her feet at the ankles, declaring that there were some late In- dian summer nights that were so perfect you could almost believe in God. No one contradicted her. Rosa stretched out her legs even fur- ther, and Gary, who sat in a chair at the end of the chaise longue, reached over and rubbed her foot, which had been stripped bare of its leather flat.

"Well," Mimi said, looking down at Rosa's ankle, "I suppose we all ought to go to bed."

"I'm not tired," Artie said.

"Maybe *they* are," Mimi said.

That was the clincher. That was all it took—those three words— to make Rosa realize that Mimi was a malevolent force, cloaked in a guise of politeness and concern. Yet it was strange how no one fought her back. Although Artie had said he wasn't sleepy, he still got up when Mimi did, and Gary, who could easily have said, "Oh, Rosa and I want to sit out here a little bit more," also followed Mimi's lead. Wouldn't Rosa look like a hardhead, the stubborn inde- pendent little pig that she was, if she continued to recline and gaze at the stars, saying, "Well, goodnight, everybody"? She got up, too.

The Fishers may have been liberals, but Rosa was the kind of bashful girl who purchased tampons and mini-pads by slipping them underneath a box of granola or a frozen pizza in the shopping cart and then racing to the check-out line, where she began the ar- duous and mostly impossible task of trying to find a line where there was both a female cashier and bagger. In short, in public Rosa was excessively modest, and she felt awkward when she and the Fishers all went upstairs and stood in the hallway to say goodnight. Mimi kissed Gary long and meaningfully on the cheek as if he were embarking on a lifetime journey. To Rosa's surprise, she also leaned over after taking Rosa's hand and planted a kiss on Rosa's cheek. "You're beautiful and charming and you have a wonderful appetite," she said. "And I can tell you make Gary so happy—"

"Mom," Gary said warningly.

"He's always gone out with these girls who were skinny as sticks," Mimi said.

"Painful to look at 'em!" Artie added. He snorted and clapped Gary on the back, then shook Rosa's hand, as if they were closing a business deal. "Great to meet you," he said, as if he did not expect to see Rosa the next morning at the breakfast table, or indeed, ever again.

The minute the Fishers closed their bedroom door, Gary breathed a deep sigh and feigned an inaudible whistle. Rosa followed him down the hallway to the guest room. "You can use the bathroom first," Gary said.

The bathroom had a sunken tub and separate shower stall. The thick, pale green and peach towels that hung on the racks made the gold fixtures shine all the more brightly against the smooth tiles. The back wall obviously butted up against the wall of the bathroom in the master suite, because Rosa, as she peed, could hear the faint noises of a sink being turned on and off, a drawer being opened and shut, and the distinctive, hinged creak that seemed part of the vocabulary of every medicine cabinet. Rosa stood up and flushed the toilet.

Gary knocked on the door. "Can I come in?" he said softly. "It's an emergency."

Rosa opened the door and stepped aside to let him in, but when she began to leave he took her by the wrists, backed her up against the tile, and reached behind him to flick off the light. The bathroom was dark before Rosa even had time to tell him he was crazy.

It was short, almost violent. A belt and zipper only. No foreplay except a rough, brushing of his beard along her neck, a brief palming of her breasts through her blouse, and a long, wet mouthful of tongue before he yanked down her pants and entered her. He pushed hard and fast and buried his face against her hair when he came, so that his *I love you, God, I love you* was breathed right into Rosa's ear, and then he pulled out, so quick it hurt, and knelt on the floor and went down on her. Rosa spasmed in a matter of seconds. She held her hand up to her mouth to stifle her own cry, then pressed her knee against Gary's shoulder and pushed him away. By then her eyes had adjusted to the lack of light, and she saw him sitting on the floor, grinning.

On the other side of the wall, Mimi's voice came through. "Artie, where is that aspirin?"

Rosa smiled and yanked up her pants. Gary whispered, "Musta been a hard day at the mall. She's got a headache."

"Get up off the floor, you fool," Rosa whispered.

"Take off all your clothes," he said.

Rosa obeyed. She stripped in front of him, piece by piece, and after she had skinnied out of her wet underpants, she held them by her fingers and purposely dropped them on his head. "Eat it," she said as she strutted out of the bathroom. She turned out the overhead light in the bedroom, pulled down the covers, and slipped her satisfied body between the cool, clean sheets on the bed.

Gary pissed with the bathroom door open. "It aches," he said when he came to bed.

"Oh, how you *suffer*," Rosa said as she cozied up next to him and lay her head on his chest.

He rubbed her shoulder, fingered her hair. "So," he finally whispered, "what do you think of my family?"

"I think it's sick," Rosa said.

"By Jove," he said, "I think you're right."

Rosa hesitated. "Does your mother always act like that?"

"No," he said. "She's usually worse." Then he laughed. "You gotta cheer up, Ro. Have some more to drink. Go with the flow."

"She doesn't like me," Rosa said.

"Oh no," Gary said. "Take my word for it. She truly does. That's why she's coming out swinging. She wants to see what you're made of, and how much you can take."

"I like your father," Rosa said.

"Well, he's obviously thrilled with you. With us. I told you, you're proof I'm not another Benny."

"I thought all your skinny girlfriends before me would have proved that," Rosa said.

Gary snorted. "That was a classic comment, wasn't it?"

"I don't like being told that I have a good appetite," Rosa said.

"She just meant—"

"Fat," Rosa said. "She meant fat."

"Oh, she says all sorts of things without being aware of what she really means."

Rosa's neck was beginning to ache. She took her head off Gary and put it down on the pillow. "What was with that remark about going to Princeton? And what did she mean when she said she could almost believe in God?"

Gary sighed. "She wants me to get married."

Rosa kept silent.

"The last time I visited, she asked me, 'What do I have to do to make it happen, pray?' " Gary sat up for a moment and fluffed his pillow. "No doubt she did, huh?" he asked before he kissed Rosa, turned over, and fell asleep.

Rosa lay awake for a long time, thinking of Venus in the dark night, and the stars.

chapter six

Rosa Salvatore and Gary Fisher were *gonna get married.* The news, that spring, was delivered by phone, since it was dangerous to do it in person. Antoinette might squeeze Gary's face like an accordion. Aldo might force Gary to smoke a cigar, bringing on a sneezing attack. Artie might pinch Rosa's arm until a blood vessel broke, and Mimi might faint.

Rosa fiddled with the modest diamond ring *(simple, but elegant!)* that Gary had given her. "Two calls," she said. "You do your parents, I'll do mine. Then we leave town."

"We're not criminals," Gary said.

Rosa put her hands on her hips. "Do you want to spend the weekend listening to the phone ring off the hook and talking to every relative in creation?"

Gary shook his head. He suggested they take an advance honeymoon. They could escape to Niagara Falls, don yellow slickers, and ride the Maid-of-the-Mist. Or they could drive into the Poconos, where Gary could poke Rosa silly, first on a heart-shaped bed covered with red satin sheets and then in a jacuzzi shaped like a champagne glass. But Rosa shook her head. She had in mind something loftier—a day at the Cloisters, listening to medieval music and musing over the unicorn tapestries. They could have dinner in the theater section and maybe attend an opera at night.

After consulting their checking accounts, they ended up bolting to the Bronx Zoo, where Rosa ate too much buttered popcorn, and Gary detailed the complete adventures of every grammar school field trip he had ever taken. A giraffe nuzzled Rosa's hand when she held out some weeds. The gorillas hugga-hugga-ed at Gary, and a chimpanzee in a tropical-looking tree, upset by Gary's rather accurate imitation, let loose a stream of clear white urine that spattered the pavement below, disgusting Rosa so much that Gary was forced to buy her a souvenir to commemorate the event. He selected a stuffed monkey suspended, by elastic, from a thin stick. Happy as a four-year-old, Rosa made the monkey dip and swing as they walked through the Primate World.

"There's something weird about apes," Gary said. "Scary. Like I look in that cage, and I swear I'm in some nightmare from the past. I see the face of everyone I ever grew up with. There's Uncle Siddy and Aunt Leila and Pinky Doyle from summer camp. See the monkey up there, scratching his balls? That's Peter Leibowitz, the kid everyone called a retard even though he wasn't, from the third grade."

Rosa watched the monkey scratch and shuddered.

"I guess Darwin was on to something," Gary said.

Although she was familiar with the phrase *survival of the fittest,* Rosa had never read Darwin. For years she had operated under the mistaken belief that *The Voyage of the Beagle* was a children's book about a nautical dog. Well, was it her fault she had gone to a third-rate college? Her fault that the nuns believed the theory of evolution would shake all Catholics in their faith? Rosa had to admit that the apes in the Bronx Zoo did make all those trips to Confession, all the penitential Our Fathers and Hail Marys, seem a little foolish and unnecessary. How could she believe in God, or heaven, after staring at an orangutan and seeing a replica of her own mother?

The Antoinette-lookalike orangutan was plucking bugs off itself and gulping them down with a toothy grin on its dark face. And at that very moment, back in New Haven, Antoinette probably was plucking lint balls off her pilly black sweater and making satisfied little primate noises as she called all of Rosa's aunts and hollered, "Guess what? Rosa got herself a lawyer!" None of Rosa's aunts would misinterpret Antoinette's message. They instantly would understand that Antoinette was referring to husband material as opposed to legal counsel to overturn a traffic violation.

And back at home, at Rosa's apartment, the answering machine was clicking on and off.

Errrrrrr, beep! *Rosa—Rosa? Zia Cenza here. I got the machine? It's the machine, I hate these machines. . . . I gotta hang up.* Errrrr, beep! *Ciao! Rosa, che dici? You really fidanzata? You getting married? God bless you! Hold on for Uncle Weegie, come on, say something, Weegie, before the machine cuts ya off*—Errrr, beep! *Rosa, dear. This is Mimi, dear. I—I can't tell you—well, I'm crying, do you believe it? We had no idea this was so serious—even though Gary told us—and—and—we welcome you*—Err, beep! *Rosa, Mimi again, as I was saying, we welcome you with open arms and I hope you'll call right back so we can start planning, Gary was completely impossible about it on the phone, such a man, you'll come to New York, we'll go shopping, just the girls*—Errr, beep! *It's Mimi, one last call, just to tell you that you really should leave more time on your machine, dear, people might have important things to say and you don't want to miss their messages.* Errrr, beep! (Connie, in a low, sexy voice) *A Yalie, huh? Bulldog, bulldog, bow, wow, WOW!*

Rosa was official now. She was a fiancée, a bride-to-be, a souvenir monkey bobbling precariously on a stick as she was petted and pawed over by her relatives and future in-laws. But at work she was a pariah. Rosa's engagement threatened the single people in the social work office. Terry and Donna and Alejandro (who had broken up with Dirk) stopped teasing her altogether about men; they did not ask her opinion of the new surgeon upstairs who supposedly was getting divorced, or confide, on Monday morning, how boring their weekend had been and how they actually were kind of glad to be back at the office, even if it meant being under the Baloney's thumb for the next five days.

"Daydreaming?" Alejandro inquired as he walked by Rosa's office.

"Mooning over your honeymoon?" Terry asked when Rosa gave her the wrong client file for the second time in a row.

"Fantasizing about Mr. Right?" Donna asked when Rosa didn't answer the phone right away.

Rosa had the cooties.

On Friday afternoons, while the Baloney was upstairs for his weekly meeting with Dr. Kahn—better known as Genghis Kahn to all who had to deal with his temper—Rosa and Terry and Alejandro all used to gather by Donna's desk to gossip and complain. Now Terry went out to talk to Donna by herself. "What are you doing tonight?" she asked Donna.

"I don't know," Donna said. "Probably go home and wash out my bras."

"Alejandro," Terry called out. "*¿Qué pasa?* What are you doing tonight?"

"Nada," he called back from his office, mournfully.

"Come to Promises, Promises with Donna and me. We'll have a drink."

"Do I have to dance with girls?" Alejandro asked.

"Just us girls."

Alejandro tssked his tongue. "I don't know. Macy's is having a shoe sale."

"Men's and women's?" Donna asked.

"¡Creo que si, muchacha! ¿Te gusta andar conmigo?"

"What the fuck did he say?" Donna asked Terry.

"If you can't get laid, you can always go shopping," Terry translated. "You got yourself a date, Ali!"

And Rosa—who lusted to go to a shoe sale—was heartily sorry that she had arranged to meet Gary for dinner. Terry and Donna and Alejandro left the office, bumping into one another and laughing about high heels and witch boots and roachstompers. Rosa was sorry to see them go, especially since Gary was in a foul mood when he picked her up that evening. Rosa rode to the restaurant in silence and quietly inspected the menu. Would she really have to spend the rest of her life exclusively with Gary, engaged in thrilling conversation about whether to have stuffed mushrooms or hearts of palm for the appetizer? Would she always have to go to the opera with someone who jingled his keys during *Cavelleria Rusticana,* yawned his way through *Pagliacci* and, at the end, burst into wild, thunderous applause and so many catcalls and whistles that Rosa, tears still in her eyes, was forced to turn to him and ask, "What do you think this is, the left field of Yankee Stadium?"

"I told you," he said, "I always went to Shea." He bent closer toward her, still clapping loudly. "Jesus, I can't believe it, are you crying just because Pagliacci did too?"

Rosa stared down at her menu. Her mind was anywhere but at the restaurant. She was at Macy's, her lusty little hands slipping another pair of Van Elis (twenty percent off) onto her swollen feet. She would hand the shoe salesman her charge card and then trot over to the accessories to find a belt to match. She would circle the cosmetic counter several times before she dared to venture up and try on a new lipstick. She would let herself be talked into some new blush, and maybe even a new shampoo (because God knew she needed *something* to tame that hair of hers). Afterwards she would eat an eggroll, fried rice, and hot green tea in the food court at the mall, putting her aching feet up on a chair and rejoicing in her freedom and independence.

That was the Friday night of the past—the Friday night of loneliness—but also the Friday night of feeling that anything, anything in the world could happen. The shoe salesman might spend a little longer than necessary slipping on that pump, and Rosa might decide to point coyly at a pair of stilettos and say, "I just got the desire to try those on." At the Chinese food counter, Rosa might make eye contact with another customer—a thoroughly handsome man whose order matched her own—and they might strike up a conversation and end up drinking green tea for hours at the little wire tables in the mall. Promises, Promises might be packed. The Brandy Alexanders would be smooth and mellow and the bar might yield a sensitive hunk, an accountant who bench-pressed 300 pounds and wrote poetry on the side, and whose deep, watery eyes were the very pools of love that Rosa was ready to dive into.

Bullshit. Rosa knew these scenarios were complete dreck. There was no such thing—except in the movies—as bright and intelligent shoe salesmen coming on to girls whose skin had putrified yellow from sitting all day under the fluorescent lights at work. The men who sipped green tea at the mall food court were handsome and extremely well-dressed, yes—but surprise, surprise, surprise! they also happened to be gay. Promises, Promises was yet another promise unfulfilled. It was dark and smoky and the booths were sticky with spilled beer. Hideous women with dark-rooted hair and black eyeliner sidled up to creepy men who wore too-tight pants.

Rosa knew that bar-hopping was nothing but heartache and herpes and too many looks at yourself in the bathroom mirror wondering if that tiny little mole on your cheek was the one thing that kept you from finding your soulmate and eternal happiness. Yet sitting across from the foul-mooded Gary in a Branford restaurant on Friday night made Rosa forget that, for a while. Gary and Rosa ate their meal, making occasional mundane conversation, and Rosa dreamed about curling up on the couch at her apartment, eating a TV dinner and half a chocolate cake while watching some dumb Katharine Hepburn–Spencer Tracy movie. Alternatives, alternatives. Rosa was happy when they left the restaurant and went out to the cool air of the parking lot.

"What's the matter with you lately?" Gary asked.

"Me?" Rosa asked. "You're the one who's in a bad mood tonight."

"I wasn't until I picked you up," Gary said.

"Oh, so blame me," Rosa said.

Gary shook his head. "I don't know. I don't know what's behind it. But I feel distinctly bad vibes coming from your direction."

Rosa felt guilty, then angry. But she was determined not to fight. She would get a grip on herself, control her emotions. Gary took the back way in to New Haven. "That's where my cousin Connie works," Rosa said, pointing to a mini-mall where the words 99 CENTS ONLY! blazed in lime-green neon light.

"Let's go in," Gary said.

"Let's not."

"Come on," Gary said. "Connie is the one person in your family I actually want to meet. Besides, I need a new potato peeler." He pulled into the mini-mall and looked at Rosa out of the corner of his eye. "What do you need?"

"A new squirt gun," Rosa said glumly.

"A yo-yo," Gary said.

"Another one of those little green copies of the New Testament," Rosa said.

"A plastic dashboard Christ."

Rosa hoped Connie wouldn't be on this shift. But her Plymouth was out in the lot, the bumper stickers proclaiming the mixed messages of *Hi, I'm your Mary Kay Representative* and *GET YOUR LAWS OFF MY BODY!* It was 8:45. When they entered the store, setting off the door chimes, Connie was standing in front of the register, her hands on her skinny hips, hollering, "Closing in ten minutes, ten minutes!"

Gary instantly recognized her from her pictures. "Hey, Connie," he said.

Connie turned and slitted up her mascaraed eyes at this guy—this prick—who had the nerve to use her name without even knowing her. But then she spotted Rosa and nodded. "Well, if it ain't Rosa. And the bulldog himself." She surveyed Gary from head to foot as Rosa introduced him. Gary laughed and made bow-wow-wow noises at her as he shook her hand. Connie responded by hissing like a cat. She told them to wait until she had checked through the last customers.

Rosa went down the first aisle and began inspecting the merchandise. Half-gallon squeeze jars of Plochman's Mustard stood next to evil-smelling votive candles in crystal holders. There were bins of waxy crayons and stacks of books called *The Truth About Male Menopause* and *How to Talk to Your Cat.*

"Look at this." Gary pointed to a group of puzzles that showed scenes from the Old Testament. "Moses in the bulrushes. Hannah and her seven sons. Jonah and the whale. The golden calf. All for ninety-nine cents."

Rosa ignored him. She went up to a key chain display. BITCH GODDESS, proclaimed one of the key tags. A CAREER WOMAN HAS

TO LOOK LIKE A LADY, ACT LIKE A MAN, AND WORK LIKE A DOG, said another. ITALIAN AND PROUD OF IT. POLISH AND PROUD OF IT. IRISH AND PROUD OF IT. DON'T BLAME ME, I GOT A DYSFUNCTIONAL FAMILY. WHEN SHIT HAPPENS, DUCK!

Gary stepped up behind Rosa and pointed to a tag that announced, WE'LL GET ALONG JUST FINE ONCE YOU REALIZE I'M GOD. Rosa, furious, searched the rack until she found a tag that offered an appropriate retort: NO THANKS, I'M ALREADY INVOLVED IN A MEANINGLESS RELATIONSHIP.

Gary laughed. And Rosa, still smarting from being denied her trip to Macy's, picked up a large pink plastic shopping basket and went down the next aisle, where she selected a three-pack of memo pads, some gift wrap that said *For Your New Baby,* and a street guide to Rome. The Muzak played "By the Time I Get to Phoenix," and Rosa hummed along and walked up and down the aisles by herself, blinking from the too-bright lights. By the time she got back to the front of the store, Gary was leaning against the remaindered book display, reading a copy of Nixon's memoirs. Connie had locked the front door of the store and was counting out the cash.

"Wait," Rosa said.

"Shut up," Connie said. "I'm trying to count."

"I have to pay for these," Rosa said.

"Too late," Connie said. "I already cashed out. Just walk outta here with the stuff. I won't tell a soul."

Had she been alone with Connie, Rosa might have laughed and walked out of the store with the merchandise. The stealing would have seemed like yet another one of their childhood pranks. But Rosa felt herself immediately look over toward Gary. Although he pretended to be engrossed in the Nixon memoir, Gary obviously was all ears, waiting to see what Rosa was going to do.

"Connie, please," Rosa said. "Let me give you the money."

"How much stuff you got there?" Connie asked.

Rosa searched through her basket. "Six items," she said.

Connie silently accepted the five and the one that Rosa gave her. Then she rolled the bills up and slipped them down the front of her shirt. "Good thing I put on a bra this morning," she said. Then she cocked her head toward Gary as she wrapped a rubber band around a stack of tens from the cash register. "He want anything?"

"Gary?" Rosa reluctantly asked. "You want anything?"

"I don't know," he said, and Rosa anticipated some smart-aleck remark. "There was a coloring book of Christ back there that really caught my eye—"

"He doesn't want anything," Rosa said. "Forget him."

"Ooooh," Connie said. "Trouble in paradise?" She stuffed the cash in a vinyl bag and zipped it up. "Better watch out, Bulldog. She's baring her teeth."

"Oh, her bark is worse than her bite," Gary said.

Rosa felt her face grow hot. She went behind the counter, ripped a plastic bag off the holder, and stuffed in her merchandise.

"So what brings you guys out my way?" Connie asked.

"I really wanted to meet you," Gary said.

"We went out to dinner," Rosa corrected him.

"Where'd you take her?" Connie asked Gary.

Gary grinned. "She took me. This time."

"The guy's supposed to pay," Connie told Rosa.

"Rosa's a feminist," Gary said.

"Rosa's a sucker," Connie said, and before Rosa could protest, Gary asked, "Don't you believe in equal rights?"

"Not when it costs me money," Connie said.

"Oh, so you want it both ways," Gary said.

"Doesn't everybody?" Connie asked.

"Connie likes real men," Rosa said. "The kind that give her black eyes."

"Yeah, I'm in love with my father," Connie said and gave Rosa the finger. She pointed at Gary. "How about you, you in love with your mother?"

"Oh, absolutely. Head over heels." Gary laughed, but then his face hardened, as if he suspected that Rosa, on the phone with Connie, might have brought such a charge against him.

"Speaking of real men," Rosa said, "how's Joey?"

"I broke up with him," Connie said.

"I guess he didn't pick up the check," Gary said.

"Yeah, and he always wanted oral sex, so what good did that do me?"

Rosa tssked her tongue and Connie laughed. She left her mouth open a little bit too long, Rosa thought, and Gary looked inside, at her tongue, a little too intently.

Rosa was more than ready to leave. "Nice to see you again, Con," she said.

"Pleasure," Gary said and held out his hand. Connie's fingers were studded with rings. Gary pretended to be stung by them.

Back in the car, Rosa stared out the window and wondered what Gary had made of Connie. Did he look at the bags under Connie's eyes, the blue eyeshadow, the thinning, frosted hair, and the hollowed-out chest, and realize that but for the grace of God, Rosa could have looked just like that? Did he admire Rosa for evading Connie's fate? Or was he appalled, having second thoughts about getting married to someone whose relatives would never climb out of the gutter?

"You two still friends?" Gary finally asked as they drove back.

"In our own way," Rosa said defensively. "We go to the beach during the summer. Sometimes we go shopping or out for a beer."

Gary kept silent until Rosa, who could stand it no longer, finally asked, "So what did you think of her?"

"She looks like she doesn't eat enough vegetables," Gary said. "Too busy eating that guy off, I guess. What was his name?"

"Joey," Rosa said. "He was a loser."

"How about her husband? The guy she had to marry?"

"Same," Rosa said.

"Oh, so she's one of those women who love men who hate women, or however the latest book title would have it."

"Don't be critical," Rosa said. "You've gone out with your share of doozy girlfriends."

"And you fucked a cop."

"I told you, he had good drugs!"

Rosa stared out the window at the darkened gas stations on Whalley Avenue, the boarded-up storefronts and corner liquor stores where men stood in the shadows out of the glare of the streetlights, scoring crack and feeling up hookers. Artie and Mimi were right. New Haven did seem past repair.

Rosa looked over at Gary, who seemed so smug and unconscious of it all as he drove the Subaru his father had given him for his twenty-fifth birthday. "Connie's father used to rape her," Rosa said.

Gary applied the brakes. A car behind them honked and passed, and then Gary picked up speed again. "Holy shit," he finally said. "Your Uncle Dino? The one I met last week?"

"Yeah, him."

"He seemed normal enough—considering your family."

"Well, he wasn't," Rosa said. "Isn't."

"He never touched you, did he?"

Rosa shook her head. "No."

Gary puffed up his cheeks with breath and then let the air out. He seemed relieved. Rosa wondered how he would have responded if she had said yes.

"You knew?" he asked. "You knew that he was doing that to her?"

"Yeah, I knew."

"So why didn't you tell somebody?" Gary asked.

"Who was I supposed to tell?" Rosa asked. "My mother?"

"I don't know. Somebody at school."

"A nun?" Rosa asked. "A priest?"

Gary shrugged. "I just don't understand keeping it quiet if it really happened, that's all."

"You don't believe it happened?" Rosa said.

"Did you see it happen?" Gary asked.

"Of course not, I told you she told me—he used to get her in the garage, he used to rub up against her—"

"Did he enter her?"

"No."

"Well, then she wouldn't have had a case."

"It *happened,*" Rosa said.

"All right, so it happened!" Gary said. "I'm not disputing it. I'm just telling you. Rape is penetration. If there's no penetration, you don't have a rape case. Maybe you could have nailed him on molestation or something—"

"What do I care about all this?" Rosa asked.

"I'm just giving you the legal definition—"

"Like we could have gotten ourselves lawyers?" Rosa asked.

"Don't say *lawyers,*" Gary said. "In that crappy tone of voice, like the way people say *doctors,* and then go crying to 'em the minute their nose starts snuffling. God, it makes me ill the way people look down on doctors and lawyers. You don't like it, do the surgery yourself! Or stand up in court and make your own case, you'd be bounced down the steps in two seconds. People get sick, people do sick things, the world is sick, but ease up on me, huh? I didn't create it."

Gary let out another deep breath. Now he would do the male thing, Rosa thought—act strong but hurt and neither talk nor look at her, until sick (and scared) of being iced out, she would cave in to him, saying, "Can't we just forget about all this?" or "Let's not fight, you know I didn't mean—"

Rosa stewed and fumed. Why was making up for fights always her job? Let him do it. His hands were on the steering wheel. He was driving. He always drove everywhere. And Rosa, who liked this, who liked to be driven, absolved of all responsibility should there be a crash, suddenly hated herself for it. She hated playing the woman, being the woman. Wasn't that her problem tonight? Yup, she just hated herself.

They were approaching the Boulevard. Here came the awkward moment when they would have to decide whose apartment they were going to return to. And it would not work, tonight, to say, "Listen, I need a little space" or "How about meeting for dinner tomorrow?" It would imply that too big of a rift had opened, that they couldn't deal with fighting. They were getting married. They would have to be together. They were stuck.

"Well?" Gary finally asked. "Should we be miserable at your place or mine?"

"Let's not be miserable anywhere."

"We'd have to pull a double suicide to work that one out." He laughed. "Come on. We'll go to your place. And torture ourselves with that loose spring on the bed."

A brown package, the size of a shirt box, was propped against Rosa's apartment door. It came from Bloomingdale's on Long Island. Rosa, always cheered up by a present, took it inside and sat down on the couch. Mimi had been making some noises about getting Rosa "something for her hope chest." Rosa anticipated dish towels, maybe placemats and napkins. But inside there was a short white cotton nightgown, the bodice trimmed with lace. Rosa almost missed the card inside the box. Inside, in forceful, precise handwriting, Mimi had written, *To Rosa—the other woman in Gary's life.*

Rosa stared at the card. Then she handed it to Gary without a word. He groaned when he read it. "What's her problem?" he asked.

Rosa picked up the nightgown by the straps. It was not her idea of sexy. The puckered bodice, which was supposed to accentuate the breasts, would make Rosa look top-heavy, and the skirt was too short. Rosa didn't have the least desire to show off her knobby knees.

Rosa dropped the nightgown back into the box. "Take it away," she said.

Gary picked up the nightgown by the delicate lace straps and held it against himself.

"It's not your style," Rosa said.

"*Au contraire.* I think it looks fetching." He folded the nightgown up, awkwardly, goofily, the way men always folded things, the wrong way. "Is the mall still open?" he asked.

"You know it's not."

"I'll take you to Victoria's Secret," Gary promised. "Tomorrow."

The thought of shopping for lingerie with Gary in tow made Rosa cringe. "I'll pass on that."

"Why? I see men in there all the time. All the time."

"You go in there?" Rosa asked.

"No, I'm like everybody else. I sort of glance in when I walk by. Sometimes I think about getting you something."

"You would go into a lingerie store all by yourself?"

"Sure," Gary said. "For you. I'd do it for you. You know, the real you. The one that loves me."

"Is there another?" Rosa asked.

"Oh, I think so," Gary said. "Yes."

Rosa nudged the Neiman Marcus box with her foot. "Then what are we doing this for?"

"You can't be alone for the rest of your life," Gary said.

"Plenty of people live alone," Rosa said.

"Yeah, but are they happy doing it?" Gary asked. "Married people live longer."

"Maybe they're just trying to outlive their spouse," Rosa said. "It's a spite thing."

"Well, men always kick off first, so you can laugh long and hard when I'm in my grave."

Rosa bit her lip. She looked down at the nightgown. The silence of the apartment engulfed her, and she felt intensely alone.

"Well," she said, trying to sound flippant, "as they say in Nashville, I love you, I hate you, I can't live without you."

"Ditto," he said. "Let's go to bed."

While Gary used the bathroom, Rosa picked up the nightgown and pressed her hands over the soft lace. She had not been generous toward Mimi. On second glance, the nightgown truly was pretty, more feminine than anything Rosa would have picked out for herself. And Gary seemed to like it. Rosa put it on in the bathroom— she refused to undress in front of Gary whenever they had argued or gotten tense with one another—and self-consciously walked across the bedroom to join him in bed.

"It's pretty," he said.

"You like it?" Rosa asked. Then tears started streaming down her face.

"Yeah. Yeah," Gary said. "Come on, cut it out, stop crying. It's okay."

Rosa snorted and snuffled and then reached over to get some Kleenex. She was glad that they had stopped messing around every night. It had gotten to be too much of a strain. Things had started thinning to a slower pace about a month ago, when Gary, once, had too much to drink, and his allergies were bothering him, and Rosa's stomach hurt, and it was a relief not to do it. "Well," Gary philoso-phized, "you can't keep up that old bunny-fucking pace forever. Sooner or later you shoot your wad and then—you know—once or twice a week, maybe more during the summer. I don't know what it is about hot weather, but it always makes me horny."

At first Rosa had been hurt by those remarks. But she too was tired of keeping up the pretense that she was hot to trot every night, and why be a hypocrite? You got married for comfort, for stability, for a little bit of company, for somebody to chat with, because your own conversation with yourself was so neurotic and inane, and be-cause God sure wasn't listening, or if He was, He was doing it like some deaf-mute sitting across the room, reading your lonely, desir-ous lips but failing to respond to them.

No, God certainly did not talk back when Rosa said her prayers. For Rosa continued to say them at night, making a furtive sign of the cross and muttering an Act of Contrition, an Our Father, and three Hail Marys before she went to sleep. Was this habit? Or hope? Rosa felt there had to be something more to life, something better than the bullshit at the office, the weekly laundry, the nightly load of dishes. There had to be something beyond even the pleasurable stuff, like eating pizza and sucking on watermelon-flavored hard candy and laughing in front of the apes cage and kissing Gary. Rosa felt there was an emptiness inside her that could only be filled by something higher. But where was this something? What was it? She thought she had heard it once, practically throbbing inside her hol-low body, that time she had placed her head on the towel at Light-house Beach and put her ear to the sand. For one gorgeous moment, her own breathing, the beating of the sun, and the lap of the water had combined into one big beautiful pulse, and Rosa had heard the pounding of the earth.

Of course, this had happened right after Rosa had downed a can of Budweiser, and Connie lay passed out beside her, half of the six-pack audibly gurgling inside her stomach.

But still . . . still . . . sometimes, when Rosa lay in bed listening to Gary breathe, or when she turned around in a crowded room and caught his eye and he smiled at her, or when she walked silently with him by the creek at Edgewood, she thought she was on the very edge of another one of those moments. Something sparked inside of her— something, for half a second, made her feel on the verge of being to-tally complete. But then Gary snored or stuck out his tongue at her or made dumb quacking noises at the ducks, and the feeling was gone. Rosa kept waiting. She kept thinking there was something inside Gary that would help her understand the world—surpass it, even.

But so far the idea of marriage—the preparation for marriage— had been anything but spiritual. In fact, it focused totally on the mundane. On their next trip to Long Island, Artie toasted their en-gagement by holding up his champagne glass and saying, "Family. I've always taught Gary, put your family first. Do good business, fair business, but don't live for the office. Remember, nobody at the of-fice is going to hold the bucket for you when you throw up."

"What kind of toast is that?" Mimi asked, annoyed. She raised her glass and looked at Gary and Rosa, who sat there like two little kids being chastised. "To love," Mimi said. "And a lifetime of hap-piness."

Rosa and Gary both downed their champagne in one gulp.

The next morning Artie went into work early and Pilar made a fabulous breakfast—hazelnut coffee, delicate almond-studded pan-cakes, and fruit cup laced with a bit of liqueur. Mimi presided over the table and began addressing the most important part of marriage: acquiring material things. Rosa accidentally had dumped too much pure Vermont maple syrup on her pancakes and was doing her best to avoid dripping all over her shirt. Mimi looked down at Rosa's plate and said, "We need to get you registered."

Rosa instantly felt like a dog.

"Huh?" Gary said.

"People already are asking what you want for your wedding," Mimi said. "Mostly on my side. On Artie's side, the tradition is to give cash."

"And lots of it," Gary said.

"Don't be crass, dear," Mimi said. "Even if they are."

"Sorry," Gary said. "Crass must be in my genes. Thank God I got your DNA, too, otherwise I, too, might be predestined to own a Cadillac dealership in Whitestone."

"It's not Cadillac," Mimi said. "Uncle Len has an *Oldsmobile* firm. He does very well for himself, even though he acts like a— peasant." She gave a little laugh, forced and fragile as a cheap crystal bell. "As I was saying, we need to get Rosa registered." Looking at Gary's blank face, she added, "*Bridal* registry. You know. Tell him, Rosa."

"Yeah, tell me, Rosa," Gary said.

Rosa picked at her pancake. "You go to a store," Rosa reluctantly said. "And you look at everything they sell and you make up a list of what you want. Then people come in, consult the list, and get something for you."

Gary hooted.

"I fail to see the humor," Mimi said. "It's a very practical concept."

"Why is handing someone a list of what you want less crass than handing someone a check?" Gary asked.

"People get to select a gift," Mimi said. "There is no exchange of money."

"Oh yeah, money," Gary said. He smacked himself on the head. "I forgot how corrupting it is! How filthy is that lucre!"

Rosa silently chewed her soggy pancake. She felt, at first, a bit uncomfortable with the whole idea of bridal registry. Rosa's relatives also gave cash, and a lot of it. Those who decided to give presents always went to the International Silver plant in Meriden, where they picked out scalloped trays, wire bread baskets, salt and pepper shakers, and candlesticks that tarnished within a year. Rosa's mother would die if she knew Rosa had registered anywhere. Antoinette's whole attitude about gifts summed up her philosophy about life. "You take what you get," she said, "and say thank you, no matter what it is."

But then a bit of greed, combined with a real fear of being saddled with hideous, useless household items for the rest of her life, made Rosa shrug and nod at Gary and Mimi.

"So where are we going to register?" Gary said.

"Rosa and I will do it this morning," Mimi said. "You can stay here and do—man things."

"What's a man thing, Mom?" Gary asked. "I don't think that was in the sex education booklet you gave me when I was nine, you know, the one with the stick figures—"

"If you're not going to stay here, then go to the shop and visit your father. Give Rosa and me some time together."

"Not on your life," Gary said. "I'm not coming back from my honeymoon to a warehouse full of china and crystal."

Mimi dabbed at her mouth with her white napkin. Little blobs of pink lipstick came off. "Then join us," she said. "But you had better behave. Isn't that right, Rosa? He'll have to behave if he wants to come with us. We'll leave right after breakfast. Right after you get dressed."

"We *are* dressed," Gary said.

Mimi looked at Gary's workshirt and Rosa's plain white button-down blouse from the Gap. "Dressed to go *shopping*," she said.

After breakfast Rosa went upstairs and put on the black jumpsuit, linen jacket, and fabric sandals she had been saving for that evening. Now she would have to be careful not to spill anything on herself for the rest of the day.

Gary took off his workshirt and khaki pants and put on a royal blue T-shirt and a pair of jeans. Rosa shook her head at him. He raised his eyebrow at her.

"Whose side are you on, anyway?" Gary asked.

That was the problem. Rosa was not on anyone's side, nor was anyone on hers. She was simply a voyeur, gazing at Gary and Mimi, who bickered and squabbled like those crazy married couples Rosa had read about in advice columns, the kind who went to parties and staged fights in front of other people, then went home and banged each other senseless. Gary and Mimi tussled about whose car to take to the store and who would be the driver. Gary finally ended up driving Mimi's Saab, and Mimi, who got carsick if she sat in the back, perched in the passenger seat, saying, *Not so fast, not so fast, you're cutting off cars, since when do you drive like such a maniac?* implying that it was all Rosa's fault that Gary had acquired some crazy boy-fantasy of becoming Mario Andretti in the Indianapolis 500.

Rosa moped in the back seat like a teenager with B.O. who couldn't get beyond the first word of a conversation: hi.

Gary was humming a tune that Rosa recognized but couldn't name. Just as they pulled into the crowded parking lot of Fortunoff's, she remembered. It was sung by Joel Grey, his face bleached Clorox-white and his lips fire-engine red, as he lewdly pranced in *Cabaret:*

Bee-dle dee dee dee dee! Two ladies!
Bee-dle dee dee dee dee! Two ladies!
Bee-dle dee dee dee dee!
And I'm the only man. Ja!

This did not bode well for the shopping trip.

The parking lot at Fortunoff's was packed. Cars were backed up in the main driveway, and the side entrances were jammed with chartered buses that had Connecticut and New Jersey license plates.

"Just another Sabbath morning in Garden City," Gary said to no one in particular. "Welcome to the biggest temple on the island."

"Don't be ridiculous," Mimi said. "This parking lot is just as packed on Sunday."

"I guess God can't compete with a white sale," Gary said. He bucked Mimi's car around the parking lot, stalling out several times before he finally found a parking space close enough for Mimi's comfort. When Rosa got out of the back seat, she felt on the verge of throwing up from the motion and the heat.

Clearly on a mission she had waited to fulfill for years, Mimi charged ahead in the parking lot. Gary took Rosa's arm and commented on the customers all the way into the store. "I haven't seen so much plastic surgery in one place since my parents took me to Beverly Hills," he said. As they rode up the escalator, passing woman after woman on the staircase going down, he whispered in Rosa's ear his sage opinion about which body parts had been fixed. "Butt," he whispered. "Boobs. Neck. Nose. Nose. Nose."

"Cut it out," Rosa said, although she had to admit she thought his guess was usually pretty accurate.

Bridal registry was on the fourth floor, in back of the silverware. Row after row of Oneida, Reed and Barton, and Towle five-place settings lined the shelves. As they passed by the display, Rosa heard a blur of voices. "Look at this spoon, you're supposed to fit this spoon in your mouth?" "The blade on the knife is too long." "Is the hostess set included?" "Take down the name of the pattern, you can find it on sale at Strauss."

The counter for bridal registry was empty.

Gary leaned forward and whispered in Rosa's ear. "Watch this," he said. "You are about to see a true fishwife go into action."

As if on cue, Mimi stood at the counter for a moment, then moved away and craned her neck, searching the sales floor. She huffed. "We're here to register the bride," she said loudly, to any and all who cared to hear. "The bride is here, but where are the salesladies?"

Someone tapped Mimi on the shoulder. Mimi turned around, ready to give the saleswoman a dressing-down. But it was only another customer, an older woman in catglasses, a turquoise housecoat, and Hush Puppies. "You can get their attention if you break something," the woman said.

Mimi looked scornfully at her.

"Go ahead," the woman said. "Throw something on the floor. The more expensive, the better."

Mimi looked at the woman as if she smelled bad. Rosa bit her lip to keep herself from laughing. Gary followed her over to the silverware display. Deliberately flouting the discreet little signs on the display racks which requested that customers *please ask the sales help for assistance,* Gary picked up a pie server in a pattern called Full Moon and pursued Rosa up and down the aisles, talking into the pie server like a microphone.

"Good afternoon, folks, this is your American talk-show host, and we're here on Lawng Island, New Yawk, where the Lincoln Town Car rules the expressway, and in the bedroom, the dildo reigns supreme—"

"Shh," Rosa said.

"We stand here at Fortunoff's, which in the American tradition, is open on both Saturdays and Sundays, so you can shop 'til you drop on the holy day of your choice—"

"Be quiet," Rosa said.

Gary lowered his voice to a whisper. "And I'm standing here in Bridal Registry with a woman who once gave serious consideration to becoming a bride of Christ and now—if I may so humbly add—has graciously accepted me as a substitute." He stuck the pie server in front of her face. "Rosa Salvatore, just a few questions, if you would. Tell us a little something about this fisherman you worship—"

"Carpenter," Rosa corrected him.

"Oh, pardon me, that's what I get for learning the gospels from Andrew Lloyd Webber! Anyway—anyhow—anywho—what light can you shed on the cult of this carpenter king? What is his mystique? Was he really a party animal, with all those loaves and fishes and vats of wine, and is his eleventh commandment really *Thou shall play Bingo?* Clear up the controversy once and for all, is he pro-family or pro-choice? And where do all those aborted fetuses go, anyway? What *can* we do to solve the population problem in—" Gary swiveled his hips and assumed an island reggae voice as he sang "—Limbo, Limbo, Limbo, Limbo, Limbo, Limbo, Limbo?"

Rosa stood there, furious. Then a tall black woman, dressed in a mustard-colored jacket and black stirrup pants, came out of the

Reed and Barton silverware display. She looked down at Gary with complete disgust. "Stop it," Rosa hissed, reaching out and swatting the pie server. It clattered to the tile floor. Gary laughed and bent over to retrieve it. When he stood up, he met the eyes of a silver-haired woman in half-glasses. She wore a name badge.

"Whatta you know," Gary said. "A saleslady."

Rosa turned and walked away. She wanted to die. She wished she could just run down the escalator and out the front door. But Mimi, who finally had found someone to wait upon her, now sat at one of the little tables by the counter, thumbing through a huge catalog. She waved Rosa over.

Rosa pulled up one of the Breuer chairs and sat down next to Mimi. "What's the matter, dear?" Mimi asked.

Softened by Mimi's solicitous tone of voice, Rosa gestured at Gary.

"You see," Mimi said. "Now you see. You see how he is."

Rosa moved her chair closer to Mimi. This felt comfortable. It was the kind of situation Rosa had grown up with, the women against the men.

But Mimi spoiled it the very next moment. "It's not too late, you know," she said. "You don't have to marry him. Don't do it, dear, unless it feels one hundred percent right."

Rosa narrowed her eyes and said, "It's completely right."

"Well," Mimi gave her little laugh, "you never know how miserable a man can make you until you live with him."

"We already live together," Rosa said.

"I see," Mimi said between very tight lips. "I might have been told. Although I might have guessed."

Rosa tried to decide what Mimi meant by this—that Gary was some oversexed animal that needed round-the-clock attention, or that Rosa was some fat, lazy slut trying to muscle her way to the top?

But Mimi merely said, "Times are changing." She idly flipped through a few pages of the catalog. "And yet you still keep your apartment?"

"I go there when I want to be alone," Rosa said.

"After you're married, you'll have nowhere to go," Mimi said. "So I don't think that's it. You must keep the apartment as a front. It's a front, isn't it, for your parents? Your parents aren't very progressive, are they?"

"If you mean do they vote Republican," Rosa said, "the answer is yes."

Mimi bit her lip. "Gary didn't tell us *that,*" she said.

"What does he tell you?" Rosa asked.

"He tells us nothing," Mimi said, and Rosa instantly felt relieved. "Naturally, Artie and I are concerned. Dear, we are concerned about all this. How *do* your parents feel about Gary?"

This clearly was Mimi's question; never in a million years would Artie believe that the whole world wasn't in love with his son. Rosa felt like telling Mimi, *My mother likes Gary because he eats a lot. But because he talks too much, my father thinks he's a faggot.*

"My parents like Gary," Rosa said, in a tone of voice that she hoped conveyed to Mimi the rest of the unspoken sentence: *more than you'll ever like me.*

"But do they *accept* him?" Mimi asked.

Rosa looked across the sales floor at Gary. He was holding a martini shaker in his hands. He opened the top, almost dropped the lid to the floor, and juggled the parts before he put them all back together again. He looked at Rosa, pointed to the shaker, and gave it a couple of hardy shakes. He's a clown, Rosa thought. God, a real *pagliacci*!

"Do *you* accept him?" Rosa asked Mimi.

Mimi looked down at the catalog. "He's my son," she said, as if she and Rosa had just slugged out nine rounds in Madison Square Garden and the sweaty referee had raised Mimi's fist in the air, declaring her the victor. "Now, let's choose some patterns. Take your time. You will have to live with these things for the rest of your life."

Rosa and Mimi hunched over the catalog. There were important decisions to be made, on everything from bath mats to pierced serving spoons to sugar shells and swizzle sticks. Flatware storage options alone seemed limitless. Rosa selected lead crystal barware with silver rims, no-iron 250-thread-count pima cotton sheets with extra deep pockets to fit today's mattresses, whistling teakettles, and round casseroles with domed lids. After a few minutes, Gary joined them, thumbing through a catalog at the next table.

"Listen," he said. "I think I've found some man things." He chose a four-speed blender, a food processor, and a combination coffee grinder and espresso maker.

"They always like appliances," Mimi whispered to Rosa. *"Men."*

There was a half-hour controversy about the plates. Rosa and Mimi combed the catalogs. Rosa loved all the patterns, the exotic ones with names like Jasmine and Martinique; the geographically inclined Bellaire, Monterey, Southern Vista, Prairie Blossoms; the ones that reminded her of her special day: Bridal Bouquet and Wedding Band; the comforting ones she felt she could happily retire with: Simplicity, Old Willow, Country Romance, Remembrance; the ones that sounded like the names a four-year-old would give her dolls: Alice, Joanna, Sabrina, Beth. Then there were the racy patterns: Momentum, Traviata, Black Contessa, Urban Twilight, Eclipse. There were patterns for the men who would be country squires and the girls who longed to look like Princess Di, with nary a blond hair out of place: Royal Hunt, Evesham Vale, Chippendale, Embassy Suite, Haverford Hall.

"I gotta have the Blue Italian," Gary said.

Blue Italian was a Spode pattern. Rosa liked it, and she was intrigued by the idea that over time, she could fall in love with it, simply because it would be on her dinner table every day.

They spent three hours in Bridal Registry. Then they went upstairs for lunch and coffee. As Rosa sipped her mocha java, exhausted and badly in need of some Tylenol, she looked down at the slip the saleswoman had run off for her on the computer. At the top of the page it said *Fisher–Salvatore. June 10 wedding.*

This, more than anything, made it seem final. It was Blue Italian all the way.

Looking back at that shopping trip a couple of years later, Rosa remembered how embarrassed she had been by Mimi's single-mindedness and Gary's deliberately obnoxious behavior. But she was most mortified by her own pettiness, which she had kept under wraps, only to have it backfire and explode on her later. What Rosa remembered—and resented—most about that afternoon was that she had let Mimi talk her into peach and sage-green towels. The colors were warm and subtle, Mimi said, and hadn't Rosa noticed how well they went together in the guest bedroom of the Fishers' home? It really would be nice if Gary had something—just something—in his new home to remind him of the house he had grown up in.

"All right," Rosa said.

Two years after they were married, Rosa got into some petty fight with Gary about where he should store his extra cans of shaving cream. Rosa pulled open the door to the linen closet, which was jammed. The towels, still unused and stored on the top shelf, fell down onto the carpet. Rosa shoved them back onto the top shelf. She hated them! She had never wanted them! Yet she could not return them, and she felt like she would have to drag them around with her, like a mortal sin that had gone unconfessed, for the rest of her life.

Rosa had wanted deep midnight blue and silver towels, the colors of the moon and stars and sky, to remind her of the sparkling, fragmented beauty of the constellations. There had been too many streetlights on Pizza Beach, and Rosa had not really seen the stars until she visited the Hayden Planetarium in high school, where she leaned back in the padded chair and gazed up in wonder at Orion, Cassiopeia, the Pleiades, the Seven Sisters. The show had left her feeling stunned, with the same kind of breathlessness she had felt that night she had walked with Gary around the Divinity School, the rain pelting quick as a switch on her face and a few solitary stars gleaming overhead. The universe had seemed to whisper some secret that night, and Rosa, remembering that evening as she moved through the linen department of Fortunoff's, had wanted midnight blue and silver to remind her of those moments. The color of the towels might fade, but when she was caught up in the drudgery of domestic chores—wondering what it was all for—she could always pull those towels out of the dryer and sink her face into their warmth and promise.

But Rosa got stonewalled. She ended up with peach and sage green. And when Gary snapped at her about the shaving cream, Rosa felt like a sponge or starfish, pulling back further and further into herself until she drowned and disappeared in the deep green sea of her own bad humor.

chapter seven

Wedding plans. Such a squabble. Such a mess.

"Do what you want to do," Artie counseled Gary and Rosa.

"You've always done whatever you want to do," Antoinette accused Rosa.

"You're gonna do what you're gonna do," Aldo said, "so go ahead and do it!"

And Mimi told Artie, "I hope you're happy, your son is doing exactly what he wants."

It would be a small wedding. In Battell Chapel. With a justice of the peace. "Whew," Gary said when they finalized the plans. "What a relief. Now I don't have to step on a light bulb."

"I thought you were supposed to step on a wine glass," Rosa said.

"No, it's a light bulb, wrapped up in a napkin. It's bad luck if the glass doesn't shatter, so they substitute forty watts of mazel tov instead."

Rosa was relieved to be spared a Jewish wedding. Although she thought it might be fun to dance the hora, she balked at taking a ritual bath. She was afraid of heights, and the thought of being carried above everyone's head in a chair gave her the willies.

But she was even more relieved to be spared an Italian wedding, a ceremony she described, to Gary's amusement, as *The Godfather* without guns. Rosa's relatives pulled out all the stops for weddings. Most American parents saved for their kids to go to college, but Rosa's aunts and uncles saved for a twenty-four-hour extravaganza that kept the florists, tailors, and caterers in steady business. Like every other mother on the block, Antoinette Salvatore started saving for her daughter's wedding right after Rosa was born. Rosa was certain of this because once, when she was ten years old, she searched her mother's drawers just to see what she could find. In the top drawer of the chest, tucked underneath five white cotton bras with wide and evil-looking straps, Rosa found a dozen laminated holy cards tied together with a grubby green rubber band, a set of pale blue rosary beads in a black box that said MURANO — CITY OF GLASS, and a small white plastic object that Rosa took to be a penlight (realizing, years later, that it must have been a vibrator). Underneath all that were two passbooks from the Greater New Haven Savings Bank, dark green with worn edges, that showed Antoinette had been making monthly deposits of twenty dollars since November of 1961, two weeks after Rosa had been born.

Rosa never forgot about that money. She thought about it more and more as she grew up and started to hint around about going to college and was told point-blank that there was no moola for such foolishness. Although the passbook was hidden, the fund was no family secret. All of Rosa's aunts talked openly about it.

"What would happen to that money if we decided we didn't want to get married?" Connie once asked.

"We'd use it to pay for your funeral," Zia Pina said. And that was that.

Connie and Rosa were never going to get married. When they were kids they used to perch their fat little fannies on the tin garbage cans behind Zio Dino's garage and purposely tumble to the asphalt, scraping their chubby knees as they recited the nursery rhyme about Humpty Dumpty. Later they sat on the same garbage cans and smoked their first cigar, a green Cuban stogie that burned Rosa's lips and turned her stomach hollow. Then Connie took the butt of the cigar and held the hot ashes dangerously close to the tender palm of Rosa's hand. "Swear you'll never do it with a boy named Rocco or Louie," Connie said. "Swear he won't be from East or West Haven, swear it, swear it."

Rosa swore it. But Connie—who grew up clipping ads from the

back of *American Girl* magazine that promised exciting careers in fashion merchandising to girls willing to relocate to Atlanta and Fort Lauderdale—was the first to break her own vow. One Friday night she went to the top of East Rock with a nineteen-year-old named Carmen Miglietti, who drove a delivery truck for the fresh fish market down on Olive Street. Four months later she let herself be stuffed into a full-length boned bra and her mother's Playtex girdle, and was yanked up the aisle at Saint Boniface Church, dragging a twelve-foot train of Chantilly lace behind her. When Zio Dino lifted the tulle veil over Connie's head, Rosa was afraid that instead of kissing her before handing her over to Carmen, he might belt her one, right across the puss. But he gruffly grazed Connie on the cheek, and Connie came up the altar on Carmen's arm, her eyes red puddles and her skin mottled green. Throughout the ceremony, Connie stifled burps that came from swilling too much ginger ale that morning and munching on too many saltines.

Rosa was the maid of honor. She kneeled next to Connie on the altar and wept during the *Ave Maria*, reviewing in her mind the events that had led them there.

"What am I gonna do, what am I gonna do," Connie kept moaning when she first told Rosa. "My mother knows, she went out back of the garage and found the throw-up."

"You can get it," Rosa said. "You know, the operation."

"How'm I gonna get it? Where'm I gonna get the money?" She clutched Rosa's arm. "You could take it. Outta your father's bank deposit bag."

"I can't," Rosa said. "It's stealing."

And Connie wept some more, twisting her miraculous medal round and round on the silver chain. "I couldn't do it anyway," she said. "It's killing. How'm I gonna tell Carmen? How'm I gonna marry him? I don't love him. I don't even like him. Now I gotta like him and love him, because I gotta marry him."

So there they all were, kneeling on the altar. As the communion wafer melted in her mouth, Rosa tried to imagine Connie and Carmen having sex. She was sure Carmen was the kind who groaned and grunted, who said obnoxious things like *Holy Mama!* and *Sweet Mary, Mother of Jesus!* as he ground it in. The thought of it caused Rosa to swallow the host the wrong way, and she had to furiously swallow for the rest of the ceremony to keep herself from retching. As she followed Connie and Carmen back down the aisle, blinking as the Sylvania blue-dot flash bulbs popped off left and right in her face, Rosa bit her tongue until she tasted blood and swore, this time to herself, that she would die before some Louie ever put his thick-knuckled paws or anything else anywhere below her waist. Nobody knew it yet, least of all Rosa's parents, but Rosa was set on going to college. College men did not deign to lower their pants on East Rock. They did not wear black leather belts with silver studs; they did not drive delivery trucks; they did not eat pizza with their mouths open. They said *please* and *thank you* and never said *bitch* or *cunt* or bragged about their big ten-inch.

Connie's reception was held out at the shore, at Tony's Villa Bari. In front of the restaurant stood a huge stone fountain that spurted blue-tinted water. Out in back there was a trellised rose garden with a white arbor, where countless brides and grooms had stood stiffly, smiles plastered on their faces, while the photographer called out, "A little smile from the groom, please. Bride, don't look so frightened, he ain't gonna bite you, that's it, everybody say *formaggio,* say *romano, pecorino, parmigiano, provolone,* I like it, I like it, here goes the click, aaah, that's nice."

For Connie's wedding, Rosa and five other cousins were dressed in tiered taffeta dresses, each tier a different pastel color, so the girls looked like blocks of spumoni or seven-layered parfaits. The ushers, all Carmen's teenage brothers and cousins, wore black tuxes and pink cummerbunds. Looking at the photographs later, Rosa was hard pressed to tell who had darker mustaches, the boys or the girls.

The reception was held on the lower level of the Villa Bari, in the Firenze Room, where there was nary a picture of Florence but plenty of crude murals that showed the crumbling facade of the Colosseum, a black gondola gliding under the Rialto Bridge, and the ruins of Pompeii. The tables were set with blood-red cloths, silverware

heavy as hammers, Chianti bottles in wicker holders, and floral cen-
terpieces to be given away as door prizes at the end of the dinner.

After the members of the wedding took their seats at the head
table, Zio Dino got up and banged his knife against the side of his
wine glass. He cleared his throat. "I wanna thank everybody for
coming," he said. "And I just wanna say—" He paused. "God bless
the bride and groom. Many happy years together." He lifted his
wine glass. *"Salute!"*

"Salute!" everyone echoed.

Then they tilted back their glasses. The Chianti was thick and bitter, but Rosa forced herself to down it in one gulp, otherwise it
would be bad luck. When she lowered her empty glass to the table,
she saw her mother glare at her from across the room. Antoinette refused to drink her wine. She would not wish good luck on any slut.

The best man took his knife and banged it against his wine glass,
and soon the whole hall resounded with the sound of silverware on
crystal. *"Baciano!"* someone called out. "Kiss, kiss!" Carmen leaned
over and Frenched Connie. The men guffawed. The women tit-
tered. Carmen's cousin called out, "Save it for the wedding night!"
Connie, already loosened up by the wine, stuck out her tongue at
him and waggled it.

Then the swinging doors at the back of the hall opened, and the
waiters and waitresses swooped in with huge majolica platters piled
with antipasto and blond wicker baskets full of hot sliced bread. The
salami, shriveled olives, and Tuscan peppers dripped with oil that
stained Rosa's dress. The antipasto was followed by a slab of prime
rib that bled all over the plate, a pile of waxed yellow and green
beans, and a baked potato wrapped in tin foil with a ball of creamy
yellow butter that oozed out of the crack. Throughout the meal, men
stood up and offered toasts to the bride and groom. The more wine
that was drunk, the more inarticulate and ribald the speeches became. People hollered and cheered when Carmen and Connie sunk
the silver knife into the four-foot-high wedding cake, and whooped
when Connie smashed the vanilla frosting into Carmen's ten-hair
mustache. He took a piece of cake and smashed it right back.

Then the microphone at the back of the hall whined and squeaked as the lead singer of the band came out on stage. "Hey there, folks. My name is Vinnie, Vinnie Hoffa, no relationship to Jimmy, wherever he is. This here's Frankie on the electric piana, and we got Georgie on the drums, and together we're called the Olive Tree. You got any requests, we wanna hear 'em. But first we'd like to lead off with a little song for the bride and her father." He took an index card out of his pocket. "Carmen? Oh, sorry, that's the groom. Connie? Where's Connie? Can I get Connie up here? Come on up here and dance with your dad. Let's have a hand for Connie and her dad, a little louder, gang, can't hear ya! And a one and a two and a—"

Vinnie plucked at his sparkling red electric guitar and leaned too close to the microphone as he launched into "Daddy's Little Girl." Connie carefully gathered up the train of her dress and let herself be led around the dance floor by Zio Dino, whose guts she had hated ever since she was thirteen years old and he had pushed her face against the wall of the garage, clawed her breasts, and rubbed himself against her butt until he got what he wanted. Then he had let her go, swearing he would strangle her if she ever told anybody.

Now, circling the dance floor to "Daddy's Little Girl," Zio Dino looked like he was going to cry. Connie's face was a triumphant mask, as if she were thinking about how her father had lost his free once-a-month pleasure, and about how he had only two alternatives left—whacking off on his own, or risking VD with the whores on Howe Street.

Vinnie Hoffa modulated from "Daddy's Little Girl" into "Never, My Love" and then called Carmen up onto the dance floor to cut in on Dino and Connie. Connie no longer looked nauseated. After dancing with her father, she looked resigned, and maybe even a little happy, to dance with Carmen. Then Vinnie called up the rest of the wedding party one by one. Rosa refused to touch the best man any more than with her fingertips as they waltzed awkwardly around the dance floor. Everyone applauded when the fat little flower girl simpered up to the dance floor and held hands with the surly ring bearer. There was dancing for about an hour, while the men went back and forth to the open bar. Then Vinnie got up and said, "Okay, all you single girls. We got any single girls in here? Front and center to catch the bouquet. This may be your lucky day."

The girls swarmed onto the dance floor. While Connie flung the baby's breath over her shoulder, the girls rushed forward, clawing and knocking one another down to catch the bouquet. Rosa purposely hung back. She noticed her mother glaring at her when one of Carmen's cousins surfaced with the crushed flowers from the mass of overly eager girls.

"Okay, the lucky girl has won her prize!" Vinnie said. "And now for the lucky man. Bride, stay right where you are. Give her a chair, somebody give her a chair. Can I have the best man up here? Best man, where are you? Over by the bar? Front and center, best man, for the garter!" Vinnie put down his guitar and took up a trumpet. Leaning over and blowing on the horn, his skinny body writhing suggestively, Vinnie gargled out the stripper song. Connie gave Vinnie a silly little smile. Then she raised her dress off the floor, inch by inch. The best man held out his hands and stroked her ankles, then her calves. The first call came out from the bar, soft at first, then louder and louder.

"Teeth. Teeth. Teeth, teeth, teeth, teeth!"

The men pounded on the table. The women groaned as the best man stuck his head up Connie's dress and dragged the blue lace garter down her thigh with his teeth, leaving a colossal run in her stocking. Everyone cheered when he yanked off the bride's shoe and held up the garter in his hands.

Rosa was mortified for Connie. But Connie didn't seem to care anymore. She clearly had drunk too much wine. She leaned on Carmen's shoulder and practically fell flat onto the dance floor as she tried to get her shoe back on.

Then it was time for the line dances. The Chicken, the Hokey Pokey, the Alley Cat, the Tarantella. Vinnie demanded that everyone come out onto the floor for the final number. Rosa crammed her way into the large circle. Her mother and aunts stayed at the table.

"Now the bride and groom are going to Niagara Falls—" Vinnie said.

Cheers, applause.

"—and to wish them bon voyage, the rest of us are going on a trip around the world! Everybody ready for a trip around the world? Okay, here we go!" The drummer launched into a dramatic roll and ended with a cymbal bang. "Join hands and everybody circle to the left!"

The circle began to go round, slowly, awkwardly. People bumped into one another. Rosa felt the best man's hips rubbing against hers and felt the sweat on his hand as the line went round and round. Vinnie sang:

Everybody circle to the left!
Everybody circle to the left!
Everybody circle, everybody circle
Everybody circle to the left!

Then the drummer let out a cymbal crash and the line abruptly stopped, sending bodies against bodies and causing people to laugh and shout at one another. "Okay, folks," Vinnie said, "our first stop is Poland, home of Solidarity and the good old-fashioned beer barrel polka. I got a couple of volunteers to get out on the floor and do the polka? Circle round 'em as they dance, folks."

The Olive Tree launched into the Beer Barrel Polka as Rosa's great-uncle Melo and his wife Louisa, who had won plaques from Arthur Murray that said *Silver Tango* and *Bronze Rhumba,* dipped and hopped around the floor. Then Vinnie called out, "They oughta teach at Fred Astaire Dance Studio! Everybody give 'em a hand and everybody circle to the right!"

Everybody circled. They went to Hawaii, land of Don Ho and blue waters, volcanoes, leis. All of Carmen's aunts went into the middle of the circle and swiveled their hips like hula girls. They travelled to Austria for a charming little waltz, and to Mexico for a hat dance. "Now, to France!" Vinnie yelled. "Where zee men are real men, except they carry purses—and zee *femmes* are so *feminine,* and we'd like to ask everybody to stand back, *s'il vous plait,* and let Carmen and Carmen, whoops, I mean Carmen and Connie, dance to this one, which is oh-so-very French indeed!"

Vinnie leaned over to the microphone and grinned as he crooned, *"Voulez-vouz couchez avec moi, ce soir!"*

Carmen and Connie did a bump and grind that made Rosa blush and everyone else hoot and applaud. Then they went to Argentina for the tango and Ireland for a jig. They ended up in Spain. Before Rosa was even aware of what was happening, Connie stepped up behind her and pushed her into the middle of the circle. And Zio Dino, that piggy old lecher, pushed Rosa's father out onto the floor with her. Aldo was completely tanked up on whiskey. Rosa's head hurt from the Chianti. "Bullfight!" Vinnie said and then launched into:

Toreador-o
Don't spit on the floor-o
Use a cuspidor-o
That is what it's for-o!

Someone tossed Rosa a red napkin from the table. Aldo put two fingers on top of his head to make bull horns, leaned his upper body down, and lunged at her. Rosa flapped the napkin. Her father lunged at her over and over again, and everyone cheered as she neatly sidestepped his advances.

Rosa was seventeen years old, two years away from the introduction to Freud she later would receive in Psych 101, taught in a fourth-floor classroom at Southern Connecticut State College. She had no inkling whatsoever of the Oedipus complex or penis envy. But she knew enough about human nature to realize that this spectacle was definitely weird. Rosa kept waving the red napkin and her father kept on charging her, over and over again, and all the faces of the crowd turned and revolved around her, until Vinnie hollered,

"So we're the Olive Tree, don't forget us next time you're throwing a wedding or baptism or confirmation, and we thank you for listening and *hasta la vista, toreador!*"

The circle stopped revolving. Rosa's father stood up and wiped the sweat from his brow. He did not look at Rosa; Rosa did not look at him. But over in the corner Rosa saw her mother sitting at the table with her lips shut tight as a zipper and a cruel, cold look on her face.

The dancing was over. The guests were starting to leave. Those who stuck it out to the bitter end were treated to the spectacle of Connie getting so close to the candles at the head table that her wedding veil caught fire. Zia Pina shrieked and descended on her, beating her with napkins and purses to put out the flames.

"That fire was a sign," Antoinette told Rosa three years later, after Connie finally left Carmen. "Bad luck. Bad luck. Anybody could have seen it. Anybody could have said."

Rosa and Gary got married in Battell Chapel, in a ten-minute ceremony spoken by a justice of the peace. Rosa's relatives were furious to be cheated out of a Catholic mass. Rosa had rooked them of candles and incense, Mendelssohn's wedding march, and a poorly sung rendition of *Ave Maria.* They were denied seven fat bridesmaids in chiffon dresses, silver matchbooks engraved with the names of the bride and groom, a chance to catch the bouquet and garter, and the ridiculous sight of Gary and Rosa being carted away from the church in a black limousine with the back windshield soaped up and the silver fender dragging behind old shoes, tin cans, and streams of white toilet paper.

When Rosa and Gary walked out of the chapel, Rosa's aunts and uncles stood at the bottom of the stone steps and pelted them with Uncle Ben's converted rice and sugared pastel almonds, symbols of everything Rosa never would find with Gary: long life and fertility.

So Rosa and Gary got their way about the ceremony. But then they were subjected to parties—separate parties given by each set of parents. Aldo and Antoinette's came right after the ceremony and was held in their backyard. The food—huge foil trays of lasagne and

baked ziti, platters full of tomato and cucumber slices sprinkled
with olive oil, black pepper and oregano, and kaiser rolls heaped in
two wicker laundry baskets—was set up on a huge plank of wood
balanced on sawhorses in the garage, and served on thick paper
plates that said *This Is Your Special Day!* Antoinette had strung
streamers and fold-out wedding bells from the rafters and set up a
"wishing well," a big barrel covered with pink and blue crepe paper,
where the relatives deposited their envelopes, stuffed with money,
for the happy couple. The guests sat out on the asphalt on lawn
chairs borrowed from neighbors and relatives. Rosa's Zio Weegie,
who was a milkman, brought crates from the dairy to use as make-
shift tables. After the food was consumed, the women sat together
under the plum tree, which was encrusted with tar to ward off some
kind of weird tree disease. The men smoked stogies and threw the
butts over the fence into the tomato patch. They played *morra* and
bocce.

Rosa kept on watching Artie and Mimi to see how they reacted to
this spectacle. Artie, somehow, fit right in. He ate two helpings of lasagne and traded stories with Antoinette and Aldo about the old
days. Then Antoinette and Artie tried to one-up each other.

"We've come a long way from Avenue A," Artie said. "My father
pushed minks around the garment district. He went to work at four
in the morning."

"*Four* in the morning," Antoinette said. "My father started work
at *three* in the girdle factory."

"We used to go to the market," Artie said, "and my mother would
buy fish skin and fry it up. We'd suck on that to hold our appetite
until supper."

"My mother broke bread into a bowl of wine and added some water and said, 'Here, here's your dinner,' " Antoinette said.

"We wore little bags of camphor around our necks to ward off
polio," Artie said.

"We washed our scalps in kerosene to keep the lice away."

Mimi watched on, impassively. She sat on a green webbed *chaise
longue*—which she pronounced in the French way, to Antoinette's

puzzlement. The metal legs of the chair were rusted brown from rain and encrusted with seaweed from all those summers spent at Lighthouse Beach. Mimi talked briefly to Rosa's cousin Michael, an accountant who was the only member of the family who had a college education, but for the most part, she sat on her own, quietly nodding as she listened to Rosa's aunts complain about their indigestion.

The sky gradually turned darker, then sunk into the grey-blue of twilight. Aldo and Zio Dino and Connie set up some milk crates in front of a bush. "What's going on now?" Gary asked.

"My mother's cousin Anthony is going to sing," Rosa said. Rosa considered asking her mother to put a stop to it. Anthony had a good voice, but he was always accompanied at these gatherings by Zio Louie on the accordion, which seemed like such a peasant instrument with its goofy shortened keyboard and wild, whining squeeze box.

Rosa went up to Connie and whispered in her ear. "Go tell Anthony not to sing *Finiculi, Finicula.*" Connie nodded. She went over to Anthony, whispered in his ear, and then reported back to Rosa. "Anthony said he'd be glad to honor your request."

"You bitch," Rosa said and pinched her arm.

Anthony stood up on the crate and to the accompaniment of the accordion, sang *Finiculi, Finicula.* Then he announced a few love songs—*O Sole Mio, Torna a Sorrento, La Donna è mobile.*

"Sing Puccini," someone called out.

He shook his head. "Verdi," he said. He told Louie to put down the accordion. It let out a loud, lamenting noise when Louie released it to the ground. Dusk settled on the backyard, the plum tree looked black against the grey sky, and Anthony sang an aria from *Tosca,* the one in which Cavaradossi looked up at the stars and thought about how he would never see his ladylove again. Rosa wiped a tear from her eye when he was through. Anthony waved his hand when people called out for more. He stepped down from the milk crate.

"What does he do for a living?" Mimi asked Rosa.

"He works for the sausage man," Rosa said. "Down on the wharf."

To Rosa's surprise, Mimi looked charmed by Anthony. She lay back on the chaise lounge, crossed her legs at the ankle, and her head fell langorously to one side. "He has a stunning voice," she said. "And I haven't heard accordion in years. Not since before we had Gary. On that trip to Italy, do you remember, Artie? At Tivoli, in the gardens of the Villa D'Este. You've been there?" she asked Antoinette.

"Can't say that I have," Antoinette said.

"It's magnificent," Mimi said. "There are fountains upon fountains, water cascading everywhere, from gargoyle heads and the ears and eyes of cherubs."

"One statue had twenty breasts and water squirting out of every nipple," Artie said.

"You exaggerate," Mimi said.

"I remember," Artie insisted. "I stood there and counted every single one of them."

Aldo guffawed. Antoinette looked momentarily shocked, but then—perhaps remembering she had had a glass of wine—she smiled. Some of Rosa's aunts, sensing a story was being told, leaned forward a little and listened.

"The light when we came up from the garden was breathtaking," Mimi said. "The whole world seemed to glow like red clay. We stayed at this little *pensione*. . . . "

"The toilet was out in the hall," Artie said. "Beautiful country, Italy, but bad plumbing. The toilets and the phones never worked."

"We went back to the *pensione*," Mimi said. "And the owner, he kissed my hand when I came in. I felt like a queen. He gave us some wine on a tray to take upstairs. I remember everything, the pink color of the walls, the green shutters on the windows. In the distance there were shouts and laughter. And then an accordion started playing, Artie, do you remember?"

"Remember?" Artie said "Look at who we have to remind us." Then he reached over and slapped Gary on the knee.

"Oh," Mimi said, recovering her composure. "Honestly."

Antoinette's eyes widened. Rosa's aunts clapped their hands together in polite applause. Mimi acknowledged their appreciation with a polite nod. Rosa grew embarrassed when Zia Pina said to Gary, "For you, too. *Molti figli.* Many sons."

"And a daughter to help you with the dishes," Antoinette added.

Throughout all this, Gary looked down at his shoes, which had become dusty from the garage. He was preoccupied, disconcerted. For once, he had nothing to say for himself. Artie and Mimi were doing all the talking. They began to laugh and trade stories about Italy with Rosa's relatives. Then shortly after that, Artie and Mimi made a move to go back to the Sheraton in downtown New Haven, where they planned to spend the night.

"This has been delightful," Mimi said, holding out her hand to Antoinette. She kissed Rosa. "Your family is so interesting!" she said, and as she took Artie's arm, there was a little gleam in her eye that Rosa had never seen before. Gary walked them back to their car. As they pulled away in the Lincoln with the license plate that said "EYES," Artie honked the horn.

Gary winced.

"Managgia!" Antoinette murmured to Rosa. "Imagine telling such a story, in front of people you had just met."

Connie sniggered. "I didn't think old people did it," she whispered. "But why do I have a feeling that they're gonna?"

Rosa cringed. She knew everyone would be having the same feeling about her and Gary when they stood up to go. This mortified her. She gave Gary the clear-out sign and he nodded. It took them a half hour to leave; everyone's hand had to be squeezed and shook, and cheeks had to be pinched and kisses planted and thanks and good luck repeated over and over, until Rosa breathed the final *ciao* to her mother and father. Aldo and Antoinette looked sad and pathetic standing on the sidewalk, waving to Rosa and Gary as the Subaru pulled away.

Rosa and Gary had planned to go back to his apartment—now their apartment—for the night, before they drove up to the Green

Mountains for their honeymoon. Gary was silent all the way back. And when they got home, Rosa had no idea what to do. This was her wedding night, after all. She had envisioned a little shyness on her part, and a healthy dose of male aggression on the part of Gary. They would have pleasant, normal sex—missionary position, of course, nothing should be too unusual or weird, because the act was symbolic, after all, and would serve to seal their union. But Gary seemed preoccupied as he followed Rosa into the bedroom. Rosa took off her shoes and sat back on the bed. Gary put his car keys down on the chest of drawers and loosened his tie. He stood there looking at himself in the full-length mirror that hung on the closet door before he said, "I'm gonna puke. I'm not kidding, I am danger-ously close to barfing the big one all over this rug, right now, and I mean right now. Why did my mother tell that story?"

"I thought it was cute," Rosa said. "Romantic."

"What, that my father got a rise out of staring at twenty stone boobs, and my mother forgot to put in her diaphragm because a ho-tel clerk kissed her hand?"

"It wasn't the clerk," Rosa said. "It was the concierge."

"Great!" Gary said. "My mother got the hots for a concierge and here I stand. God. I'm a freak. I'm half Italian."

"You are not," Rosa said. "She did it with your father, not the guy who kissed her hand."

Gary shuddered, "Ugh," he said, pulling free the knot on his tie. "I can't handle it. I bet your family got a bang out of looking at my parents coo-cooing at one another, like a couple of birds on the first day of spring, and then taking off early and honking the car horn!" He threw his tie on the chest of drawers. "I'm putting a stop to this nonsense. My father is sixty-five years old."

"Your parents do sleep on a waterbed," Rosa reminded him.

"My father has a bad back," Gary said.

"What about all those mirrors in their bedroom?"

"What about 'em?" Gary asked. He looked in the mirror again. "Shit. The last time those two did it was the night Nixon resigned. They rocked the whole house down and then they slept until eleven o'clock the next morning. My father came downstairs whistling and turned on the news. My mother ate two bowls of granola sitting in front of the TV set, watching Tricky Dicky dissolve into tears. 'Well, Gary,' she said, 'I hope you will remember this historic moment.' Little did she realize why. I'm the only person on the planet who can look at Richard Nixon and think of sex." He picked up the phone. "I'm calling the hotel."

"Don't you dare."

Gary starting flipping through the Yellow Pages. "I'm gonna call their room—"

"You will not."

"—and bring on a massive case of *coitus interruptus*—"

"I thought that meant pulling out," Rosa said. Then she lunged across the bed for the phone as Gary began to punch in the numbers. "Leave 'em alone, leave 'em alone!" she said. "What's it going to look like, you calling them on your wedding night? They'll think you have nothing better to do."

Gary's finger paused in midair. He looked at her with utter despair, then put down the phone and sat on the bed.

"My sinuses hurt," he said.

The Green Mountains were lush and verdant. The sun beat down on the maple leaves, the clover bloomed, the butterflies flitted from flower to flower, and after twenty-four hours on their honeymoon, Gary and Rosa grew massively bored gawking at all the trees. But neither dared to express their dissatisfaction. They got up from bed and put on their khaki shorts and drove from one charming little country inn to another, past little white churches and weathered barns and those black-and-white cows—Rosa wasn't sure if they were used for milk or for meat—that gazed dopily at the Subaru from behind the wooden fences. Then Gary and Rosa arrived at yet another New England hamlet and Rosa got out of the car, feeling as conspicuous as a giant crashing through one of those miniature porcelain villages nestled beneath the Christmas tree at Macy's. Rosa was the only person wearing black spandex. Gary's voice seemed awfully loud in comparison to everyone else's in the restaurants.

And wherever you looked there was wallpaper, imprinted with horses and cows and Queen Anne's lace and whales.

They went hiking. Rosa got blisters from her new Chukka boots; Gary carelessly pissed against a tree and it splashed back and stained his white socks. They went canoeing on a lake. Rosa couldn't figure out how to use the paddle; Gary got aggravated and Rosa yelled, "What do I look like, Pocahontas?" That evening Gary had an allergic reaction to the wildflowers and Rosa ate a piece of apple pie that incapacitated her for the next twelve hours. They holed up on the four-poster bed, Gary sneezing like a banshee and Rosa occasionally rolling off the mattress to make yet another trip to the toilet. Gary honked into a Kleenex and turned on the TV. He used the remote to flick back and forth from channel to channel, a behavior that Rosa considered particularly male, not to mention rude and obnoxious. From the bathroom, she heard clips from PBS (*Indeed, I should say so, James*), the shop-by-mail channel (*These are called butterfly sleeves, and they flatter all figures*), MTV (*Yeah. Yeah. Yeah. That was wild, man. Yeah*), and a rerun station (*All my life I've wanted to be a cop*) before Gary seemed to settle on a show called "Let's Get Personal."

The topic of the call-in talk show was "everybody's favorite subject—sex!" Rosa cracked the bathroom door and peered through as she washed her hands for the tenth time in the past hour. The host was a tall, dark-haired man who looked too earnestly into the camera, as if to prove he was not embarrassed to talk frankly about such a sensitive subject. The guest, a sharp-looking woman with pink lipstick and frosted blond hair, was the director of a sex institute. Dr. Nancy Gutten wore a navy-and-white polka-dot dress. The polka dots shifted back and forth as she gestured, also a little too earnestly, at the camera, as if she were truly trying to reach out to Tiffany from Alabama, Cindy from Florida, and Steve from Illinois.

Cheryl from Montana, you're on the air!

"Hey, Rosa," Gary called out from the bed. "Somebody actually *lives* in Montana—"

"That's her problem," Rosa called back, clutching her stomach.

Dr. Gutten, my name is Cheryl and I'm from Montana and my hus-
band doesn't like oral sex——

Receiving it?

No, performing it.

"Outta luck, babe," Gary said.

"Dump him," Rosa recommended.

Bill from Missouri? Go ahead, Bill.

I'd just like to know——

"Spit it out, Bill," Gary said.

Well, my wife and I, we masturbate in front of each other, and I'd
like to know how much is too much——

How much are we talking about, Bill?

Two or three times a day.

Gary whistled. "Holy mother," he said.

Well, if it's mutually satisfying and not interfering with work or
friends or other family commitments——

No, we have hobbies, Dr. Gutten. And we go to church.

Rosa came out of the bathroom laughing. She flopped down on
the bed next to Gary, curled up, and put her head on his stomach.
He stroked her hair. Then he took in a deep breath and sneezed.

"Ssshh," Rosa said. She didn't want to miss the next question.
The show fascinated her, although she could not explain why. She
would never dream of making such confessions on the air. Yet she
was more than willing to listen to them. Was it pure prurient interest, or maybe some aid to self-discovery, a standard to gauge herself
against, to reassure herself that she was normal? Was it comforting—or depressing—to know that there was a woman in Wisconsin
who wanted more emotional commitment from her boyfriend, a
man in Maine who wanted sex four times a week instead of just one,
a Michigan woman who wanted to do it outdoors (Gary suggested
she move to a more tropical climate), and a California man who
tried and tried—really tried—to get over this problem, but he just
couldn't get beyond it, the only way he could come was in between
a woman's breasts?

All of the callers wanted something more than what they were getting, except for Joe from Maryland.

Dr. Gutten, my wife says prayers after we have sex.

Dr. Gutten looked intently at the camera and her polka dots seemed to widen with her eyes.

Um, how does she say them? Out loud, on her knees?

No. Quiet. All by herself. I see her doing it. In the dark.

Have you talked to her about this?

No. I'm not religious.

But she obviously is.

She never was before. She never said nothing about it.

I think you need to ask yourself why she's doing this. She might feel guilt about something. Or maybe she's just thanking God for having such a wonderful lover!

I don't think so.

Hmm. You don't talk. You don't know each other's opinions about religion. And you sound uncertain about your sexual performance. You may have some things to work on in your relationship, Joe.

I just don't think God's got anything to do with it—

Thank you, Joe from Maryland. And now we invite you to call our toll-free line and register your opinion for tonight's viewers' poll: Do You Want Your Partner To Be More Sexually Aggressive?

A commercial for roach spray came on and Gary pushed on the remote. The TV made a crisp snapping noise as the power went off, but the screen remained grey for about half a minute afterwards. Rosa watched the color fade and recede, like the landscape in a dream. And she suddenly felt embarrassed for herself, for Gary, and for all people and their sad, lonely problems that they could not confess, except to some woman in polka dots who blinked too much when someone mentioned the connection between physical love and a higher force.

It was a relief to check out of the bed-and-breakfast in the morning. "I don't think I'm cut out for the country life," Gary said as they packed their bags. "I don't like crickets. They make me nervous. Screeching at you all night long. And what's with all those plaid shirts? Everybody in Vermont wears 'em. They look like they should be on the cover of a tin of maple syrup. Or chopping wood in some Robert Frost poem. Jesus, everybody looks so normal, it's neurotic."

On the long ride back, Gary said he never thought he would miss New Haven. He swore that when they got back home he would get down on his hands and knees and kiss the first blob of pigeon plop that he saw. Rosa said she would not go that far. Still, she longed for a cup of hot, bitter coffee, a bagel from Zacky's Deli, and a scoop of gelato from Claire's.

So it was a relief to come back to the filthy city. But Gary and Rosa did not seem quite at ease with one another. They were excessively polite to one another all the way up to the next weekend, when the big doo-rah was scheduled at the Fishers', an event that proved excruciating even beyond Rosa's wild imagination.

There were no milk crates or mandolins for Mimi. Waiters in black coats whisked around the Fisher home with bottles of champagne; waitresses in white caps offered darling little cucumber sandwiches and spicy canapés. There was a string quartet that no one listened to and a lifeguard by the pool to fish out drunken guests. In the foyer, Artie pumped hands, Mimi pecked cheeks, and Gary suffered repeated slaps on the back, which later translated into big business for his chiropractor. Rosa could tell Gary was totally clueless about the identity of half the guests. Whenever he accepted congratulations from someone he didn't know, he turned to Rosa and said, "I'd like you to meet—well, I'd like you to meet—my wife, Rosa Salvatore!" Rosa wished she had a dollar for every person who said, "You mean Rosa *Fisher!*" and then another buck for every time Gary had to say, "No, Salvator-ay, you pronounce the last *e.* Yeah, that's right, Italian."

The men molested Rosa as they congratulated her. The women sucked face. As Gary took out his handkerchief to wipe a violet lipstick print off Rosa's face, he stopped in midair. *"En garde,"* he whispered. "It's the kamikazi kisser!"

No introductions were necessary for Aunt Sylvia. She swooped into the foyer, all four feet nine of her shimmering with fuchsia and black sequins, and the smooching began. "Artie!" Suck. "Mimi!" Smack. "Gary! Mmmm!" She squeezed Gary's face with great satisfaction. "Another bachelor bites the dust. So introduce me. Is this her? Is this the girl who'll keep you from eating Stove Top Stuffing for the rest of your life?"

Rosa received a full-body massage. Then Aunt Sylvia went back onto the front porch and retrieved a battered black portfolio and a bright red amplifier and microphone designed for eight-year-olds who wanted to pretend they were famous pop singers. "I brought my music," she said.

"You shouldn't have," Mimi said. She reached out and firmly clasped the portfolio, pulling a little too insistently upon it. "We want you to enjoy yourself."

"I enjoy my singing," Aunt Sylvia said.

Mimi pointed to the living room. "I hired the quartet. They're students at Juilliard."

Aunt Sylvia grasped Gary's elbow, stood on her tiptoes, and peered into the next room. "Are they made in Japan?" she whispered. "Last week I was at a party and the musicians, they didn't know any Rodgers and Hammerstein except *The Sound of Music,* what good did that do me? This time, I brought my music, all of it." She squeezed Rosa's hand. "Got any requests? Frank Sinatra, you like Sinatra? Jerry Vale?"

"Rosa likes the opera," Mimi said.

"Opera!" Aunt Sylvia snorted. "They fall in love and die! I gotta have plot."

"Like they fall in love and live?" Gary asked.

"That's more like it. How about it, Rosa?"

Something about Aunt Sylvia made Rosa melt. She smiled her first genuine smile of the day and Aunt Sylvia rewarded her with a big smack on the cheek. Then she squished Rosa's lips into a figure eight between her orchid-colored fingernails, reminding Rosa of a stupid game the third graders at Saint Boniface used to play. The kids squeezed each other's cheeks into accordions and grunted out, "Please! Mr. Bus Driver! Open the back door!"

Just as Rosa felt ready to suffocate, Gary reached out and extricated her face. "Stop raping my wife, will you?" he said. "Jesus, go get a drink." He gave Aunt Sylvia a little shove that divested her of half a dozen fuschia sequins. She immediately disappeared into a crowd of pastel sports jackets, white shoes, and low-cut dresses. The sharp smells of White Linen, Poison, and Eau My Sin wafted back toward Rosa and sharpened her headache.

Just as Gary had predicted, Artie's brothers stormed the party all at once: four troll-like men, each one tinier and uglier and kinder than the next. Uncle Len led the way. He pressed a check written on blue safety paper into Gary's hand. "They say married couples have two big problems: money and sex," he said. "Here's a little something to help you out with the first category."

Uncle Len was followed by Uncle Sollie, who insisted that the roots of all domestic strife could be traced to children, and by Uncle Sammy, who claimed that the biggest bugaboo was real estate. Then came Uncle Siddy, who looked over at Artie and Mimi, smiled sadly at Rosa, and assured her that the top difficulty was in-laws. "Take my word for it," he whispered in her ear. "Every time."

After the reception line was over and done with, Gary snagged a waiter and grabbed two glasses of champagne. Gary downed his in one gulp and Rosa did the same. Before they had a chance to exchange a word, Mimi nabbed Gary and Artie grabbed Rosa, marching them away.

Rosa was pushed and pulled from one group of guests to another. With difficulty, she managed to convince the men that her father did not own a pizza joint. With greater difficulty, she convinced the women that she was not a *career girl* and that she intended to have children someday. "So," they asked, "when?"

Totally carbonated on champagne, Rosa looked longingly at the waitresses who whisked around the hors d'oeuvres. But they passed by without stopping, convincing Rosa that there was a conspiracy to keep her from having anything to eat. Rosa gripped and grinned, trying to concentrate on what people were saying, but bits of other conversations kept distracting her. *She lost it with Weight Watchers.*

What we need are the Democrats, let's get the Democrats back. They took a balloon and blew up her kidney. Benny's in Spoleto. You gotta buy it in the nitrogen-flushed can, remember, nitrogen-flushed for freshness. Did you hear your son, Artie, listen to what your son is saying, what'd you say, Gary, I didn't hear you!

Outside, by the pool, Aunt Sylvia began to sing reckless arpeggios in the beach cabana. Mimi closed the sliding glass door. "Well, I have to admit, I was afraid he'd *never* get married," she announced to a group of women. "I even asked him once, do you want to turn forty years old and still be sleeping on a futon? It's your choice, of course, I won't interfere, I've never interfered. You're happy, I'm happy." Mimi began to weep. Rosa watched two rivers of mascara run down her face, curious to see if the flow would lead to Mimi's hidden plastic surgery stitches. She was on her fourth face lift, Gary said.

Just as the quartet finished some rousing Beethoven, Aunt Sylvia marched back into the living room and rapped the first violinist on the shoulder with her fake book. "Enough of the classical," she said. "Now for the kind of music people *want* to hear. I'm gonna start with some tunes from *Show Boat,* I got a paper clip here on the page, and the rest of you—" She waved her hand at the cellist. "You, over there on the double bass, take a bathroom break."

Aunt Sylvia turned on her little red amplifier and scratched on the microphone with her nails to get the attention of the crowd. "This first tune is for the bride and groom!" She snapped her fingers and called out, "And a-one and a-two and a-three." The violinist sawed out the opening and Sylvia's sequins shook like castanets as she launched into

Oh, why do I love you?
Why do you love me?
Why should there be two
Happy as we?
Can you see the why or wherefore?
I should be the one you care for?

Rosa sat through "Make Believe" and "Can't Help Lovin' Dat Man." "Where's the Mate for Me?" was the last straw. She slipped behind the other guests and sneaked into the kitchen, where she found the rest of the string quartet swiping up the salmon mousse with chunks of dried pumpernickel bread. The waiters and waitresses laughed as the cellist performed a whispered rendition of Aunt Sylvia's dancing and singing.

They fell silent the moment Rosa stepped in. Rosa looked blankly at everyone. She walked across the long galley kitchen and passed through the swinging door into the hallway that led to the maid's room. Then she climbed the narrow staircase to the second floor. She followed the long hallway to the room where she and Gary slept, then shut herself in the bathroom.

The room was cool and dark and quiet. Rosa locked herself in and turned on the light. She felt breathless, as if she had just performed a bellyflopper off the high board and was crashing through a wall of chlorine blue. Her stomach was hollow, her chest was tight, and her heart pounded in a panicked rhythm that reminded her of the childhood rhyme, *A peanut sat on the railroad track, his heart was a-a-a-ll a-flutter!* How did the rest of it go? Rosa put her hand on her chest. *The five-fifteen came rushing by, toot, toot! Peanut butter!*

Yes, the peanut got creamed. Rosa put her palms on the vanity and watched the faucet drip steady little beads of water into the marbled sink. She took deep breaths until the panic began to pass. Then she looked at herself in the mirror. Her black hair, which she had carefully curled under that morning, had reversed its angle to an insouciant flip. Her makeup was yellowed and her coral lipstick was faded to the color of a dead seahorse. Her sleeveless black shift—billed in the Spiegel catalog as *a sophisticated sheath—this season's fabulous little black dress*—hardly seemed worth the 220 dollars Rosa had paid for it, not counting shipping and handling. The model in the catalog had looked chic and thin and elegant. Rosa looked like something straight out of steerage, a *paesana* walking down Grand Avenue to seven o'clock Mass on a summer morning, who had to don a black crocheted sweater to cover her flabby upper arms before she entered the church.

Downstairs, the hubbub momentarily stopped. There was laughter and applause, and then the sad strains of *Sunrise, Sunset* began.

Rosa stared at the lines creased into the thick skin on her neck, the four or five wiry white hairs at the front of her scalp that she had forgotten to yank out with a tweezer, and the cracks on her dry lips. She raised her hands and placed them on the mirror, just as she used to lay her palms on the shiny blue ball that sat on the plastic pedestal in Zio Dino's backyard. She and Connie used to spend hours playing fortune-teller, gazing into the ball and foreseeing nothing but glamour and fame for themselves, a life full of sophistication and carefree happiness.

Now Rosa looked in the mirror and saw it all, and it was nothing like she had ever imagined it would be.

Rosa is married. The first week of her marriage is marked by a conspicuous lack of sexual activity and an overabundance of politeness. Gary suppresses his burps at the dinner table and washes the dishes. Rosa cleans the stray strands of her pubic hair out of the bathtub and makes furtive, unsuccessful attempts to hide the minor fortune she has invested in feminine hygiene products. They both brush their teeth before they set foot in the kitchen in the morning.

Little by little, this all changes. Gary belches; Rosa nags, until Gary has to ask, "What'd you say?" every time Rosa says something. There is an unspoken moratorium on French-kissing. Too wet and gross. They peck each other good morning and good night, like a couple of chickens halfheartedly trying to search out that last little bit of seed on the cold, damp ground. Sex is a once-a-week chore performed, most of the time, to the satisfaction of each, and always with the help of a little bit of bubbly.

Gary works hard, goddammit. Rosa works hard, but she does not say goddammit, and she does all the housework, too. So Rosa gets lazy. She stops making lamb chops and lasagne and chicken paprika for dinner. Instead, she fixes frozen waffles, Jimmy Dean sausage links, and scrambled eggs. Weekends they go to restaurants, where the conversa-

tion runs like this: "What are you going to order?" "I don't know, what are you going to order?" Dinner is followed by a concert at Woolsey Hall, where Gary and Rosa are only slightly amused by the merry pranks of Till Eulenspiegel and thoroughly disgusted by some dingdong twentieth-century mood piece that involves the percussionist making random whacks on a washboard with a wooden spoon, the concertmaster bowing on a Stanley saw, and a boy soprano howling like a cat being dragged to a veterinarian. After the intermission (which Rosa spends standing in line in the ladies' room, to the disgust of Gary), they resume their seats. It takes the opening strains of the New World Symphony—so full and rich, so drawn out with longing— to strike a chord in both their hearts. Rosa crosses her legs and focuses on the conductor. Gary looks around the stage as he shifts his weight in his chair. By the time the horns announce the second movement, Gary is blissed out from an imaginary blow job performed by the petite Japanese bassoonist, and Rosa is on her third round of multiorgasmic sex with the maestro and his very interesting little baton.

They are married. They buy a house, a split-level behind Lake Whitney. To make the mortgage, Gary works late. Rosa gets pregnant and quits the job she has complained about for years and which she sorely misses the minute she stops doing it. During the first three months of her pregnancy, she acquires an intimate knowledge of all the hairline cracks and cleanser-resistant stains of the toilet bowl as she leans over the rim and retches herself empty every morning, her knees scraped raw as a penitent's on the cold tile floor. Then one morning she wakes up hungry, a veritable human vacuum cleaner, and for the next six months she sucks up canisters of Pringle's potato chips, waxed bags full of chocolate-covered doughnut holes, raw potato flakes from the Idaho Spuds boxes, and spicy Swanson Dinner buffalo wings before the microwave can even defrost them.

Rosa gets just a bit chubby, then pleasingly plump, then plain old fucking fat. She has the baby and then another. Bleary-eyed from lack of sleep and one common cold after the other, Rosa watches the babies squall, open-mouthed, until their tongues vibrate like hummingbird wings and the back of their throats turn purple, and she fantasizes *about tossing her offspring into the clothes dryer, grinding them to pieces in the garbage disposal, or dunking their sweet, defenseless little heads over and over again into the toilet. She looks in the mirror and sees she is yet another hag from Hamden. She reads magazine articles that suggest she take time for herself, make that trip to the beauty salon, go shopping and buy a sexy little dress or even just a zingy new shade of lipstick. "Schedule time with your husband!" the articles command her. So Rosa does. Gary needs a couple of Heinekens before he can begin to think about sex. Rosa requires an entire six-pack before she can even tolerate it.*

The children are boys. They barf and piss on Rosa. They scatter Lincoln Logs and He-Man figures all over the carpet until Rosa feels like she is crunching through the bones of a mass grave every time she walks around the house. The boys throw tantrums every time Rosa tries to pack them in her dark green Volvo station wagon and cart them to music lessons, art classes, and intellectually stimulating events like the Ice Capades. They follow Rosa around the house, talking about Dr. Spock and Dr. Who, and telling one knock-knock joke after another. "Knock, knock, Mom," they say. "Knock, knock. Who's there, who's there?" Why, what do you know? It's Louis Pasteur, Marie Antoinette, Yogi Berra, Julius Caesar, Baby Beluga, Roll Over Beethoven, William of O-range-you-glad it ain't Princess Di, Elvis the Pelvis, P.D.Q. Bach, Punch and Judy, Mamma Mia, Pepe le Pew, Baruch Adonai. "Knock, knock," the boys say. "Knock, knock, Dad. Dad, what's the capital of South Dakota? Who's Charles de Gaulle, Dad? What's Einstein's theory of relativity, Dad? We need ten dollars to go bowling, Dad. Dad, Dad, do we have to be Jewish? Saturdays is pee-wee hockey!"

When the kids aren't locked in cahoots against Gary and Rosa, they are beating each other black and blue. Rosa is a full-time referee of their constant fights, hugging and kissing the sobbing younger brother when the oldest one rips off the largest piece of the wishbone, until Gary, who has made a career out of defending homosexual rights in the New Haven courts, warns Rosa to stop coddling the kid, Jesus, does she want to turn him into a fag or what? Rosa accuses Gary of having no compassion. He accuses her of having no common sense. Gary works later, and Rosa puts the kids to bed every night, slightly gratified that they look so much like their father and truly appalled that they act just like him, too.

And so, the kids. Little shits.

The sun rises; the sun sets. Rosa develops migraines, ulcers, endometriosis, pernicious anemia, and spontaneous nosebleeds. Gary gets a hernia and he knows he keeps on complaining about it, but he'll say it one more time: his hernia hurts, his hernia hurts. *Somehow these symptoms always seem to coincide with holidays. Where will these holidays be celebrated? On Long Island with Artie and Mimi? On the shore with Aldo and Antoinette? Or should Gary and Rosa invite their respective parents to their own house, where everyone can be miserable together? Such merry gift-giving almost seems to require witnesses. Rosa smiles and says thank you after Gary gives her weird presents—Dirt Devils and bonsai trees—that indicate a thorough misreading of her character. "Just what I always wanted," Gary says after Rosa gives him two cement gargoyles for his bookcase and ten free trips to the chiropractor to straighten out his suspiciously bad back.*

The seven-year itch comes—and goes. Gary and Rosa no longer connect. *At the office, Gary sexually harasses the new junior partner, some hot chick straight out of Fordham Law School. The junior partner gets reprimanded; Gary gets promoted. Meanwhile, back at the ranch, Rosa makes it with Phil Donahue, Mr. Yoga and You, and the Frugal Gourmet. She dreams of practicing highly unsafe sex with the plumber, the electrician, the painters, and all the other men who troop in and out of their new home in Mount Carmel. Because after Artie and Mimi die and leave them more money than any two people morally should possess, Gary and Rosa buy another, bigger, and better house at the base of Sleeping Giant Mountain, where the only black face within a ten-mile radius is at the top of the totem pole at Brooksvale Park, the site of the Boy Scouts annual statewide jamboree. Yet their neighbors all are liberals—doctors, lawyers, and Yale professors—self-proclaimed Marxists who squat in half-a-million-dollar* mansions, physicists who tinker with the neutron bomb, feminist theologians who worship ball-busting tropical sun goddesses, and anthropologists who study synchronized menstruation among the Mayan Indians. "Academics," Gary says, shaking his head as he drives by their homes. "What a fucking racket."

Gary works later and later; Rosa gets fatter and fatter. She goes for long walks on the still country roads, ostensibly to shape her waist and trim her thighs, until one evening, toward dusk, she comes full circle in the neighborhood and looks up the driveway of her own home, where Gary and the boys wait for her, and she keeps on walking. She walks until the dogs barking in the distance and the mournful calling of the owls from the woods sound too melancholy to bear, and then she reluctantly turns up the drive to her own home and enters by the back door, to be greeted by Gary, who is leaning against the Corian countertop munching on Funyuns straight from the bag. "Hey, Ro, what's cooking?" he innocently asks. Then Rosa loses it. She blows her cork with more whop and wallop than a bottle of Mumms; she clenches her fists and beats on Gary's chest like some heroine from a silent movie trying to fend off her attacker. She cusses Gary out. "For years!" she hollers. "For years I've wasted my life and put up with your crap and cracked my ass every time I sat down in the bathroom and now—now—I'm warning you!" Rosa's voice lowers to the depths of her being. She sounds like a cross between Louis Armstrong and a deranged succubus. "PUT DOWN THE TOILET SEAT!"

Gary looks truly alarmed by this outburst. And upstairs, the boys—who by day are star pupils at Hamden Hall and by night, confirmed dope addicts and petty thieves who steal snack-sized Doritos and Visine eyedrops from the Seven-Eleven—yes, these oversexed, underworked teenagers who have the gall to translate years of Suzuki violin into a neighborhood rock band called The Tenured Radicals—these alienoids now laugh scornfully at their mother's menopausal rage and their father's clear-cut impotence.

The next year the youngest son is ensconced in a juvenile detention home in South Norwalk, the oldest begins to squander his trust fund as a first-year film student at Harvard, and Gary and Rosa become em-

broiled in a bitter custody battle over the two children neither one of them is sure they ever really wanted in the first place. Gary moves into the old Taft Hotel downtown. Rosa, on the edge of suicide and desperate for a date, rejoins the local Catholic church and answers a personal ad in the New Haven Advocate.

Then one night the phone rings. It's Gary.

"What do you want?" Rosa barks.

"You answered my ad," he says. "In the paper."

Rosa imagines him putting his feet up on his desk and leaning back in his ergonomically correct office chair. "So," he laughs, "where you been all my life?"

Rosa is temporarily at a loss for words. Then she finally settles on motherfucker, *and the fight begins.*

"You said in your letter that you were a sensitive woman! Ha!"

"You said in your ad that you were forty-something! Well, you're fifty, buster, you are fifty!"

"You said our marriage was loveless. Torture, maybe, maybe hell on wheels, but loveless, I don't want to hear."

"You said you were a bachelor!" Rosa hollers. "Dream on!"

"You said you were a divorcée! Who served you the papers?"

"You said 'enjoys quiet evenings, dinners, classical concerts.' When was the last time you stepped your big, fat, lazy philistine feet in Woolsey Hall?"

"I don't know," Gary says. "Too long, maybe."

There is silence. Pregnant expectation. Could it be? A spark of interest? A little sexual tension, after all these years?

"You wanna go?" he asks. "On Friday?"

Rosa wraps the phone cord around her hand. "Oh, I don't know," she says.

"We could sit in the balcony," he says. "Like we used to. And then, you know, afterwards. Maybe I could come home. Fucking kids'll be out. We could have, you know, champagne. And then—"

Silence. Rosa wraps the phone cord another time around her hand. She begins to purr. Gary's heavy breathing results in a hiccup that he apologizes for, profusely. "Will you make me a big plate of Ronzoni for breakfast?" he asks. "The spiral jobs, with the meatballs, you know, the kind with the fresh parsley and the ground-up bread from Lucibello's Bakery? Would you? Mmm. I got a thing for your carbohydrates, Ro."

Rosa sighs. *"You're still the same old asshole."*

"Hey, love me or leave me," he says.

"I already left you."

"You're still living in the house," Gary says. *"I'm still paying for it."*

"So what?" Rosa says. *"I'm still cleaning it."*

And so, their marriage. Holy cow. They were in for it.

Rosa looked in the mirror, with all the forlornness of an animal gazing out of the bars of its cage. She was married. The band was on her finger and she could not pry it off even if she wanted. She clenched her puffed-up fist and curled her lip at her heavy face. Aaah, she rued all that Danish on her coffee break, the mounds of French fries for lunch, and the 220 bucks she paid for this *schmatta,* which made her look like a piece of shit!

Rosa turned off the light, put down the seat, and lowered herself onto the cool green porcelain of the toilet. She put her head on her knees and waited for the sick feeling in her stomach to pass. Instead, she was overwhelmed by *déjà vu.* She had sat just like this after she first got her period. She had hid in the bathroom, shocked by the dark brown sticky blood on her underpants and the dull ache that came from below her stomach. She had doubled over and pressed her forehead onto her thighs, wishing she could climb into her knees and disappear off the face of the earth. Then Rosa had finally mustered up the courage to come out of the bathroom and tell her mother, who cracked a slap across her face that brought Rosa to her knees. *"Ora, sei donna!"* Antoinette said. *Now you're a woman.* Antoinette stuffed a sanitary napkin in Rosa's hand and pushed her back into the bathroom, leaving Rosa to figure out the logistics. When Rosa finally waddled out of the bathroom, walking as if she had a twelve-inch zucchini stuck between her legs, her mother stood in the kitchen with a pair of red-handled sewing scissors. Without a word, she turned Rosa around and clipped off Rosa's long, wavy black hair, which fell to the linoleum in tufts. Rosa instantly felt lighter, but no freer.

"Now the boys will know," Antoinette said. "Hands off. Don't touch."

Antoinette swept up the hair, made it into a thick braid, wrapped it in green tissue paper, and put it in her bottom drawer, where she kept the black rosary beads she had picked out for her own funeral and the hospital bracelet that belonged to the baby she had lost, years ago, to spinal meningitis. Rosa's sister's name was Regina Theresa, but for years Rosa had the impression the baby was called "God's will," because that was the only reference anyone ever made to it.

Downstairs Aunt Sylvia sang *L'chaim!*

Rosa let out a sad whimper of fear. And someone knocked on the door.

"Rosa?" Gary asked softly. "Hey Ro, you all right in there? You got the runs again?"

Rosa shook her head.

"I said, you got the—"

"NO!" Rosa said.

Silence.

"Did you drink too much?" Gary asked. He burped. "Whoops. Sorry. God, I sure did."

Rosa didn't answer.

"Hey," he said. "You crying in there?"

Rosa's voice was muffled by her thighs. "What do you think?"

Gary tried the doorknob. "What's the matter?"

"I'm miserable!" Rosa choked out between sobs.

Rosa heard him lean against the door. "Could this be the jolly voice of PMS I hear speaking? Stay tuned next month, folks, when this episode will be rerun for the pleasure of none involved."

"You're a stupid sexist pig!" Rosa said.

Gary gave a cocky laugh, then oinked and snorted. "Hey, correct me if I'm wrong, but isn't this getting to be a pattern?" he asked. "Me on one side of the door, you on the other?"

Rosa held her head in her hands.

"I think we've got a communication problem here," Gary said.

Rosa heard him close the bedroom door. There was a loud scraping sound, then the creak of wood. Rosa was trapped. Gary had pulled up a chair.

After a moment, there was an imperious knock on the door. Gary cleared his throat. "Doctor Zigmund Freud here. Ze good doctor to zee Rosa."

"Fuck off," Rosa said.

"Ze good doctor finds it ve-lly in-ter-est-ing that ze plumber's daughter always hides in ze bathroom ven she has a problem vith ze vorld."

"I have a spastic colon," Rosa said. "I've been diagnosed. By a medical doctor."

"Could dis indicate a dark and repressed love for ze vater, or perhaps a deep hatred of ze mutter? Could dis indicate a resentment of men in general, or perhaps one *mensch* in specific?"

"It means I go to the bathroom," Rosa said, "when I gotta go to the bathroom!"

From downstairs came a round of applause and calling out of requests. The violin began again. June, according to Aunt Sylvia, was busting out all over.

Another knock on the door, this time more timid.

"Who's there?" Rosa asked.

"It's your pal," Gary whispered. "Adonai. Heard you were looking for a definition of *Kumbaya.*" He snorted with drunken laughter. "Heard you and the Tidy Bowl man were having an existential crisis. Either that or one hot tamale of a love affair. So which is it?"

Rosa bit her lip. "The affair," she said.

"Something wrong with your *caro sposo?*"

Rosa shook her head. "No, no. I like you. Don't ask me why. But I do like you."

"Thanks. I'm on fire for you, too."

"But—" Rosa said. "I mean—"

"What do you mean?" Gary asks. "What do you mean in there?"

"I mean, I'm thinking my parents must have liked each other once," Rosa said. "Yours, too."

"Who-o-o-o-a," Gary said. "Let's put on the brakes right there, right there. We don't have to take them as role models." Then he added, "Do we?"

Silence, while they thought of Aldo and Antoinette, and Artie and Mimi. So ludicrous. So loveless.

"Hey, Ro?" Gary asked. "Your mother try to give you any—uh— advice? About marriage?"

"No," Rosa lied.

"My father did. Can you imagine? We were in the hotel waiting to go to the chapel. My mother was dicking around in the bathroom with her powder puff and mascara. She was in there so long I was afraid she would come out with ten eyebrows and fifteen pairs of lips. My father was pretending to read the *Times*. I could tell he was on the verge of something, you know, by the way he kept fiddling around with those hideous cufflinks he had on. Then he looked up and said out of nowhere, 'I want to give you a piece of advice,' and his face was all red like he was offering me a piece of tail or something. Whew, man, the whole thing was too weird for words.

"So I said, 'Dad. Don't. Please. Just spare me the big one, in a major way.' And he said, 'No, let me speak my piece.' So I stood there fiddling around with the hotel matches, waiting for these great pearls of wisdom to come raining down from the sky and my father goes to me, 'There were times in my marriage when I thought your mother was out to lunch, and at the most *meshugenah* deli in town, but I stuck by her. I stuck by her.'

"And that was it," Gary said. "Think of it. He was actually proud of it, bragged of it, that his marriage was like an Oldsmobile stuck on a sand dune at Jones Beach, the back wheels screeching and spinning."

Rosa held her head in her hands. She did not dare—no, she could not divulge—what her own mother had said to her. Antoinette and Aldo had come over to Rosa's old apartment the morning of the wedding. Rosa had spent the night at Gary's. She overslept. When

Rosa pulled up in front of her apartment building, her father's Chevrolet Caprice was already parked on the street.

For a moment, Rosa contemplated restarting her car. Yes, she would go down Whalley Avenue and pick up a dozen doughnuts and then return to her apartment with a bright smile and a cheery "I just had a craving for a few glazed crullers." But just as she was about to turn the key in the ignition, Rosa caught a glimpse of her mother's face in the hallway window of the apartment building. She had been spotted.

Rosa reluctantly got out of the car. Upstairs, outside her apartment door, Antoinette waited like a sentinel, in a peach lace mother-of-the-bride's dress and shoes dyed to match.

"Where's Dad?" Rosa asked, not looking her mother in the eye as she fumbled with the lock.

"I sent him down Whalley. To Dunkin Donuts. I saw your car wasn't out there and I said, 'Go get your daughter some of those jellies she likes so much—' "

"I like the crullers," Rosa said.

"Whatever!" Antoinette said. *"Managgia a mi.* If he hadn't found you here. Couldn't you wait?"

Rosa was uncomfortably aware of her wet hair as she bent over the lock and threw open the door.

Rosa had moved out of her parents' house when she was twenty-two. In all the years that she had lived on her own, her mother had never once set foot in Rosa's apartment. Now Antoinette entered the living room and looked around with her lips curled, as if she were surveying the scene of some evil crime. Half the furniture already was gone. The closets were empty and boxes lay everywhere. In the bedroom, draped across the conspicuously double bed, lay Rosa's wedding dress. Antoinette did not approve of the dress because it was off-white and did not graze the floor. Rosa refused to wear a veil. "You're gonna look like a divorcée," Antoinette said.

Yes, Antoinette disapproved. But she still insisted on coming over that morning and doing what mothers were supposed to do before the wedding: help their daughters get dressed.

Aldo came back with the doughnuts. Rosa felt obliged to thank him and eat one of the sugary buns that squirted raspberry jelly all over her teeth and tongue. Aldo ignored his wife and daughter. He sat on a kitchen chair and turned on the nine-inch black-and-white TV Rosa intended to donate to the Salvation Army. The Yankees were playing the Red Sox. But the cable had been turned off and the reception was fuzzy. Aldo found some aluminum foil in Rosa's kitchen cabinet and fashioned it into two bows, which he attached to the TV antenna. The picture still was fuzzy, so he turned up the volume to compensate.

Rosa and her mother went into the bedroom and closed the door. Rosa was dismayed. She did not want to spend the morning of her wedding with a splitting headache that came from eating too much sugar, fighting with her mother, and listening to Phil Rizzuto call out "Line drive to right field!" Rosa did not want to undress in front of her mother. She did not want her mother to watch her pull on her French-cut silk Underalls. She did not want her mother to see the Berlei push-up bra with the seed pearls that she quickly had picked out at the Victoria's Secret shop in the Stamford mall with the unsolicited advice and assistance of his truly, Gary. But most of all, she did not want her mother to look at her belly button and remember her as a child, and yet see everything about her that had changed so much since then, that marked her as a woman.

Fortunately, Antoinette looked out the window and stared down at the street. Rosa was the one who did the watching. Rosa watched Antoinette gaze down at the sidewalk and knew, for a fact, that her mother was counting the black people who walked by. Any moment, Rosa just knew it, Antoinette was going to turn and tell her, "*Managgia,* all these years you've been living in a *melanzana* neighborhood!"

But when Antoinette did speak, it was in a complete spill of Sicilian, so raw and involuted that Rosa, who had learned what should have been her native language from a textbook, at first had difficulty understanding it. Antoinette looked Rosa up and down, from the reinforced toe of her Underalls to the straps of her push-up bra, said what she had to say, then turned back to the window, while Rosa connected nouns and subjunctive verbs and supplied nonexistent consonants and vowels. The final product she came up with was, *Remember, after you have kids, you can tell him to keep it zipped.*

Rosa stood there, shocked and embarrassed. How was she supposed to answer her mother? It was impossible. *Non capiscono.* They did not speak the same language. Rosa climbed into her wedding dress. "Zip me up," she commanded her mother. As Antoinette slowly, carefully pulled the two sides of the dress together and raised the tab of the zipper, Rosa suddenly remembered that she had forgotten to remove her diaphragm. She felt the spermicide she had used the night before leak out onto her Underalls, cold and clammy, and realized that all of her problems with the world—the stupid, slimy world—began right there with her mother.

Rosa's mother's advice was so ridiculous, so uncalled for, so bad enough spoken once that Rosa was damned if she would repeat it to Gary, who stored away everything she ever told him and threw it back up to her face.

"My mother didn't tell me anything," Rosa said.

Gary laughed. "You lie."

Rosa lifted her head from her thighs. "How do you know?"

"You're a very moral person, Ro. Your voice gets strangled when you fib, like you're trying to talk with a big, fat macadamia nut stuck in your windpipe."

"Don't act like you know everything about me," Rosa said.

"I admit," he said. "I admit I don't know the half of you. But that's *your* problem. You think you know the all of me."

He was right. Rosa already felt she knew too much about Gary. He told too many tales on himself. He confessed he once stole five bucks out of his father's cash drawer and blew it on licorice whips, Good-n-Plenties, Mike-n-Ikes, and Jujubees that stained his teeth and tongue red, black, and yellow. He admitted, actually admitted, to unbuttoning his shirt to his waist and using his mother's hairbrush as a microphone as he performed imitations of Jim Morrison writhing out "Come on baby, light my fire" in front of the full-length mirror in his parents' bedroom. He even confessed that Mimi caught him once. She simply held out her hand and said, "My hairbrush, please." He told Rosa he used to sit in the public library and look, for hours, at photographs of the concentration camps. *There was this story in one of the books,* he said, *about some Polish soldiers who forced some Orthodox Jews to mow a field by eating the grass. I used to lie in bed at night and imagine myself ripping away the soldiers' guns and mowing them down with bullets. But the whole time I had the fantasy, I had this sick feeling inside, like the grass was already in my stomach.*

Who would tell such sad stories on himself, and then (this was what made Rosa love him) laugh afterwards? Only Gary.

Rosa, on the other hand, was secretive, cunning, and becoming more so. But when Gary said, "Come on, tell me something I don't know about you, and I'll tell you something you don't know about me, come on, I dare you, I dare you," she could not resist the challenge.

She thought. She would have to be careful. At the beginning of their relationship, she confided to Gary that she once had given serious thought to becoming a nun. Big mistake. For months afterwards, he sang "Dominique—eeky—eeky" on those rare occasions when she went to church.

Another whopper error was the time Rosa told Gary that her mother believed Jesus Christ had been Italian.

"Come again?" Gary asked.

"You heard me," Rosa said.

"But how the hell did she get that idea?" Gary asked.

"Because the church is in Rome."

"The Pope's a Polack, am I right or wrong?"

"She doesn't trust this one," Rosa said. "When the smoke came out of the Vatican, she predicted Armageddon."

"But doesn't she listen? When they read the Gospels? *Out of Egypt have I called my son. And Joseph also went up from Galilee,* out of the city of Nazareth, not out of Naples. Not out of the canals of Venice!"

Gary snorted with laughter. Rosa sensed danger ahead. "I'm warning you," she said. "Don't make anything out of it. Don't start anything with my mother about it."

"Oh, I wouldn't dare presume," Gary said. "It's too moronic."

But what did he do the next time Antoinette cooked them dinner? While Rosa washed the dishes, Gary cornered Antoinette in the living room. "You know, I've been meaning to ask you," he said. "Just out of curiosity. Who do *you* think are the top ten Italians of all time? Besides Madonna and Pavarotti?"

Yes, Rosa had to be careful what she told that husband of hers. She had to choose carefully. She was tempted to put him right into his place by telling him that immediately after he asked her to marry him, she had spent the rest of the ride to Long Island subjecting him to her cousin Connie's "Is He Mr. Right?" test. The quiz consisted of three simple questions: Is he worth shaving your toe knuckles for? Every day? *Every* day? Rosa had given some hard hours of thought to the answer.

Rosa could tell Gary that she, too, had sung with a hairbrush, the summer that *Jesus Christ Superstar* was such a hit. She and Connie had stuck out their chunky little butts and moaned like that ultimate slut, Mary Magdalene, "I don't know how to lo-o-o-o-o-ve him, What to do, How to mo-o-o-o-o-ve him." They were caught, too, by Zia Pina. But were they sent to a shrink? No. They were told to stop acting like Puerto Ricans. Connie had her pants yanked down and her bare bottom spanked with the bristle side of the hairbrush, while Rosa ran home and escaped.

What to tell Gary? What to say, what to say? Rosa pondered admitting to the recurrent nightmare she had of a man climbing in through her bedroom window to rape her. The man wore a top hat and white gloves. He had the face of Captain Kangaroo! Rosa screamed with terror.

Then she thought about disclosing something shameful. After Gary and Antoinette had gotten into a shouting match about the ethnic origins of Jesus Christ, Antoinette sent Gary outside with a bushel of tomatoes. "Put that in the garage," she told him, "you

crazy nut, you. Take your time. Get a little fresh air. You need it."
After he left the kitchen, Antoinette turned to Rosa. "You know
what that *pozzo*-head you're gonna marry told me? *Christ è mat-
achrist.*" Well, if that wasn't a tautology to beat the band: Christ was
a Christkiller. Rosa was tempted to laugh. But then, disgusted by her
mother's ignorance and prejudice, she simply squeezed out the
sponge in the sink and kept silent. She let her mother say it.

Gary was right. There still was a lot left to be revealed. But Rosa
and Gary had a whole lifetime ahead of them. Plenty of time to let
down the guard, slowly, slowly.

So Rosa called out to the closed door, "I Xeroxed my butt once."

"Say *what*?" Gary asked.

"At work. Terry and I got furious at Doctor Kahn, so after hours
we made a photocopy of my butt on Yale–New Haven stationery.
Then, on the top, under the seal that says *Lux e verita,* we typed
'MEMORANDUM: from one asshole to another'."

Gary sounded dismayed. "You put your naked tush on a Xerox
machine? You exposed yourself to what could be radioactive elements? You could be sterile!"

"Your turn," Rosa called out. "Your turn."

Gary hesitated. "I like to take—" He put his mouth up to the
crack in the door and whispered, "I like to take baths."

Rosa was grossly disappointed. "Is that all?"

"I like to take them with—" he whispered again, "—Mr. Bubble!"

He laughed. And Rosa knew he was bullshitting her, because he
was using his smooth-talking voice, his educated voice, the voice he
took to Yale and to cocktail parties, grammatically correct and de-
void of all the layers of New York accent.

"Try me again," Rosa said.

Silence. Gary mumbled something that Rosa didn't catch. "Speak
up," Rosa said, impatiently. And the answer came back Avenue A-
style, loud and clear:

"I said, I believe in GAWD!"

Rosa sat up. This, from the man who ruined Easter Mass for Rosa by pointing to the crucifix and asking in a loud whisper, "Why do they always paint him that sickly yellow color, like the worm at the bottom of the tequila bottle?" This, from the man who once took a paper yarmulke home from a bar mitzvah and used it the next morning as a coffee filter? Rosa saw him do it. It was the mocha java from Macy's that Mimi had given him for Christmas. "Adds a certain *je ne sais quoi* to the flavor!" he said as he sipped the coffee. Rosa, who at first was horrified, laughed long and loud when he burnt his tongue.

So he believed in God. "Prove it!" Rosa called out.

"What? That He exists?"

"No, you *stupido*. That you believe."

"How? How can I prove it? You want me to go downstairs, right now, and grab that microphone away from Aunt Sylvia and yell, 'YAHWEH'?"

"That won't be necessary," Rosa said.

Rosa heard his chair scrape back. "I'm gonna do it. I'm gonna do it. You watch. Educated people don't like God. It'll be like hollering fire. Everybody will go flying for the nearest exit—"

"Stay here," Rosa said. "I believe you."

"Do you really?"

"What the hell do I know what you're gonna do?"

"So why don't you stick around a while and find out?"

"I'm not going anywhere," Rosa said. "You've got me trapped in here."

"You locked yourself in!"

Rosa considered the significance of this. Downstairs, Aunt Sylvia began to hyperventilate on a string of Yiddish syllables.

"Goddamn that Sylvia," Gary said. "How can somebody so ugly be so happy? I was just standing there in the living room, listening to her, and I felt like my heart was going to break. Just from being alive."

"I felt that way, too," Rosa said.

"I just wanted to hug somebody," Gary said.

"I just wanted to hide," Rosa said.

More laughter and applause from downstairs. Then the violinist scratched out the beginnings of the "Miami Beach Rhumba."

"Hey, Ro," Gary said softly. "I got proof."

"Of what?"

"God. God's existence."

And the story unravelled like this: when Gary was growing up, Artie used to play 78 records on the wind-up Victrola that was a relic of his own childhood on the Lower East Side. His favorite song was about destiny, torturing him day and night. The song drove Gary so crazy that he took a nail file and made a small scratch in the record, so the singer called out, "Des-des-des-des-des," until Artie popped the needle and destiny could be fulfilled.

Eventually, Gary grew up. He forgot about the song until the first time he went over to the hospital to talk to Rosa. The garage at Yale New Haven Hospital was full that morning, and Gary had to walk up from the hill. Gary didn't mind telling Rosa he was sweating it as he walked past those charred houses with the bullet-ridden holes, thinking about how he was liable to get mugged or shot, all because he had agreed to defend this poor black guy with the absurd name of Ivory White who couldn't pay his frigging hospital bill, and all because the Master of the Universe saw fit to give the poor schmuck only one kidney. Why couldn't He have just given him two like everybody else—and while He was at it, why couldn't He come on down and fix up this ghetto back here and *tout de suite,* too, before it turned into an even bigger mess?

Anyway, Gary got to the hospital. He found Rosa's office and talked to her. Rosa knew that part of the tale. What she didn't know was that he became instantly obsessed. He went back home, and when he went to bed, he kept on hearing that stupid Destiny song in his head.

He memorized the cracks in the ceiling, trying to think of who Rosa reminded him of. Because in that blue turtleneck sweater and those gold hoop earrings—and with those big, sweet eyes—Rosa resembled someone from Gary's past. Then Gary finally put his finger on it. It was the Ed Sullivan show. Remember? Every Sunday night

Mimi let Gary stay up until nine to watch it. Gary would wait and wait. He used to lie on that zebra-striped couch, you know, the tacky one that was in the family room now? and he used to pray. He clenched his fists and said, *Please, God, please, God, let him come on, please God.* And Gary's faith was confirmed, he truly believed in God when Ed Sullivan came out and said, "And now, a really big treat for you boys and girls, Topo Gigio, the Italian mouse!"

Then that little mouse puppet came out, remember? in the striped pajamas and the tasseled nightcap, and he tiptoed and preened around his little brass bed. It didn't matter that Ed Sullivan was short and dark and hairy and ugly. Topo Gigio's voice was all soft and gentle and there was this look of—Gary didn't know what to call it, maybe just pure love—yeah, pure love in Topo Gigio's eyes as he said, "Eddie. Kiss me goodnight?"

Gary's voice was subdued when he finished the story. "Hey, Ro," he whispered through the door. "I hate to tell you this, but you look like Topo Gigio. And if you're Topo Gigio—okay, so I've had too much to drink out here—then Somebody sent you to me, right, right?"

Rosa crinkled up her forehead. Jesus. It was worse than she thought. She had married a man who wanted to make it with a mouse. And after he made it, he tried to act like it was a religious experience!

Rosa sighed, got up from the toilet, unlocked the door, and opened it. Gary was sitting on a wooden chair, his eyes all boozy as he looked up at her. He held a blackened Chiquita banana in his hand, which Rosa assumed he meant to offer as a cure for her diarrhea.

Rosa took the banana, sat in Gary's lap, put her arms around him, and buried her face in his neck. She couldn't help it. She loved the way he smelled. This was comforting. It was out of her control. It was all atoms and molecules and complex chemical reactions. It was destiny, and destiny was in God's hands, not Rosa's.

Or was it? Rosa remembered that just last week, Gary had been complaining about how the cost of cleaning and pressing his shirts had gone up from a dollar twenty-five to a dollar fifty at the Wiseguy Laundromat. Rosa panicked. She sunk her nails into his shoulders. "Promise me you'll never change dry cleaners," she whispered in his ear.

Gary shrugged. "You're the boss, babe," he said, just as Aunt Sylvia finally launched into the theme song from *Exodus*.

chapter eight

I n Rosa's family, the men always seemed to die first, leaving their wives behind to mourn them. Zio Dino was the first of Rosa's uncles to go. He was standing on the back porch, jingling the change in his pocket and whistling the theme song from "Gilligan's Island" when a blood clot in his brain ruptured, killing him instantly. After that, Zia Pina made a sign of the cross whenever she heard mention of Gilligan. Connie was so shaken by her father's death that she could not watch Channel 8 at three o'clock ever again.

Zio Paulo came next. *Cancer,* Rosa's aunts all whispered. He had it—*of all places*—in the *penis,* and it got out of control and spread and then it was *all over. It ate him up, like leprosy, may his soul rest in peace.*

Rosa's father came in third. Aldo died a year after Rosa and Gary got married. His heart gave out, in the garage, on a Sunday when Gary and Rosa were visiting for dinner. It was over an hour before anybody found him.

Rosa, for once, had looked forward to dinner. She had good news for her parents. The stick had turned pink. She was pregnant. And Gary was treating her with a tenderness he had never shown before. He did not criticize the way Rosa parked her car, either too close or too far away from the curb, or the way she washed both the counters and the dishes with the same sponge. He did all the laundry and walked down three flights of stairs to toss out the garbage. He insisted on balancing the checkbook and paying all the bills, as if performing simple subtraction would interfere with the gestation process. Every morning he held out his hands to pull Rosa up from the bed. "Sweetie," he called her. "Lovey." And he buried his face in Rosa's mongo boobs, which, like hothouse blossoms, had burst out of her body into 40C practically overnight. "Mmmm. Aaaah." He rubbed her belly. "Mommy."

Rosa pushed him away. He aggravated her. He was incompetent. He put her bras in the dryer. He made pathetic spaghetti—worse than Chef Boyardee—for dinner. He bounced checks. He let spider webs dangle from the molding and hairballs collect on the bathroom floor. It drove Rosa crazy. But what could she do? She shrugged, yawned, told him to make her some tea, and then flopped down on the couch. Why not? She was exhausted. She would lounge on the couch like a lazy slut, thank you very much, while the man who was responsible for her appalling and debilitating condition could trot up and down three flights of stairs toting groceries and garbage and laundry. Let Gary go out at ten o'clock at night, risking getting shot on Whalley Avenue as he ducked into the corner Seven-Eleven to buy more ginger ale and orange soda.

Because the pregnant Rosa was thirsty. She had never been so thirsty in her entire life, and she drowned the someday-heir of the Fisher family fortune with Poland Springs mineral water, Donald Duck apple juice, and the Stop & Shop version of V-8, as if the fetus' sole form of nourishment would come from liquids. Rosa drank and peed, drank and peed, all day long. She hadn't thrown up once (knock hard on wood), but the thought of easing pantyhose over her swollen ankles, thick thighs, and spread hips made her want to lose it. Rosa felt ready to wear a tent, and not just one of those pup bubbles out of the L.L. Bean catalog, but an enormous structure, Barnum and Bailey's Big Top, or the Sheik's house in the *Arabian Nights.* She felt enormous. But she only had put on three pounds, and Gary assured her no one else could tell yet, unless they brushed up against her and copped a good feel, in which case her rock-hard boobs would be a dead giveaway. So she could relax. Until the way she *looked* truly matched the way that she *felt,* she planned to keep the whole deal a secret. Except for family, of course.

"I gotta tell my parents," Gary said. But Rosa wanted to tell hers first, and not by phone. No. She would do it in person, since her parents, for once in their lives, would be happy for her. According to Aldo and Antoinette's logic, a woman who had a baby stood less chance of getting divorced. Besides, everybody loved a chubby, squalling little infant—mmm, it smelled so delicious, like fresh-baked chocolate chip cookies, and its silly, toothless smiles, plump-dee-dump belly, and smooth knees were enough to melt the most miserly of men. Even Rosa's uncles, usually so gruff and noncommunicative, liked to lean over the bassinet and chuck the chins of the latest additions to the family, cooing stupid things like "*Bello, bello, what a fellow!* Eenie, weenie, three cheers for *bambini!*"

It would make everyone so happy, this joyous event, this careless mistake! For—it must be admitted—Rosa had been too lazy to get up and put in more spermicide when Gary—who probably had been perusing Rosa's Victoria's Secret catalogs an hour before—initiated a second round of sex with a thumb applied slowly, languorously, to just the right spot. It felt so *good,* too good to stop, and Rosa took so long to come that Gary was more than ready to enter her right afterwards, and Rosa—transformed by orgasm into a sweaty, panting, ferocious beast—certainly wasn't going to call time-out for something so mundane as another shot of unscented Koromex.

Oh well, Rosa thought afterwards. It wasn't her most fertile time of the month. Still. . . . She turned over and silently whispered an entire Rosary before she went to sleep, just to remind God that she was still down there, needing a little extra help every now and then—like *right now, right now.* Then she fell into a restless sleep and worried for days and nights afterwards.

Three weeks later, a scared and horrified Rosa was holed up in the bathroom, staring at the pregnancy detector stick turning an ominous pink right before her very eyes.

"Motherfuck," Rosa whispered. "Sonofabitch! Shit!"

Gary was in the bedroom getting dressed. "What'd you do, stab yourself in the eyeball with your mascara wand?"

"I don't use mascara," Rosa called out. "Your mother does! And too much of it!"

Rosa heard Gary's belt rattle as he pulled on his pants. She heard the neat zip of his fly and then she heard him come by the bathroom door, singing in clipped British tones the tune from *My Fair Lady* that asked: oh, why can't a woman be more like a man? Rosa, furious, flung open the bathroom door and threw the pregnancy detector, still dripping with urine, straight at his smug little face.

"That's why!" she said and slammed the door shut, sitting down on the toilet.

What she heard next were the sounds of confusion: Gary saying "Huh?" and footsteps on the hardwood floor as he searched for the object she had thrown at him. Then his "What the hell—" and then, "Who-o-o-o-o-a, man. Oh my God!" Then, quieter, more serious, "Oy."

Gary opened the bathroom door and leaned on the doorjamb. The pregnancy detector stick was stuck in between his lips. "Have a cigar," he said.

Rosa looked at him. "Don't put that in your mouth," she said, "there's germs on there!"

He took it out of his mouth. "You already sound like a mother," he said.

"That's what I'm scared of," Rosa said and lapsed into her standard response to chaos. Rosa began to cry, and Gary put his arm around her and told her, "Come on, it's not so bad."

"So what?" Rosa said. "It's not so good, either."

"You said you wanted to have kids."

"Kids are vicious."

"I know," Gary said. "I've read *Lord of the Flies*."

"You just want to see yourself replicated," Rosa said. "Men always do."

"That's a sexist thing to say."

"Well, show me a woman who would wish her own face on someone else, except as a curse."

Gary scratched his head. "But you wanted to have kids," he repeated.

"Not now, you dorkhead!" Rosa held her stomach, as if she were in danger of puking up the fetus. It was the worst possible timing. She was up for a promotion at work, which the Baloney undoubtedly would screw her out of, and Gary was almost done with law school and getting ready to study for the bar, and Rosa never would be able to quit her job. She'd have to drag her fat self into work at nine o'-clock every morning because they needed the health insurance, and now she'd never get to go to Europe or Montana or even just go out to the movies; it would be nothing but pee-pee and poo-poo and wee-wee and ca-ca for the next eighteen years, until the baby got old enough to pack his bags and cart his neurotic self to Harvard.

Gary shrugged. Rosa could quit her job. And Gary could borrow money from an unnamed, but very reliable, source on Long Island, i.e., the parents—

"Never!" Rosa said.

Well, then Gary would get a job. That was it. One of his professors had asked him to take on a course at University of Bridgeport. He would teach the class and they would live like a king and queen forever on a lousy two thousand dollars. Paradise. Bliss. In the meantime, everyone would pet the expectant Rosa, kiss her and pat her and love her, and she could eat all the ice cream she wanted, and the whole thing would be more fun than a tonsillectomy.

"Oh, fuck you," Rosa said. "Big time."

"That's the spirit," Gary said. "I knew you'd come around."

Gary went down to Dunkin Donuts and got Rosa half a dozen crullers, which she polished off, with two cups of coffee, in ten minutes. Then Rosa went back into the bathroom and carefully examined her diaphragm for pin pricks. She was dying to blame this whole thing on somebody else. She would not put it past Antoinette—or Mimi, for that matter—to snoop around in the bathroom to find the birth control method of Rosa's choice and then sabotage its effectiveness. Antoinette believed abstinence was the only acceptable form of birth control. And Mimi—who was dying to see Rosa get huge as a sperm whale—several times had said, "Well dear, you don't want to be going to the PTA when you're fifty." Yes, that was it. Two anxious mothers, one miniature yellow safety pin pushed through the rubber of the diaphragm, right under the rim, and so much for the barrier method.

But there were no holes in the diaphragm. Rosa held it up to the light to examine it, then filled it with water to see if it dripped. No. No. The pregnancy was all Rosa's fault. No, it was all Gary's. Oh, why had he wanted it twice, he hardly ever wanted it twice, it had always been good-and-plenty on the first round before, then suddenly he had gotten hornier than a weasel in heat, and there was Rosa, fat, fat, fat. And thirsty. And there was nothing but disgusting New Haven municipal tap water to drink. Rosa wanted root beer. Ginger ale. Dr. Brown's cream soda, with a scoop of Häagen-Dazs butter pecan floating on top. . . .

Rosa sighed. She pressed her hands on her stomach, as if it were a Ouija Board that would help her communicate with the fetal world. What did Baby want? S-L-E-E-P. M-I-L-K. M-A-M-A.

That silent little voice from the netherworld melted Rosa's heart. She was going to be a mama. Yes, she would be a good mama to her little girl (boys were so unruly and unpleasant.) She would dress her sweetie up like a baby doll, in a straw hat with a ribbon, a velvet pinafore with a fluffy crinoline petticoat underneath, fishnet tights, and black patent leather Mary Janes. Gary would call the baby *Princess.* Rosa would kiss the baby's chubby cheeks over and over, like a plunger sucking water out of a drain. She would love her baby to death, with the kind of passion Antoinette never, ever had shown Rosa and did not display even when Aldo died and Rosa was transformed into half an orphan.

The Sunday that Aldo died, Antoinette commanded Rosa, "Ring the bell out the back door. It's almost chowtime."

Rosa was perturbed by her mother's loud voice. And what was wrong with saying *please? Would you? Dear? Honey?*

"I've told you a million times, I'm not ringing that bell out the back door," Rosa said. "It's mortifying. Daddy isn't a cow. He doesn't need to be called back from the pasture. Besides, he isn't in the garage anyway."

"Of course he's out there," Antoinette said.

"We didn't see him when we walked in," Gary said.

"Maybe he went over to Dino's," Antoinette said.

"Stop calling it Dino's," Rosa said. "Dino's been dead for six months."

Antoinette threw a dirty spatula into the sink, marched over to the china cabinet, and grabbed the bell. She threw open the back door and ding-donged with all her might.

"You want something done around here, you better do it yourself," she said.

Rosa stuck out her bottom lip in protest. Gary sighed and looked longingly over at the grocery bag that held the champagne. Rosa and Gary had planned to pop the bubbly after they made their announcement. But so far, nobody had been overly festive or cheery.

Antoinette plopped a pile of rigatoni into a bowl and held it out toward Gary. "For you," she said. She held out another bowl for Rosa. "And *you*. And if your father doesn't get in here in two seconds, he can go to the devil. Let's eat."

"Mother, wait for Daddy—"

"I rang the bell," Antoinette said stubbornly.

Rosa looked at Gary. He shrugged. "Get it while it's hot," he said and went into the dining room. He sat down at the table and waited for Antoinette and Rosa to join him before he sunk in his fork. Rosa began to chew on her rigatoni. She kept listening for the slow creak of the stairs and the slamming of the screen door, but she heard nothing.

Something was not right.

It only took another couple of minutes for Gary to reach the same conclusion. He looked at Rosa and raised his eyebrows. Then he got up from the table. "Where are you going?" Antoinette asked.

"I'm gonna put more sauce on the pasta," he said and took his bowl into the kitchen. Rosa watched him set the bowl down on the table, then slip out the door.

"Where's he going?" Antoinette asked Rosa. "He said he was—"

"Maybe he forgot to bring in something from the car," Rosa said. She fiddled with her macaroni, then ripped off a piece of bread and nibbled on the crust. Antoinette kept eating her pasta. She seemed completely unperturbed by Aldo's absence at the dinner table. What was the matter with her? Rosa thought. Did she already know and accept that something had happened?

That's what Antoinette claimed later. At Aldo's wake and funeral and at the party afterwards, she kept on saying, "I had a premonition. Something didn't seem right. I felt a dark cloud over my head all morning. I could hardly concentrate."

Yet she was halfway through her bowl of rigatoni when Gary came back into the dining room and said softly, "Antoinette. Listen. I've gotta tell you something. Something important."

Antoinette slit her eyes at Rosa. "I knew it," she said. "You're getting divorced."

"Huh?" Gary asked. "What?" He looked at Rosa, and Rosa shook her head at him. *Drop it,* Rosa silently told him.

And Gary let it pass. Because there were more important things at stake. Aldo was in the garage. His body was slumped over the work table, his face in a pile of washers. He must have had a heart attack. His body was stiff. He was dead.

Antoinette stood up and took off her apron. Then she walked past Gary and turned off all the burners on the stove. Rosa got up to follow her downstairs.

Gary shook his head at Rosa. "Don't go," he said. "You don't want to see your father like that."

"You come down and say a prayer," Antoinette told Rosa. "You, call an ambulance."

Gary obeyed.

Rosa went down with her mother. It was fall, and the crisp air smelled heavy down by the garden, where too many tomatoes had fallen off the vine and rotted. Antoinette and Rosa walked in through the open garage door. Aldo was hunched over the work table, his face flat on the wood, one hand dangling down by his side, the other flung across the surface of the table, grasping the far corner. He looked as if he were doing exactly what Rosa, so fatigued these days, was tempted to do every afternoon at work—put her head down on her desk and konk out into a deep sleep.

Antoinette's voice shook. "Well, God bless him," she said, forgetting that just five minutes before she had said Aldo could go to the devil. Antoinette made a sign of the cross and began to whisper her prayers. And Rosa, who was not sure what to do, just stood there, until a sharp, skidding sound came from the corner of the garage, and a black-and-white cat—a neighbor's pet—jumped down from a pile of lumber, trotted by Aldo's inert body, crossed in front of Antoinette and Rosa, and went out into the backyard.

The cat scared Rosa. It had green eyes speckled with yellow and a long tail that stood straight up in the air. Rosa's heart began to thump crazily. Her ears rang until she felt almost completely deaf, and her voice sounded like it came from far, far away as she said, "I feel like I'm going to faint," then fell to the floor.

When she came to, Gary and Antoinette both were bent over her, and Antoinette was scolding Gary over the sound of a nearby siren. "You shouldn't have let her look, how could you let her look at a dead person? And a black cat crossed in front of us, *managgia,* it's bad luck, it's all bad luck for the baby."

"Are you all right?" Gary asked when Rosa's eyes flickered open. "I told. I had to tell."

Antoinette stood up when the paramedics came up the driveway. "In here," she said. "No, not her," she shook her head at Rosa and pointed to Aldo's body, "him, him!"

After they found that nothing could be done for Aldo, one of the paramedics lifted Rosa up and walked her out to the garden, put her on the bench, and told her to keep her head between her legs. Antoinette finally came out of the garage and sat beside Rosa.

"He was going to do something about those tomatoes," Antoinette said mournfully. "Now, too late. Ah, me. Ah, me."

Antoinette made a wonderful widow. She had all the right clothes—the sleeveless black dresses, dark pilly cardigans, and sturdy low-heeled shoes with laces thin and black as licorice whips. She had the black rosary in her black purse—you know, the one Bruno's wife brought back from the pilgrimage to the National Shrine?—along with the Jesus nightlight that plugged directly into the socket, which had saved Antoinette from many a fall when she had to get up to pee in the night, which at her age—well, *Madonna mia,* let me tell you, you hit sixty and you may as well start wearing the diapers all over again.

Antoinette already went to Mass every day, so putting in a few extra prayers for Rosa's father proved no problem. Of course, now she had to pay extra to have Aldo's name mentioned at Novena and All Souls Day, and the cost of lighting candles—well, one of the big ones alone cost a buck fifty. But now Father Bruccoli treated her with respect. Last week at Confession he only gave her one Our Father for penance. And the week before he let Antoinette lead the procession when they trooped around the church for the Stations of the Cross.

Antoinette's daily routine remained the same. She cooked and cleaned and scowled at the transvestites who appeared on the Phil Donahue Show. She played dumb about everything that had to do with Aldo and his business. Rosa's brothers took care of it all. They sent the extra plumbing supplies back to the manufacturer and did the income taxes. They sat down every Saturday, combed through the bills, and went to the bank for Antoinette. They gave her seventy-five dollars in cash for the week, twenty-five of which she usually managed to save in one of Aldo's old cigar boxes beneath the bed, just in case another dust bowl developed, the stock market crashed, and the country suddenly plunged into depression.

Aldo's death turned Antoinette into an Oracle of Doom. "You never know," she predicted. "These days, you never know what's going to happen *these days!*" Anything, anything could happen. Antoinette could slip and fall on the back porch and break her neck. A crazed drunken driver could crash into Gary's Subaru and total it. One of Rosa's clients, cranked up on crack, could reach out and strangle Rosa to death. *Madonna mia,* what was the world coming to? The country was going to hell on a handcart, New Haven was the city of sin, Gary had better watch out and convert to Christianity before it was too late, and that's all Antoinette had to say about the state of things, amen, except for God have mercy and protect us.

But failing God's protection, let a dog do it for you. One Sunday afternoon when Gary and Rosa climbed the long back staircase to her mother's house, Rosa thought she heard a weird sort of scuffling going on in the kitchen. When she opened the back door, a huge German shepherd woofed and lunged at them.

"Look out, it's a Nazi dog!" Gary said.

Rosa, who had a mortal fear of canines, screamed, pushed Gary in the path of the ominous beast, and immediately climbed up on one of the kitchen chairs. Well, fuck it. Just *fuck* being feminist! Let Gary get bitten by that smelly, hairy, salivating, flea-bitten creature.

But Gary was defending himself quite nicely. "Come on, make nice!" he said as the German shepherd leaped up and licked his face. He caught the dog's front paws in his hands and waltzed it around the kitchen table, singing, "Hava, nagila hava, nagila hava—"

Antoinette rushed in from the living room. "Get off that chair before you have a miscarriage!" she hollered at Rosa. "And put my Theresa down," she told Gary.

Gary raised the paws of the dog slightly higher and glanced under its belly. "This is a boy dog," he pointed out.

"What are you talking about?" Antoinette said.

"I'm talking Theresa has herself a very fine three- or four-inch—"

Antoinette covered her ears.

"Stop talking about penises," Rosa said. "It's impolite."

"Your mother's got to grow up sometime," Gary said. He turned the dog toward Antoinette. "Come on, Antoinette, open your eyes and look at it—it's all there!"

"*Santa Maria,* what do I want to look at one of those ugly things for?" Antoinette said. "I'm done with that stuff."

Gary puckered up his lips at Theresa and made loud kissing noises as he backed the dog around the room. "One, two, cha-cha-cha! Strut your boy-stuff, cha-cha-cha!"

Theresa stuck out his long stippled tongue and salivated. His tail wagged excitedly and his nails skidded on the kitchen tile. The porcelain in the china cabinet began to rattle, the floor creaked, and Gary accidentally cha-chaed Theresa right into the jelly cabinet, which skidded against the wall. Antoinette drew in a breath. "Watch out for my Lourdes water cross!" she hollered.

Too late. The translucent blue glass crucifix, which purportedly was filled with water from the famous grotto, fell off its hook onto the floor. The glass shattered. Before anyone could stop him, the dog twisted out of Gary's grasp, leaned down his head, and lapped up the water.

Antoinette shrieked. Gary looked horribly, incredibly guilty, like a four-year-old caught messing around with some highly toxic substance. He bent down to pick up the metal Jesus that had been attached to the cross. "Body of Christ," he silently mouthed at Rosa as he cupped the Jesus and gently lowered him onto the kitchen table. Rosa tried not to laugh as Gary apologized to Antoinette over and over, picking up the blue glass pieces and promising to buy her a new cross, next time he went to Belgium or France or wherever the hell Lourdes was.

"Save yourself a round-trip ticket," Rosa told Gary. "They sell those crosses at Spencer Gifts in the mall."

"How much?" Antoinette asked.

"Too much," Rosa said.

"I'll get you one," Gary said.

"Wait 'til they go on sale," Antoinette told him.

"Then he'll end up buying two," Rosa said.

"Don't you want one?" Gary asked. "I think all American consumers should have one hanging on their kitchen wall. Sort of like a fire extinguisher. You never know when you'll need an instant cure for leprosy." He scratched his arm. "Think it cures fleas?"

Theresa stuck out his long pink tongue at Rosa. Then he trotted over and nuzzled Rosa's legs. Rosa shrieked. "Eeew. Eeew. Gary, get this dog away from me, it's smelling my crotch."

"Hey, get your nose outta there!" Gary grabbed Theresa by the collar and yanked him away.

"Mother, get rid of that repulsive beast," Rosa said.

"I just got her," Antoinette said.

"It's a he," Gary insisted.

"He or she, that dog is gross," Rosa said.

"Frankie gave it to me," Antoinette said.

Rosa groaned. "I might have known."

Antoinette leaned over and smooched Theresa on his hairy snout. Then she picked up the metal crucifix from the table and sucked face with Jesus, too. She said to Rosa, "Frankie was over here last Saturday, and he goes to me, 'You oughta get a dog, Ma.' And I said, 'What am I gonna do with a dog? Listen to it bark all day?' And Frankie said I had to be careful because I was a widow. He said men were watching me, out on the street. They watch me come in and out of the house the same time every day, Frankie said. 'You better look out, Ma,' Frankie goes to me, 'or they'll come in and clean out the whole house some night when you're at Novena.' And I said to him, 'I can't give up Novena, I gotta go to heaven.' So now I got a dog, I named it after a saint, maybe I'll get some points for that. If it doesn't count, it can't harm, what do you think?"

Rosa turned away, disgusted. In the corner, Gary was kneeling by Theresa, feeding him some of Rosa's Manischewitz matzoh crackers, which she carried everywhere to counteract morning sickness.

Theresa crunched his big jaw down on a matzoh. He chewed, looked puzzled, then took another bite.

Antoinette look horrified. "Isn't that a sin?"

Gary looked at Theresa and shook his head.

"Not for the dog," Antoinette said. She pointed at Rosa. "For *you* to eat *that*."

"Oh, goys can eat these," Gary said. "Some goys—like Rosa— even like 'em."

Antoinette marched over and grabbed the Manischewitz box. She squinted her eyes at the label, which announced in capital letters, NOT FOR PASSOVER USE. "Isn't eating this like eating Communion?"

"Oy," Gary said in his finest little-old-Jewish-man accent. "I should hope not."

"Then what does this stand for?" Antoinette demanded.

"It's sort of a historical artifact," Gary said. "Once upon a time, the Jews were in a rush to get out of Egypt. Centuries later, B. Manischewitz discovered he could make a fortune by keeping the myth alive."

Antoinette looked at Gary like he was nuts.

"It's supposed to be unleavened bread," Rosa translated.

"This isn't bread," Antoinette said. "It's a cracker."

"And now for a reading from the post-structuralists," Gary announced. He held up a cracker toward Antoinette. "This signifies the unleavened bread, just like the Communion host—or wafer, whatever the hell you call it—signifies the Body of Christ."

"What is this *signify* stuff?" Antoinette asked. "It doesn't signify. Either it is or it isn't."

"Ah, but what is *is*, to the nonbeliever?" Gary asked. "What is being? What is nothingness?"

"What is his problem?" Antoinette asked Rosa, who simply shrugged.

Gary kept on going. "What is the nature of the universe? What is evil? Is there a Satan? And how can we solve the big mysteries of the universe, like who really buys all those enemas they sell in the drug-stores?"

"My aunts," Rosa said, and Antoinette said, "Shush your mouth and have a little respect, why don't you?"

Antoinette knit her eyebrows. Rosa, who thought she knew her mother like a book, sensed that Antoinette was about to ask Gary something pointed. But Antoinette simply pushed up her eye-glasses. "You married a crazy kookalootz," she told Rosa.

"Don't I know it," Rosa said.

For the next two weeks, Antoinette reported that she spent the major part of her day trying to confine the rambunctious Theresa to a sudsy bathtub. She chased the dog around the house with flea powder and a big wire hairbrush, then covered all the furniture with Saran Wrap and set off one bug bomb after the other, until Rosa refused to visit on Sunday unless her mother detoxified the house. "All right, that's it!" Antoinette announced. She took her broom and swept Theresa into the backyard, where she kept the dog chained in the dusty alley on Aldo's old horseshoe post. "Ugly hound," Antoinette muttered. But every day at noon she cooked Theresa an all-beef frankfurter, hollering, "Chowtime!" as she tossed the hot dog out the back window. Theresa went wild, gobbling up the wiener in two greedy bites. Gary thought this was amusing. Rosa thought it was sick, especially since Antoinette made it clear that an extra pack of hot dogs a week was an enormous strain on her budget, and from now on, her kids could bring over the pastries on Sunday, thank you very much.

Antoinette had changed. Without Aldo around, she became more outspoken. "We ought to go out to lunch sometime," she told Rosa. "I see it all the time on TV, these women who go out to lunch. Their daughters take 'em."

So one Saturday Rosa made the trip over the Ferry Street Bridge by herself and took her mother out to the corner pizzeria. At Il Giardino, Antoinette and Rosa sat across from one another at a laminated table for half an hour, neither one of them saying anything. The food was slow to come and lukewarm by the time it got there. Antoinette shook her head at the skimpy salad, the limp manicotti, and the overly buttered garlic bread. "A waste of money," she said, after Rosa paid the bill. "I don't know what these women see in this lunch business."

Rosa left two singles on the table. Antoinette stared at them.

"Fifteen percent, Mother," Rosa whispered.

"One dollar's good enough!" Antoinette said, reaching over her doggy bag to pluck the extra single off the table.

"Mother, leave it!"

But Antoinette already had crumpled George Washington into a tidy little ball and was whispering at Rosa to take the money back.

"Non faro!" Rosa said.

"*Stai zitte* and take it!" Antoinette hissed.

Why were they bothering to speak Italian, as if it were a secret language that would veil their confrontation? Everyone in Il Giardino understood Italian, and those who didn't understand knew very well that it was the language all neighborhood families used when they were having a fight. Rosa felt like everyone in the restaurant was staring at them. Four months pregnant and already showing it, she turned her big belly in the direction of the exit and stormed out. Antoinette, clutching the dollar bill and her purse in one hand, and her doggy bag in the other, caught up with Rosa and trotted next to her on the cracked sidewalk, oblivious to Rosa's anger.

"I forgot to tell you, I'm going on a trip," Antoinette announced. "The Holy Family Shrine in New York, we're going to see it with the Rosary Society. Frankie's paying for half of it. But I don't know. It's a lot of money. Maybe I should tell him to cancel."

"Go," Rosa said through gritted teeth. "Do something with yourself. You never do anything."

"Who's gonna visit my *compare* in the nursing home?" Antoinette asked.

"Let someone else visit him," Rosa said.

"Who's gonna feed Theresa?"

"Mother, forget that mangy dog," Rosa said. "It salivates and has fleas and Frankie can feed it a hot dog every day, if he's capable of boiling water."

"Why should Frankie boil water when he's got Patty to do it for him?"

"He should learn how to cook," Rosa said. "What would happen if Patty died?"

"Don't even say it," Antoinette said. "I never liked her, but don't say it."

"Frankie would have to go to Kentucky Fried Chicken every night—"

"*Managgia,* he's still got a mother. You think I wouldn't go over there and cook for him?"

Rosa walked faster. "You baby Frankie," she said. "Frankie and Junior, you babied them both, did whatever they wanted, cooked them whatever they pleased, and now look at them."

"What's wrong with them?"

"They're *guinea,* Mother."

"Who's guinea? We're all guinea. Why be ashamed of it?"

"They're guinea *men,* Mother. Just like Daddy. They're not American. They've got an attitude, that shitty wait-on-me-because-I'm-a-man way of acting."

Rosa was aware that she was starting to shriek. She looked up and down the street. Across the way, the Guidicis and the Paratoris had cracked their windows, even though it was forty chilly degrees out. A Chevrolet moved down the street slowly, a clear indication that Rosa and her mother were making an official scene.

But that didn't stop Antoinette. She trotted along, clutching her purse and doggy bag until they came to the driveway. "Who's got the attitude?" she said. "You do. You got the problem with yourself. You live for yourself. You always have. You gotta be different. You gotta have a job. You gotta pay twenty-five dollars to get your hair cut. You gotta shop at Macy's. Caldor's isn't good enough for you. I could starve to death—"

"I just took you out to lunch," Rosa said. "And you stole a dollar from the waitress!"

"I work hard and take what's mine," Antoinette said. "Not you. You spend your life giving yourself away. You work for the government—"

"I don't work for the government," Rosa said. "I work for the hospital."

"You spend all day talking to those people, who don't even belong here. You're nicer to them than your own family."

"So why isn't my family nice to me?" Rosa asked.

"You don't like your family," Antoinette said. "You gotta be different. You gotta marry a man from New York. You gotta drive a foreign car—"

"Gary isn't a Subaru!" Rosa said. "He isn't a Toyota!"

"You gotta have a baby and—and—not even baptize it!" Antoinette said.

"How do you know?" Rosa said. "How do you know we're not going to?"

"I asked him," Antoinette said. "That Sunday you were over and he fed those crackers to the dog. After dinner, you were in the john with the diarrhea—"

"Skip it, Mother!"

"—and I thought I'm just gonna ask him, just see what he's got to say for himself. And he laughed, the way he laughs at everything that has to do with God, you know how he is, and he tells me he wants nothing to do with those voodoo rituals, but if it makes me feel any better, I can dunk the baby under the faucet when he's not looking." Antoinette shook her head. "Imagine!"

Rosa pushed out her lip, vaguely aware that between her petulant mouth and large belly, she looked exactly like Benito Mussolini. Truth to tell, she was concerned. If Gary didn't let her baptize the baby, it might die and float around in Limbo for the rest of eternity, and Rosa herself would go straight to hell or be condemned to twiddling her thumbs for thousands of years in the grey area known as Purgatory. Rosa was planning to douse the baby with water the moment the cord was cut. She was terrified that she would give birth, and three seconds later the world would end. After all, when she was in third grade, a nun had told her the world would end on Thursday. Now every Wednesday night Rosa said an extra set of prayers, then woke up in the morning with a vague feeling of fear in her stomach. All day long the thought of Sister Peter Simon's predictions—and the very idea of Nostradamus and his prophecies (which Connie sometimes read to her over the phone)—sat upon her chest like a big, fat burp that wouldn't come up. Nostradamus had predicted that mothers who gave birth just before the millennium would gnash their teeth and dash their babies to the ground, the fire and ice would be so all-consuming. Rosa had faith. She believed it.

"Gary never said we couldn't baptize it," she told her mother.

"You better talk to him," Antoinette said. "You better get this all straight."

"It's none of your business, Mother."

"Then whose business is it?"

"Forget it, Mother. You don't get it. You don't understand anything."

Antoinette crooked a finger at her. "You say that to me too much," she said. "But you'd be surprised. I *capisce* more than you think."

Just at that moment, the sun came from behind a cloud. The sidewalk was flooded with light and the lenses of Antoinette's silver eyeglasses turned impenetrable. Antoinette's eyes had disappeared. Rosa saw only herself in the thick lenses.

What did Rosa's mother know? What did she *capisce*? Was she wise to what was going on—and not going on—between Gary and Rosa? Or was she just acting like she knew something, just as she had pretended to have had a premonition about Aldo's death when the truth was, all she really had cared about that Sunday afternoon was sitting down to dinner? If Antoinette really knew something, Rosa thought—if she were a *real* mother—she would take Rosa inside and make her a cup of coffee. She would begin by apologizing—treading lightly on the troubled waters—before she told Rosa, *Dear, you hold grudges. Too many grudges. You remember too much. You hate yourself. And now you have a hard place in your heart that no man or woman can ever melt, and if you're not careful, it will be the death of you.*

But Antoinette did not say any of that. She did not tell Rosa what Rosa already knew about herself but wanted her mother to say, so Rosa could feel free to put her head down on the kitchen table and bawl her eyes out, just like a baby, and receive the comfort only someone so mean and nasty needed.

Rosa was tired of playing mother and daughter. She wanted to *be* mother and daughter. But how could she, when Antoinette was such a sham? Antoinette stood there acting like she knew Rosa, when really she was nothing more than just another bewildered parent, another Great and Powerful Oz revealed to be nothing more than a shabby human being, pushing buttons and pulling levers behind a tattered curtain.

Antoinette shrugged, and Rosa grew even more furious. Wasn't it just so predictable, so hotheaded, so TV-movie Italian, to holler and scream vile things at one another and then forget about it all the next minute? Antoinette walked Rosa to her car, the infamous foreign car that had irked her just seconds before. "Well, who's to say?" Antoinette asked. "Who's to say a little change isn't for the better? You got your family now. And I got my life. I got Theresa, I get to play Bingo every Thursday without your father grumbling about my going out at night and having to eat leftovers from the night before. I'm going on a bus trip. I'm doing all right for myself. I thought I'd fall apart, but look at me. Look at me."

Rosa lowered her heavy body into the car and looked at her mother. Antoinette stood proudly on the curb, clutching the doggy bag, which was soggy on the bottom. Rosa noted that tomato sauce was starting to leak onto her mother's black pilly coat.

"She never loved my father," Rosa said to Gary after she related the afternoon's events—censoring certain key phrases, of course—to make herself look good and her mother look worse than ever. "He was nothing but habit. She's glad he's dead. She likes that disgusting dog better than she ever liked him."

"You've really got it in for that dog, don't you?" Gary said.

"It has bad breath," Rosa said. "And it's always sniffing my crotch."

"Cheer up," Gary said. "It'll probably get cancer from all those Oscar Mayer wieners."

Small consolation, Rosa thought.

chapter nine

One day a dead baby was found in the hospital lobby, beneath the benches, in a half-zippered nylon gym bag. A desk clerk noticed the bag had been sitting there for several hours and called the security guards, who cleared the lobby. Inside the bag was not a bomb but a puny baby, all black and blue and bloody, the stub of its umbilical cord still attached, dead on discovery.

Well, wasn't that an item! Top story on the six o'clock news, front-page material for the *Register,* something for people to talk about in their cozy, well-heated homes in Wallingford and Madison and Spring Glen. "Jesus, that's creepy," Gary said when Rosa came home from work and told him about it.

"Too bad you didn't find it," Antoinette told Rosa. "You could have gotten on TV."

The dead baby bothered Rosa. At night, just before she fell asleep, she thought she heard the baby clawing at the zipper of the abandoned gym bag. In her dreams, she heard it sizzling in an incinerator. She heard it calling from Limbo, far beyond the grave.

While the dream baby haunted her at night, Rosa's real baby grew and grew and grew. Because Rosa ate and ate and ate. Everything bulged. Her rear end spread; her boobs boinged out to double D. Rosa's skirts hiked up her hips as she made constant trips to the store to buy new and bigger underwear, pants with elastic waists, tent tops. The doctor told her to put on the brakes—curb her appetite—or she'd find it hard to shed all those pounds afterwards. He had the nerve to say it in front of Gary, who told Rosa to forget about it, you're the mother, listen to your own body and eat whatever you want. So Rosa ate. And Gary left her completely alone except for the nice little hugs he doled out before she went to bed—earlier, of course, than he did. She was exhausted.

At the A&P—a required stop on the way home from work—Rosa stalwartly pushed the cart past the crackers and cookies. She passed by the deli cheeses and the freezers full of ice cream. The bakery, at the end of the store, was her downfall. *Ah,* sang the doughnuts, the Danishes, the cakes, the cookies (in perfect four-part harmony), *eat me, eat me, eat me, eat me!*

Trained to listen to authority, Rosa simply had to obey. She slowly wheeled her shopping cart by the glass bakery cases, then whipped it around, causing a three-cart collision and provoking comments such as "Watch where ya going, why dontcha?" Rosa looked up and down the aisles to make sure no one she knew was around before she snatched one of the wax paper sheets, pulled open the glass door, and selected a cheese-stuffed pastry slathered with icing and sprinkled with slivered almonds. Rosa breathed heavily in the check-out line. In the parking lot, she pulled her Honda around to the back of the store. She slipped the pastry out of its wax bag and devoured it as she stared morosely at the overflowing green Dumpsters.

Rosa dreaded going home. At work, at least, she could help herself to ice cream and frozen yogurt from the hospital dairy bar, and cheddar cheese popcorn—sometimes two or three bags—from the vending machine, without listening to anyone's criticism. In fact, Donna, Terry, and Alejandro egged her on to eat. "Go on, go for it!" they said. Rosa suspected her chubby face and spreading thighs made them feel better about themselves.

But back at the apartment, Rosa had to watch it. Gary was usually home, studying. The slightest rustle of a potato chip bag, the mere soft thud of the freezer door, annoyed him. He bent over his books, his mouth silently moving as if in prayer, and Rosa could not help but think he looked far older than his years with his shoulders stooped and his head bent under the lamplight. He did not want to be disturbed. He did not want to hear Rosa chomping on Fritos or spicy chicken wings. He did not want her to chew celery. He did not want her to chew anything. He wanted her to starve to death! She was fat and he wanted skinny, skinny, skinny!

So Rosa stuffed her face in the grocery store parking lot and then went home. The second-floor tenant, La Luigi, stopped her in the hall. "You got bags under your eyes," she told Rosa. "You should sleep more. And what's the matter with him upstairs? He sick?"

"He's studying," Rosa said.

"He's got the TV going all afternoon."

La Luigi said Gary watched the same soap opera as she did—she knew, because she heard the theme music coming down the heating vent. Did Rosa know? Did Rosa know what Gary's opinion was about Monica? Was she really going to leave that two-timing son-ofabitch Cameron for the safe and dependable Garth, or was she going to make a clean break of it all and run away to Los Angeles, where she planned to pursue a career in acting?

Rosa steamed with anger while La Luigi prattled on. Gary was watching TV when he was supposed to be studying. Meanwhile Rosa was shelling out five bucks a week for Excedrin, which Gary claimed he needed to fight off his headaches and chronic fatigue, which supposedly came from reading all the fine print of his books but really came from straining his eyes in front of their twenty-four-inch color Quasar, a first-anniversary present from Artie and Mimi.

Of course, Gary was entitled to his secrets. Everybody was. Rosa, for instance, had a comely stash of Baby Ruth bars in one of her many shoeboxes in the closet. And underneath her camisoles, in the bottom drawer, she kept a steady supply of licorice whips that she chewed upon, slowly, as she soaked in the bathtub on Saturday nights after sternly warning Gary to leave her alone for half an hour because she needed to do some long-overdue beauty treatments. Still, Rosa wondered. She worried. Gary was acting weird. He sneezed too much. And he had stopped telling stories. He was as clamped shut as one of the mussels Rosa's grandfather used to pick off the rocks at Lighthouse Beach. Rosa simply did not have the strength to pry him open. She was too busy fussing in the kitchen. She was too busy living from doughnut to doughnut—the life of a desperate woman—and Gary couldn't even begin to understand.

In a blur of excessive eating, Rosa's pregnancy passed. Perhaps the only event that stood out—and this only with retrospective significance—was a party she and Gary went to, given by one of his law-school buddies in a second-floor apartment over by East Rock, on Canner Street. Rosa was one of only three women who attended. There was a lawyer-to-be named Lisa and a woman from Sweden who had long, stringy blond hair. She was somebody's girlfriend. Her name was Ilse. She was so thin she reminded Rosa of the Halloween song that went *Oh dem bones, oh dem bones, oh dem jee-umping bones!* Rosa, as soft and fat as bread dough, was seized by the wild urge to feel up Ilse's sharp little hips. But she contained herself.

After just a few sips of forbidden beer, Rosa sat back, all boozy in the Barcalounger, and watched Gary make an ass of himself by drinking too much, talking too loud, and initiating a game of charades. Rosa vaguely enjoyed the spectacle. Gary kept offering clues that no one understood, and as he shook his head and gesticulated wildly with his hands, he reminded Rosa of one of the thieving monkeys in the children's story *Caps for Sale* that shook its fists and chattered nonsense when the peddler demanded, "You give me back my caps!"

Charades—and the rest of the horsing around at the party— seemed lost on Ilse, who came over and sat by Rosa, nimbly pulling her thin legs into a lotus position. Her tiny T-strapped shoes looked like doll's slippers to Rosa, perhaps because they were an unlikely shade of red.

Through some polite but disjointed conversation, Rosa found out that Ilse had grown up far outside Stockholm—the only Swedish point of reference Rosa knew, besides massage—in a rural area that Rosa imagined looked like the landscape in *Heidi*. Ilse was a research associate in the Child Psychology lab. She was running a long-term study of the effects of divorce on pre-adolescents. Rosa thought Ilse's job sounded interesting (she heard herself saying in a fake, party voice, "Isn't that fascinating?"), but Ilse confessed she was tired of looking at pubescent children. "Their heads are too large for their bodies," she said. "And they're always moping." She looked around the room. "Which one is your husband?" she asked, and when Rosa somewhat reluctantly pointed to Gary, Ilse said, "Oh, *him*," and went back to nursing her beer. Rosa wondered what that was supposed to mean. Then she decided she didn't want to know and promptly forgot about it.

Since Gary had done justice to an entire six-pack, Rosa was the designated driver on the way home. Gary flung himself on the bed and fell asleep instantly, with his clothes still on. Rosa slept fitfully. She dreamed that she reached out, in slow motion, and placed her hands around Ilse's waist. Ilse shattered, like a thin-stemmed wine goblet that once slipped out of Rosa's hands and smashed into slivereens in the kitchen sink.

In the morning, Gary had a hangover and lingered too long in bed. Rosa, who was under threat of being fired if she got to work late, felt an unaccountable rage toward him, an urge to nudge him in the small of his back with her Van Eli patent leather flats, which no longer fit very well because her feet were swollen. How easy it would be to give him a swift kick and rupture his spleen, like a knife split open a watermelon!

Listening to him breathe heavily in bed, she hated him. She could not say why, but she did.

All morning long Rosa felt sluggish and bloated, not entirely herself. The baby was still, but pressed hard against her bladder, making her groin and thighs ache. At the lunch table in the employee cafeteria, Rosa gnawed on her grilled ham and cheese sandwich and picked through her cole slaw as Terry told her the latest installment in the ongoing quarrel between the Baloney and Genghis Khan. "Who cares?" Rosa felt like saying. But she nodded and smiled wanly. She tried to remember the last time she had felt the baby kick. On the way out of the cafeteria, she got a cup of coffee to go. That would get him moving, she thought. That would wire him.

Rosa went back to her office and tried to work. But it was impossible to concentrate on the computer screen. Was it the cole slaw or her depression that was making her feel slightly nauseous and eager to park herself in the rest room, just in case? The coffee . . . it tasted so dark and bitter and warm, and seemed to slide straight down her throat to her stomach to her aching bladder. Rosa stood up, and a filmy green haze came over her eyes. She walked past Donna down the hall to the bathroom. Safely inside a stall, she pulled down her clownish maternity pants. A second after she began to piss, she realized her underwear was covered with blood.

Rosa felt light-headed. Her ears began to ring, and then the eardrums seemed to close off. She looked into the toilet. Red, bright red. She swabbed at herself with toilet paper. More red. Aah. Oh my God. She tried to clean herself up as well as she could. Then she quickly washed her hands and walked back to the office. She passed by Donna, closed the door to her office, and picked up the phone. She called Gary at home and hung up when the machine answered. Then she punched Terry's number. "Can't talk now," Terry said.

"You've got to help me," Rosa whispered.

"What's the matter?"

"I think I'm, like—having a miscarriage or something," Rosa said.

Terry hung up the phone. Rosa sat down and put her head on the desk.

They came down with a gurney and wheeled Rosa up to the operating room. After the nurse undressed and prepped Rosa, an anesthesiologist—two watery blue eyes between a cap and mask—leaned over the gurney. "Just a little prick," he said. Then he injected something warm into her arm, and her whole body instantly felt like it was dissolving.

Twilight sleep, they called it—half awake, half asleep, like being in a spooky, slow-moving dream. Rosa's legs were spread. Something cold was slipped inside of her. And later—how much later?— a vague image, of something white and waxy, like a blob of melted paraffin, being lowered into a green-blue basin, and the backside of a nurse as she carried it away.

The vacuum they used to clean her out made a soft, whirring noise. Rosa dreamed she was a child, sitting in the corner by the radiator playing with a doll, while her mother pushed the Hoover back and forth over the living-room carpet.

Rosa opened her eyes in the bright lights of the recovery room. She immediately shut her eyelids and then opened them again at the insistence of a nurse who held Rosa's wrist between her fingers and said, "Come on, you're awake now." The nurse then declared to an orderly across the room, "This one should be ready to clear out now, any minute."

Rosa felt limp and useless, almost carsick, as the orderly pushed her out of Recovery, stopping every once in a while to maneuver the gurney around a corner. She stared up at the ceiling lights, then closed her eyes. She did not talk to the orderly, who was young and thin and had the same kind of high cheekbones as some of Rosa's clients who came from the West Indies. On the elevator, Rosa turned her head and watched him push the button for the third floor. It was official. The baby was dead. Sixth floor was maternity.

In the double room at the end of the hallway, the other bed was empty, so Rosa had the luxury of crying long and hard after the doctor—who was he? what was his name, again?—finally came down in his scrubs and presented his theory of what had happened. A mild case of food poisoning, perhaps. Or a flu that had weakened her immune system, causing her to reject the baby. Or perhaps the fetus itself was ill or deformed, although he certainly had looked normal. Spontaneous abortion, he said, was more common than most people thought—a perfect illustration of natural selection.

The doctor told Rosa to make an appointment with her gynecologist. She should use birth control for the next sixty days; it was dangerous to get pregnant again so soon. In the meantime, she could rest in the hospital for the next twenty-four hours and look forward to all the other children she would have. Sometimes these things just didn't work out.

Rosa pictured Gary's response to the doctor: *You missed your calling—should have gone to law school, you callous fucker!*

No one could find Gary. "Donna called your house and left a message on the machine," Terry told Rosa when she came up around four o'clock. "Donna said she'd stay late in the office until he called back—now there's a girl who's really devoted to her job, don't you think?"

Rosa tried to smile.

"I'll stay until Gary gets here," Terry said.

"You don't have to."

"You want me to call your mother or something?"

"God no," Rosa said.

Terry looked around the room, at the cold tile floor, the yellow curtains, the metal bars on the bed. "You know, it's funny," she said. "We come to work here every day, but we don't have any idea what it's like, do we?"

Rosa nodded. On the first floor—where the halls were carpeted and the pale walls were decorated with soothing, bland art—it was easy to forget that more floors existed, each of them full of patients lying passively in beds, slumped over in wheelchairs, dragging IV trees behind them as they shuffled down the wide halls. It was more convenient to flip on the computer each morning and pretend the patients were numbers, individual files that could be called up and dismissed at random, as opposed to living, breathing human beings who needed round-the-clock care.

Groggy and still slightly nauseous from the anesthesia, Rosa fell asleep. When she woke, the sky outside the windows was a deep and ominous black purple, the dusk just beginning to swallow the silhouette of the Knights of Columbus tower. The room was dark, with just a patch of light coming in from the hall, and it took a moment for her to realize that Gary sat in a chair at the foot of the bed.

"Hey," he said.

"Hey," Rosa said.

Gary dragged his chair up closer. "How do you feel?"

"All right, I guess."

He shifted in his chair. "I'm sorry."

"Me, too," Rosa said.

"Were you scared?"

Rosa nodded. "It was a boy," she said.

"I know," he said. "We saw it on the ultrasound, remember?" Then he paused. "Oh, you mean they showed you—?"

Rosa shook her head. "They took it away. In a basin. Like it was throw-up."

Gary winced.

Rosa fell silent. "It was odd," she finally said. "The whole thing. I was asleep, but I was still awake. I saw things, I heard people talking, and I kept on thinking this is like those experiences you read about, the kind people say they have when they die and come back to life. I saw myself. I was in my body, but I was outside it, too."

"Were you scared?" Gary asked again.

"No. It all seemed so insignificant."

"Sounds like some sort of coping mechanism," Gary said.

Rosa shrugged. She did not want him to reduce the experience—so mysterious, almost otherworldly—to some mundane term from a psychology textbook.

She looked outside. The sky was completely dark, except for the glow from the streetlights below. The room seemed cold and empty.

"I want to go home," she said.

He shook his head. "You can't. I asked. Tomorrow, maybe, one of the doctors will discharge you."

Rosa started to cry.

"Come on, don't, or I'll lose it, too," Gary said. "You know me. I'll lose it."

"Okay, okay."

Gary switched on the little lamp by the bed, opened up the nightstand drawer, and found Rosa some tissues, which she used to blow her nose. "We'll have another one," he said.

"But we'll never have *that* one," Rosa said. "I wanted that one." And then she fell silent once again. Her own voice appalled her. She sounded like a toddler whining for some toy that had been taken away or a piece of candy or a cookie that was off limits. She hated herself, so she took it out on Gary. "Where were you?" she asked him. "We tried and tried to call—"

"I was over at Dave's."

"You were just over there. At the party. Last night."

"We were cramming. For an exam. In the Public Policy class, you know, the one I've been telling you about? The killer?"

"I thought you took that last semester."

"It's a year-long course."

"Oh," Rosa said. She closed her eyes. Seduced by the darkness, she felt everything melt away, except for one last thing—Gary's quiet kiss, planted on her forehead.

One in six, Mimi told Rosa on the phone next morning. "I called my doctor last night, and he said one in six babies get lost," Mimi said. Rosa thought *get lost* was an extremely odd choice of words, making the whole experience sound as if Rosa had taken her eyes off her child in a department store.

Mimi urged her to come down to Long Island. It had been so long. "Artie is dying to see Gary," Mimi said. "He needs to see Gary. He simply *has* to have his Gary fix." Pilar would cook all of Rosa's favorite dishes, the gumbo with red rice and the Belgian waffles studded with almonds and dressed with fresh fruit and maple syrup. Gary and Artie would do *man* things, while Mimi and Rosa would go shopping—just the girls. Mimi would treat Rosa to lunch. She would buy Rosa a new outfit.

I don't want a new outfit, Rosa felt like saying. I want my baby back.

Yet the next weekend Rosa stood in the elegant dressing room at I. Magnin's, trying on one of several "casual but chic" dresses that Mimi had yanked off the rack. Rosa could barely stand to look at herself in the full-length mirror. Her hair looked dull and flat and her pale skin was yellow under the fluorescent lights. Her breasts were squeezed into a dingy white bra, her flaccid stomach rolled over the top of her cotton underpants, and her thighs looked like someone had flattened them out with a rolling pin. The sight was hideous enough without having any spectators. But Mimi insisted on following Rosa in and sitting on the little stool in the corner of the dressing room. This was Rosa's worst nightmare—Mimi seeing her fat body; Mimi evaluating her dowdy underwear; Mimi witnessing the embarrassing bulge of the sanitary napkin Rosa would be forced to wear for weeks until her body finally decided there was no more need to bleed; Mimi saying, "My stomach sagged so horribly after I had Gary that I was afraid Artie would leave me."

Gary was right: Mimi Fisher really *was* radioactive waste. Rosa pulled the dress over her head and buttoned the front.

"I thought I'd lose my figure completely," Mimi said. "But if you get right to work on it, you'll snap right back, just like I did."

Rosa pulled the belt of the dress as tight as she could and buckled it.

"Well? What do you think?" Mimi asked.

The dress was rayon, striped in neutral tones that did nothing to make Rosa look thinner or any less like a living corpse. "Fine," Rosa said. "I'll take it."

"Don't you want to try the others on?" Mimi asked.

"No," Rosa said in a sharp tone of voice that even Mimi had to accept as the final word.

In front of the cash register, Rosa watched as Mimi paid two hundred and forty-seven dollars for an outfit Rosa never had any intention of wearing. The dress would hang in the closet, too ugly to wear and too expensive to give away, and Rosa, rifling through the closet on Monday mornings for something—anything—that was comfortable, would keep on coming across it, causing her to remember what Mimi had said, and to picture, once again, her own ugly body. Rosa accepted the dress not as a gift, but as a punishment. As for the money—now wasted—such extravagance had ceased to shock Rosa. That was Mimi's concern. Rosa felt guilty only when she thought about Artie, who had worked hard to support all these trips to I. Magnin's and Lord and Taylor's. But Artie probably didn't care. Shopping, just like snooker, took Mimi off his back.

When they returned to the Fishers' house, Mimi insisted that Rosa go upstairs and model the dress for Gary. "Isn't it lovely?"

Mimi exclaimed after Rosa reluctantly had donned the dress. "Gary, say it's lovely."

Gary looked at Rosa, who stood there slump-shouldered in the new outfit, and Rosa saw on his face both pity and contempt and some implicit knowledge of what had taken place that afternoon between Rosa and his mother. "You look great," he told Rosa in a thin, liar's voice.

Then why do I feel like shit? Rosa felt like crying.

A week after the miscarriage, she went back to work. Soon she was obsessed with a patient, someone whose case she was handling, someone she had never even met before.

His name was Bright, Baby Boy. He didn't have a first name because neither parent wanted him. They were going through a divorce and each refused to sign the adoption papers, hoping to foist custody on the other party. Rosa was supposed to work with the state and the parents—who hung up the phone every time she called—to negotiate a settlement.

In the meantime, Bright, Baby Boy remained in neonatal ICU, racking up a bill that already was close to a quarter of a million dollars. He was born with a leak in his heart and some brain damage from lack of oxygen during delivery. At three months old, he already had survived several surgeries: a neural shunt, a mitral valve patch, and a hernia repair.

Sitting at her computer, processing his paperwork, Rosa liked to whisper his name to herself: *Bright, Baby Boy.* The sound soothed her and made her whole body relax deeply, just as she had relaxed only twice during her life: during the twilight sleep and once, long ago, during her field trip to the Hayden Planetarium. There, Rosa had leaned back on the soft, cushioned chair, staring up at the light show on the ceiling and feeling she could lose herself forever—float down the Milky Way, ride a comet to the outer reaches of the universe, and whirl with the planets.

The next day in the classroom, Sister St. Paul had tried to discount the theory of the Big Bang which had been presented by the planetarium. Sister told them that God made heaven and earth and that the Earth was the only planet that truly existed—the rest was just a show that God put on for man's benefit, to prove He was all-powerful and that his reach was infinite. She told them that every time a child died, God put another star in the sky; thus man would continue to discover more and more galaxies far beyond the Milky Way.

If Sister's theory were true, then Bright, Baby Boy—the baby who reminded Rosa of a star each time his name appeared in bright white type against Rosa's green computer screen—was still of the earth. It was Rosa's baby who hung in the heavens. Bright, Baby Boy had been born the day before Rosa had suffered her miscarriage. So perhaps the very moment Rosa had pulled down her underwear in the bathroom and found the blood, the doctors were wheeling Bright, Baby Boy in for his first surgery, anesthetized and pinned down on the tiny cart, like a butterfly or moth killed with chloroform and pinned onto a corkboard for inspection.

Rosa wondered what the parents—who sported very desirable addresses in Hamden and Guilford—were really like. Why didn't they want their child? Why did each try to foist the baby on the other? How did they justify their behavior to themselves? How did they explain the situation to their families and the people they worked with?

Rosa despised their selfishness, but at the same time, she did not want them to sort out their differences. She liked the idea of Bright, Baby Boy cloistered in his incubator, waiting and struggling on his own, proving the human race could survive on just some animal instinct to live, as opposed to parental love and encouragement. If Rosa speeded up the paperwork, the baby eventually would be released into foster care. He might even be ruled a ward of the state and then adopted, in spite of his medical problems. Why not? Enough people were desperate. The *Register* was full of ads placed by couples who wanted children. The ads were targeted toward high school girls too scared to have abortions, coeds who drank too much and picked up the wrong guy at the Thanksgiving mixer, working girls in trouble who might be eager to quit their jobs as receptionists or cashiers. *Place your baby in our loving home. Dad an accountant, Mom a registered nurse, will give up career to care for your child full-time in warm, supportive atmosphere.*

Rosa sometimes looked at those ads and wondered how the pregnant girl—the biological mother—was supposed to choose one couple over the other. Look at us, each ad seemed to say. No, seriously, look at *us*—we are white and wealthy, warm and supportive, we can and will pay for elaborate birthday parties, summer camp, private school, four years and maybe more of college education. We believe in family prayer and a well-stocked refrigerator. We would never say *Shut up, you brat!* or *Go fry your face in front of the TV!*

Rosa knew these potential parents were out there, waiting to snatch up Bright, Baby Boy and provide him with corrective eyeglasses and special education classes. She did not want anyone to get him, because she herself wanted him. She fantasized about adopting the baby, quitting her job, and leaving Gary. Was she crazy? Or just totally hormonal? In any case, she couldn't control herself, so why worry?

One day after work, instead of exiting the doors of the front lobby, Rosa took the elevator to the neonatal ICU. She happened to have on her navy suit that day, the skirt held together in the back by a couple of large safety pins. She clipped her hospital ID onto her breast pocket and strode past the nurses' desk, hoping she would pass for one of the hospital's top administrators. The blinds of the ICU were closed. Visitors had to sign in and don a surgical mask and gown just to stand in the observation area.

After hesitating for a moment, Rosa signed herself in as Mrs. Toni C. Ballone. Then she went into the prep room, scrubbed her hands at the sink, took a yellow gown off the hook, and awkwardly fastened it in back. She felt short of breath as she put on the mask. When she glanced at herself in the mirror over the sink, she thought she looked like a fool, an impostor, a fat version of the Lone Ranger.

The door to the observation room was made of thick blond wood, and the latch clicked behind her after she went in. Behind the large glass window were two rows of cribs, seven occupied and five empty. The babies—all puny and pasty as lumps of Silly Putty—were hooked up to elaborate equipment with pulsing lights and beeping monitors. Saline dripped down the long, transparent coils of the intravenous tubes into a small, bandaged patch on each baby's arm.

The cribs were labeled. Bright, Baby Boy was in the back corner—nothing but raw, red legs, a flat diapered rump, and the back of a bandaged head. He was sleeping on his tummy. Rosa instantly fell in love with him.

Behind the glass, a nurse was tending to another baby. After nodding to Rosa, she did not pay her further attention. Rosa continued to stare at Bright, Baby Boy until the observation door opened and another person in a mask and gown came in. Not until the person spoke was Rosa sure it was a woman.

"Which one is yours?" the woman asked.

Rosa looked down at herself. Underneath her gown, she still bore all the traces of a woman who recently had been pregnant—a wide rump and swollen breasts. And so Rosa—liar!—pointed to the crib in the corner.

"Mine is that little girl," the woman pointed to a baby in a full-body cast. "Hip correction. Aren't the doctors wonderful?"

"Oh," Rosa said vaguely, "the doctors don't do the real work. I prefer the nurses."

"We have Dr. Kasvinicz, do you know Dr. Kasvinicz?"

"Is he Polish?" Rosa asked.

"No, he speaks English," the woman said.

Rosa despised her. She wished she would go away. Yet the woman obviously wanted someone to talk to. Keeping her eyes on her baby, she said, "We came here because we heard Yale was the best. We're from Tolland. I drive in every day from Tolland. Have you ever even heard of Tolland?"

"Yes," Rosa said. "That's the place where the girl was kidnapped when I was in third grade."

The woman nodded. "I was in fifth grade. They never found her body! I used to feel so sorry for the girl. Now that I've had a baby, I think more of the parents, I feel so sorry for the parents." Beneath her surgical mask, her lips raised in a smile. "Don't you think being a mother has changed your whole outlook on life?"

"Yes," Rosa said.

"Are you going in?" the woman asked Rosa.

"No," Rosa said. "I'm checking out." She grabbed the handle of the door and walked back into the prep room.

Oh, God! Rosa thought to herself. She was nuts, whacked out, completely *pozza*. The prep room was stifling hot and Rosa perspired as she struggled with the knots on her mask and gown. She threw them into the laundry bin and walked quickly down the hall. She considered stopping in on the eighth floor and checking herself into the psychiatric ward. She was sick. She was a degenerate. She lived in a fantasy world. How could she even contemplate going into the office tomorrow, even think of advising others, when she so desperately needed help herself?

"What's the matter with you lately?" Gary asked her in an irritable tone when she got home, and Rosa was surprised to hear herself say, "I miss my father."

It was true. Although she had not loved him—nor even much liked him while he was alive—Rosa always found herself looking for her father, peering through the panes of the garage door windows as she went up the driveway of her old house. When she walked around downtown New Haven, she sometimes fantasized about seeing his truck rumbling by the Green, or waiting at the light on the corner of Church and Chapel. It did not hit Rosa that he was truly gone until after the baby ceased to exist. And then his grave became a special place for Rosa. She visited it often.

Rosa's father was buried in Saint Lawrence. The cemetery seemed the only peaceful green space left in New Haven. Gravel roads wound up and down the hillside, willow trees lined the creek, and the grey and white headstones seemed to go on for miles. A tall iron fence, topped with spikes, was supposed to keep the wrong people out.

But it didn't. You name it, Antoinette said, and these men do it.

They climb the fence and swipe the wreaths right off the graves. They topple headstones, just for a joke. They attack women and— *Madonna mia,* can you imagine?—rape them right over the bodies of their dead husbands. Rosa should not visit the cemetery alone, her mother cautioned. Even Gary, who usually laughed at these horror stories, told Rosa he didn't think it was such a hot idea for her to plant flowers in Saint Lawrence by herself. "I'll go with you," he said.

Rosa didn't want him along. She liked being by herself more and more these days, especially since she was prone—no, addicted—to wild and melodramatic jags of weeping. But if she broke down in front of Gary, he would tell her to get a grip, so she stifled it.

They went to Saint Lawrence after work, on one of the first spring evenings any kid would welcome—a warm, play-outside-after-dinner night. Rosa insisted on driving. She couldn't stand the idea of Gary bucking the Subaru up and down the narrow roads of the cemetery. She pictured him honking the horn at a squirrel or gunning the motor as they passed by headstones that had amusing names on them like Fifi Macaroni or Stanislaus Stanislawski.

The zoning system in Saint Lawrence mimicked the segregated neighborhoods of New Haven. The Irish were buried at the bottom of the hill, where the plots were larger, the grass greener, and the headstones more elaborate. The Italians and Poles—with their plain and thrifty grave markers decorated with American flags and yellowed fronds from Palm Sunday—were crowded at the top of the hill. Blacks were buried at Beaverdale and Fair Haven, and Jews in the cemetery on the far side of Saint Lawrence, beyond a wide stone wall implanted on top with tiny, sharp rocks.

Gravel crunched beneath their feet when they got out of the car. Gary carried the plastic flat of bulbs—tulips and hyacinths—and Rosa carried a roll of paper towels and a shiny, new, silver hand spade. Her father's plot was at the end of the row, a long rectangle of light, fresh green surrounded by coarser grass. Someone had left a potted geranium in front of the granite headstone. The petals had shattered. Rosa picked them up one by one and put them back into the pot.

When she moved the geranium to the side and tried to sink the spade into the soil, she met only stubborn, firmly packed earth. "I can do it," Gary said. Rosa stood up, relieved to get off her knees. She could only imagine what she looked like bending over, her shirt untucked because her jeans only zipped up halfway. Her backside, she was convinced, was monstrous.

It took a few minutes for Gary, who was no more a gardener than Rosa, to clumsily dig a narrow trough. Then they both knelt down and puzzled over the bulbs, wondering which end was up and how far apart they were supposed to be planted. "Didn't you ask at the garden center?" Gary said.

"I asked for tulips," Rosa said defensively. "I expected them to bring out flowers."

"And here we sit, two city kids with a bunch of weird onions."

"I think the green part goes at the top."

Rosa had been too embarrassed to ask the man at the Whalley Avenue nursery any questions. He had shaken his head when he brought out the flat of bulbs from the back, telling her that tulips planted in early spring grew very short, and sometimes didn't even flower. He had tried to sell her on geraniums or potted mums, but Rosa, who hated being condescended to, stuck to her original plan.

They planted the bulbs about four inches apart. Gary wiped his hands on a paper towel, then walked down to the end of the row. Rosa used the spade to sprinkle dirt around the bulbs and pack them underground with a thick soil layer. She tried not to look up at her father's name, which was chiseled in plain block lettering on the headstone. But she couldn't help but see it and repeat it inside herself, like some useless prayer—one more bead, maybe, on the rosary, muttered over and over in the night: *Aldo Salvatore, Aldo Salvatore, Aldo Salvatore.*

Down there was her father. Yes, he was down there, cold beneath the ground. Yet it was not him. Not for Rosa. He still burned in her memory, like stubborn, charred coal that blushed hot orange hours after the fire supposedly was put out. He was the man with the grease-splattered pants and the smudgy hands, who dirtied the brass doorknob when he came home late from fixing leaking faucets and faulty toilets. He was the man who merely grunted hello as he stepped out of his muddy shoes and sighed as he took a ten-dollar bill out of the grey-blue cash bag he brought back every evening. He folded the cash bag and stuffed it inside his right shoe. Then he stood on a stepstool and reached up to the top shelf of the hall closet, where he tucked the ten-dollar bill into the black tweed hat he wore to funerals and weddings. The money was for Antoinette—her household allowance, deliberately placed up high so she had to think twice before she reached into the till.

For their entire marriage Aldo had put everything worth having out of Antoinette's reach—a nice vacation, a wad of cash, a little love, a happy family. Antoinette still resented him. Some of the things she said—*Why I married him, God only knows! Always a cross word, never an apology!* and *Today, who would have children with a man like that?*—made Rosa blush and Gary give out a low whistle. Later, alone with Rosa, he laughed and said, "Must have been love, right?"

"Right," Rosa said.

Gary and Rosa had thought they were so superior to Rosa's parents. They had thought their marriage was above all that, until a pall of boredom had settled in, dark as the cloth laid over a coffin. Gary studied all the time. Rosa went shopping too much. And the baby—hadn't it been nothing but the result of too much wine on a Friday night? For four months or so, maybe the thought of him had pulled Gary and Rosa together. But with him gone, what was left? Just moment after moment of loneliness, when Gary and Rosa looked at one another and had nothing to say, or looked at one another and said too much.

Rosa spilled the final mound of dirt onto the bulbs and put down the spade. Gary was standing at the end of the row, looking down the hill. Rosa wiped her hands and went over to him. Down the hill, by the creek, a stone angel kneeled on a pedestal. The sun, which already hung low in the greyish sky, illuminated the half-spread wings of the angel at just the right angle. She seemed to radiate.

"You can see that angel from inside the Mishkan Israel cemetery," Gary said.

"How do you know?" Rosa asked.

"I went in there," Gary said. "Once."

"What for?"

"Just to see what it was like."

Rosa shook her head. She didn't believe him.

Gary looked down at his hands and rubbed some of the dirt off his palm with his thumb. "I thought they would let us bury the baby, didn't you?"

"They have to be full-term," Rosa said. "The nurse told me. Besides, we would have fought over where to bury him."

"That's not true."

"Of course it's true. You would have wanted it buried over there and I would have wanted it buried over here."

Gary shrugged. And Rosa, who felt the need to slug this issue out, continued. "You told my mother we wouldn't baptize it."

"Jesus, have a heart, Ro. My parents would have flipped. And do you really think people are born with original sin, just because some guy wanted to eat an apple? You really think your soul can be shook clean, like an Etch-a-Sketch?"

Rosa bit her lip. She herself had not gone to Confession in years, and the last time she did it was because she was serving as a bridesmaid in a wedding and had to take Communion.

"You know I hate all those rituals," Gary said. "The incense aggravates my sinuses, and all that voodoo, I don't care if it's Catholic or Jewish, it's all the same to me, seems like a hoot and a half. Did I ever tell you about this *bris* I went to in Far Rockaway? The *mohel* circumcised the baby boy and then gave the foreskin to the father to bury in the front yard of the house, as a fertility symbol. The poor guy had to use his car keys to dig a hole in the petunias. And later, the neighbor's dog came and dug up the foreskin, carrying the damn thing off in its mouth."

Rosa laughed in spite of herself.

As they walked back to the car, Gary carrying the spade and Rosa carrying the empty plastic flat, Gary grew serious again. "Sometimes, when I sit at my computer, I think about the baby being put into an incinerator."

"Don't," Rosa said.

"I can't help it. The screen is amber and it reminds me of flames."

The screen on Rosa's computer was a deep, dusty green—the color, maybe, of a woman's beautiful eyes. Rosa had been staring intently at the computer screen that afternoon when she felt like she had indigestion and stood up from her desk to stretch, only to realize, in the bathroom, that a gush of blood was running down her legs. It was hours before Gary turned up at the hospital—and it would be months before Rosa finally remembered, like a image from a suppressed dream, that he had smelled clean, but different, when he leaned over the bed and kissed her, as if he had used another kind of soap in the shower.

Rosa's memory catalogued and repressed the smell of that soap. Yet the vague fragrance—and the wild suspicions it engendered—stayed with her (the way her father's smell still lingered in the house for more than a year after his death) all the way up until the time she came home from the beauty salon and found Gary lying in bed.

"I've got cancer," he said.

"Oh," Rosa said.

And he said, "Jesus, what'd you do to your hair?"

chapter ten

The next few months were awful. Gary went through two surgeries, some radiation, injections, and a short round of chemotherapy that, amazingly, left most of his hair intact and made him only slightly dizzy and listless. Yet Rosa remained calm. She felt strangely prepared for it all.

Rosa had grown up believing in signs, in everything from the *mal'occhio* to the message of Fatima, from Nostradamus to the Ouija board, an item which had been forbidden in her house as a sign of the devil but which became a staple at every birthday party in the neighborhood once the Saint Boniface girls got past seventh grade. The girls consulted Ouija strictly about boys, reinforcing the fact that the male half of the species, at least on the East Haven shore, seemed to live in another world.

At Angie Ianuzzi's fourteenth-birthday party, Rosa had asked Ouija if she would ever get married and watched, with great relief, as the pointer beneath her fingers began to veer toward the Y, then the E.

"Ask if you're gonna be *happily* married," Angie insisted.

Rosa reluctantly intoned the question, watching with horror as the pointer hesitated beneath the pressure of the girls' fingers, then slowly stopped between the N and the O.

"No," Angie said, triumphantly.

"It didn't spell out no," Rosa said. "It just stopped in between the two letters."

Gary, too, had consulted the Ouija at Mark Fink's house, one sunny Saturday afternoon after the first batch of MIA soldiers came back from Vietnam. Gary had asked Ouija if he would be rich and famous. Ouija said no. When Gary asked why not, the pointer began to move underneath his hands and spelled out D-I-E.

Of course, it was just that dumbo Mark Fink pushing the pointer wherever he wanted it to go. Gary had found the whole thing amusing—until, of course, Mimi overheard him talking about it on the phone. Then there was hell to pay. Mimi grew incensed. She hammered Gary until she had gotten the entire story from him, including the Ouija's bad predictions. Then Mimi called Fink's mother and made it perfectly clear that even though she was neither religious nor superstitious, she did not feel that such dealings with the occult were healthy for children. After all, what if Mark or Gary or any of the other boys in the neighborhood asked if they were going to get into Harvard, and this Ouija board told them no? Why, then they might conclude that Yale and Princeton also were beyond their grasp. They would stop studying, fall off the honor roll, and within no time at all, they would be wandering the streets, homeless heroin addicts.

After Mrs. Fink deposited Ouija—with his dark black cape and hooded brow—into the trash, the pointer that had predicted Gary's illness was silenced forever. Rosa imagined it buried in the bowels of the earth, in some Long Island landfill, sandwiched in between a decaying copy of the Garden City Yellow Pages and an empty wax box of Banquet Southern Fried Chicken.

Rosa's belief in signs comforted her, because she thought it helped her cope. But it also made her sick, because it confirmed she was Antoinette's daughter.

"I knew it," Antoinette said when Rosa finally, reluctantly, called and told her that the tumor they had removed, along with Gary's prostate, had metastasized to his bones. "I knew when you married him that something would go wrong," Antoinette said.

"Stop it, Mother," Rosa said.

"You never know," Antoinette kept repeating. "You never know when your number's going to get called. I'll light a candle for him."

Rosa imagined the candle burning by the altar night after night. "You do that, Mother," she said. "Please do that."

Rosa couldn't decide which was worse: Antoinette's passive acceptance of death or Artie and Mimi's inability to accept the fact that their son was going to die, and no doctor—no treatment, no matter how expensive—was going to save him.

"That's a disease for old men," Artie had said when Gary told him about the prostate tumor. "Only old men get that." And Mimi: "Surely there's some mistake. Who is your doctor? Is that an Indian name? I don't care if he is at Yale—Artie, tell him to go to the right kind of doctor—" And Gary, hollering back: "I hate Jewish doctors—they always ask you if you get good grades!"

Second opinion. Mimi insisted on a second opinion, which Gary was anxious to get, provided it didn't turn into a third or fourth or fifth. They did it in Long Island. Mimi set up the appointments, and she and Gary made the rounds of the doctors while Artie went to work and Rosa stayed alone in the Fishers' house, uselessly trying to read a magazine. All she could do was turn pages.

Late morning stretched into the afternoon, and afternoon stretched into early evening. Rosa dropped her magazine on the mattress, spread out, and fell asleep on the bed. The room was bathed in grey light when she woke. She got up, splashed cold water on her sleep-wrinkled face, and went downstairs. The lights were on, but no one was in the living room. Rosa fantasized about making a quick escape—slipping out the foyer and going for a long walk around the neighborhood, past the well-groomed lawns, now dead and brown, the redwood decks and cheerful gazebos cold and spindly in the winter air, the swimming pools covered with blue tarps. But at the bottom of the stairs, Rosa heard the disconcerting crack of a pool cue and the thud of balls falling into pockets. Mimi was playing snooker.

Rosa peeked through the door and saw Artie sitting in the game room. He motioned her in. Before Rosa could even ask how the appointments had gone and where Gary was, Mimi turned around. She was crying, and streams of mascara fell freely down her face.

"I always thought it would be Benny," Mimi said. "It should have been Benny. For months, for years now, I've been expecting a phone call from Sylvia telling us that Benny has AIDS. Why couldn't it have happened to Sylvia? She has three boys. I only have the one."

Artie nodded glumly. He slumped in his chair. "Well," he said. "You work really hard all your life. You never think something like this will happen." He looked at Mimi. "Put down that pool cue, Meem."

"Why should I?"

"Because of Rosa. What will she think? It's not right. At a time like this."

"What do you want me to do? Read the newspaper, as if it were any other night of my life? I have to do something."

Mimi looked like she was going to explode. Rosa wondered what would happen if she totally lost her cool. Maybe she would shoot all the balls down into their pockets, except for one red ball which she would turn and hurl into one of the mirrors, smashing the glass into a million pieces. What if she did do that? It would be an empty gesture. In the morning, Pilar would come in, kneel on the floor, and sweep up the glass, clucking to herself, taking it only as upper-class bad humor.

But Mimi did not throw any snooker balls. She washed the mascara off her face and pulled herself together. Artie stopped sighing, and Gary came back from the very walk Rosa had wanted to go on, his face grim. They sat down, like civilized people, and ate a tasteless dinner. The mirrors—all of them, and there were a lot of them in the Fisher house—stayed intact. As he backed the Subaru out of his parents' driveway for the trip back to New Haven, Gary told Rosa that Jews traditionally covered the mirrors in their houses after a funeral. "I always thought that after my father died—I always saw my father dying first—my mother would have to call in Christo to wrap up the whole frigging place in sheets," he said.

After his prostate was removed, Gary's hormones were delivered once a week, through an injection in his arm. The hormones bloated his body, making his cheeks and neck look heavy and unpleasant. They controlled—and derailed—his behavior, making his moods flash faster than MTV. Sometimes he sat silent and immobile in an armchair by the window, his eyes focused on the sky and the branches of the trees, as if he were watching a time-lapsed movie in which the days and seasons played themselves out over and over within the span of half an hour. Other times he followed Rosa from room to room, talking non-stop about his fatigue, his voracious thirst, his brittle bones, and his incontinence—which Rosa knew was really a way of *not* talking about his impotence. He told more and more tales from his childhood, which made Rosa suspect there was something from his adulthood that he was eager to repress—or confess.

Rosa listened. A social worker always knew how to listen. She knew how to dole out good—and bad—advice. She tried to get Gary interested in something different—the gossip she reported from work, the eleven o'clock news, the benefits of a vegetarian diet, the writings of Moses Maimonides—but he refused to be distracted, until he found the perfect diversion.

The tables were turned. Now Gary Fisher was suspicious of Rosa Salvatore. When she came in the door—whether she was returning from a day at work or a five-minute trip downstairs to throw out the garbage—he immediately looked at his watch.

Rosa was on trial. Her crime was being female and being interested in men. Never mind that she was more attracted to men in general rather than the specific. Gary was out to nail her. He made her swear she would never sleep with anyone else while he was still alive. He tried to make her swear she would never remarry after his death.

"I don't want to get married again," Rosa said. "Marriage makes me miserable."

"There, you see," he said. "You hate me. But I still want you to be happy."

At night, he lay back on the bed, watching Rosa undress. "I'm watching you," he said, propping himself up on a pillow and putting his arms behind his head. "I've *watched* you. Don't think I don't notice when you're interested in a man. You pass your tongue under your upper lip like you've just eaten a big, fat, salty kosher pickle."

Rosa pulled her flannel nightgown over her head. "I despise pickles," she told him. "They make me burp."

Gary gave a triumphant little snort. "You like 'em short," he said. "Men, that is. Packed like pistols. Dark and strong, like black coffee."

"I take cream," Rosa mildly reminded him. "Sometimes even sugar."

"You got a thing for Greeks," he said, a little dreamily. "Italians. Men with last names that sound like an archeology site or some obscure kind of vegetable that nobody except people in California want to eat." Then his voice sharpened. "Admit it—you lust after the waiter with the mustache at the Athenos Diner, the one who looks like he goes home and plays the balalaika after he's done counting his tips!"

Rosa bit her lip. Nikolas Theodos always wore a clean white shirt that went charmingly unbuttoned at the neck. When it was her turn to pay, Rosa left him twenty percent. Gary stiffed him.

"I'm on to you," Gary said. "It's the arm muscles."

"Drop it," Rosa warned him. But in truth she was fascinated to listen, to see how accurate he could get.

"You like waiters," he said. "Carpenters. *Musicians.* You get the hots every time we go to Woolsey Hall. I can tell just by looking at your feet. Some guy is up there pounding on the piano or sawing away on some violin, and you're sitting back with your legs crossed and your shoe slipped off, dangling from your toe. You've got wistful-looking ankles. And they whisper, *Take me to the Motel Six!*"

"You're completely crazy," Rosa said. "Stop it. Stop torturing yourself."

Gary blew out his breath and punched Rosa's pillow. Then he picked it up and threw it at her, catching her square in the gut. Rosa was furious at him. She was sorry for him. She also was a little bit scared of him. Because he couldn't do anything more than just look, his eyes were always on her, paring her down quicker than a metal peeler stripped a cucumber. He searched her behavior the same way Antoinette, transformed by menopause into a sweaty, raving shrew, once searched Rosa's drawers and purse and came up with damning evidence of her daughter's decline into slutdom, a tampon.

"Che cos'è?" she confronted Rosa. "What is this? What *is* this? Where did you get this? *A scuola?*" She spit *school* like it was a dirty word. "You got this at *scuola!*" She threw the tampon onto the red-tiled kitchen floor, turned around to the counter, grabbed the first thing she saw—a metal colander—and winged it at Rosa, missing her by half an inch. "Sticking things up yourself! The next thing you know you'll have more holes poked in you than a *collino*—and end up with something cooking in your oven!"

Then there was Rosa's father. The moment Rosa's breasts began to burst like bombs through the green-and-black plaid of her St. Boni-face School uniform, Aldo had accused her of carrying on with prac-tically every boy on the block. She came home late from a birthday party once and he grabbed her by her waist-length hair, winding it around his wrist like a belt. Rosa felt her neck snap back again and again. She felt her father's breath on her ear as he made incoherent grunting sounds, like some crazed rhinoceros or wild pig. When Aldo got mad he lost control of both his tongues and sputtered in an absurd mix of Italian and English. Although his words were all bro-ken, Rosa knew how to translate them accurately: she was grounded, for good.

Gary, her mother, her father—what evidence did they have that she was up to mischief? She was too fat to wear anything provoca-tive. She did not flirt. She kept her body language under tight check. But put in a crowd, she often sat in the corner, nursing long silences.

They suspected her of thinking. Of imagining. And it was true that Rosa led a rich and sick fantasy life. She saw men on the street and they returned to her in her dreams. They were faceless, identi-fied only by a strong forearm or a large, rough hand. They were de-livered to her, heaped naked on green wheelbarrows, like the zucchini in her grandfather's backyard. They sat behind the steering wheel of an unknown car, and she sat in the back seat, ready to ride anywhere they were willing to take her. One moment they stood next to Rosa at the altar rail in Saint Boniface church, exchanging wedding vows. The next moment their lips were grazing her ears and neck, and their fingers were slipping along the insides of her thighs, stripping her of her tummy-control pantyhose. They made her come like gangbusters! They went down on her as she lay on her mother's kitchen floor, underneath the velvet painting of the Last Supper, in which the apostles gesticulated as wildly as Rosa's relatives did when they tried to agree upon whether or not to order the pizza with anchovies, while the dream Rosa made low, guttural noises, like a toaster that was stuck and wouldn't pop up until someone came along to flip the handle.

Yes, it was true. Rosa was completely crazy for men. How had it all started, these fierce attractions coupled with the lack of courage —or the overabundance of good sense—not to act upon them? Had Rosa reclined on Freud's lush black leather couch, she might have discovered it had all begun on the beach. The Salvatore family used to go to Lighthouse Point on Saturday evenings at sunset. The coarse, dark sand was strewn with seaweed, broken white shells, and desiccated crab husks faded pale orange in the sun. Rosa sat on a piece of rotting driftwood, watching her grandfather wade in the water. He plucked mussels and snails off the jagged shoreline rocks and dropped them, with a clink, into his tin pail. As the sun began to sink into the horizon, Rosa's father and uncles took off their shirts, rolled up their pants, hoisted their heavy rope nets, and moved silently through the water, dragging for eels. They did not talk. They spoke with hand gestures, cocks of their heads, and low, whistling noises to indicate moving to the right and left.

When they returned home, Rosa's grandfather sat at the kitchen table and broke open the mussels and snails with a burnished pewter nutcracker, eating them raw. Out in the backyard, under the yellow glow of the porch light, Rosa's father and uncles skinned the eels onto the Sunday edition of the *New Haven Register*. Rosa's grandmother took the long tails of meat, chopped them into half-inch pieces, and dropped them into huge aluminum pots of boiling water. She pickled the chopped eels in brine and displayed the jars on the window sill—to make the neighbors jealous, she said.

It was all that unabashed, swaggering action that made Rosa lust after the men. They took off their shirts and *did things.* They had the nets; they used the sharpest knives. In the dining room, they were served Sunday dinner first and ate whatever they damn pleased. After they had gorged themselves, they went out on the steps and lit up their cigars, leaving behind a mound of garbage as evidence of their gluttony—heaps of walnut shells, corn cobs, mussel husks, artichoke leaves, orange and banana peels. Then Rosa was sent in to clean up the mess, to bring it all back to the kitchen, where her mother and grandmother stood at the sink, watching the world go by as they washed dish after dish, and the eels glistened on the windowsill, pale and fishy in the sun.

And there Rosa's troubles began. She refused to stand at the sink. Yet she could not go out on the steps. Where did that leave her?

It left her standing there, in some schoolmarm flannel nightgown, in the bedroom with the only man (of all those she had desired) whom she ever had loved, a pillow pressed against her stomach, as if it could hold back all her distress. She considered winging the pillow right back at Gary. But he wore such a sorrowful, penitent look on his face that suddenly Rosa smelled soap. She smelled the soap he had on his neck and collar when he leaned over her at the hospital, and she heard Ilse say, *Oh, him,* and it all became clear. He was the guilty one. He had the nerve to accuse her, when really he should confess.

"Gary Fisher," she said, her voice trembling on his name. "Tell me the God-honest truth. *You* had an affair. With that—that stringy-haired Swedish *woman,* in the little red shoes that looked like doll's slippers."

Gary swallowed. Then he nodded.

Rosa let the pillow slide to the floor.

After Gary assured her that it was only once or twice ("I don't know, it could have been three times, twice on one night, I don't remember except for the last time, when I couldn't even do it—shit, it wasn't that good, sweetie, really, I swear it, I don't know what got into me, it was just this—you know—*sex* thing"), he told Rosa that for months the guilt had been killing him—he had longed to tell her, because he couldn't stand the thought of her maybe finding out— you know, *afterward*—and now he really felt so much better having gotten this off his chest. Then he fell asleep, and he actually snored.

Rosa cried. She pressed her face into her pillow and wept like a colander, all her sorrow leaking through in a steady, patterned stream. She cried because she had been betrayed, because she had had a bad childhood, because she could not find God, because she was frightened of being alone, because she wanted to be loved, be- cause she had fallen in love with a man who abandoned her. She cried because she had lost the baby but not the weight, because her thighs were wider than tires and she couldn't find a bra that fit, be- cause the moon wasn't on her side, because the moon was *never* on her side. But most of all, she cried because the tampon had been a Super Plus and because she had been only eleven years old when her mother threw the *collino* at her and because she still had all the heart and yearning of that young girl but no longer knew where that girl had gone, the one who had picked up the colander from the floor and thrown it right back at her mother, yelling, "I just wanted to swim! I got a right to go swimming!"

The next morning the sky was the color of eggplant, and the rain whipped against the windows in jagged rhythm. Rosa awoke with eyes bruised from lack of sleep. Her face in the bathroom mirror had more crinkles than a balled-up rayon shirt waiting to be ironed. Gary was still asleep—a fact Rosa greatly resented—when she went into the kitchen.

The tile floor, which hadn't been mopped in months, was sticky beneath Rosa's slippers. The counter was spotted with coffee rings, and crumbs littered the table. Rosa stood at the sink and thought back upon the first morning she had woken up next to Gary. They had laughed and kissed and made love like a couple of suction cups. It had hurt to pry themselves off the mattress. In this very kitchen, on that long-ago morning, Rosa had felt so happy that the refrigera- tor's hum sounded like a symphony and the faucets seemed plated with real silver. Gary had pulled out the GE waffle iron with the frayed cord, and Rosa, her biceps swollen with hope and love, had beat the batter senseless. The mixture had been thick and porous, and the waffles had come out as crisp and stiff as the petticoats Rosa used to wear beneath her Easter dress. Now Rosa craved those waffles, their deep pockets heavy and sweet with maple syrup, and full of the promise of everything wonderful yet to come.

The Cheerios Rosa eventually settled upon were stale and gritty as sand, and the coffee she made tasted like it had been fixed by some little old lady at a church bazaar who forgot how to measure out the grinds—dark and oily and gritty. Rosa vowed to drink every drop as penance for her undesirableness. She sat there and grimaced as she heard Gary rustling around in the bedroom, opening and closing the bathroom door, flushing the toilet. Her intestines cramped with anger. She loved him like a big war. Call a truce and what would be left?

Rosa clutched her coffee mug as Gary came to the door. He cleared his throat.

"About last night—"

"Don't mention it," Rosa said.

"I didn't mean to tell you all that—"

"I already knew," Rosa said. And to make herself sound more interesting, she added, "On a very unconscious level. So you can stop saying you're sorry."

"I'm not saying I'm sorry." He stood in the doorway. "I mean, I *am* sorry—"

"You're sorry you told me, that's all."

Gary shook his head. "Forget it."

"How can I forget it?"

"You remember everything," Gary said.

"So do you," Rosa said. "And you tell me every last detail."

"Yes, but I don't hold grudges. You hold massive grudges."

"I'm sorry I'm human."

"Forgive and—"

Before he could even mouth *forget,* Rosa asked, "God, why did you tell me? If you hadn't told me, then I could have ignored it.

Now I've got to live with it." At the word *live*—a problem word these days—Rosa lowered her face to avoid his gaze.

Gary pulled out a chair and planted himself in it. He cleared his throat again. "Look, Ro, it all started when you threw that EPT stick at me—"

Another one of his stories! Rosa gave him some bad body language—pressed lips, folded arms across her chest—to show him she wasn't very receptive to his ideas.

"The minute I saw that EPT stick, my whole *Weltanschauung*—my complete outlook on life—"

"I went to college," Rosa reminded him. "I know what *Weltanschauung* means."

Gary cleared his throat again. Okay, so his worldview changed, completely changed. He just wanted Rosa to know that he felt as if the past had been sucked down a glugging drain. There was only the future: dandling the baby—or whatever the verb was—on his knee, patting the baby's tender shoulder blades and waiting for the big burp, chucking the baby's three little chins, diapering his chubby tush, and getting a dumb, toothless smile in return. But right in the middle of some fantasy about feeding the baby pureed carrots and strained prune juice—or whatever it was that babies actually ate—Gary had this horrible vision.

"I kept on seeing this William Blake print that we had to study in one of my English Literature classes," he told Rosa. "It showed some Greek god—Kronos or one of those bozos—devouring his children. The god was all ghostly white with his big teeth chomped down on the kids' heads, and the bodies of the kids were hanging out of his mouth, stretched like saltwater taffy. But the horrible thing wasn't the image, it was the way I saw it. I mean, I identified not with the children, but with the god. All of a sudden I was the father. I was a cannibal, eating my kids before they could eat me alive."

Rosa looked scornfully at Gary.

"You said you were happy," she reminded him. "You whooped when we had the ultrasound and the technician showed us the stump between the baby's legs. All the way home in the car, you sang, *Found a penis, found a penis, found a penis last night!*"

Gary grimaced. "But inside I was miserable. The baby looked like my father. I thought, I'm perpetuating a race of midgets, the Jolly Little Fisher Men—"

"Melodrama," Rosa said.

But was it melodrama, Gary asked, that one minute he was just me, myself, and I—Gary Alan Fisher—and the next minute part of some vast continuum? "I looked in the bathroom mirror, right after you told me you were pregnant, and I swear I saw my great-grandfather, cutting leather in Warsaw. I saw my grandfather, pushing minks down 32nd Street. I saw my father, blinking his eyes behind his glasses as he said, *Customer satisfaction is the key to success!* Then I saw myself, father of my own kid, saying, *Education is the ticket, my boy.* And the worst—man, the worst—was when the kid appeared in the mirror and said, *Fuck you, Dad, who wants to be a nice Jewish boy, anyway?*"

Worthless, useless, good for nothing but bringing home money and paying the bills—that's what Gary feared most in life. "I remember being a kid and hating when my father came home in the afternoon," he told Rosa. Gary would be sitting under the black upright piano the Fishers had in their house in Flushing, messing around with his trucks and toys when all of a sudden he would hear the front door click. Artie was home. He would crawl underneath the piano and want to play with Gary. It ruined everything. Killed all his imagination. Gary couldn't be a cop. He couldn't be a fireman. He couldn't be a cowboy on the dusty Texas plain. He just had to be Artie's son, acting like it was the greatest thing in the world when Artie wanted to follow directions for the Tinkertoys and pretending he didn't notice when Artie put the log cabin roofs on backwards.

"One day my father crawled under the piano with me," Gary said. "The sleeves of his white shirt were rolled up and he had on a black tie because my grandmother had died maybe a week or so before. I was screwing around with Matchbox cars, and I got ahold of an ambulance and kept pushing it around the carpet, making that whining siren sound. Then something—I don't know what—clued me in that he didn't like the noise—so I did it even more. 'That's enough,' my dad said. 'How about playing with one of those fire trucks or this sports car?' and I kept on pushing the ambulance around, going 'EEEEEERRRRR, EEEEEEER,' until finally he put his hand over my hand and said, 'I asked you to stop, didn't you hear me?' and I said, 'I heard you'—real snotty-like. He just blinked his eyes—you know, those blue eyes of his, God, how'd they get so blue?—and he said, 'Sometimes you are nothing but heartache.' When he crawled out from the piano, he bumped his head on the bench. 'Why do we have this goddamn piano, anyway?' he said to my mother. 'No one ever plays it.' "

Gary looked expectantly at Rosa, as if she could translate all this information into a cogent moral. Rosa wrinkled up her nose to show her confusion.

"Come on, Ro," he finally said. "Don't you get it? I didn't want to be a piano that nobody wants to play."

"So you had to screw somebody else, and tell me about it?"

"I felt doomed, trapped. I swear, I can't explain it." Gary curled his hands into fists. "Now I'm doomed for real. I don't even get to be like my father. I don't get to be anyone."

Rosa's throat ached with sadness. The refrigerator clicked off, and in the silence of the kitchen, through the vents that led downstairs, Rosa heard La Luigi's TV—a Sunday morning mass, a choir singing "O Lord I Am Not Worthy." Gary crinkled up his forehead and pointed at Rosa's cup. "Can I have some of this coffee?" Rosa pushed the cup toward him, and he took a sip, then stuck out his tongue. "Tastes like crap," he said. "I need a fix. Come on—baby, baby, don't cry, it's you I love. Let's go to the Seven-Eleven."

After the Seven-Eleven—and Dunkin Donuts—and a stop at the bagel joint on Whalley—Gary and Rosa walked around the Brewster Estate, then went to the Peabody. The museum was full of dinosaur bones, shells of ancient sea turtles, fossils, arrowheads, stuffed bison and elk and a fat dodo bird that reminded Rosa of the dentist who had removed her wisdom teeth. Gary had to keep excusing himself to use the bathroom, and Rosa toured the tall, empty rooms on her own, trying to resist the urge to reach out and touch the brown bones, dessicated feathers, and moth-eaten fur on display. Somehow Rosa found it comforting to be surrounded by all these dead things. It seemed okay to die, to become part of natural history.

By the end of an hour, Rosa felt better. She went down the cold, dark stone stairwell, her Bruno Magli pumps clacking on each step, and stopped in the gift shop to wait for Gary. The display case was full of turquoise and silver jewelry, glossy minerals, and exquisite sea shells packaged in charming little boxes. Rosa rummaged through a sale basket on the counter, selecting cheap plastic dinosaurs as souvenirs for her nieces and nephews. But as her fingers lingered on the spiked backbone of a Stegosaurus, she suddenly remembered an elementary-school field trip to the museum. As all the Saint Boniface kids had filed out the wide, high doors onto Whitney Avenue, a funeral procession had gone by, a grey hearse followed by a long line of cars with their lights on. Connie had begun to sing:

Did you ever see a hearse go by
And wonder if you're gonna die?
They wrap you up in bloody sheets
And throw you down about ten feet deep!

Rosa put her hand down on the display case to steady herself as the second verse came to her: *The worms crawl in, the worms crawl out, and green salami comes out of your mouth. . . .*

"Can I help you?"

Rosa looked up into the concerned eyes of the woman behind the counter. She nodded at the plastic dinosaurs, and the woman began to ring them up. When Rosa removed her hand from the counter, five perfect fingerprints—her own mark, her fossil, white and anxious—remained on the clean glass. One good swipe of Windex and she too would be swept away.

chapter eleven

Rosa finally couldn't take the stress anymore. She opened the Yellow Pages, once again, and this time she called a shrink.

On a bitterly cold Monday afternoon, Rosa parked far down on Trumbull Street and walked two blocks to the brownstone Dr. Fine shared with a podiatrist and a CPA. On the first floor, she looked longingly at the frosted glass doors that led to the other offices. Bunions, ingrown toenails, even an audit from the IRS—all seemed like desirable problems now.

The stairwell was steep and wide and covered with a muddy red runner. Rosa's knees felt hollow by the time she got to the top. She averted her eyes and identified herself to the receptionist only as "the three o'clock appointment."

In the empty waiting room, Rosa hung up her coat and sat down on one of the light tan sofas. She noted the simplicity of the furniture, the hushed, muted tones of the tastefully framed photography, and the non-neurosis-inspiring reading material on the coffee table—*Harper's, The Wilson Quarterly, The Economist*. Within seconds, Rosa felt nothing but scorn for the entire decor. The sisal rug got on her nerves. The Southwestern-style lamp that sat on the glass end table gagged her. If Dr. Fine had come out of his office at that moment and held out his hand in greeting, Rosa surely would have said, "Excuse me for a moment while I puke all over this nice potted fern you got here." And she would have said it in her mother's voice, which she suddenly heard whispering in her ear: *You gotta be* pozza, *going to a psychiatrist, paying good money to be a crazy!*

Oh, God, what was she doing here? She was a practical woman, a working-class girl. If she wanted to spill her guts to a stranger, she should have made an appointment with her hairdresser. If she wanted advice, she could have consulted Ouija or the I Ching, or stopped in at the fortune-teller's house on the Boston Post Road, the one that had the big poster in the window that claimed *Madame Estrella Knows All.*

Rosa picked pills off the sleeves of her black sweater. *A therapist?* she could just hear Gary saying. *Christ, if you want to be happy, sign up for tap-dancing lessons.*

Rosa eyeballed her coat and considered making a bolt for the stairs. Her heart beat loud and fast, the way it used to thump when she entered the confessional and knelt down in the dark, waiting for Father to slide back the window and hear the litany of her sins. But an hour with Dr. Fine would be far worse than five minutes with Father Bruccoli. Dr. Fine would interrogate her. He would look her in the eye and ask, "Why did you spend hours, as a child, staring at the pictures that accompanied 'The Emperor's New Clothes'? Did you really strut up and down your bedroom belting out 'These Boots Are Made for Walking'? Tell me how you *really* feel about penises. And what about this fantasy you have of dancing naked in a cage?" At the end of the session, he would sit back, shrug, and offer his diagnosis. "Patient wore platform shoes in the eighth grade. She is warped for life."

Rosa might sit there, stunned. Or she might sweat and salivate and stutter and try—unsuccessfully—to defend herself with a couple of swift kicks to Dr. Fine's shitty little ego. She might say, "You want a medal, or a manly chest to pin it on?" or "What's your idea of good bedtime reading, *Twilight of the Gods*? And speaking of penises, there's this great Italian word that translates into English as 'a very big little prick.' If the shoe fits, wear it."

The more pills Rosa picked off her sweater, the more pills she found, and the more she felt her rage against Dr. Fine rising. "You know, shrinks are useless," she would tell him, "absolutely pathetic, the product of a material culture. You're worse than Toys R Us.

You're living evidence that people have too much money and don't know how to spend it right. God may be dead, but the human race has survived centuries—outstripped famines and earthquakes and wars and plagues—without your kind." Then Rosa would reach into her pockets and pull out a handgun purchased down on Dixwell Avenue. "Get out of my life, boogerface," she would threaten Dr. Fine in a gravelly voice, "and I mean by sundown."

The door to the office suddenly swung open. Rosa dropped a couple of lint pills as the real Dr. Fine came out. He was in his forties, with a close-trimmed beard greying around the edges. Bad eyeglasses, Rosa thought. Too small for his face. Rosa approved of his corduroys and the olive-colored shirt he wore beneath his brown herringbone jacket. But his yellow tie looked like cheap stone-ground mustard, tempting her to ask, *Ou est le Grey Poupon?*

Rosa kept silent. She shook Dr. Fine's hand and followed him into the office, hesitating in the center of the room as the doctor closed the door. She looked around for a couch, but there wasn't one.

"You may sit wherever you like," Dr. Fine said.

Rosa chose a wing chair with a straight back that—moments later—she realized was meant for the doctor, not the patient. But Dr. Fine didn't correct her. He sat down in the softer, lower chair, armed with a yellow legal pad and a pencil. Using a line Rosa had heard only in pick-up bars, he said, "So tell me something about yourself."

Rosa's mouth went dry. "What's to tell?" she asked.

"Tell me why you're here."

Rosa looked down at her hands. How to answer? What to say? *Mine was a desperate childhood. My husband ain't nothing but a hound dog. Ever since I got married, I look at knives funny. I saw a nun in Kentucky Fried Chicken the other day, and I envied her. I envied her!*

Rosa swallowed. "I come home from work," she finally said, "and I sit there. I just sit there, and I think, 'God, is this all there is?' "

"What is the source of that feeling? Do you know?"

"Doesn't everybody feel that way?"

"Let's concentrate on you."

Rosa rolled her right hand into a fist and covered it with her left hand. "I'm depressed," she said. "God, I'm depressed. And I'm so—hungry. All the time."

"Why don't you eat?"

"What do you mean, why don't I eat?" Rosa asked. "What do you want me to do, get fat?"

"Do you see yourself as fat?" Dr. Fine asked.

"Do *you* see me as fat?"

Dr. Fine crossed his legs. "Let me rephrase the question. Do you think *others* see you as fat?"

"You think I'm fat," Rosa said. "Great. Look at me. I'm fat."

Dr. Fine nodded. "I think it's safe to say you see yourself as overweight," he said.

No shit, Sherlock! Rosa felt like saying. *Brilliant, my dear Watson!* She looked up at the wall over the desk, where Dr. Fine's diplomas hung, and noted with satisfaction that he hadn't made Yale or Harvard, just Haverford and Penn. *So just how cracked is that Liberty Bell?* Rosa felt like asking. *Did you eat your Quaker Oats this morning?*

"Do you work?" Dr. Fine asked.

All of a sudden Rosa felt like a greasy-haired adolescent moping in the corner. She answered, "Yeah."

"What do you do?"

"I'm a social worker."

Dr. Fine noted this on his legal pad. "Married?" he asked.

"What's that got to do with it?"

Dr. Fine smiled slightly, as if he had just found out something significant. "What is *it*?" he asked.

"What is *what*?"

"What does *it* stand for to you?"

"What are you talking about?"

Dr. Fine nodded patiently. "Let me replay the scenario. I asked you if you were married and you replied, 'What's that got to do with it?' And then I asked you, 'What is *it*, what does *it* represent to you?'"

"This isn't a philosophy class," Rosa stated. Dr. Fine looked impassively at Rosa, who felt compelled to keep on talking and fill up the silence. "I don't like Duns Scotus," Rosa continued. "And I don't give two shits about how many angels can hop around on the end of a pin."

"I take it you grew up Catholic?" Dr. Fine asked.

"Who else would envy a nun?" Rosa asked, forgetting that she had not talked out loud about Sister Kentucky Fried Chicken, who, incidentally, had ordered the twelve-piece dinner with six extra biscuits, a large and greasy meal Rosa easily could have sucked up, solo, in a matter of five minutes if someone gave her half the chance.

Rosa saw Dr. Fine write "Catholic" on his legal pad. From Rosa's point of view, he may as well have written *leper. Freak. Self-flagellator. Sexual fuck-up,* with a whopper inferiority complex. Dr. Fine probably scorned Catholics, thought they were undereducated, superstitious, anti-intellectual, responsible for three-quarters of the potholes on the New Haven streets. Or maybe he didn't disdain them. Maybe he liked them. Maybe he had a thing for Catholic girls. Maybe he was sitting there thinking about how much gold Rosa had on underneath her blouse and wondering just how hot those miraculous medals got in her cleavage.

Dr. Fine looked at Rosa. Rosa looked back, listened to the quiet in the office, and had the bizarre urge to break out into song—*The Sound of Silence, You're a Grand Old Flag, Saturday Night Fever.* What would Dr. Fine do if Rosa jumped up from her chair and bleated like Art Garfunkel or a sheep in heat, oom-pah-pahed on an imaginary tuba, or cavorted like a disco dancer? Would he simply take another note on his legal pad or would he lay down his pencil and politely say, "Excuse me while I book a padded cell for you at Yale New Haven Hospital?" Oh, if only Rosa had gone back to Mr. Charles! He would have bent over her with his blow dryer and scissors and said, *You don't need psychiatric help, honey, you just need more fats in your diet.*

Rosa stared at Dr. Fine. From the other corner of the room, she heard the digital clock slip onto the next number. Jesus! Another minute, another two dollars wasted. Rosa gulped, then blurted out, "I'm lonely. My father died. I had a miscarriage. My husband cheated on me. My life is miserable, I hate my job, I drive back from work and fantasize about turning the steering wheel and smashing myself right into a telephone pole. I want to eat Twinkies and Swiss Rolls and Ho-Hos. If I don't get some potato chips and french fries and onion rings, I'm gonna kill myself, that's it, I'm just going to kill myself or do something desperate, like sleep with some stupid guy I don't even like or—or—or—have plastic surgery!"

"What part would you fix?"

"My face."

"What's wrong with it?"

"It doesn't look happy."

Dr. Fine took detailed notes on all of this. He went to his desk and fetched a box of Kleenex. Rosa ripped one of the pale blue, slightly perfumed tissues out of the box and tried to honk her nose into it. But she wasn't crying. Her eyes, for once, were dry. Rosa crumpled up the Kleenex and threw it down into her lap. *You probably could lower your rate five bucks an hour if you just bought generic,* she felt like telling him.

"You seem to be a very angry person," Dr. Fine said.

Rosa could have let out a primal scream. She could have reached up on his desk and winged his precious cut-glass paperweight across the room, like shotput in seventh-grade gym. But it was important to get a grip. So she confined herself to a polite nod.

"We may want to devote our first few sessions to finding the source of your anger," Dr. Fine said. "Later, we might want to look at ways to channel your anger into constructive action."

What do I look like, Rosa felt like saying, some macaroni-and-glue Girl Scout project? But she kept silent. Because for now—according to the great Dr. Fine—it was more important to talk about Rosa's feelings toward herself and others.

"Tell me something about your husband," Dr. Fine said.

"He has severe sinus problems."

Dr. Fine duly recorded this on his legal pad. "Any other characteristics you'd like to mention?"

"He's dying."

"What is the—uh—problem? The illness?"

"Cancer."

"How does this make you feel?"

"Oh, like a million bucks, you can imagine."

"Are you angry at him for being sick?"

Rosa looked down at her lap. "How can I get mad at him? I get mad at God."

"Leaving your concept of God aside for a moment, do you feel anger at your husband for leaving you behind?"

"He would have left me anyway," Rosa said.

"How do you know?"

"Jesus, take better notes, I just told you he fucked somebody else!"

"Has he continued to have relations with her?"

"He said it was a fling."

"Did you know her?"

"She was skinny. And she wore red shoes, do you believe it? Tacky."

Dr. Fine nodded—in agreement? Or just to show sympathy? "Have you ever had an extramarital affair?" Dr. Fine asked.

"I told you, I'm Catholic."

"Have you ever *wanted* to have an extramarital affair?"

I lust for men, Rosa felt like saying, *as I lust for Ring Dings!*

She shook her head vehemently.

"What sort of emotions do you feel toward your husband?" Dr. Fine asked.

Rosa hesitated. "You know that scene in *Fiddler on the Roof,* when Tevye asks Golde if she loves him, and she shrieks back, *WHAT?*"

Dr. Fine stared at Rosa.

Stupid asshole, Rosa thought. No sense of humor. Stupid Rosa. Acting like a jerk!

"I don't know why I just did that," Rosa said. "I mean, that's the kind of thing Gary would do, start acting out some musical number when you ask him a serious question. God. He drives me crazy."

"Have you ever considered leaving him?"

What do you need, a date on Friday night or something? Rosa felt like asking. But she said, "How am I going to leave him? My mother's still alive."

"Tell me, briefly, about your mother."

Rosa looked at the clock. At breakneck speed, she launched into her anti-Antoinette spiel. "She's always got tomato sauce stains all over her clothes. She says *Mamma mia* way too much, you couldn't put it in a book, people wouldn't believe you. She used to keep mittens together by clipping them with a wooden clothespin. She doesn't like black people, the Irish have too much money, she thinks all Jews are going to hell. She likes her dog better than she likes me."

Dr. Fine took copious notes. At the end of Rosa's speech, he asked a series of mundane questions, the answers to which he could have gotten through a patient questionnaire had he bothered to give one to Rosa. Then he flipped back the pages of the legal pad and said, "I think we've made quite a bit of progress here today."

Rosa tried to keep her lip from curling in disgust. *You're a cheat,* she could have said, *a charlatan, a magician who slides his hands into a man's pocket and steals his wallet, a phoney, a fake-o, a misogynist. You've got the moxie, sitting there passing judgment on me. You're probably a closet alcoholic, your wife pops Valium, your kids snort Ready Whip, your rec room has an orange shag rug. Physician, heal thyself.*

Dr. Fine held open a door—a different door than the one Rosa had entered—and Rosa stepped out into the lobby. Dr. Fine suggested that Rosa wait until the receptionist got off the phone so she could schedule another appointment for next week. He shut the door and went on to his next looney-tune for the day. For a moment, Rosa simply stood there. Then, realizing she wasn't obliged—she didn't have to come back, she didn't have to listen to his bullshit—she grabbed her coat off the rack and bolted for the door. He had the nerve. And a fucking ugly tie, all it needed was a hot dog to match and he could have opened a wiener stand downtown on the Green.

Rosa ran down the steps, afraid the receptionist would follow in hot pursuit, shouting, "Mrs. Salvatore, Mrs. Salvatore!" to which Rosa might reply, *That's Ms. to you, bitch!*

Out on the street, Rosa held her breath as she passed the overflowing garbage cans by the curb. She hurried to her car. Her hands trembled. She dropped her gloves, and then her keys, before she finally got into the Honda and leaned her forehead on the steering wheel. She started the car with a roar (Gary's voice: *Jesus, how many times do I have to tell you, don't flood the engine?*) and charged out of the parking space.

She could not go home. Yet it was too cold for a walk. The art museum was closed on Mondays. She could not deal with the mall. She might purchase a giant-sized bag of caramel corn from the little red snack wagon by the fountain and eat the entire thing, paper bag and all. She might take the escalator up to the second level and station herself right in front of the potpourri shop that always stunk like a week-old vaseful of lilies of the valley. She would plunge herself off the balcony and land splat on the tile in front of the Victoria's Secret window, rueing the fact that she had lived on this fine planet for over a quarter of a century and had never purchased—or worn—a leopard-skin bra and matching panties.

Rosa pulled up to the stop sign on the corner of Trumbull and Orange. Suddenly the decision to turn right or turn left felt like a clamp on her head. Was this it? The real thing? Had the crazies finally come home to stay? Well, swell. Fine. Rosa would just go with the flow. She would go berserk. Why not? The world wanted berserk, expected berserk, she'd show 'em berserk. She would go to church.

Over by Whitney Avenue stood a black stone church, Saint Somebody or Other's, that Rosa once attended, years ago, to hear a harpsichord concert. The performer was a tiny man with long fingers and a head of fiery-red hair. He had reminded Rosa of a water globe she used to own that depicted Santa's workshop. When you shook the globe, pellets of white snow bombarded the workbench and tools and old-fashioned toys, all crafted by a solitary red-haired elf.

Rosa parked on Audubon and walked up Whitney, past the run-down storefront of Clark's Dairy, the underground bookshop, and the music stores that displayed gleaming black grand pianos in the windows. The cold gnawed at her ears and fingers, and by the time she finally reached the iron gates of the church, she realized the building probably would be locked. The last time Gary and Rosa had visited her mother, Antoinette had gone on and on about how people were defiling the churches in New Haven. "These days," Antoinette said. "These days they gotta lock the doors of the church to keep the homeless people out. They say there are dope addicts making drug deals in the vestibule, can you imagine? They steal the robes and the candles, the water and the wine. They go into the tabernacle and—" she crossed herself "—defecate the hosts."

"I think that's *desecrate,*" Gary corrected her.

The iron railings that surrounded the church were coated with ice. Rosa hesitated before she climbed the steps and pulled at the handle of the heavy wooden door at the top. To her surprise, the door opened. It gave a hushed thud as it closed behind her.

The vestibule was dark, lit only by a small bulb above the holy water fount. Rosa dipped her finger into the cold water and crossed herself. At the front of the church, the votives glowed on both sides of the altar, casting flickers of light on the statues of the saints in the alcoves. Rosa walked to the back pew and let her eyes follow the red carpet all the way up the center aisle to the table draped in cloth that stood behind the altar.

For a moment, she was suffused with the memory of being the maid of honor at Connie's wedding, of standing in the vestibule, her bouquet pressed tight against her stomach as the organ modulated and sighed and began to bellow out the opening chords of the wedding march. Someone shoved the ring bearer forward, and the flower girl trotted behind. Then the bridesmaids began to march, one by one, until Rosa stood flanked by the vestibule doors, paralyzed by the thought of walking all the way down the aisle. What an enormous distance it seemed to the altar. How far and yet how near! Why, it could have been her, marching up the aisle on one man's arm and coming back down it on the arm of another. Why was the organ moaning? Why was the organist prolonging each dah-dah-dah-dah, so that Rosa, who wanted to rush up the aisle and get it over with, was forced to walk very slowly, the bouquet trembling in her hand, everyone's eyes upon her, not daring to look behind to see if Connie and Uncle Dino really were following her, and half-hoping Connie would stay behind. . . .

Rosa put her hand down on the smooth wood of the back pew. She had never—and now, never would—walk up the aisle for any man. She had slept with Gary the night before they got married. She had raced home and gotten dressed and met him in Battell Chapel, and even though Antoinett: tried to hide her from him, claiming it was bad luck for the groom to set eyes on the bride, Gary walked right up to her and said loudly, "Hey, haven't I seen you somewhere before?"

Rosa smiled weakly at him. And when Antoinette glared and moved away, Gary whispered in Rosa's ear, "Didn't we have a close encounter recently? Like, just last night?"

Rosa pinched him and told him his tie was crooked, which it was, and he said, "Turn around, lemme see if your slip is showing," and Rosa suddenly felt as happy as a clam. To think that there would be a whole lifetime of this intimacy, of whispering in public, *Missed your belt loop in the back,* or *Pssst, your bra strap's showing,* or *En garde—big booger, left nostril.*

Now, nothing. Never. The days of the fashion police, the snot patrol, were numbered. So maybe it hadn't been so hot the past few years. Maybe they had fought like a couple of animals locked up in too small of a cage. But they also had some good times together— just tossing dried Challah crumbs to the flock of pigeons gathered on the New Haven Green, yodeling off the top tower of Gillette's Castle, munching on crinkled fries and buttery lobster rolls out at Jimmy's on Savin Rock. God, Gary was all Rosa had besides her own stupid self. He was all she ever loved. And God, he irritated her, but at least he made her feel like she was alive, and soon she would be among the living dead, left with nothing but voices, the memory of him saying all sorts of disjointed things. *Nice neighborhood you got here. I think your mother's got the hots for me. It's your pal, Adonai. You fucked a cop? I can't believe it, you fucked a cop!* The voices would fade down to a whisper, and then even the whispers would go dead. Rosa would be left trapped inside her silent self, in a body that felt empty and longed to be filled in.

Rosa slowly walked up the center aisle of the church, passing the pews, the stations of the cross, the stained-glass windows muted dark green and purple from the lack of light. At the front of the church the candles flickered and flowers perfumed the air. Behind the altar, on the cross that seemed too huge and superhuman, hung a porcelain Christ, his head limp and turned to the side, the crown of thorns pressed into his temples, the muscles beneath his arms and shoulders stretched tight. His abdomen dripped blood. Nails punctured his graceful feet.

Rosa knelt at the altar rail, the way she used to go down to receive Communion before they ruled that parishioners should stand while taking the host into their mouths. *Body of Christ,* the priest used to intone over and over. *Body of Christ. Body of Christ.*

Wasn't that what she really wanted, needed?

Rosa clasped her hands on the altar rail. "Oh God," she whispered, "enter me."

chapter twelve

Rosa began her leave from work when Gary grew too tired to even get out of bed in the morning; when the very suggestion of moving from the bedroom to the living-room couch produced a look of doubt and despair. "I'm fine where I am," he said as he lay on the mattress. "Pop open the shade, will you, so I can look out at the trees?"

Rosa popped the shade to the top of the window. The black branches of the maples glistened with water from the March drizzle; the sky looked grey and thick as schoolroom paste. Rosa thanked God that spring always came late in New Haven. She thought of how painful it would be to leave the world just as the air became scented with lilac, forsythia, dogwood, and magnolia, and the noontime church bells seemed to ring with wild abandon. How sad Gary would be to look outside and see the whole world turning those joyful colors—bright yellow and soft, light green. How mournful he would be, denied a walk around the duck pond at Edgewood Park or the long drive on the Hartford Turnpike to the Wadsworth Atheneum, where he and Rosa would sigh over the hushed tones of Eakins' portraits and back away from the black holes of Rothko's despair. In Hartford, Gary and Rosa would buy a bag of popcorn outside the museum and eat it down to the old maids as they strolled around the wide green lawn, while the daffodils bobbed in the breeze and the gold dome of the state capitol glinted in the warm sun.

But this was not to be. The trees were bare; the sky was grey; and WYBC, sensing the listeners' anxiety for the arrival of spring, over-played *The Four Seasons*. At least it seemed like Vivaldi was aired once a day during the week Rosa stayed at home with Gary. Rosa turned on the radio for Gary every morning. She got him some water and held the back of his painfully thin neck as he leaned forward to drink. Then he sank back onto his pillow and drifted in and out of sleep, while WYBC's announcer reported the dates and times of concerts that neither Gary nor Rosa could ever dream of going to, concerts where musical pieces would be played that Gary likely would never hear again.

"Well," he said after one announcement, "I always hated Shostakovitch anyway."

Rosa hardly knew what to do with herself. While he slept in the bedroom, she sat in the living room, waiting for something to happen. It seemed like a sin to eat anything, to turn on the TV (where everyone looked overly made-up, well-dressed, and disgustingly healthy) or to glance through a magazine, thick with ads for material goods that Rosa now quite clearly understood you couldn't take with you. Rosa gazed out the window at the dull grey sky and thought about vanity. Why had she spent so many hours puckering her lips in front of the mirror as she applied three coats of Raspberry Rose lipstick? Why had she walked the mall until her heels burned, just to find the right pair of sandals to match a particular dress? She was disgusted with herself—and yet she wanted that old self back, vain as she was, because that vanity—that desperate hunt for the lipstick and the shoes—seemed a sign of caring about herself, of desiring to live.

To keep herself occupied, Rosa got up and straightened the kitchen. She put the dishes away and scrubbed the sink with a Brillo pad and blue abrasive cleanser. She checked on Gary—asleep. She checked on Gary again. Then she returned to the chair by the living-room window and stared at the same trees that Gary, every morning, seemed so eager to look at. The only difference was that Rosa could lean her head against the pane and see not only the wild, bare branches swaying in the March wind, but all the way down the rough trunk to the gnarled roots that had worked their way through the cracked sidewalk.

Rosa found herself waiting for the mailman. She watched him troop down the opposite sidewalk and then work his way back up the street, arriving at their house just before noon. Rosa took a long time going down the three flights to fetch the mail. She usually met La Luigi somewhere on her way down or way back up. Funny how wonderful, how comforting, La Luigi seemed to her now. La Luigi always asked after Gary, and Rosa reported on the little things: Gary had drunk half a glass of water. He had trouble sleeping. He had hummed a little bit of the Beethoven symphony played on the radio that morning. He had talked on the phone to his parents for all of ten minutes the night before.

La Luigi listened to it all. Then she told Rosa to wait. She disappeared into her apartment and came onto the landing holding a Rubbermaid container full of minestrone, a pan of eggplant parmigiana, or a loaf of Easter bread baked in the shape of a basket, with a couple of hard-boiled eggs squatting inside. Rosa always looked reluctant to accept her gift, and La Luigi always looked offended that Rosa would even dream of denying it.

"What else do I got to do with myself?" La Luigi asked. "After your husband dies, there's so much time."

Rosa nodded. She balanced the mail on top of the food container and went back upstairs.

"La Luigi made fried peppers," she told Gary.

"Mmm," he said. But his voice had no enthusiasm.

"You want some?"

"Nah."

"You want anything?"

"Nah."

Rosa waited, on the verge of tears. And to comfort her he always said, "Bring your lunch in here, you want to bring your lunch in here?"

Rosa brought her lunch in on a tray and Gary shared bits and pieces—a little bit of bread, some pea soup, a bite of chicken left over from the night before. Then Rosa set the tray aside and crawled into bed with him, turning her back and letting him put his arm around her. "You're getting skinny," he whispered as they drifted, together, off to sleep.

Rosa loved napping with Gary—snuggling against him, listening to him breathing, while the radiator clanked and whistled and the digital clock clicked as she sank into sleep. It was the best part of her day. But waking from the nap was the worst part. She always turned right over, quickly, to check on Gary. She was terrified he would die in bed next to her with his arms locked around her, and the stiffness of his dead body would not permit her to escape. She imagined herself trying to disengage from his embrace. She heard the crack of his bones; she felt the beating of her own broken heart. What a relief it was to turn over and find his fingers clutching his pillow, his thin shoulders rising almost imperceptibly as he breathed in and out.

When she woke she called the oncologist's office and reported on Gary's progress to the nurse. She had to keep track of how much he ate and how much he *eliminated,* a word that never failed to amuse Gary. "Makes taking a crap sound like a boxer knocking someone out," he said.

Finally, one day Rosa had to admit to the nurse that Gary hadn't downed a crumb and had eliminated even less. Dr. Makoff called her back.

"You could leave him at home," the doctor said. "Or you could bring him in. He might hold on longer at the hospital. A week, two weeks, perhaps." His voice was hurried. Rosa imagined the reports stacked up on his desk, his four examination rooms each populated by a shivering man or woman in a paper robe. She hesitated, and in her hesitation the doctor read assent. "You've done a wonderful job, now let the nurses do theirs," Dr. Makoff said. "I'll get him a bed."

Before they left, Rosa helped Gary into the bathroom, then went to search for her purse. Gary was in the bathroom for a long time. For as long as Rosa had known him, he had had the habit of peeing, flushing, and then combing his hair. Rosa heard the pee, a sad, weak dribble. The flush. The creak of the medicine cabinet, the scratch of the comb pulled through what was left of his matted, wiry hair. Then she heard a dull thud, a sickening sound. He had thrown his black comb into the wastebasket.

"I'm ready," he said when he came out.

The drive down Whalley went fairly quickly. Rosa kept thinking, *The last time, this is the last time . . .* that he would ever be outside, that he would see the streets, that he would drive past Saint Lawrence and Mishkan Israel cemeteries, that he would hear the bells of the churches on the green ringing out into the afternoon. When they stopped for a red light at the intersection of Whalley and Dixwell, Rosa looked over at him. His eyes looked dreamy.

"What are you thinking about?" she asked.

"Something stupid," he said.

"What?"

"That I've never, in my entire life, liked anyone named Steve." Gary smiled weakly, and Rosa noticed how yellowed his teeth had become. Tears came to her eyes. The light changed. Cars began to honk. "Come on, cut it out," Gary said. "You're the driver now. Put it into gear. Drive."

Artie and Mimi insisted on paying for a private room. For this, Rosa was grateful. There were no roommates for Gary to acknowledge, no other families trooping in and out, no TVs blaring basketball games or talk shows. There was just a large, grime-streaked window that looked out over George Street, a high bed with thick metal rails, and the comforting drip of the IV, like rain sliding down the window on a Sunday afternoon.

While Gary was in the hospital, Artie and Mimi came in from Long Island and stayed at the downtown Sheraton. Artie praised the buffet breakfast. Mimi criticized the service. "But after all," she told Rosa, her eyes bloodshot and dry, "we don't expect to stay there long."

"Yes," Rosa said.

"It's horrible to say so, but it will be a relief." She looked hard at Rosa, obviously wanting her to agree. "Don't you feel, sometimes, that it will be a relief?"

Rosa nodded, and each little movement of her head seemed a betrayal of Gary.

Yet Gary turned out to be one of those people who hung in there much longer than anyone could have imagined. One week on the IV and increasingly larger doses of morphine stretched into two. Occasionally he woke up and called Rosa's name, expressing the thought that was on everyone's mind: *Oh. I'm still here.*

No one did a very good job of hiding their surprise and impatience. After the first few days, they all just sat around the hospital room, no longer trying to put a good face on things or keep up any extended conversation. Rosa sat by the bed, dozing off every once in a while in the big armchair. Artie sat by the window. He sighed and looked at the *Times.* Mimi had a book called *Picking Up the Pieces: Help for Life's Big Changes.* She seemed to be reading the same page over and over again.

Antoinette, who came every afternoon, hovered in the hallway until Artie or Mimi invited her in. "I don't want to intrude," she said. Then she picked the hardest, most uncomfortable chair in the room and squatted on it for at least two hours. She crocheted pot holders for the church bazaar. Rosa stared at the ugly squares of yarn—bright orange and green and pink surrounded by black borders—and could hardly bear it.

Antoinette became very officious when someone she knew was on the brink of death. She was all ready to go. She had her black dress ironed and her bid for Masses put in. She told Rosa that she wanted to pay for a grave wreath, but she wasn't sure what kind. What sort of burial did Artie and Mimi have planned? Were flowers even allowed? What color should she choose?

"I don't know, Mother," Rosa said. "Just tell the florists not to put a cross on it."

"A cross," Antoinette said. "*Madonna,* what do you take me for? I know better than that."

Sometimes, to break the monotony of the afternoon, Antoinette and Artie struck up a conversation. They exchanged stories about their own childhoods, and then Artie told stories about when Gary was young. Rosa was grateful he did this only when Gary was asleep, because Artie overdid it, in a way that would have annoyed Gary to no end. Artie showed Antoinette all the pictures of Gary he carried in his wallet—from the first picture of baby Gary, taken in the hospital ("Imagine, I've carried it around with me all these years"), to the picture of Gary posing with a scooter in front of the brownstone in Flushing, to the picture of a long-haired Gary in his cap and gown at Columbia. Rosa hated that graduation photo. The golden tassel of the mortarboard hung too far to the front and cast a shadow on Gary's face; he squinted into the camera and sported the sort of obnoxious smile children always wore when their overly proud parents were the ones behind the camera.

Artie showed these photos as if they could contradict the picture right in front of their eyes of Gary's sunken cheeks on the pillow and skeletal hands on top of the white hospital sheet. Then he began to eulogize Gary.

"I always knew he was a genius," Artie said. "His first word was *Chekhov.*"

Antoinette nodded blankly. "That something you people eat?" she asked.

Mimi pressed her lips together with disgust. "His first word was *bubba,*" she corrected Artie. "For bubbles. Remember, we were at Jones Beach? Sylvia had one of those magic wands. She knelt in the sand—she had on a turquoise bathing suit with yellow flowers, and bright pink lipstick that smeared all over the wand when she puckered her lips and blew the bubbles all over the blanket. Gary was delighted. He clapped his hands and said *Bubba, bubba.* And Sylvia was furious because Benny was two months older and still couldn't do anything but grunt."

"Gary had on a sailor hat," Artie said.

"You had on the sailor hat," Mimi said. "And then you put it on his head and his whole face disappeared and he giggled."

"He had a full head of black hair when he was born," Artie said.

Mimi did not contradict this.

"His right big toe seemed unusually large," Artie continued. "I always thought there was something strange about that toe—"

"It is big," Rosa said.

Mimi sighed. "I was so embarrassed when Artie asked the doctor, 'Look at this toe. Do you think this kind of toe is normal?' "

"I just wanted to know if he would need special shoes."

Mimi gestured at Artie. "He actually took Gary in to see one of his customers who owned a Buster Brown shop."

"I wanted a second opinion," Artie said.

"You were crazy about him," Mimi said. "Wild about him. Absolutely spoiled him."

"Well," Artie said. "Why not? That's what it's all about."

Rosa noted, with bitterness, that Antoinette looked mystified by that comment. She kept fiddling with her glasses as she peered at the photos of Gary, until Artie pointed out to her that her bifocals probably were crooked. He took out the little gold screwdriver set he always kept in his pocket and adjusted Antoinette's frames.

"What do you know?" Antoinette said to Rosa, as if she had doubted Artie ever had worked for a living. "He fixed it."

To show her gratitude, Antoinette offered Artie the sports section from the newspaper. While he read the scores, Antoinette clucked her tongue over the crimes reported on the front page of the *Register.* "What is the world coming to," she kept repeating, until Rosa, sensing the force of Mimi's disgust and disapproval, finally said, "Mother, stop it. Just stop it."

The presence of Gary's parents, and Rosa's own mother, annoyed Rosa to no end. They hovered. They never left her alone with Gary, except during lunch. Since there was an unspoken agreement that someone would stay with him at all times, except during the night, they went to lunch in shifts. Rosa considered herself lucky if Gary woke up during the hour she had alone with him. But even if he were awake, she could not count on him saying anything.

The morphine, at first, made him babble. Late at night he told long, circuitous stories. Then his verbal ability began to shut down.

He spoke only in short questions: *Where are my parents? Did the doctor come?* After that, he asked for things in one word only: *Water. Washcloth. Piss.* If no nurse was around, Rosa had to hold the red bottle over his flaccid penis and keep it there until he could muster the energy to concentrate and let the piss out. Then the nurses put him on a catheter. His urine came out infrequently, tinged with brown. Rosa watched it slide down the tube on the side of the bed. It seemed the saddest sight in the world.

Rosa found herself picking up the *Register* every night, just like her mother, to read the obituaries. Rosa's first lay teacher of catechism, Mrs. Anita Ponciroli, died of cancer. A man who lived down the street from Aldo and Antoinette—known, for some unnamed reason, as Brutus—died of natural causes at age ninety-four. Rosa looked at the picture of Brutus' wizened face and remembered how he used to sit in his backyard, perfectly still, in a green lawn chair. He smoked a pipe, and the smell of his fragrant tobacco seemed to permeate the entire neighborhood. Rosa once had gone inside Brutus' yard because she was selling tickets for the Saint Boniface spring raffle. She went up to his chair. He did not acknowledge her. Rosa turned and ran, frightened by the grey hairs growing in his ear.

One afternoon there was a short notice in the obituaries for Ivory White. Rosa was not surprised. When Gary first was checked into the hospital, Rosa had gotten off on the wrong floor. As she walked down the hallway to take the stairs another flight up, she bumped into Ivory in the hallway. He sat out in the lobby in a wheelchair, his body skinny and wasted.

"Lady," he said. "You come to visit me." He smiled at her.

And Rosa—who had no intention of visiting Ivory, who had not even known he was in the hospital—nodded. She sat down next to him on an easy chair.

"How you been, Lady?" he asked.

"Fine, Ivory."

"Long time," he said, and repeated, "How you been?"

Rosa took this as a cue to tell him the truth. "Do you remember the man who helped you at Legal Counsel?" she asked Ivory.

He squinted, then shook his head.

Rosa sat back in her chair. How insignificant each person was! Someone who had played such a large role in her life now was hardly memorable to Ivory.

"We got married, Ivory," Rosa said. "I married him."

"Lucky man," Ivory said. "Children?"

Rosa shook her head. "He's sick," she said. "My husband is sick, he has cancer."

Ivory held out his hand. Rosa took it tentatively, then, remembering he had AIDS, quickly let it go. She immediately was ashamed of herself. She burst into tears. She felt like she was expressing the crux of everything, the whole human condition, when she said, "I'm scared to die."

Ivory nodded.

A week later he was cremated by the state. There was no service. Rosa wished there had been. She wished she could have put on a black dress and gone to a storefront church on Dixwell Avenue, where the women keened and moaned and the men yelled *Say it, brother!* as the preacher spoke, and behind an out-of-tune piano played by some ninety-year-old woman, a choir in white robes swayed and sang "Amazing Grace." Rosa would have gone to that service. Then she would have come straight from the church to see Gary, still wearing her black dress.

In this fantasy, Rosa was all alone in the hospital room with Gary.

Ivory White died, she would say.

Oh.

They cremated him. I went to the service. It turned out he had family, brothers, sisters. They sang gospel music. I was the only white person there.

You look pretty. Are you going to wear that? That dress. For me.

I guess. I hadn't thought—

You look pretty.

Stop saying that.

Listen, I don't want cremation. I want to be buried.

Okay, okay.

*And my father. He has this prayer shawl. He showed it to me once.
It was my grandfather's, he brought it over from Poland. Ask him—
don't ask my mother—if I can have it—you know—they drape it
around your shoulders. Tell my father. Tell my father I want a real service, I want a rabbi, I want him to say Kaddish. Tell my father. He said
I could have whatever I want, whatever I wanted. He said he would
take care of it.*

Okay, Rosa would say.

If only they could have some kind of talk like that. Then what
Gary wanted would be clear. But it was not so easy. Artie and Mimi
seemed to be bickering about the arrangements. "What kind of ceremony did he tell you he wanted?" Mimi asked Rosa out in the hallway one morning. "Artie said Gary told him he wanted to have a
rabbi, and I said nonsense, he's never believed in anything before."

"He believed," Rosa said. Then, catching a glimpse through the
doorway of Gary's feet in the hospital bed, she corrected herself.
"Believes."

"He never told me anything about that," Mimi said. "And if he
really wanted it, why did he tell Artie? He should have told *me.* He
should know that I'm the one who does everything around the
house—"

"A funeral isn't *around the house,*" Rosa said.

"—and I'm the one who always makes the arrangements," Mimi
said.

Mimi's head quivered with anger, and Rosa once again had the
impression that she was a puppet or marionette. "Gary told me that
Artie had a prayer shawl from Poland," Rosa said. Then she ventured to lie, because she knew the lie would annoy Mimi and would
have given intense pleasure to Gary. "He said he wanted to be buried in it."

"I don't believe it," Mimi said.

Rosa shrugged. "Then don't listen," she said. "It's on your head."

Rosa left the hallway and went back into Gary's room. She sat beside his bed and refused to look at Mimi. Mimi came back in a few
minutes later and refused to look at Rosa. In his chair by the win-

dow, Artie kept clearing his throat so much that Mimi snapped, "If you're going to say something, then say it."

"I have a frog in my throat," Artie finally said.

"Then get a drink and stop tormenting us with those noises!"

Rosa chewed the inside of her mouth to keep from screaming. Gary opened his eyes, for a second, then closed them. The IV continued to drip, like that phenomenon Rosa once had read about in *Reader's Digest:* Chinese water torture! The sound was enough to drive anyone insane.

When Antoinette showed up in late morning, earlier than usual, Artie finally had someone to talk to. "Come to lunch," he told Antoinette.

Mimi tapped her shoe on the floor to show her displeasure. "You come, too," she said to Rosa, clearly thinking Rosa's presence would help her deal better with Antoinette. "Gary's asleep now. We all need a break."

"Yes, we all need a break," Artie said.

"Come," Mimi said. "It will do you good."

Rosa refused. She could not wait for them to clear out of the hospital room—their yakking and bickering sickened her; their very breath got on her nerves. She felt like applauding as she listened to their voices fading down the hall. She prayed they would not return to fetch something forgotten—a purse, a glove, a car key. After two or three minutes, she finally relaxed. The nurses were done with their morning rounds, and the room was completely silent except for the soft, barely audible sound of Gary's breathing and the trickle of the IV.

Gary's eyes flickered, then opened. He turned his head toward her. "Hey," he said.

Rosa stood up and leaned over him.

"Everybody here?" he asked, looking up at her.

"They went to lunch."

"Why not you, too?"

"I wanted to stay with you."

He was quiet for a while. Rosa sat down again.

"I'm having weird dreams," he finally said.

Rosa stood up and leaned over the bed rail again. "What of?"

"I can't remember." He stared at the ceiling. "Aren't you hungry?" he asked. "I can tell you're hungry."

Rosa, who had a strong gnawing sensation in her stomach, suddenly felt as hollow as a dried gourd. "I'll go when they come back."

He looked at her, and his glazed eyes seemed too big for their sockets. "Go ahead now," he said. "Go on. Go. Eat something big for me." He turned his head. "Think I'll sleep a while."

Rosa watched his eyes close and his hands freeze in one position, like dried clay, on top of the sheet. It reminded her of how she and Connie, who once saw a made-for-TV movie about a quadriplegic, used to hole up in Rosa's bedroom and play Paralysis. "Pretend you can't move," Connie said. "Your whole body is there, but it isn't there. It's not even numb, like when your foot falls asleep."

Rosa lay perfectly still on the mattress. "I feel like I'm in a plaster cast."

"I feel like I'm a looney-tune in a straitjacket," Connie said, lying perfectly still beside her.

"I feel like a person who's going to die," Rosa said.

"I feel like I'm already dead," Connie said. She closed her eyes. "I'm in the pits of hell. Here comes the devil. He's got a pitchfork. He's going to stick it in my butt." Connie leaped up on the bed and began giggling and writhing on the mattress. "Ants in my pants!" she hollered.

"Saint Vitus' dance," Rosa shouted as she stood up and joined Connie on the mattress, shaking and shivering her limbs. And nothing had seemed more amusing, more full of fun, than doing what Antoinette strictly had forbidden because they would break their necks and cost their parents millions of dollars in medical bills: jumping up and down on the bed.

While the Fishers and Antoinette had been in the room, Rosa had longed for nothing more than being alone with Gary. But now that she was there with Gary—watching him sleep and thinking about paralysis and death—the room suddenly seemed as claustrophobic as a telephone booth on a hot summer day. Rosa craved to get out. Hadn't Gary even told her to go?

She hesitated only for a moment before she got up, fetched her purse, and took the elevator down to the basement, not to the employee cafeteria, where the food was better and cheaper, but to the snack bar that was for the families of patients. There she wouldn't bump into anyone she worked with; she would not have to suffer from Donna's pitying glances or Terry's tough facade of concern. She could simply be who she was: the family member of yet another patient, who took a plastic orange tray off the stack and slid it along the metal bars that lined the counter, surveying with no enthusiasm the wilted lettuce with the perfect little scoop of cottage cheese on top, the grilled cheese sandwiches glowing under the warmer lights, and the solitary brownie on a chipped porcelain plate.

Rosa got coffee and a tuna fish sandwich on whole wheat. The sandwich came on a white paper plate with some stale potato chips and a slice of kosher pickle. She sat down at a corner table meant for two and stared morosely at the specks of catsup left behind on the laminated tabletop. The cinderblock walls were painted a tannish color that reminded Rosa of her father's old polyester suit, worn only to Easter Mass and weddings. He had worn the suit with a red tie and lace-up shoes, bright white with too many coats of polish. That outfit had never failed to embarrass Rosa.

Rosa chewed on her potato chips. Too salty. Through the windows, set high up toward the ceiling, Rosa saw green buds on some of the bushes, and a robin pecking at something on the lawn. Then she saw people—or rather, people's calves and feet—walking by. Purposefully by. They had somewhere to go. They were outside. They were not trapped within the walls of the hospital, where the air smelled like Band-Aids and overcooked broccoli, where the minutes seemed like hours and the hours and days moved so slowly that Rosa felt suspended, like an insect trapped in honey, forever in one time and place.

Watching those feet, Rosa felt a pang of intense loneliness, an indescribable yearning, a feeling of being cut off from herself and the whole world that reminded her of what she used to feel when she returned home from work and sat in her apartment all by herself, thinking, *God, is this all there is? Is this all?*

Rosa ate her sandwich. She sipped her coffee and felt herself slipping into despair. *I need something,* she thought. *I need somebody.* She thought about Dr. Mehta, about the time he had come out of the operating room after Gary's last surgery, wearing those turquoise-blue scrubs, the surgical hat and mask hanging behind and in front of his neck. His black hair was ruffled and his face was red and sweaty, like a boy who had just spent the whole afternoon at hard play. He had sat down with Rosa in the lounge and explained the whole surgery to her in great detail. Then he had asked, "How are you holding up? Is there anything we can do for you?"

Ah, there was plenty, Rosa thought. Plenty! For starters, she needed an exorcist. She felt inhabited. Gary was in her bones, and Rosa was sure that with his spirit in there she would never be able to do the most important thing in life—*love*—ever again. Forever, his voice would be in her ear. Rosa would look at other men, maybe even date them, and in the middle of some already awkward first dinner, while Rosa dribbled olive oil on her lap or tried hard to keep up her end of the conversation without seeming too eager, Gary suddenly would be doing all the talking. *You've got nothing in common with this one, sweetheart,* he would whisper. Or *Jesus, what a weenie, look at him, he doesn't even laugh at your jokes. En garde, this one needs a green card. Check out this dope, too dumb for Harvard and Yale, so he goes to Dartmouth, forget him. All right, so this one's got an ugly mug, but he rakes it in, you've gotta be practical, sweetie, I've told you a million times Social Security is going bankrupt, so smile, smile, go for the bucks, you need somebody to support your shoe-buying habit.*

How would Rosa ever forget Gary? How could she be herself with anyone else ever again? She would never be able to say *belly button* or *booger* in front of another man without blushing, never be able to tell him her father had a portrait of Mussolini and a stockpile of toilets in the garage, never be able to serenade him when he came out of the shower with her favorite childhood song: *I see your heinie, it's nice and shiny!* This imaginary man never would be able to fully appreciate the absurdity of her life. Only Gary, who had his own private mythology to share, could understand the feeling of forever being haunted by these childhood memories.

Rosa finished her sandwich, chewed pensively on the pickle, and ate the last potato chip. She looked down at her empty plate and then looked around the cafeteria. She thought about going back through the line for something else to eat—a brownie or maybe even a chocolate chip cookie. Right in front of the register, she had even seen a display of king-sized Milky Ways and Three Musketeers bars. Rosa felt hollowed out, ravenous. But she did not dare leave Gary for too long. She crumpled up her plate and tossed the coffee cup in the wastebasket.

The elevator was slow. Rosa waited a long time for it to drop down to the basement. On the way up, the elevator stopped on every floor except the second. On the fifth floor, she went down the hall and stopped outside Gary's room.

The door was open, but the yellow curtains were drawn around Gary's bed.

Rosa paused for a moment. Maybe the doctor was in there, making his rounds, or the nurse was by his side, adjusting the IV. But then the curtain jerked back, the metal rings scraping on the rod, and a nurse, a tiny Filipina with a wide face and vibrant pink lips, practically jumped when she saw Rosa. She closed the curtains behind her.

"I just found him," she said.

"Oh," Rosa said.

"I just happened to check."

"Oh."

Think I'll sleep a while.

"Do you want to—?" the nurse asked. "Be alone for a few minutes? You can go in. Someone will come in later and—straighten him out."

Rosa stepped inside the room. And the nurse did just what Rosa dreaded she would do. She closed the door. Now there was just Rosa, staring at the yellow curtains, dreading parting them, the way she once stood outside the burgundy velvet drapes of the confessional, terrified to pull them back and go inside. Rosa took a pinch of the yellow curtain in her hand and held it back. Then she stepped inside.

The IV bag dangled from the metal tree. The nurse had disconnected it and wound the plastic hose around the spoke at the top. Gary lay on his side with his back toward her. How had he found the strength to turn over? Maybe he had wanted to spare Rosa the sight of him dead. Or maybe he deliberately had turned his back on her, renouncing her and all the world.

In any case, now he was just a form—a body—a back and a pair of shoulders, inert legs, a head that never would lift from the pillow. He no longer was anything to her. He was only what he was not: black, wiry hair that no longer would scratch her face. Hands, big hands, that no longer would reach out and grab her around the waist. A foot that no longer would bump her in the night.

Rosa stared at his form on the bed, and for some odd reason, she began to remember all the goofy things Gary had done with his body. The way he stuck his finger in his ear and shook his head, like a dog, when he climbed out of the Fishers' pool, sending a shower of water all over the tiles of the patio. The way he sometimes pulled his beard into a point, pretending to be one of the swashbucklers from a Gilbert and Sullivan show, or the way he clucked his lips together and said, "The Great Poo-bah has spoken!" The way his tongue rolled, all pink and wet, when he belted out those crazy, rollicking songs along with Mickey Katz and Moishe Oysher. The way his naked butt waggled against the towel when he sang the Toreador song from *Carmen* after he had gotten out of his morning shower.

Then there were the hands—the hands that dropped Ivory White's folder on the floor, the hands that gripped the Subaru's steering wheel and the oar of the canoe in Vermont, the hands that wiped Aunt Sylvia's lipstick off Rosa's face, that gestured, wildly, that night at the party when they played charades. Expressive hands. Now his left hand lay useless on the sheet, the skin a pale, luminous color, the fingernails white as wax, the thumb grazing the iron rail on the hospital bed. Rosa wanted to rearrange his hands, fold them—in the posture of prayer—on top of Gary's stomach. But he was all curled up, and Rosa could not bear to touch the heaviness and uselessness of his body.

Don't look at me when I'm dead. It won't be me. It's the real me you should remember.

Rosa's head began to ache. She felt increasing pressure in her ears, the way she once felt when she flew with a cold, and her ear canals seemed to contract and fill with all the compression of the atmosphere as the plane descended into the airport. Now the pressure grew and grew and then, suddenly, popped. Rosa heard music—not the music of the angels, but the music of the real world—the wild, wracking sobs that came at the end of an opera, the desperate sounds Gary once had claimed were so unbelievable. Yet there they were. They came from Rosa herself. She could have crumpled to the ground, just like a diva.

Must have been love, right?

Through the haze of her own tears, Rosa took one last look, then turned and walked away, pulling the curtain behind her. She opened the door. Two nurses stood in the hall. They gave Rosa embarrassed looks, then came forward. "Okay," Rosa said, not knowing what she meant. "Okay. All right."

Down the hall, across from the nurses' station, there was a small conference room. The nurses told Rosa to wait there, and they would send her family in. They put a box of Kleenex on the large table in the center of the room. Rosa sat down in one of the plush, padded chairs at the table. She stared at a chart, hanging on the wall, which diagrammed the gall bladder. On the green chalkboard, written in white, were the words: *Cholecystectomy. Bile ducts. Japanese.*

Rosa went through half a box of the Kleenex before the nurses finally ushered in Artie, Mimi, and Antoinette. Antoinette looked grim and serious. Mimi looked haughty, as if something very important had just happened to her and her alone. Artie was the only one who seemed to have the appropriate response. He sat next to Rosa, at the head of the table. Then he put his head down in his arms and wept.

When Rosa was small, her mother used to shred old sheets and underwear and make them into dust rags. Artie's crying reminded her of that sound: each sob was like a rip. And Rosa remembered what Gary had told her, that at funerals some Jews tore their clothes to express their grief. When Rosa asked why, Gary shrugged and said, *It's in Genesis. You know: Jacob rent his clothes and mourned his son for many days.*

Artie's shoulders shook in precise rhythm, like the vibrating fingers on a therapeutic mattress or reclining chair.

"Stop that," Mimi finally said. "Get a grip."

Artie continued to cry. His voice came up from the table all muffled. "A grip on what?" he said. "He was my son. My only son. You were too caught up in other things—too busy with your life—too concerned with your figure—to have other children."

Mimi turned away and examined the chart on the gall bladder.

Artie continued to weep. Rosa held his hand. "I just had all these hopes," he said. "I had these hopes—for him."

"You can forget them now," Mimi said. "Now there's nothing left. There's nothing."

Artie reached for the Kleenex box. He took off his glasses and wiped his eyes with a tissue. He looked so vulnerable without his glasses that Rosa had to look away.

Artie picked up his glasses but did not put them back on. He stared down at them, as if they reminded him of something. "I hit him once," Artie said. "We got into a fight. I mentioned—just mentioned to him—that maybe he might want to come into the business after he graduated from college. And he said, 'I'd rather die than sell eyeglasses, Dad.' " Artie clenched his fist. "It made me so angry. He thought he was too good! He said, 'I'd rather die than have your life, Dad!' "

"He never said that to you," Mimi said.

"He did. And I got so furious, I hit him! He was fifteen years old, and I hit him. Afterwards I heard him crying in his room, and I was so mad at him, I didn't go in. If only I had gone in—"

"Stop doing that to yourself," Mimi said.

Artie looked up at Rosa. His eyes shone with tears. "I just wish I had gone in."

"We all have regrets," Mimi said.

Artie put his head down on the table and wept again. "All those years," he said. "All those years I worked. I did it all for him. And now—" He held out his hands. "Nothing. There's no one to leave it to. I would give it all up. I would. All of it. What does it matter?"

Mimi turned to Rosa. "You see," she said, gesturing at Artie. "You're lucky you didn't have children. This is what it comes down to. It all comes down to this."

Rosa looked at Mimi. Then she looked at her own mother. Antoinette sat in a chair by the door, her mouth moving in silent prayer. In her hands she held her black rosary beads.

"Put that away, Mother," Rosa hissed.

Mimi looked scornfully at Antoinette. Then she went up to the chalkboard, and in what Rosa considered an extremely odd gesture, she took an eraser and rubbed out the word *Japanese*.

After a half hour—after Artie and Mimi went down the hall and spoke to the doctor, and Rosa mechanically signed the paperwork the nurse put down in front of her—the Fishers went back to the hotel. Rosa would go back to her own apartment, with her mother along for company, and pack a suitcase. Later, she would drive back with Artie and Mimi to Long Island and stay with them. ("For however long you want to, dear," Mimi said.)

Rosa knew she would not stay long. And she knew this stay would be for the last time. After this, she would never go back to the Fishers' house, never return to the guest room where she always had slept with Gary, only to remember him pressing her against the tile in the bathroom or to feel his ghost beside her in the bed. She would weasel her way out of the Fishers' life as deftly as she had weaseled her way in. Artie and Mimi would call her from time to time—just to check and see how she was doing. Mimi would invite her to meet them in New York for dinner and a show. Rosa would go, because (as Mimi said) it would make Artie so happy. But it would kill her to sit next to Gary's parents, to sense their bodies beside her in the dark. After the curtain opened, Rosa would fall into the dream world of the stage. She would laugh and clap and only remember her anguish when she turned away from the Fishers to the next chair and saw a stranger. It would not be him, ever again. She would never again sit next to Gary.

Then the calls would become less and less frequent, like a friendship undergoing a slow death. Just as the Friday-night pal became the occasional lunch partner, and then just another name on the Christmas card list, the Fishers would cease to consume Rosa. But somehow they would still be a hidden force in her life. The very thought of them would fill Rosa with remorse for not maintaining the relationship and relief for letting it go.

Before they left the conference room, Rosa and Antoinette picked up all the used Kleenexes, dropping them into the wastebasket.

"I've never seen a man cry before," Antoinette told Rosa as they waited for the elevator.

"Well, now you have," Rosa said. "Congratulations."

The elevator clunked down to the fifth floor. The doors opened. The elevator was empty. Rosa got on first. Antoinette waited until the door had closed before she turned to Rosa. "Did you do it?"

"What?" Rosa asked.

"You know," Antoinette said. "Baptize him."

"Are you crazy?" Rosa asked.

The elevator began to drop.

"You could have done it," Antoinette said. "I could tell he was slipping away. Why do you think I went out to lunch with them? While we were gone, you could've given him both, baptism and last rites."

Rosa looked at her mother in amazement. But Antoinette didn't seem to clue in. "Well," she said. "I guess God takes care of everybody. God bless him. I'll miss him." She leaned down and buttoned her black cloth coat. "His parents, they took me to a restaurant downtown," she said. "The waiter was colored. A bowl of soup cost five bucks. A cup of coffee, no refills, two-fifty!"

Rosa stared at the pale buttons on the elevator panel. She heard Gary's voice.

Man, your mother reads the menu like Hebrew—from right to left.

Frightened of being trapped in this small space with just the tight, hateful voice of her mother, with Gary's voice rapidly becoming just a memory, Rosa inflicted upon herself the worst form of self-punishment. As the elevator sank to the lobby, Rosa reached out and smacked her palm against the red emergency stop. The car jolted and ground to a halt. Antoinette gasped, reached for the rail, and said, "Holy Mary!" Then the high-pitched alarm began to ring and Rosa, feeling crazed and slightly nauseous, just stood there, suspended in midair with her mother, waiting.

epilogue

It galled Rosa that so many cheap consumer goods survived Gary—a chipped brown coffee cup full of nineteen-cent Bics, a pair of scruffy sneakers with the soles split open, three cannisters of yellow-green tennis balls, a sliver of blue Dial soap, a translucent red Oral B toothbrush (the bristles all roughed-up and bent), and a jockstrap that had lost all its snap. The kitchen cabinets were stocked with foods that Gary alone liked to eat (lentil soup, heart-shaped Lavosh, pale-green shav, and Cuban coffee), and the medicine cabinet was stuffed full of drugs that were supposed to save him, as well as the everyday medicines he had relied upon—Chlor-Trimeton, Seldane, Sudafed. The drugstore always had been Gary and Rosa's downfall. Turn them loose in the Rexall and within two minutes they could blow a hundred bucks—Gary on stuff to clear his sinuses and Rosa on products to either clog or jog her intestines.

Rosa tossed everything in the medicine cabinet, from Gary's testosterone replacements to the trusty Immodium, the stalwart white cannister of Metamucil, the sickly pink plastic bottle of Pepto Bismol, and the discreet foil wrap of Extra Strength Gas-X. She did not want to die and let the whole world know she had been plagued, for years, by alternate bouts of diarrhea and constipation, which (mysteriously and quite miraculously) had ceased upon Gary's death.

Rosa no longer had a body. She no longer had headaches or stomachaches; she no longer felt hunger or thirst or desire. She was neither in the world of the living nor in the world of the dead. She was simply a guardian of Gary's things, waiting for a respectable amount of time to pass before she could take out the brown paper shopping bags and fill them with all his clothes, books on Nietzsche and Hume and jogging and organic gardening, French and economics texts, pictures of his old girlfriends, and postcards from his mother that showed sunny pictures of Buenos Aires, Johannesburg, Florence, Sydney, and other far-flung cities. A month after Gary died, Rosa filled over seventy bags. Then her brother Frankie came over, with Aldo's old Plumb Easy truck, and took it all away.

Gary might have found that amusing.

Rosa kept very few of Gary's things, and like a child, she hoarded her treasures in one of her father's old Dutch Masters cigar boxes. She held onto Gary's silver Cross pen, the keys to his Subaru, the black Seiko watch his parents had brought back from Hong Kong, the brown leather wallet that had conformed to the curve of his butt, and his gold wedding band, which, in all her confusion, Rosa had forgotten to bury with him. The ring had become too loose for him to wear after he lost all the weight. Rosa, too, had dropped ten pounds, enough so she could work her own ring up over her knuckle with just a little bit of soap and a minimum of twisting. She put her ring next to his at the bottom of the cigar box. Her hand, bald and wrinkled, was the only part of her that looked old enough to be widowed.

The word *widow*—so ancient and melodramatic—made her feel as repulsive as a spider. Yet when she put her head down on his pillow every night—that thin, feathered pad that was old and soft and still smelled like him—the appropriateness of the word became clear enough. The bed was too big, and she woke up too often, with the vague and unhappy feeling that she had heard him snoring.

Rosa used to scoff at her mother when a cold draft came into the room and Antoinette made a hasty sign of the cross to ward off ghosts. Yet she was tempted to do the same whenever evidence of Gary popped up, as it did from time to time, making her shiver. Cleaning out the purse he had given her for her birthday, Rosa found a 1961 penny Gary had planted in the zippered compartment for good luck. Vacuuming the bedroom, she saw the Hoover suck up a tiny white button from one of his shirts. When she scrubbed the bathroom floor on her hands and knees, she found a toenail clipping, big, broad, and creamy yellow. Once, in the lobby of Yale New Haven Hospital, she thought she saw a man—a scruffy, dirty old man—shuffle by in one of Gary's plaid shirts donated to the Salvation Army.

It skewered her.

The eaves of the house creaked on windy spring nights, and branches scraped against the window. Like a teenager, Rosa played the stereo constantly, with all the adolescent longing for love and overwhelming loneliness that made her believe the lyrics were being sung especially for her. Her favorite record—all because of that night they had played Charades—was *The Mamas and the Papas Sing Their Greatest Hits.* The tritest of phrases, sung in the big, belting voice of fat Mama Cass, seem to shine with more meaning than any brilliant philosophy. One song in particular killed her. It began, *I call your name, but you're not there.* Rosa knew it was stupid, but when she heard them sung over and over, the words sounded almost religious to her, like a lament from the Psalms or the cry from the prayer that Mimi finally had allowed to be spoken at Gary's funeral: *Out of these ruins I will rebuild you.*

It used to drive Rosa crazy when Gary left up the dust cover of the turntable while the record spun. Now she left it up, too, because it made it easier to flip the record and begin the music again that much faster. She wanted to drown out Gary's voice, because when the apartment was silent she heard him talking in her head—usually a recap of that wild spill of information he offered late at night in the hospital, right after the pain woke him up and before the nurse came in, like an angel of light, with more morphine. He clutched Rosa's hand. He rambled. *So much has happened to me, I can't help remembering. I remember so many things. Once I had a nightmare about a green fire engine and my mother came—I was in a crib—and she lifted me up and she smelled all powdery and beautiful, and she said, shhh, shhhh.*

My parents took me to the west coast when I was ten. We went to Carson City and the ghost towns. I stood on the porch of an old saloon with my hands slouched in my pockets and grit in my eyes, and I felt like an honest-to-God miner, a real forty-niner, until I heard my father ask my mother, "You seen a bathroom, Meem? God, I gotta make."

Another time we went to L.A. to visit my mother's cousin, and we walked on the Palisades, these huge cliffs that overlook the ocean, and there was an earthquake, a little one, and the whole ground groaned and shook like a bust muffler.

At Benny's bar mitzvah, my Uncle Len hired a juggler and a klezmer band and Henny Youngman to tell godawful jokes. I remember standing by this table piled high with pastries, listening to the microphone screech and looking at this tiered crystal fountain piled high with fruit. On the very top there was a bronze cherub that peed Hawaiian punch all over the oranges and pineapples and bananas. I remember standing there staring at his stinky little wiener and wishing I could just be normal, just be American—Jesus, just be anything in the world but Jewish!

When I graduated from college my parents wanted to take me to Bermuda. I went to Auschwitz. It's unforgettable. You walk into this room where there are glass cases heaped high with all the stuff left over—the suitcases and clothes and jewelry and books. And the shoes—piles and piles of black boots with the toes facing every which way and the laces all undone because they were yanked off in such a hurry. Then you come out of the building and stand on the field. The ground and the buildings are all brown and desolate. Even the barbed wire looks dusty. But the sun is shining on the railroad tracks, and you wonder what it's all for. God, the world is such a beautiful and appalling place! There has to be some reason for it. Why can't you find it? I thought I did when you got the ultrasound. I couldn't get over the way the baby was sucking his thumb. And remember how his eyes were squinched shut, like he couldn't bear the thought of eating any more broccoli? I never told you, when I told my father you were pregnant he said to me, "Now I can die happy," and it pissed me off no end and I told him to put a lid on it, when really I was thinking something not so different, I thought, God, now I finally have something to wake up for in the morning.

I never felt so lousy in my life as when you called me from the hospital. I never told you, on the way to meet you I had to pull over on Whitney Avenue between the Peabody Museum and the Kline Lab—I've always thought it was so funny that they should put those two buildings together, the dinosaurs and the nuclear experiments—and I put my head down on the steering wheel and cried like a baby. I cussed out God, I called him a motherfucker! because I had believed in him for half a second and he let me down. I walked back there, back to the same spot, after they found the tumor went to the bones. It was windy and cold and the leaves were raining down on the sidewalk and the bark seemed all old and rutted on the trees. Everything looked so separate and unnatural, and I kept on thinking how it all meant nothing if there was nobody there to look at it, and then I thought, how can there be a world without me, without me? Hold my hand tighter, I can't feel it. Ring the call button again, will you? Listen, I bought the baby some of those little white knitted things, you know, booties? They're underneath my sweaters in the bottom drawer. Keep them. I couldn't bear to throw them out. I don't know. Give them away, give it all away, give it to somebody else. There's no point in hanging on to anything.

Rosa found the booties and kept them in the Dutch Masters cigar box. She kept the silver Cross pen, the Seiko, the car keys, the wallet, the wedding band. But of all the things she held on to, it was Gary's reading glasses that got to her the most. She found them under his side of the bed, on top of a stack of books that included *Crime and Punishment* and *The Joys of Yiddish*.

She remembered, too vividly, the afternoon she and Gary had picked up the glasses, just a month before they found out he was sick. They stood in Artie's optical shop, neither speaking nor looking at one another. Then Artie came out of the back, wiping the thin lenses and the wire frame of the glasses with a soft blue cloth. He proudly held out the glasses and shook his head when Gary reached out to take them. "No, let me put them on you," he said. "My pleasure. I ground and polished them myself." He winked at Rosa.

As Artie slipped the glasses over his ears, Gary closed his eyes. When he opened his eyes he said, "Dizzy."

Artie took the glasses off Gary and bent the frame forward. He fiddled with the ear pieces before he put the glasses back on Gary. "Well?" he asked.

Gary picked up a brochure that described the benefits of disposable contact lenses. He peered at it for a moment, then nodded.

Artie beamed. He stood back. "Look at him," he said to Rosa. "Perfect." He put his arm around Gary and pointed to the mirror. "Who'd of thunk I'd have such a handsome son? I go places with him, people can't believe we're related. I laugh. I'm proud of it! I've always been proud of him, Rosa. I always knew he was special. He could read when he was three years old. He played piano when he was four. We used to have people over for dinner, and he used to tell jokes, funny ones, too. In the fourth grade, they had a public-speaking contest at his school—"

"Don't, Dad," Gary said.

"He won first prize," Artie said. "He stood right up there at the microphone and he announced, loud and clear, 'My name is Gary Fisher and the name of my speech is "Why Jews Don't Drive Volkswagens." ' "

"Come on, Dad," Gary said. "Cut it out."

"He gave a great speech! He won the whole crowd! I sat there in the audience. The guy sitting next to me, he leaned over and said, 'Is that your son? He oughta be a lawyer.' And now look at him—a lawyer!"

"I still have to pass the bar, Dad—"

Artie shrugged. "So, almost a lawyer. I'm a lucky man, Rosa. And you're the lucky girl."

And what had Rosa answered? Ah, Rosa, stubborn as a mule, skull thick as a donkey's! She had not replied. Because just that morning she and Gary had had another blow up. Gary was studying in the bedroom. In the kitchen, Rosa sorted through the mail and paid their bills, dreading the trip to Long Island that afternoon. Gary's MasterCard showed one hundred dollars was owed to a florist. Rosa stared at the amount and could not for the life of her think of what occasion had warranted such an extravagant charge. Then she remembered it was January. The previous month had been Mimi's birthday.

Rosa was furious. Gary was hardly working, teaching only one class. They were living on her salary, the measly income of a hospital social worker. A hundred dollars equaled a week of groceries, one-seventh of their ridiculous rent! And for whom? Mimi, who frowned when she went into the kitchen and found Rosa speaking Spanish with the maid, who pursed her lips together when Rosa came downstairs dressed for dinner in a denim shirt and jeans (the shirt hanging out because Rosa could not fully zip the fly), who took Rosa to I. Magnin's and insisted she buy a new dress, who squatted on the tiny upholstered stool in the dressing room and watched Rosa take off her blouse and pants, oh-so-casually remarking, "My stomach sagged so horribly after I had Gary that I was afraid Artie would leave me."

Rosa was incensed. One hundred dollars for a woman who had eyes only for Rosa's flabby gut, who could not see beyond Rosa's ugly body!

Rosa took the bill back into the bedroom and held it out toward Gary.

"What is this hundred dollars?" she asked. "For a florist?"

Gary looked up from his books and shrugged. "My mother's birthday," he said.

"Did you have to spend so much?"

"I only have one mother."

"Thank God."

"Look, be more understanding, will you? I can't explain it. I had to do it. She expects it."

"Don't you think it's sick, the way you show love in your family—by spending money?"

"So how do you show it in your family? With a slap in the face?"

Rosa felt her cheeks color. "Flowers wilt in a day."

"So my mother could drop dead tomorrow."

"You once called her the kind of woman who never dies."

Gary threw down his pencil. "What are you really fighting about?

It isn't the money." He glanced down at his book, and when he stared back at Rosa he wore the beginning of that look that Rosa hated to see on his face, that triumphant smile that usually signalled the end of the argument. "You're jealous. That's it. You're jealous because my mother has always made a lot of me and because your own mother won't give you the time of day except to criticize you for asking."

Rosa tried her best to assume a haughty tone. "Spare me the analysis, Dr. Freudy-Fraud."

"No, I won't. You're like a textbook psychology case. The woman who hates her own mother so much she starts to act like her."

Rosa bristled. "And you act like your father," she blurted out, even though it wasn't true. The only thing Gary and Artie had in common was the fact that they both talked far too loudly.

Rosa felt herself making the same kind of stony, ugly face Antoinette had made when she had fought with Aldo. To keep Gary from seeing it, she turned and walked back into the kitchen. She cried as she made out the check. She muttered stupid, inane things she halfhoped he would hear. *Fuck you, too. Honest to God. Just get lost. Get out of my life. Drop dead!*

Over and over Rosa relived this argument and the drive to Long Island that afternoon, mortifyingly long even though Gary, as usual, floored the gas pedal on the Subaru and took the majority of the ride in the fast lane. It was drizzling. Then it began to pour. Rosa watched the wipers scrape back and forth as she listened to *Pictures at an Exhibition* on the car stereo. Every time they passed a truck and a spray of water covered the windshield, Rosa wished for an accident, for one swift pileup on the highway that would put her out of her misery.

Neither Gary nor Rosa said anything until they crossed the bridge into Queens. When Gary finally spoke he had to clear his throat first. "Do you mind if we stop at my father's store?" he asked. "I want to pick up my glasses."

"Fine," Rosa said.

Over and over Rosa saw herself getting out of the car in front of

Twenty/Twenty for Less. She remembered the way Gary, in spite of his anger, still opened the door of the shop for her and motioned her inside, and how foreign—totally New Yorkish—his voice sounded as he told the receptionist, "I'm looking for my father." Then she saw Artie coming out of the back with that hopelessly wondrous and loving look on his face, polishing the glasses one last time before he presented them to Gary. "I'm a lucky man, Rosa," he said. "And you're the lucky girl!"

Over and over Rosa remembered what followed, the way she had bit her lip and held her tongue, the uncomfortable silence, the horrible moment when she caught Gary's eye, and they gave one another looks that were so fierce and animal-like, they made Rosa feel as though she and Gary did not belong in the twentieth century at all, but should be back in the wilderness, dressed in furs and feathers and living in a cave.

Standing there looking at her husband, Rosa had felt consumed with disgust and desire. She wondered how she ever could have thought him attractive. She knew she never wanted him to touch her again. And yet she knew she would probably let him back her against the wall in the upstairs bathroom that very evening, while downstairs Artie and Mimi watched the evening news hour with a bowl of mixed nuts and a couple of stiff drinks. And afterwards she would tell him she loved him and then push him away, because he knew far too much about her, and yet so little.

How could I ever have married you? she thought. And then, the next moment: *How could I not have?*

So Rosa looked at Gary and Gary looked at Rosa. And even Artie, who was usually so obtuse, noticed something. "Hey," he said. "What's going on here? Lighten up." Then he took Gary's hand in one hand and Rosa's in the other. He shook their arms as if to shake all the demons out. "You kids," he said. "You cra-a-a-a-zy kids."

Gary looked down and Rosa looked away. And all the mirrors in the shop, the hundreds of pairs of glasses neatly lined up on their trays, became thousands of eyes watching them, like a silent chorus that already knew the end of the story and that simply sat back, waiting to see it happen.

After Gary died, Rosa felt so lonely that there were times she believed she would give up the rest of her life just to relive that second, so she could say, "Oh, I guess I am kind of lucky," or so she could shrug or half smile at Gary, just enough to make him shrug or half smile back.

Whenever she opened the cigar box and saw his glasses, Rosa thought of this moment, of how it was now closed to her, shut tight as a coffin, unavailable for replay. She thought of it when the record she was listening to ended, when the arm of the turntable skidded and the needle popped onto the empty tracks, dragging out that empty, breathy noise—whop, whop, whop, whop—that sounded like a helicopter ready to take off, or a fetal heartbeat. The record spun dizzily, crazily, and against the heavy breathing of its emptiness, Gary's voice pierced her: *Everybody should die sometime, Rosa. God, the things you remember! The things you regret!*